Marsali grew up near Edinburgh, Scotland. Her family holidays were spent in a remote cottage in the West Highlands, the region where her detective Gavin Macrae lives. Like her sailing heroine, Cass, she has always been used to boats, and spent her gap-year earnings on her first sailing dinghy, *Lady Blue*. She studied English at Dundee University, did a year of teacher training and took up her first post, teaching English and French to secondary-school children in Aith, Shetland. Gradually her role expanded to doing drama too, and both primary- and secondary-school pupils have won prizes performing her plays at the local Drama Festival. Some of these plays were in Shetlandic, the local dialect.

Death in a Shetland Family is the fourteenth novel in her much-loved Shetland Mysteries series.

By Marsali Taylor and available from Headline Accent

The Shetland Mysteries

Death on a Shetland Longship
(*previously published as* Death on a Longship)
Buried in a Shetland Tomb
(*previously published as* The Trowie Mound Murders)
The Shetland Night Killings
(*previously published as* A Handful of Ash)
Grave of a Shetland Sailor
(*previously published as* The Body in the Bracken)
The Shetland Poisonings
(*previously published as* Ghosts of the Vikings)
Death in Shetland Waters
Death on a Shetland Isle
Death from a Shetland Cliff
The Shetland Sea Murders
A Shetland Winter Mystery
Death in a Shetland Lane
Death at a Shetland Festival
An Imposter in Shetland
Death in a Shetland Family

DEATH IN A SHETLAND FAMILY

Marsali Taylor

Copyright © Marsali Taylor 2026

The right of Marsali Taylor to be identified as the Author of the Work has been asserted by her in accordance with the Copyright, Designs and Patents Act 1988.

First published in 2026 by Headline Accent
An imprint of Headline Publishing Group Limited

1

Apart from any use permitted under UK copyright law, this publication may only be reproduced, stored, or transmitted, in any form, or by any means, with prior permission in writing of the publishers or, in the case of reprographic production, in accordance with the terms of licences issued by the Copyright Licensing Agency.

All characters in this publication are fictitious and any resemblance to real persons, living or dead, is purely coincidental.

Cataloguing in Publication Data is available from the British Library

Paperback ISBN 978 1 0354 3627 9

Typeset in 10.5/13pt Bembo Std by Six Red Marbles UK, Thetford, Norfolk

Printed and bound in Great Britain by Clays Ltd, Elcograf S.p.A.

Headline's policy is to use papers that are natural, renewable and recyclable products and made from wood grown in well-managed forests and other controlled sources. The logging and manufacturing processes are expected to conform to the environmental regulations of the country of origin.

Headline Publishing Group Limited
An Hachette UK Company
Carmelite House
50 Victoria Embankment
London EC4Y 0DZ

The authorised representative in the EEA is Hachette Ireland,
8 Castlecourt Centre, Dublin 15, D15 XTP3, Ireland (email: info@hbgi.ie)

www.headline.co.uk
www.hachette.co.uk

Dedication

To John, and all who use their experience of alcohol addiction to give strength and hope to others, and to spread the belief that recovery is a reality.

The Shetland 'horse' proverbs are taken from *Shetland Proverbs and Sayings* by the late Bertie Deyell, by kind permission of his family.

I
Horse

Tuesday 23rd August

Morning tide times in Lerwick

HW 01.51 (2.4m)
LW 08.06 (0.2m)

Afternoon tide times in Brae

HW 12.32 (2.1m)
LW 18.14 (0.5m)

Sunrise 04.35; moonset 10.22; sunset 19.36; moonrise 20.02.

Waning gibbous moon.

Chapter One

Der mony a göd horse snappered: *Misfortunes or mishaps can occur to the best.* [Literally, *There's many a good horse stumbled.*]

I was on my way back from Bergen to Lerwick. We'd not long sighted the cliffs of Noss, a misty triangle on the horizon, when my phone pinged: two messages from my partner, Gavin. The first one said *Mother's had stroke call me asap xxx* and the second one was *Heading for Inverness xxx*.

I moved away from the trainees and called him. 'Gavin?'

'Cass, thank goodness. I wasn't sure if you'd get me before the flight. I'm on my way to Inverness. Mother's had a stroke.'

I looked out at the shifting sea and didn't know how to comfort him. 'Oh, Gavin. I'm sorry.'

'Pray for her. I'm going down now.' His voice shifted to organisation mode. 'I don't know how long I'll be. When do you expect to be home?'

'ETA midday, to Lerwick. We can see Noss.'

'I've organised Rainbow to call in and feed the animals tonight, in case you didn't get in as expected, but she's back at school, so she can't do it all.' He hesitated. 'I was looking at your trips . . . I've got a week's compassionate leave.'

'I'll sort it,' I said firmly. 'You just worry about your mother, and helping Kenny.'

There was a bing-bong in the distance behind him, and

the sound of an airport voice. Gavin listened. 'That's me,' he said. 'I'll phone you once I get there. Once I know more.'

I put the phone down and stared blankly at the shining water. Gavin's parents had married late, and his father had been dead for a long while. Morag, his mother, had been forty-three when his brother, Kenny, was born, and forty-five with Gavin, so she was in her early eighties now, but she was always so busy about the farm, between hens and cows, washing and baking, that I couldn't imagine her lying in bed. Gavin hadn't said whether she was still at home. *I'm on my way to Inverness.*

That could be the flight, or the hospital there.

'Cass?' Anders said from behind me. 'Is something wrong?'

I nodded, and turned slowly to face him. 'Gavin's mother's had a stroke. He's flying down there.' I realised how little I knew. 'He didn't say how bad it was. He was at the airport, on his way. He'll phone me once he gets there.'

Anders made a sympathetic face. He was the engineer for this trip, and Kathleen, standing aft beside a trainee on the helm, was our skipper. We'd sailed Shetland's tall ship *Swan* over from Lerwick to Bergen three weeks ago, with ten trainees squeezed aboard, and set off for home from Leirvik on the Søgnefjord the day before yesterday. Now the trainees were on deck watching Shetland appear in the distance: the cliffs of Noss outlined on the horizon, Sumburgh Head to the south, the hill of Saxa Vord in Unst to the north. Gannets flew around us, paper-white against the blue sea.

I put my phone back in my pocket. It would be a couple of hours before Gavin got to Inverness. Meanwhile, I had sightings to take with the trainees and a course to plot. I needed to radio the Coastguard and Lerwick Port Authority to let them know we were on our way in. I squared my shoulders, nodded at Anders and got on with it.

I kept worrying all the way through the journey in, the bustle of berthing, immigration control and waving the trainees goodbye. When the last of them had gone, we sat down for a mug of tea on deck, and I told Kathleen the news.

'Do you want to go down there?' she asked.

I shook my head. 'Not immediately, anyway.' I wanted to be with Gavin, but if Morag was in hospital, there wouldn't be much I could do. 'I need to be in charge of the animals. Gavin usually does that. I'm not sure I can be a night away from home, and of course I won't have road transport.'

Kathleen nodded. 'Let's think . . . we all have tomorrow and Thursday off while the volunteers do a deep clean. Friday's the weekend trip to the Unst show.'

I'd planned it: a day's sail up the east coast, Friday night in Fetlar, on to Unst, Shetland's most northerly isle, for a day at the Unst Agricultural Show, then Sunday either going over the top of the British Isles, weather permitting, or along the top of Yell and back down the west coast to Aith. I'd been looking forward to it, but now it was three days away from the house. There were the cats, the hens, the horses, the sheep; I couldn't do it. I shook my head, and met her eyes in a dismayed look.

'Never worry,' Kathleen said. 'I bet Magnie can do it.' Magnie was a retired fishing skipper, a regular *Swan* volunteer, and one of my best friends.

'But I can do the school trips from Aith,' I said, 'and the sail round to Walls with all the P7 bairns. I'll find a way of getting back to Aith.' It was ten miles, too far to walk. 'Isn't it a Walls man who drives the school bus?'

'It's Trevor Mullay crewing,' Kathleen said. 'The lifeboat second coxswain. He bides in Aith, so as to be handy for a shout. I'm sure he'll run you back there.'

'That'll work,' I said. 'I'll speak to him tomorrow or Thursday. Then the women's weekend trip to Scalloway, St Ninian's and back to Lerwick . . .' I shook my head, as if the movement would clear my brain and let me think.

'Don't fret,' Kathleen said. 'That's a week and a half away. Focus on now. Phone round for a substitute skipper. Tomorrow and Thursday, at home for us all. Anders, you're welcome to bide onboard, if that makes life easier.'

'I'm going to Cass's,' Anders said. He put up one hand to caress his pet rat, who'd emerged from the cage he'd had to stay in during the crossing and was now comfortably ensconced on Anders' shoulder. He'd had to be left with Anders' parents in Norway for the whole length of the fjords voyages, because of passenger sensibilities, but Anders was staying on in Shetland for the Unst trip and then a Warhammer three-day competition, so he'd insisted on bringing Rat back with him, and Kathleen had agreed, on condition that he stayed in the crew's quarters. They were a striking pair: Anders was a classic Norwegian seaman, of medium height and muscular build, with shining fair hair, tanned skin, blue eyes, a straight nose and a neat Elizabethan beard. It was a great pity for Norwegian girls that he was also a serious engine nerd. Rat was an equally handsome specimen: nearly sixty centimetres from nose to tail-tip, with black and white markings, intelligent dark eyes and whiffling whiskers at least ten centimetres long. Anders took him everywhere, tucked inside his shirt or curled round his neck inside his hood. Most people had a moment of thinking he was a cat, then realised and were either fascinated or recoiled in horror.

Thinking about Rat brought me a whole new set of problems. The plan was, as Anders had said, for him to stay at our cottage. Rat and my Cat had been friends from when I'd found Cat as a tiny, starving kitten, but I feared that Cat's sidekick, Kitten, might have other views, especially as she had a kitten of her own to defend. I hoped it would be okay if Rat stuck with Anders, or went out with Cat to charge round the garden.

Then, I realised, there was getting home. I'd been expecting a lift home with Gavin once his police shift was ended, but that wasn't going to happen. I didn't even know where our car was - probably down at Sumburgh Airport - nor if Anders could sit as passed driver for me to fetch it back.

Kathleen echoed my thought. 'How are you going to get home?' She glanced at her watch. 'Five to one.'

'That's good,' I said. I took a deep breath and found the world starting to click into place in my head. The car could stay wherever it was; my own yacht *Khalida* was waiting for us in Brae, a convenient hundred metres from the bus stop, and home, the Ladie, was only two miles by sea from there. 'There's a bus to Brae at ten past two. We'll go there and sail *Khalida* home to the Ladie.'

Anders nodded, and rose. 'Then we'd better get on with tidying up this ship.'

'I'll phone Magnie now,' I said. I visualised him as the phone rang, into his seventies now, with a round cheerful face, pebble-green eyes and red-fair hair only just starting to grey. He'd likely be in the house putting the kettle on the Rayburn for a lunchtime cuppa – and on the thought, the ringing cut out, and his voice sounded in my ear. 'Aye, aye, Cass. I was about to phone you. I've been watching you dock on the Marine Traffic tracker. Your man got hold of you then?'

'Just as we spotted Noss. Nine o'clock.' I glanced up at the clock and realised that was four hours ago. 'I haven't heard back from him yet.'

I must have sounded worried, for Magnie cut in quickly. 'The Inverness flight goes by Kirkwall, and then he'll need to get to the hospital . . . no point in calling again till he has news.'

'No,' I agreed. 'And they might have taken her to Fort William, that's nearer the loch than Inverness, but further for him to go.'

'And folk get over strokes, even someone the age of Gavin's mam. Wi' good physio she'll come at, God willing.'

I nodded, and got to the point. 'But it means I can't go jauntering off to Unst this weekend. Are you free? Could you skipper in my place?'

'No bother, lass. I was hoping you'd ask me. The bag's ready to be packed, and I've had a word wi' me neighbour to look after my animals. He's got a teenage lass always blyde for some pocket money.'

'Thanks,' I said, and fell into formal old-fashioned Shetland. 'I'm truly obliged to you.'

'You'll be vexed to be missing the trip,' Magnie said. 'Your first shot at skipper too.'

'Can't be helped,' I said.

'And you'll be giving me that young Anders as engineer?'

'He's looking forward to it.'

'And his rat too?'

'Confined to the crew quarters during the voyage.'

Magnie grunted, which I took to mean acceptance. 'I'm just about to come into town. I could easy give the two of you a lift out west.'

'Oh, that'd be great!'

'About half past two, mebbe?'

Half past two would give us time to tidy up in good order. I thanked him again, reported the good news to Kathleen, then flurried round shoving my gear into bags. I'd just stuffed the last of my dirty washing in when the phone went. I snatched it up. 'Gavin?'

'Hey, Cass. Mother's holding her own. She's in the Fort William hospital. I got a quick look at her. I'll go back in a moment. The nurses say she's stable. She's conscious. She can't speak or move her left arm, and she's on a drip to keep her hydrated until they can check her swallowing mechanism, but I could see she recognised me. She lifted her other hand, and her lips moved. I haven't seen a doctor yet.' He paused to take a breath. 'It all happened so fast – I just leapt into the car and drove. It's still at Sumburgh.'

'Don't worry about that. It can sit till you get back. Magnie's doing the Unst trip, so I'll be at home all weekend.'

'Good.' His voice was distracted. 'That's a doctor. Dear Cass, I'll speak later.'

Magnie's mustard-coloured Fiat arrived on the pier on the dot of half past two. 'Aye, aye,' he greeted us. 'Fine to see you back. So,' he added, coming forward to take one of my bags, 'how was Norway?'

'Grand,' I said. 'We were lucky with the weather, only two days of rain, and the fjords were thatna bonny in summer. The trainees had a great time, and the Viking festival went down well. It was a bit of a marathon. I'm no' sure I'm sorry for a weekend off.'

'Any word o' Gavin's mam?'

I nodded. 'She's in Fort William, and stable. She can't speak or move one arm, but Gavin said she recognised him. He was about to talk to a doctor.'

'That's all good.'

We had a cup of tea with Kathleen, and Magnie checked through the Unst trip with us and took over the paperwork, then we squeezed our bags and ourselves into the car and headed off west: between the houses, past the power station, up the hill and into the country at last. I'd insisted on Anders taking the front seat, with Rat inside his shirt. I relaxed in the back, and looked out at the passing scenery.

I'd left in the height of summer, and come home to early autumn. Even though it was a bonny day, blue and warm as summer, the colours had turned. The orange hens-and-chickens along the Tingwall verges had withered to brown lollipop heads, and the royal purple of the heather on the hill behind them had bleached to a creamy white, with blue pincushions of scabious growing through. There were swans with cygnets as big as themselves by the pool of Nesbister. The house beside where the Loch of Strom flowed into the sea had set up a tidal generator. I looked at the turbulence it was causing in the water, and betted it probably made the house self-sufficient in electricity. There were the small wind turbines too, I reflected. Nearly every village hall had one, to back up the heating when the hall was closed, which was most of the time, and save the cost of keeping it damp-free in winter. I wondered how far Shetland could get back to the self-sufficency of a century ago, if need be. I suspected folk would manage, with lambs on the hill, several dairy herds, hens in the yairds and fish in the sea. The problem would be fruit and vegetables; Shetland didn't have a market gardening climate.

Now we were properly on the westside. At Weisdale there were immaculate lawns surrounded by curved feathers of pampas grass, and two fishermen had set up tripods at the loch. There were three Mirror dinghies sitting at the Tresta pier. We came through Bixter, up the brae, and were just past the Twatt turn-off when suddenly there was a whirl of something black at the corner of my eye, and at the same time Magnie slammed on the brakes. The car slid sideways onto the hard shoulder and juddered to a stop. We were all jolted forwards.

'Sorry, folk,' Magnie said. His face was white as he turned around. 'There's a horse running loose on the road. I came as near as dammit to hitting it.'

I rolled the window down and leant forward to look. It was a black Shetland pony charging along the road at full gallop, mane and tail flying. It was the quiet time now, but the school buses would be along at any moment, and the cars of parents collecting children. It definitely wasn't a good place for a loose horse. Magnie followed it cautiously as it reached where the road narrowed to thread between the houses. There was a field of horses there; it slowed as it saw them, and they came over to the fence. The black horse paused, tossed its head, then sidled towards them, nostrils flaring. I heard squeals as two noses touched, but they couldn't harm each other on opposite sides of the fence, and at least the black one was on the verge, instead of in the middle of the road. A man in a boiler suit came down from one of the houses to stand at the side of the road, one hand out. The horse flung its head up, then shied away to the other side of the road, kicked out as he took a step towards it, and clattered on, tossing its head. It galloped around the bend, past the Vementry turn-off and headed straight for the school, where the buses were lined up in the car park, with the first one starting to move towards the exit.

Magnie pulled into the Michaelswood car park, and took out his phone. 'Aye, aye, Aidan, it's Magnie here. There's a black horse loose in Aith, heading for the school right now, and just at bus time too. It's no' your Rainbow's?'

I realised he was talking to Aidan, father of Rainbow, who was feeding our animals tonight. I should have thought of her. I knew her because she was one of my sailing pupils, and best pal of my schoolfriend Inga's oldest lass. She looked after several ponies belonging to her granny's stud, including the five who lived in our back park, and a beauty of a black stallion, Redsand Yahbini.

Aidan's voice came over clearly. 'It's no Yabbi, for he's in the park right now, grazing peaceably. That main road's no place for a loose horse. I've got the trailer hitched on anyway. I'll come and get him.'

He clicked off. The pony had got as far as the school turn-off and paused, then when the bus came out of the gate towards it, it set off again, around the school. The turn-off to the hill road was opposite the kirk; it might go up there. If not, the road was fenced right to East Burrafirth, and I had a feeling there was a cattle-grid between us and the scattald.

Magnie echoed my thought. 'There's a cattle-grid at East Burrafirth, where the hill-grazing ends. The state he's in, he'd break a leg in it, if we can't get him stopped.' He put the car back into gear. 'We'll follow him along, slowly, and try to pass him. The Cake Fridge horses'll maybe divert him.'

Since it wasn't Yahbini, I wondered where the horse was from, and how it had come to be loose. Most crofters were particular about their fences. It had been just past the Twatt turn-off when we'd met it; maybe it had come up from there. We lost sight of it as it went on northwards, but when we came around the Purliegert corner it was standing in the middle of the road, head turning uncertainly, flanks heaving.

'Good,' Magnie said. 'He's tiring himself out.' He opened his car door. 'Anders, you take the car. No more as five miles an hour, just drittling behind him to keep him going forwards. If he goes to the side, see if you can pass him and keep going at the same steady pace to stop him running again. Cass and me, we'll coax him along to where the Cake Fridge horses are, and by then Aidan'll be here wi' the trailer.'

I slid out of my side of the car and closed the door gently.

'Careful now,' Magnie said. 'No sudden movements, and dinna try to close in on him. Just walk along with your arms spread, so that he doesn't try to go back into Aith again. The school bus is ahint us, that's one good thing, and the driver kens there's a loose horse, so he'll be on the lookout. Easy does it, now.'

The horse was shifting nervously sideways, eyeing us up. He'd got himself into a right state, poor beast: his brown eyes were showing their whites, his mouth was open, gasping for breath, and his black coat was streaked with white foam. He flung up his head and jumped sideways as we came towards him, but didn't try to run again. Magnie was talking soothingly to him in a low rumble of words: 'Now then, boy, this is no place for you to be, and a fair way from home too, I'll be bound. Easy now. I'm no trying to catch you. Let's just walk along gently.' He took a step forwards, and the horse eyed him uncertainly, then wheeled round so his powerful back legs were towards us. He stamped one hoof, striking a spark from the tarmac, then began to walk forwards, still in the middle of the road. Magnie and I closed in behind him at a respectful distance, with Anders behind us, and we daandered our way along the road in procession.

'This might be a chance for you, Anders,' Magnie said, as we reached the bend where the road widened, above the house with the grassy roof. 'Geng ahead and block the road at the Cake Fridge, just before the car park. Aidan can turn in there.' He moved to the verge, and I followed suit. Anders slid the car quietly between us and slipped past the horse, which startled backwards as the car came round, forelegs braced. For a moment I thought he was going to whirl round and run back again, but he'd tired himself out. He snorted, then plodded on, and Magnie and I continued behind him, making encouraging noises.

Even I could see he was a beauty. He was big as Shetland ponies go, his ears at my shoulder level, and shining black all over. He had a neat head, a lot of mane on a broad stallion's neck, muscular shoulders, rounded quarters and a metre of thick tail. Somebody had to be worrying about him.

A distant rattle of a car and trailer going over the cattle-grid echoed from around the corner: Aidan to the rescue. By the time we got to where we could see, Anders had moved out of the way and Aidan was busy reversing the horsebox back from the Cake Fridge car park. He parked so that it filled the road, gangway end towards us, gave a quick, assessing glance at the horse and began unhooking the ramp. Once it was down, he took a headcollar and began walking towards us, speaking soothingly, just as Magnie had done. The horse flung its head up again and dodged him, swinging its quarters round again.

Aidan shook his head. 'He's got himself into that high state where he wants things to be back to normal but doesn't quite know how to get there, like a toddler refusing to go to bed. We'll try the bribery approach. He'll likely be thirsty.' The pony watched him warily as he went into the box and came out with a yellow bucket and a two-gallon container of water. He poured a bucketful, making sure the pony saw the clear water going into the bucket, then put bucket and drum to the back of the box. The horse flared its nostrils as if it was smelling, took a tentative step forward, then startled back again. 'I wonder if you'll take a few pony nuts?' He reached into the cab for a bag of pony cubes and began sprinkling them in a line up the ramp and into the trailer, then came out and went around the side of the trailer, leaning against it where the horse could see him.

The horse watched warily, forelegs braced, tail swishing, and for a moment I thought he was going to swirl round, shove Magnie and me aside and run back the way he'd come. Then he snorted, sighed and dropped his head to the scattered cubes, hoovering his way along them until his hooves clattered on the ramp. Inside the trailer at last, he drank thirstily, and while he was doing that, Aidan lifted the ramp and Magnie and I scurried forward to push the pegs home.

'That's a relief,' Magnie said.

'I recognise him,' Aidan said. 'He was the one who beat Yabbi to the top prize at the Viking Show last weekend. I can't remember who he belongs to, but Rainbow'll know all about him. Meantime, I'll take him home. He can calm down in the box until we find out where he belongs.'

Chapter Two

Der mony a pellit röl come ta be a göd horse: *Many a rough youngster becomes a good adult.*

'I was thinking, Anders,' Magnie said, as we pulled away, 'that you'd be very welcome to come and bide wi' me for this couple o' nights. I hae a spare room, and it would be handier for you getting back to Lerwick on Friday morning.' He looked doubtfully at Rat. 'You might need to leave Rat aboard Cass's yacht. I doubt Tab wouldn't take to a rat on her territory.'

He didn't say *since Gavin's not here* but it was hanging in the air. I realised he was right. Much as Gavin wouldn't mind Anders staying over at the Ladie, as we'd planned, it was quite a different thing for him to bide when it was just him and me. I couldn't have village gossip thinking I was having an affair with Anders while Gavin was away looking to his mother.

Anders came from a village outside Bergen, and understood the unspoken words. 'I was going to ask Cass if she'd let me sleep aboard *Khalida*, at the marina.' He put a hand up to his pet. 'I'm not sure your lady cats will take to Rat.'

'I was worrying about that,' I admitted. 'Yes, of course you're welcome to *Khalida*.'

'And then after that,' Anders said, 'I can be aboard *Swan* at night.'

'In that case,' Magnie said, 'how's about we head straight for Brae, instead of going into the Ladie, and you can get Anders settled aboard, make sure he has everything he needs, then I can run you home in my boat.'

I looked doubtfully at Anders. 'It seems very inhospitable.'

'It sounds good to me,' Anders said. 'The last three weeks have been over-close quarters with too many people. I'll have a hot shower at leisure, and a fish supper from Frankie's.'

He seemed to mean it. 'Well, if you're sure . . .'

'I am certain. If I get bored, I can check over that engine of yours, see what you've done to it since I serviced it last.'

I didn't rise to that.

'That's settled then,' Magnie said. 'There's a washing machine at the club, if you need clean kit.'

'And we can take her for a sail tomorrow,' I agreed. I gave Magnie a sideways look. 'If you don't think that'll cause comment.'

He gave one of his rare smiles. 'Lass, we're all used wi' you. Nothing you'd do in that boat of yours would raise an eyebrow.'

I felt I'd come home as soon as we stepped out of the car. This was the boating club where I'd learned to sail, and there was *Khalida*'s mast rising among the taller ones.

We lugged our bags along the pontoon. I dumped mine in Magnie's old-fashioned double-ender, then climbed aboard *Khalida* and opened the washboards. The familiar smell of diesel met me. I looked with pride into the main cabin, a wooden space two metres wide and three long, with shelves set in the slope of her sides, a settee with navy cushions on one side, chart table, cooker and sink on the other, and my quarter berth projecting back under the cockpit. I'd shift the sails piled up in the forepeak into my berth, so that Anders could have the larger bunk, but otherwise she was neat as I'd left her: the chart table clear of all but chart and logbook, the cooker clean, sink empty, dishes stacked in their rack, little prop-leg table ready for use. Being aboard her again made me want to go sailing. Tomorrow; we could take her out tomorrow. I checked Anders remembered how everything worked, and left him to it. Magnie dropped me off at the cottage pontoon and waved away the offer of a cup of tea. 'We'll catch up soon enough. You go and phone your man. Tell him I was asking after him.'

'I'll do that,' I said. 'Thank you for the run.' I shoved his boat off and raised a hand in farewell, then turned and looked around me.

The Ladie was the last still-inhabited house in the narrow sound between Brae and Aith. It wasn't ours; the owner had her own house, but she had the vision of setting up a croft attraction here at the Ladie, with the native animals for children to learn about, and visitors to see. The hens and coloured sheep were hers. Up to my right, beyond the ruins of the cottage called Houbansetter, there was the rusted-brown heather curve of Linga, with the boating club and marina just visible two miles beyond, and Magnie's house on Muckle Roe opposite. The island of Papa Little sheltered us from the open sea. The township of Aith lay to the south, past the roofless walls of Millburn and Quienster: the White City, Aith was called in Brae, after the way the houses shone in the sun. The Sound of Houbansetter lay spread before me, the sea rippled with the light wind. Three seals were basking in the sun, watched by a dozen herring gulls and five shags, two of them with their wings extended, like washing hung to dry. There was a whirling of terns in the air above, gathering for their long flight to South Africa.

Cat had spotted Magnie's boat coming in, and was already halfway down the drive to meet me, bounding through the grassy park from the garden wall. He was a beauty, my Cat, smoke grey with faint stripes of silver, a long coat and a magnificent white ruff and plumed tail. He charged up to within a metre of me, then remembered that I'd been away for ages, and took three steps forward to sniff disdainfully at my shoes. I crouched down and made a fuss of him, and at last he unbent enough to let me tickle the creamy fluff behind his ears.

We walked together up to the cottage. The path led alongside the vegetable garden, sheltered from the north wind and getting full sun for most of the day. I paused for a moment to look around, and was astonished at how everything had shot up in such a short time. The tattie shaws were knee-height, the carrots nine inches of bright green fronds, and the knobbled white cauliflowers visible in the furled leaves. Gaps between the plants showed Gavin had been harvesting the spinach and lettuce in the fishboxes. The spiky shoots of the bramble that grew up against the shed were covered with green berries, and the apple tree above it was hanging with palm-sized fruit.

There was a catflap clack from ankle level as I put my key in the door, and Kitten charged out, followed by her daughter, Julie, who jumped over her and then stopped, eyeing me up with Cat's grumpy look. They were both torties; Kitten was the colours of spices shaken over a worktop, ginger and nutmeg and cinnamon all mixed together, with delicate white paws and ruff, and an apricot tail tip. She looked small and fragile, but climbed trees and scrambled onto rooftops to startle sparrows who'd thought they were safe up there. Julie was four months now and almost the size of her mother, but darker in colour, and with Cat's white ruff and impressive tail. She squawked at me, obviously remembering that she knew me, then went off to harass the hens pecking their way around the paths between the vegetable beds. There were six of them, plus the cockerel: three brown, three black, and they each had a funny tuft of feathers on their heads. I knew they were locked into their house at night, because of polecats, and let out in the morning, and that was about it. I'd have to get Rainbow to show me how much mash they got, and when.

I wasn't on much surer ground with the ponies, but Rainbow would know all about them. Fergus, the waist-high black-and-white gelding, was on his look-out hummock, enjoying the sun, the two mares were grazing peaceably, and the foals were sleeping, stretched flat out on the ground. I turned my back on them and headed into the house.

There were all the signs of a rapid departure: mug and bowl abandoned on the work surface, a fishing book left open on the table, a porridge pot filled with water on the stove. Upstairs, the bedclothes were flung back and the chest drawers weren't quite shut. I gathered up Gavin's washing and got it and all my own into the machine, then sat down in the sitootery with a sigh of relief, and took out my mobile.

He took several rings to answer. 'Sorry, Cass, I had to move out of the ward. There are notices everywhere about no mobile phones. Everyone's ignoring them.'

'How's your mother doing?'

'The doctor's pleased with her. It'll take a few days for them to know more, maybe weeks, but she seems already to be getting movement back in the fingers of her dead arm. The physio lass is on her case. She's called in twice already, just to do exercises, arms, legs and breathing noises, you ken, *aaaah*, and we've to keep them going.'

He paused. 'That sounds good,' I said.

'I've got a B&B in Fort William for the rest of this week. I'll go home with Kenny on Thursday evening, if all's going well. He's judging the Highland cattle at a show this weekend, at Strathardle, in Perthshire. I've told him to go to it. It'll take him the best part of three hours to get there, so if I hold the fort he can go down on Friday and come back on Sunday. Luckily it's the quiet time of year: harvest in, no sales or weaning. Just keeping the hens fed and the cows milked.'

'I wish I was there with you. I could be a help.'

'You would be, *mo chridhe*, but you're needed at home. Mother's going on fine. It's just patient work now.' He lowered his voice. 'I'm sorry not to have seen you before I left, after these weeks apart.'

'You're in my heart,' I said, surprising myself with the flowery language. 'In my prayers, all of you.'

'And you in mine,' Gavin said. There was another silence. I knew how he felt; he needed to go, but we both wanted to hang on to this thin contact between us. 'I must go back in,' he said. 'I'll phone you from the B&B. There's stew in the fridge, for your tea. I'm no' sure there's enough for Anders too, but you could maybe bulk it out with potatoes.'

'He's staying onboard *Khalida*, and getting a fish supper from Frankie's.'

I could feel him smiling. 'Your idea or Magnie's?'

'Magnie's,' I admitted. 'Oh, and he said to tell you he was asking after your mother.'

'Give him my thanks, and tell him she's doing well.' He said goodbye and rang off, and I was left to potter around. My first task was to go down to the pontoon and check on Gavin's little motorboat, the *Herald Deuk*. There must have been rain in the last few days, for she needed baling out. I sloshed out two bucketfuls of water, supervised by all three cats, then sat in the cockpit for a bit, enjoying the sun on the water and the sea smells of home, and the beautiful solitude of no trainees. I watched an otter swimming round the point and disappearing into its holt, then walked up and was about to go back in when the horses in the park raised their heads and turned landwards. Fergus gave a ringing neigh. Pony hooves scrunched on the other side of the hill. Cat jumped up on the gatepost to look; Kitten and Ketling Julie appeared from under the bushes. Two riders came over the top: Rainbow, on black Yahbini, and her best friend Vaila on one of her other ponies. Yahbini was sidling sideways at the sight of the other horses, but Rainbow insisted he walked down the slope instead of charging, and Vaila's one followed sedately behind. Rainbow jumped off neatly as they came level with the others, and unwound a long rope from her waist, to tether Yahbini to the telegraph pole by the track. I was pleased to see her tie the bowline she'd learned at the sailing classes. The rope looked to be a stout one, which was just as well, as he and Fergus were snorting and squealing at each other. Vaila slid off her pony and knotted its reins behind its ears, then let it loose. It went over to sniff at the others, then put its nose to the grass.

'Never leet,' Rainbow said, over the noise of Yahbini and Fergus squealing. 'They'll soon give it up. He's just reminding Fergus that these are his mares. I'm pretty sure they're both pregnant to him.'

'Hard to tell,' I agreed. The normal shape of a Shetland pony was round-bellied. I went up to join her, keeping well clear of Yahbini's hooves and teeth.

She was peerie-make, Rainbow, not even as tall as me, which was an advantage for riding Shetland ponies, and she had that indeterminate colouring, not quite blonde, not quite brown, with shoulder-length straight hair framing a sweet-natured face. She tended to fade beside Vaila's showy dark hair, dark eyes and definite manner, but even Vaila, who knew her own mind and shared it generously, paused to think when Rainbow suggested caution. Anyone who could manage a Shetland stallion had plenty of gumption.

'Hi, Cass,' Vaila said. Rainbow echoed it with only a quick glance in my direction; she was watching the foals capering round with excitement at these visitors. 'Did Gavin tell you Caedoc took Junior Champion at the Viking Show last weekend?'

I shook my head. 'The signals in the fjords were patchy. We barely managed to say good morning and goodnight. Well done, young Caedoc.'

'He's entered for Walls too. The truck's all hired. Are you up for it?'

'Walls Show? Hasn't it been?'

Rainbow shook her head. 'They had to postpone. You should have seen the day of dirt two Saturdays ago. Wind and rain. They couldn't even get the marquees up the day before. The Viking Show was the following weekend, so the horse folk had a get-together and agreed that if Walls would wait a week, we'd still go to support them, even if it was after the Viking Show, with the top prizes done and dusted.

'It clashed with Unst Show,' Vaila said, 'but that can't be helped.'

'I'll give it a go,' I said. 'Come into the garden.'

Cat came to meet us as we came down the drive and in by the gate. Vaila bent to stroke him.

'How's Gavin's mother?' Rainbow asked.

'Stable. In hospital in Fort William. She kent him, and he thought she was already getting the feeling back in her dead arm.'

'That's good. So . . .' She looked at me uncertainly, not wanting to sound as if she thought I was stupid. 'Are you okay for feeding them, and all?'

'No,' I said frankly. 'That is, yes, I'm here to do it, but no, I haven't a clue what I'm doing.'

'I told you,' Vaila murmured.

I ignored her. 'I'm very glad you're here. Let me get paper and a pen, then I can write it all down.'

We went round the beasts. The foals had concentrate food and special hay; I had to coax them into a small enclosure made of pallets for that, then feed the mares their pony mix in the main field. 'Try not to let Fergus share the mares' mix. He's not pregnant, just fat.'

The hens went in at night and came out in the morning, as I'd remembered. 'Gavin reckons Cat would see off a polecat, but better safe as sorry. You do ken they're special ones, Shetland tappit hens?'

I shook my head.

'They're descended from an old Spanish breed, supposed to have come off the Armada ships.'

I looked at them with more interest. *Tappit* came from the funny topknot, I supposed. Vaila had got bored and wandered back to the horses; Rainbow kept speaking. Water was essential, a gallon between them, morning and night – 'Birds can't regulate their temperature. The container's in the shed, and Gavin ran up a tap on the side of it.' If it got very hot, which was unlikely, I'd need to put screens on the hutch instead of doors, and create a fountain with a watering can, for them to bathe in. She showed me their pellets and a separate bag. '*Larvae for Ladies?*' I read incredulously.

'They love it. Nine containers of the pellets to one of that. Oh, and one of oyster shells too. Eggs . . . Gavin was talking of letting them incubate a clutch of eggs each, to increase the flock and share among other breeders, but he's no' done it yet, so just collect the eggs each morning and stick them in the fridge, for eating.'

9 pellets to 1 larvae, 1 oysters, I scribbled. *Eggs, fridge.* 'Okay. Sheep?'

We turned to look at their park. They were a traditional breed too, the size of a small dog, with even smaller lambs, and in a variety of colours: grey, rust-brown, black and spotted.

'Fill the trough with sheep feed in the morning, check there's water in the burn and leave them in the park to get on with it. Keep an eye on them, though. Count them each time you're looking that way. Sixteen yowes and twenty-seven lambs. The sheep can stumble into a ditch, and if they get stuck on their back they can't get up, so you need to roll them over, and the lambs wriggle through the fence, then forget how to get back and run up and down panicking. You should be strong enough to lift them back in. Watch out for them kicking, they have sharp hooves.'

16 U, 27 lmb, feed in morning. Sheep not on back, lambs wrong side fence, watch hooves. 'Got that.'

'That's it, then.' She took a step towards Yahbini. Vaila turned around and straightened up, ready to go. Rainbow paused in mid-step. 'Oh, Dad said to let you ken about Ebony. The loose horse. He's still trying to get hold of its owner.' Rainbow laughed. 'Yabbi's mad as fire about it, another stallion in his yaird, even in a trailer. That's why I rode him over, to give him something else to think about.'

'He wasn't pleased about coming,' Vaila added, tuning back into the conversation. 'Leaving his mares unguarded. He went sideways for the first mile.'

'And Ebony? Did you ken him?'

'Oh, yea. He belongs to an Arthurson man fae Clousta, Keith Arthurson, and there was a bit o' a fanfare when he bought him, you ken, in the Landwise pages o' the paper. *Klaufister Stud heir buys 3,000-guinea stallion in private sale* and a picture of him. He's from the Minstead stud, in the New Forest, Minstead Ebony, and he's a real beauty. He got Senior Champion at the Viking Show. It's such a shame—' She stopped abruptly, as if her enthusiasm had led her to say more than she meant. 'Anyway, he'd taken no harm.'

I wondered what was *such a shame*, but I could see she didn't want to say more. 'I don't ken the owner's name. Keith Arthurson?'

'He took over the Klaufister stud when his dad was killed,' Rainbow said. 'In a car crash, back at New Year.'

'He's a creep,' Vaila said. 'Slimy, with city-slicker clothes, and a knapping voice. One of these men that think they're God's gift. He was at some event at Busta when I was waitressing, and he leered at me when I was serving at the tables, then came up behind me and felt my bum.'

'What did you do?'

'Accidentally stood hard on his foot.' She grinned. 'He got the message.'

'That's my girl,' I said. 'So where does this creep live, and what sort of fences does he have, that his three-grand horse is running wild on the main north road?'

'They're at Clousta.' A shadow of uncertainty moved across Rainbow's face. 'It was odd . . . something must have given him an awfu' gluff.' A fright, she meant. 'Odd he got out in the first place, because the fences were fine, but mebbe someone left a gate open.'

'The brother drinks,' Vaila said. Country children were used to stating the facts. 'And maybe once Ebony was out, a tractor came up behind him, and set him off running.'

'Yea,' Rainbow agreed. 'Something must have done that, because otherwise he'd have grazed a bit, then he'd've wandered down to talk to the other horses. He wouldn't have gone right along to the main road. It's a fair way too. Must be three or four miles.'

'An insurance job,' Vaila said. Rainbow gave her a warning look, and she shrugged and walked over to her pony, busy stuffing as much grass as it could hold before it had to work again.

Rainbow undid Yahbini's tether then paused, as if she'd remembered something. She nodded at the foals in the park. 'Isn't Caedoc's VVE visit due soon? Friday?'

I gave her a blank look. 'Might it be on the calendar? Hang on, I'll go and look.'

I nipped into the kitchen, and there it was. 'Friday, VVE, ten thirty,' I said, when I came back out.

Rainbow made a face. 'Gavin was going to be there for it.' She gave me a doubtful look. 'Can you catch him yourself, and put his headcollar on? The vet'll do the rest. You'll likely get Annie, the young one. She's really fine.'

'What is a VVE?'

She paused, sorting out the facts in her head, ready to explain to a rookie. 'Do you know about the Shetland Pony Stud-Book Society?'

'Only the name.'

'Okay. Well, it keeps the stud-book for all registered Shetland ponies. Names, breeders, ancestors, heights, what they look like, progeny, all that. If a pony's in the stud-book, it's a guarantee that it's pure bred. They're really careful about it. All the stallions have to have a DNA profile, and a couple of years ago they made it that the mares have to have it too. They recommend as well that you put any colts you're thinking of keeping as a stallion through the VVE – voluntary vetting examination. It's a pretty thorough examination, to make sure they don't have any hereditary conditions that they might pass on to their offspring.' She flushed, and gave Vaila an awkward glance, then caught herself up again and continued. 'They have to pass the stallion examinations as well, of course, once they're older. Only one colt in a hundred makes it to be a breeding stallion. If they've not been through the VVE, then their foals cost more to register. And Gavin was thinking of buying him as a stallion, so he offered to pay for the VVE.'

'Ten thirty,' I said, sticking to the important bit. 'Friday.'

'Then Walls Show on Saturday,' Vaila said. She unglued her pony's head from the grass by hauling upwards and scrambled onto its bare back. 'We'll come over in the evening and help with horse washing.'

Rainbow made a doubtful face. 'We have all the others to do as well.' She brightened. 'But school stops at two, so we'll have time. I'll get Dad to run us over. Say five o'clock.'

I glanced at Yabbi and was reminded of the loose stallion. 'And hopefully your visitor will be gone by the time you get back home.'

'S'pose so, if Dad managed to get the Arthurson man in.' She used the fence to spring onto Yahbini's back. 'Good luck.'

Chapter Three

Dey knappit as da horse aets hay: *They spoke in an affected manner, using English in order to impress.*

It was strange being alone in the cottage as the shadows lengthened, and the sun descended towards the west hills of Aith. Normally I'd be preparing a meal for Gavin to come home to. It hardly seemed worth the bother when it was only me, but I wasn't going to fall into a moping melancholy. The little clock said quarter past five; nearly time for Radio Shetland. I'd listen to the news, hang the washing out, reheat the stew and eat it, go for a walk, then have an early night.

Rainbow's words recurred to me as I did Gavin's abandoned dishes. *It was odd . . .* You did see horses on the roads in Shetland from time to time, but only where the roads weren't fenced. I looked out at our ones, peacefully grazing. One or other of them occasionally shoved their way out but only went as far as the nearest patch of grass, as Rainbow had said. Maybe there had been mares in a park on the way towards the main road, and then he'd panicked when he found himself with fast-moving traffic around him. *An insurance job*, Vaila had said. I'd like to ask her why.

And how come he got out in the first place? *The brother drinks.* Even so, a three-grand stallion would jog anyone's memory about shutting gates. Maybe the fences hadn't been kept in good order . . . but it wasn't the drinking brother's stud, it was Keith's, who'd inherited it from his father.

Clousta. I knew where it was by sea, of course, but only vaguely by land: off the Twatt turn-off, and along the single-track road till you met the sea again. I went over to look at Gavin's wall-map, hung up for instant police officer reference to where trouble was now. Aith . . . Bixter . . . Twatt. There was supposed to be a Press Gang officer buried under the kirk doorstep there. I followed the road along with one finger. Four miles. There were a couple of houses beyond the main village, and the name Klaufister. It was a good distance for a horse to run, especially with verges of summer-rich grass on each side.

I didn't know the horsey people, and Magnie likely didn't either; he was a seaman to his bones, for all he had the croft and sheep. Walls was a horsey area, with a good dozen studs and a serious number of ponies at their annual show. I was trying to think of who I'd know among the Walls sailors when my phone rang. I leapt for it, thinking it might be Gavin, but the screen announced *Maman*, and she appeared, elegant as ever. '*Salut, Cassandre.*' She continued in the French we had always spoken together. 'You're home? How was your voyage?'

'Great,' I said. 'But have you heard about Gavin's mother?'

She nodded. 'We thought, your father and I, that you might like to come over for dinner. Dermot can come and fetch you.'

I hesitated.

'I have Normandy pork, and floating islands.'

She knew the right buttons to press. I thought about Gavin's no doubt nutritious stew in the fridge, and was sorely tempted. 'I'd really love to come,' I said. 'It's just that I'm in charge here, and the cats are so pleased to see me. I don't like to go off and leave them when I've only just arrived.'

'No problem. They can come too. Gavin always brings all three of them for Sunday lunch – they are well accustomed to it.'

'Sure, she's got the fat trimmings all ready for them,' Dad said, appearing in the screen over her shoulder. He paused to think about it, and managed, '*Elle a restes* for *les chats*. I'll come and fetch you, will I?'

'Yes, please!'

'See you soon, then,' Maman said, and rang off.

Suddenly the day was brighter. I raced round feeding the horses and shutting the hens in their run, then ran upstairs and found my one bonny dress and a pair of flip-flops. One of Maman's non-negotiables in my parents' renewed marriage was decent heating in the house, to be switched on at all times, even in summer.

I brushed my plait out so that my dark hair hung in a curling cloud down to my shoulders, and put on basic make-up. Cat watched with interest; he knew this meant going out. He and Kitten normally travelled in their boat harnesses, but I wasn't sure about Julie – in their basket, maybe? I tried getting it out, and she hopped into it straight away, with the air of a cat expecting a treat.

We were nearly ready when I heard a car coming down the track: not Dad's black pick-up, but something heavier that clanked like a trailer. I looked out of the bathroom skylight, and there was a small horsebox being reversed by a grey pick-up into the parking space. Our ponies lifted their heads and trotted over to the nearest bit of fence, nostrils flaring. Fergus gave his ringing whinny, and there was an answering neigh and a thump of hooves from inside the box. Ebony, I surmised, on his way home.

An apparition got out of the pick-up. He looked like someone strayed from a horsey show down south, in a flat tweed cap and jacket, dark trousers and polished leather riding boots. He glanced around, assessing our set-up as if he was thinking of buying it, then began striding down to the gate. I pulled a face at the mirror, and went down to deal with him.

He was on the doorstep when I opened the door, cap in one hand, the other hand raised to knock. Just the way he eyed me up told me this was undoubtedly Vaila's creep. In his mid-twenties, I reckoned, and he had an oddly disproportionate face, his eyebrows set halfway down below a high brow, and his eyes, nose and mouth squashed into the lower half. The eyes were watery blue, and he had a sandy clipped moustache, like an officer in an old war film. The general effect was like someone acting a laird for an Up Helly Aa skit. He oozed superiority, but if he really felt that far above us all, he wouldn't need to try so hard. I stretched the back of my neck to give me an extra inch of height, and reminded myself that until three months ago I'd been Acting First Officer of a Norwegian three-master. 'Yes?'

'Cass Lynch? I'm Keith Arthurson.' He held out his hand. I shook it, reluctantly, and suppressed the impulse to wipe mine afterwards. His voice was somewhere between Shetland and England, a local intonation scarred by carefully cultivated English vowel sounds. 'I just wanted to thank you for having caught Ebony, and I'd be grateful if you'd pass on my thanks to Magnie, and – Anders, was it? He's come to no harm, thanks to you all.'

A squeal and thud from the horsebox up above emphasised that. Fergus answered with a quick charge round his field, kicking out with both back legs. The foals shifted nervously behind their mothers. Keith leant one elbow on the house wall, ignoring the disturbance above. I added another mental black mark. It was good of him to call in and say thanks, but I'd have betted my best anchor rope that he wouldn't have bothered if I hadn't been DI Macrae's girlfriend. What Ebony needed was his own park, not a detour up gravel tracks for a simple good deed that barely warranted a phone call. 'We haven't met, but I own the Klaufister stud in Clousta – Klaufista was the old name for Clousta, you ken.'

I didn't, but I wasn't being talked down to by a wannabe youngster. 'Of course. I grew up here.' I motioned behind me. 'On Muckle Roe.' I gave it the local pronunciation, Roö. 'You're come back to Shetland to bide, then?'

He gave me a sideways stare, as if he wasn't sure whether he should be pleased I was recognising his south town polish or annoyed I'd spotted his Shetland origins, then gave a lordly wave. 'My family needed me, so I transferred to a firm here.' He glanced behind me into the house. 'I met Gavin when he came to give us a talk.'

Gavin? 'He enjoys being out in the community,' I said truthfully.

'He's not home yet. I'll tell him you called.' I indicated my dress. 'We've been invited out to dinner.' That wasn't quite a lie; the cats had been included.

He gave me an admiring look which was closer to a leer, but there was a funny mechanical feel to it, as if he'd got in with a laddish crowd and was copying behaviour that wasn't natural to him. 'You look great.' There was no conviction in the compliment either. Vaila had judged him as encroaching, but I had the feeling that if she'd smiled back, he'd have retreated to the safety of company and not bothered her again. 'Well, I won't keep you. Just wanted to say thanks for your trouble.'

'You're welcome.' I let him turn then added, 'How did he come to get out?'

There was a split-second pause. He hadn't expected that from someone dressed as I was. His eyes narrowed, then he answered, smooth as cream, 'Oh, someone left a gate ajar, and he wormed his way out. Have a good dinner, and give my regards to Gavin.'

I watched as he started the pick-up and headed off. Give him his due, he was good with a trailer, though that wasn't surprising since he'd grown up on a croft.

A creep. Insecure, under the bluster. I wondered if he had a girlfriend, some poor, impressionable lass who took him at face value, and was impressed that he'd been someone important in a city. I didn't believe for a minute that he'd admit to being anything less than the CEO's right-hand man.

In short, I hadn't taken to him, and when there was the sound of a car on the track again, I gave the place where the road disappeared over the hill a black glare. However this time it was Dad's pick-up hustling its way down. I went out to the gate to meet him, and reached up for a hug. 'Hi, Dad.'

'Now, then, Cassie!' He left the engine running and opened the back door. 'In you go, then, the pair of you,' he said to Cat and Kitten, then turned back to me. 'Fine to see you, Cassie. You're looking a picture, so you are.' Over thirty years in Shetland hadn't smoothed out his Dublin accent. He looked Irish too, that ruggedly handsome Pierce Brosnan style. He was six feet tall, and it annoyed me very much that I'd inherited the knee-high-to-a-grasshopper height of both my grandmothers. He'd started life as a builder, in his father's family's firm, moved to a Scottish enterprise and risen to become the head of it, then got involved with oil construction work up at Sullom Voe. He was retired now, in theory, but he was one of the directors of a firm building a massive windfarm in central Shetland, which we discussed as little as possible.

'What's the latest news from Gavin?'

I passed it on. By this time, both Cat and Kitten were waiting in the back seat, and Julie was squawking indignantly from inside her basket. I picked her up and put her in the back footrest, secured the others, then clambered up into the front seat. 'This is grand. Thanks, Dad.'

He waved that away. 'It's time we had a catch-up. We haven't seen you since Easter. Your mother was a great hit in America. Grand folk, the New Yorkers. Irish everywhere, made me feel right at home.' He chatted amiably about that all the way to Voe, then speeded up on the main road to Brae. 'And you leave your phone on now, in case Gavin has news and wants to ring you.'

'I'll text him to say where I am,' I agreed, and did. A ping gave the reply: *Heading for B&B soon will phone at bedtime. Txt me when you get back xxx*

'A fine man, he is,' Dad said. He gave me a sideways glance, then visibly remembered Maman had told him not to nag me about marriage. 'And being aboard the *Swan* means you'll be home all winter.'

'It does,' I agreed.

'That'll be fine for you both. It's a lonely life for a man, stuck in the wilds of nowhere evening after evening, these long dark winter nights.'

He was pushing his luck. 'You mean, between pipe band evenings and late nights at the station, and fishing, and the occasional game of golf, and visiting Father David for a meal?' I asked sweetly.

He took the escape route. 'Father David's a fine man too. He preaches an interesting sermon. You'll be wanting a lift to Mass on Sunday, then.'

'Yes, please.'

'I'm glad you've kept up the faith. And you'll come for Sunday lunch afterwards? It's no bother to drive round and pick up these cats on the way home.'

'That'd be fine. Thank you.'

'And you have a treat on Sunday afternoon, did Eugénie tell you? She'll be singing at the Harvest Festival in Aith. One of the committee heard she sang, and asked if she'd give them a tune.'

I tried to imagine Eugénie Delafauve, international soprano whose doomed heroines moved hardened critics to tears, giving Aith Harvest Festival a couple of tunes, and suppressed a smile.

'Of course I said yes,' Dad added. I hoped he'd asked her first.

We were almost into Brae now. Dad slowed to just over the legal 30, negotiated two cars coming out of the garage, one more going from the other side into Frankie's, and a large lorry making heavy weather of the entrance to the Co-op. We passed the Boating Club, with *Khalida* peaceful in her berth. Magnie's car was outside, so I suspected he and Anders had gone for fish and chips together, and were now propping up the bar. Dad turned into the Busta House road, and slowed to go behind Busta House and over the bridge to Muckle Roe, the island where I'd grown up. This was the road I'd taken in the school bus, from my first nursery days up to S3, when Dad had gone off to the Gulf, and I'd been sent to Maman in Poitiers. Town life hadn't suited me, and I'd been as out-of-place among the sleek, sophisticated French teenagers as a seagull in a flock of budgerigars. I'd disowned the family and run away to sea - but those bridges were re-built. I had to work on becoming a land person. *Home is the sailor, home from the sea . . .*

Dad swung the car into its place in the driveway of their 80s build bungalow, and stopped. I let Cat and Kitten out, undoing harnesses as they passed, and opened Julie's basket. Cat led the procession into the house.

'Cassandre!' Maman said, coming out of the kitchen, with a checked pinnie over her black-and-white chic, and a wooden spoon in one hand. She always dressed as if the paparazzi might be around the next corner, dark hair in an elegant chignon, a sweep of eyeliner, and scarlet lipstick. We kissed on both cheeks. 'You're looking well. Go into the sitting room. Cat, you know very well that you're not allowed underfoot while I'm cooking.'

Cat might not speak French, but he knew the drill, and turned right to where the fire was. Julie followed; Kitten paused to check out the bushes for sparrows. I rounded her up, and we all headed into the elegant sitting room, with a big picture window looking out over the voe, a dark-green Chinese rug on the polished wooden floor and Maman's baby grand piano taking up one corner. I'd emailed Dad a photo of his Acting First Officer daughter in full uniform, taken during one of the Tall Ship parades, and was embarrassed to see it practically life-size in pride of place beside their wedding photo on the piano.

The cats crowded round the fire. Ours hadn't been lit since April. I sat down on the couch; Dad got busy opening a sparkling white, and Maman appeared with a plate of pastry rounds spread with pâté and topped with an olive. 'And there are scraps for the cats, but not till we are at table.' She sat down on the couch beside me and spoke in English, for Dad's benefit. 'So, they were how, St Kilda, and Norway?'

'Both beautiful. St Kilda was amazing, but melancholy, and Norway was a lot of fun. Good weather, and we visited one of those Vikingfests, with swordplay, and Viking food, and people in costume everywhere. The trainees loved it.'

Dad passed me a fizzing glass. 'You had your pal with the pet rat as engineer, Gavin said, and coming back to stay for several days.'

'Anders. Yes.' I added clearly, 'He's sleeping aboard *Khalida*.'

Maman nodded. 'Yes, that's better for the . . . *les convenances*.'

'The look o' it,' I translated, helpfully. 'But,' I added with a touch of defiance, 'we're taking *Khalida* out tomorrow, before he goes off to Unst on Friday.'

Dad echoed Magnie. 'Ah, nobody'll think anything of that. They're used to you charging round the voe.'

I ate another pastry, and asked after New York.

'They were very sympathetic,' Maman said. 'And there were no concepts of designers. I had a beautiful robe that I could sing in, and not any stupidity of hat. The other singers, of course . . .' She dismissed them with a wave of her hand. 'I am to go back two times next year in cameo roles, and in two years' time they will stage a new version of *Acante et Céphise,* especially for me. Now, I think our principal plate must be ready. I will give to eat to these cats. You sit at the table.'

She came back with three saucers of scraps, which she put in front of the fire. The cats launched in as if they'd forgotten they'd gobbled a sachet of Gourmet each not two hours earlier.

The meal was wonderful: melt-in-the-mouth pork roasted with cider and apples, and covered with perfect crackling, followed by thin custard with whipped egg-white and sugar, cooked in milk as we sat at the table. I hoped Gavin had managed to find somewhere decent to eat, and wasn't having to survive on hospital canteen food. While we ate, I told them the story of the escaped stallion.

'Keith Arthurson, from Clousta?' Dad frowned for a moment, then his face cleared. 'Yes. The couple that were in that car crash at New Year. The *Shetland Times* was full of it.'

I shook my head. 'I'd have been heading back to the *Sørlandet* just then.'

'The parents of this Keith. They'd been south, taking advantage of the New Year sales, and they were driving back to the ferry. The husband was driving, and he misjudged pulling out onto the main road, and caused an accident with a lorry that didn't manage to brake in time. He was killed, and the wife was pretty badly smashed up.' He frowned for a moment, then got the names. 'Arthur and Patsy, from Klaufister.' He looked at me. 'I remembered them because Ertie, the other son, the brother of Keith that you just met there, well, he was one of our workers, and we'd had difficulties with him. A fine man in himself, but he drank.'

I refrained from pointing out that he wasn't squeaky-clean about a drink before driving himself. He caught my expression, and held up one hand. 'You're not to be imagining him reeling drunk, now. It's often not like that. He was a functioning drunk. He likely spent the evening with a bottle, then got up, showered, had a dram with his breakfast or instead of it, and came in to his work. I wouldn't say he'd ever pass the little bag, and he was driving a digger, so that was a concern, but he was up in the hills, not on the road, and he seemed able to do his work fine. There was no sign of him bringing drink on site. We couldn't have had that. He worked, he went home, he drank there. He wasn't quite settled and sober, but he didn't seem to be getting worse either. Then there was the accident, with his father killed, and his mother badly injured.' He sighed. 'I'll tell you the truth, we were worried. We took him off the evening shift, kept him on the days. Then about a month ago his drink consumption accelerated, and the foreman saw him with a half-bottle in his pocket. Well, that was the finish of it for us. You can't have a man in that state operating plant, even on his own in the hill.' He made a regretful face. 'I found out afterwards his wife had had enough, and showed him the door.' He shrugged. 'But he'd been a good worker, and it was an awful thing to go through, the loss of his father, and the mother in intensive care for several weeks, and then needing help for months, and all the croft work on his shoulders, and then his marriage too. I sent him a letter saying that if he could sort himself out, we'd find him a job.'

'Wasn't the other brother there to help? Keith?'

Dad shook his head. 'Came up for the funeral, then went again.'

'I remember me that you recounted it,' Maman said. 'There is a daughter?' She smiled at me, and added in French, 'They are a great comfort, daughters.'

'Two,' Dad said. 'I was at the funeral, on behalf of the firm. The mother couldn't be there. There were two daughters, two sons, and Ertie's wife, and the husband of one of the daughters, and their boy, maybe eight, all solemn in a suit. Ertie's children would be too young to be at the funeral.'

'And it's the other son who has the croft now?'

Dad shook his head. 'No, no, Ertie's the oldest son. He'd get the croft. The other son looked a bit of a city slicker to me.' He frowned. 'Or putting up that image, to impress the hicks at home. I barely spoke to him, just the condolences at the graveside.'

The oldest son who drank and should have inherited the croft, the city slicker who apparently had, and who was indubitably Vaila's creep, and two daughters, one married. *An insurance job . . .* I reminded myself that it was none of my business.

All the same, there'd been a nagging feeling since my last visit home, when I'd hoped not to have to follow a motorboat into Clousta, that there was something not right about there being a bit of water in my territory that I didn't know. It would be an idea to visit there while I had Anders as a spare pair of hands and eyes. I could check out Klaufister Stud while I was at it.

I enjoyed the evening. It was good being back in the home of my childhood, with Maman and Dad obviously happy together after their years apart. Their shared life was complicated, but it seemed to work, with summers being spent here, winters in France, and Dad accompanying Maman to her singing appearances as the critics' favourite Sun King soprano. They weren't old yet, but it warmed my heart to see them heading for a contented old age.

The sky was bright with stars as Dad dropped us off at the cottage. It would have been a beautiful night to have taken the boat out, with the rising half-moon making a gold path on the water, but I was too sleepy. I waved Dad off and followed the cats into the house.

I sat down in the sitootery and texted Gavin: *Home now xxx* He rang back straight away.

'Cass, *mo chridhe*. Good evening?'

'Very good. Parents on good form, and roast pork with crackling and a cider sauce.'

'I'm sorry I missed that. My dinner was hospital café food.'

'How's your mum?'

'Woozy, but brightening. I went in to see her again this evening.

She still can't speak, but I could see she was glad to have me there. I chatted away. Told her about your Norway voyage, the house, how the garden was doing, all that. She was listening and nodding.'

'That's good. So what next?'

'Waiting. Keeping up the physio. I'll visit as often as they'll let me over the next couple of days. Stimulation's good. I'll get a copy of the *West Highland Free Press* and read it to her.'

'Good luck. How's your touch with cows, for when you go to the farm?'

'I hope I haven't lost it. And I'll need to start getting the ponies fit, for the stalking. How's everything at home?'

We talked for a bit longer, then I put the phone down and stared in front of me for a moment. The house felt very bleak without him here.

I sighed, pulled myself together, and looked at the clock. It still wasn't late; just before ten. I looked at the map again, considering. My charts were onboard *Khalida*, but I had the older version of the *CCC Shetland Islands Sailing directions*. The helpful chart inside wasn't encouraging. The narrow entrance, Cribba Sound, had only two metres of water at low tide and a sprinkling of rocks all round the edges on both sides. The way going around Vementry looked clearer, if I went straight between the Black Stane and the islet off Gruna, keeping to the islet side, or even came right around the Black Stane and in towards Milder Ness on the 115 degree heading they suggested. The coast was foul with rocks all the way round Linga too, but there was a clear way between, until the narrowing of the voe at the entrance to the North Voe o' Clousta, where there were the submerged rocks known as the Icelanders on the Vementry side, an isolated rock off the Green Holm on the other, with only half a cable between them, and a depth of four metres. Half a cable was around a hundred metres. I snicked on my laptop to look at the satellite view. The road ran in from the turn-off above Aith and ended in a cluster of houses around the very head of the voe, with what looked like a pier jutting into one geo, except that the chart had all that blocked in as pale blue, too shallow to take a keeled yacht into. I didn't know what state of tide it was in the photo, but there was no sign of the Icelanders, unless they were a dot off the Green Point o' Vementry. The reefs from Green Holm rock showed as a cloudiness underwater. There was a fair distance between them. It would be an interesting place to explore, if Anders was game.

I might even get a look at the Klaufister folk, who'd let the younger son inherit the croft, and loosed a three-grand stallion on the roads.

II
Croft Work

Wednesday 24th August

Tides at Brae

HW 00.35 (2.3m)
LW 06.48 (0.3m)
HW 13.14 (2.0m)
LW 18.58 (0.6m)

Sunrise 05.41; moonset 12.10; moonrise 20.05; sunset 20.32.

Waning gibbous moon.

Chapter Four

Branks: *A halter made with rope and a block of wood on each side of the face.* [Old English, **branks**, *a scold's or witch's bridle.*]

I woke to a shepherd's warning; the glass of the window reflected a red light onto the white shade of the overhead lamp, and the window framed thin cirrus tinged coral-gold which faded as the sun rose. A grey shroud lay over the hills, somewhere between a summer heat haze and an autumn mist. In the garden, a last magenta rose flared among the cloud shape of the daisy bushes.

It would clear as the day went on. I got up, fed the hens, and collected five blue-green eggs from their nests. I filled the sheep trough, checked the burn and counted heads, which wasn't so easy with the lambs rushing round like mad things. I set down food for the cats to ignore. Finally I fed myself: scrambled eggs with a touch of cheese stirred in. By the time I'd finished all that, the sun had broken through. The wind would be too light for the *Swan*, but it was perfect for exploring new territory in *Khalida*. It was blowing gently from the south, giving us a reach for the dodgiest bit, between the Icelanders and Green Holm, and by the forecast it wouldn't rise till the evening, giving us plenty of time to potter gently into Clousta and out again.

Cat was on the alert. The minute I came out carrying my jacket in one hand and the electric battery in the other, he went charging down to the *Deuk* and leapt aboard. Kitten was too busy keeping an eye on sparrows to want to come too, to my relief; the more I saw of her, the surer I was that she'd see Rat as a natural enemy. I unclipped the mooring ropes and we set out towards Brae. The stillness of the water made it easy to spot the remaining birds: terns on the water around the mussel buoys, and black and white shalders on the Blade. The guillemots, razorbills and puffins were already gone; the scarfs and blackbacks would soon have the shore to themselves.

Anders was up when we arrived, and busy taking the mainsail cover off. The engine was running softly, with a smoother purr than the last time I'd used it. I parked the *Deuk*, and Cat and I came aboard. There was mutual whisker-sniffing between Cat and Rat, then the pair of them headed below. I heard the sounds of paws scrabbling on my varnished fiddles, followed by charging about, then they both came up once we'd raised the mainsail. Cat crouched in his usual corner, in the shelter of the cabin wall; Rat imitated him. It was good to see that curled mix of silver-grey and black-and-white again, with Rat's pink nose against Cat's lifejacket, and Cat's grey head on Rat's flank.

'I knew they wouldn't forget each other,' Anders said.

It was a bonny, bonny day for a sail, with the sunlight sparking gold on the water, and the hills a soft green. We tacked our way out of Busta Voe and into the Røna, then rolled away the jib, got out the red, blue and white striped geneker and skimmed along on a reach till we'd passed Vementry. The down-side of the south wind was that taking the shortcut down the side of Vementry Isle would have had the wind on our nose, so we kept going past the Stoura Baas and Black Stane, then tacked around and took up the 115 degrees course that would take us between the small isles of Gruna and Linga.

'The Black Stane,' I said, nodding at the dark lump of rock being washed by the swell on our port side, 'that was where the Clousta folk put a witch. Her name was Maggie Black.' Now I was saying it, I was dubious about that surname; the stone was obviously black with water, not named after Maggie, poor woman.

'They put her there?'

'Left her there,' I said, more precisely. 'Her body was washed up two days later on the beach in Suthra Voe on Vementry Isle.' I nodded past the isle of Gruna, ahead of us. 'In that inlet. I suppose they buried her there. And this headland here, that's the Neap o' the Neeans.' I hadn't been this close before. I looked up at the shadows on the red cliff, and thought I could see a darker one, like an opening. 'Da teif o' da Neeans,' I said to Anders, 'lived in that cave.'

Anders looked up, squinting against the sun. 'And who was he?'

'A sheep-thief. He lived in the cave, and climbed out at night and stole sheep to eat. And then as he got older he kidnapped a young lad to help him, and the lad tricked him into going back to his own house for a cow for a Christmas feast, and woke his brothers to capture him.'

'An exciting life you lead, here in Shetland. How long ago was this?'

'Goodness knows. The witch would have been four hundred years ago, poor soul.' I imagined the terror she must have felt, being grabbed by her neighbours and shoved into the boat, the gradual realisation, then being pushed onto the rock, and watching as the boat went away. She'd have been left alone with the tide rising. The Black Stane was always uncovered, but breaking waves would have gone over her. Maybe she'd clung on till she was unconscious from cold, or maybe she'd decided drowning in the sea was quicker than waiting for rescue that was never going to come. I shuddered, thinking of it.

'A good long time ago,' Anders said. 'Do you want to drop the coloured sail – what did you call it, geneker – and put the engine on?'

'We're still moving.' I nodded over the side at the V-ripple from the bows.

We drifted gradually past Gruna into clear water, and came nose-on to the wind once more. 'Now,' I said. I reached over to the controls and got the engine going. The thunk, thunk noise was horrid in the silence, but it didn't make sense to go tacking here, with underwater rocks all along this side of Vementry Isle.

The geneker was on an old-fashioned brass roller, fixed at top and bottom. I gave Anders the tiller and hauled on the line. It went halfway, then stuck, leaving the coloured nylon flapping in the wind from the forward motion. I nipped below for a bungee, slowed the engine to crawl and went forward to secure it in an untidy bundle. I'd sort it properly once we got past the Icelanders and into the inner voe.

In the end, it wasn't too bad. We had four metres depth of channel and another metre of flooding tide, so we bisected the smooth water between the Green Point of Vementry and the Green Holm, passed the end of the three lines of mussel buoys, with the inevitable scarfs sitting on the top of them, and came in good order into the enclosed waters of Clousta Voe.

The houses were all round the South Voe. There was a cluster here, then the ruins of several stone-built houses along the headland, then another new house opposite, one of the big double ones, with picture windows looking out on a spectacular view seawards over the channel. A flock of coloured sheep watched with interest as we came past them.

Now we were chugging between cliffs towards Clousta proper. The channel ended in a pool of water between grazed green hills with jagged lines of rock poking like bones through the cropped turf. A curve of houses ran along the shore and in a line up on the north hill, and every one of them had windows facing seawards. Suddenly I felt most horribly exposed. It was like we were about to park in somebody's back garden. Every spyglass in the place would be on us as we ate our lunch. There were probably photos on Facebook already, asking who we were.

Unhelpfully, my larger-scale chart stopped at the north voe, but the smaller scale one showed a couple of isolated rocks on the outside of the little island. I looked at the depth gauge. We had four metres of water still, and there was a long bay to starboard, with only a couple of houses on it, and a rectangular floating pontoon stretching out from them. From my memory of the map, that had to be Klaufister. Twenty metres in there would take us behind the headland, where we could struggle with the geneker without having every retired seaman in the place saying how much better he'd have done it. After that, we'd eat lunch in this peaceful green corrie, then I was getting us out of here, back into safe waters.

We crept in cautiously, and dropped the lightweight kedge anchor on a short chain. I took a couple of meids, to make sure we weren't drifting, then went below to dump my jacket and set the kettle on to boil. It was bonny, looking out through the windows at the shore: the sweep of green hill down to where it ended abruptly in the metre-high banks of the shore. There were geese on the hill, a great flock of them, maybe a hundred or more, and a clump of them on the water: one of the problems of warming temperatures. They no longer flew south, but overwintered here, and destroyed the grazing they colonised. There was an oilskin jacket and trousers hung on a scarecrow frame, but they were paying no attention to it.

A young woman came into view, walking from the house, a rope branks in one hand, a bucket swinging from the other. She called upwards, and a herd of horses came thundering over the hill, short legs going like pistons, manes flying. The geese scattered with alarmed honking and a rattle of wings. There was a black horse leading the charge: Ebony. The woman put the bridle on him, then tipped a bucketful of tattie peelings in a line along the grass, and presided as they shoved each other to get at them.

The two houses on the map were diagonally in front of us. I peered ahead as I waited for the kettle to boil. Klaufister had been a bigger place once, and better cared for – though, I reminded myself, they'd had a tragedy here, and now they had one man gone, another not coping, and the wife injured and not yet able to look to things. There was a litter of blue plastic drums in a hollow on the shore, and bigger containers further up, orange and grey, in front of the ruins of an older, larger house, the length of two houses, with a substantial gable and most of the front still standing. A pile of rubble suggested someone was working on it, and the front was fenced, as if it was used to hold sheep and early lambs during the coldest weather. The nearest of the lived-in houses was a small cottage above the pontoon, a simple but-and-ben, in reasonable repair, but with flaking whitewash and a moss-spotted felt roof. I saw someone shift behind the glass, then move to stand by the window, looking out at us: a man. The son who drank? It didn't look like a house with small children; there were no toddler toys around it, and no washing line of miniature onesies wafting in the light breeze – then I remembered Dad had said his wife had left him.

The second house, past the pontoon, was a newer build, and in better repair. It was square, with two windows in each side of it, a pitched roof running up to a short ridge from each wall, a felt roof, recently tarred. A trickle of smoke came from one chimney, and there was a peat stack by the door. Hens pecked around the short track leading down to the shore.

The kettle began to whistle. I brought the tea up, and went forward to see what had gone wrong with the geneker. We'd want it for going home again, so I was loathe to put it away altogether, but I could drop it, sort out whatever had snagged it, and secure it on the deck with bungees, ready to hoist again.

I uncleated the rope and began to drop the sail. I mustn't have had a good enough grip on the rope, for it began to slither quicker than I meant, and before I knew it the heavy bronze furler was hurtling downwards towards me. I ducked away from it, too late, and felt a hard blow on my head, then the guard rail caught the back of my legs and put me off balance, and then for what seemed like a long moment I was falling backwards, hands stretched back towards the boat, legs flailing in the air. I hit the water back on with a splash that echoed round the whole voe. I went under, scrabbled my way back up and trod water, gasping for breath. The cold hit me as the water seeped through my gansey. Above me, Anders was trying not to laugh as he threw down the end of one jib-sheet for me to catch. 'What happened there?'

My head was spinning and for a moment I saw two ropes. I fumbled for the nearest one and let it take my weight. My best sailing boots were pulling me downwards, but I wasn't going to kick them off unless I had to. 'There's a rope ladder in the aft locker, with a loop to go round the jib cleat.'

Anders moved quickly to hang it over the side while I sploshed over, the weight of the water making my movements uncoordinated. There were a couple of rungs below the water, and with the help of the jib-sheet wound round my hand, I managed to get one foot on the bottom one and shove myself unsteadily upwards until Anders grabbed under my oxters and hauled me over the guard rail. I sat down on the cockpit bench, dripping, and bent forwards to haul my boots off and tip the water out.

'You're bleeding,' Anders said.

I put my hand up to my head. It came away red.

'I'll get a cloth,' Anders said, and clattered below.

'Hey!' the woman onshore called, her voice carrying clearly over the water. 'Are you okay?'

I turned around to look. She was only fifty metres away now, at the edge of the land, Ebony's rope grasped with one hand, and older than I'd thought, twenty-six or -seven, with short dark hair and dark eyes in a thin, tanned face. The movement brought a fresh gush of blood. I clapped my hand to it, and grasped the kitchen cloth Anders held out from the doorway. I pressed where it hurt and felt the blood trickling into it and dripping from my fingers. A red pool was forming on the light blue paint of my cockpit floor.

The woman gestured towards the jetty. 'My mother's a nurse. You could come and let her look at it.'

'Heads always bleed,' I called back. All the same, professional help was tempting. I could sit still in this wavering world and let her deal with it. 'How deep is the water at your pontoon?'

'Two metres.'

'Two metres?' Anders looked ahead at the pontoon. It was a rectangle of walkway on orange floats, similar to the marina pontoons, and it would certainly hold *Khalida* in this wind, so long as it really had two metres of water, with another metre to flow in over the next three hours. Then he looked at my scarlet hand clutching the cloth to my brow, and went back for a basin of cold water, and another cloth.

I wrung the cloth out and pressed it to my head again.

'If we can lie up at the pontoon there,' he said, 'it'd give us thinking space. I'll start the engine and get the anchor up. You steer us in, I'll leap about.'

I nodded, and wished I hadn't. Sparks flashed in front of my eyes.

'We'll come in,' Anders called to the woman. I sat quietly as Anders moved around me, giving me the occasional concerned glance. Within a minute he had the geneker bundled up and attached, the kedge on the foredeck beside it, and the engine running. I put her into gear and edged forward to the shifting pontoon, one eye on the depth. Four metres, three point eight, three point five, three, and we were there. I put the engine into reverse, then neutral, *Khalida* stopped obediently alongside, the woman caught her guard rail, and Anders leapt ashore, rope in hand, and tied her up.

I cut the engine and stood up, still clutching the cloth to my forehead. The woman put out a hand to help me onto the pontoon. 'I'm Irene. Come you wi' me. Mam's joost in the house. We're about to hae denner, if you fancy some soup.'

'I wouldn't say no,' I said. I hadn't felt cold while I was worrying about blood, but now my teeth were starting to chatter, and the land was swaying around me.

I felt the atmosphere of the house as soon as Irene led me in: a hard feeling of bitter unhappiness. The man had died in a car crash, the wife had been badly hurt, and the son who drank had been made worse. This Irene who was supporting me with such ready kindness must be one of the daughters. 'Mam!' she called, as we came through the door, 'I've a patient for you.'

She helped me into a warm kitchen, a country kitchen with a Rayburn at the gable end, and a workmanlike wooden table below the window looking out on the voe. There was an armchair on the other side where her mother sat: a woman in her fifties, with a face lined with pain. I saw no resemblance to either of her children; her greying hair was neither Irene's dark, nor Keith's fair, but a mousy brown, and she had a low brow, a sharp chin and pale green-blue eyes. She wore a cherry-red yoke jumper which matched the patterned walking stick beside her, but whose bright colour drained her face. It was from her that the bitterness came; her face was sharp with it, her mouth set in angry lines, and it echoed in her voice as she greeted me. 'Not only injured but wet through. Have you dry clothes aboard?' Her hooded eyes had dark shadows under them, as if she didn't sleep much.

I tried to think. Now I no longer lived aboard, I had a box with extra jerseys and gloves, but no spare jeans or thermals; I only took those aboard for longer trips, and right now most of my wardrobe was hanging out in the garden, drying. 'Jerseys,' I managed.

'Well, let's sort that first,' the mother said. Her voice was low and soft, but with a sharp edge that made it a command. She nodded at Anders. 'You'll maybe go and get her two jerseys.'

'Box by the engine,' I said. 'Tupperware.' He nodded and left.

'Irene,' the mother said, 'go you into my bedroom and get out a towel, and my clean dressing gown from the press. Then you can help the lass get the wet stuff off, and while I'm looking to her head, you can find her dry clothes, and put her own in the washing machine.' There was something mechanical about the way she spoke, as if she was determined to do her duty by this bleeding stranger thrust upon her. I felt mortified, but leaving now would only make it worse. I'd have to accept her kindness with grace, and pretend I didn't see how reluctant it was.

'I'm wearing thermals,' I said. 'They'll dry quickly.'

Irene went out and upstairs, her footsteps clattering above us.

'I'm Patsy,' her mother said. 'Patsy Arthurson. And you must be the lass that sails. My other son, Ertie, he works to your dad, driving plant.' Her face twisted to anger. 'Worked.'

'Cass,' I said. My hand was too bloodstained to hold out. 'Cass Lynch.'

Irene hurried back down the stairs with a folded towel and a blue towelling dressing gown. 'This is my daughter, Irene,' Patsy said. 'Irene, this is Cass. Pass me that, and give her a hand wi' those wet clothes, then get a bowl of water for her to wash.'

With Irene's help, I managed to get most of my wet clothes off without making too much mess on the lino. The towel Irene held out was blissfully warm, and the dressing gown covered me nicely. I tried to give Irene a hand picking up my clothes, but the room began to spin around, and I sat down abruptly. 'Sorry,' I said.

'You just sit,' Patsy said. 'Irene can manage.'

It seemed that Irene was expected to manage everything. I sat in silence as she took my bundle of clothes into a side room. There was the click of a tumbler, a few bleeps, then running water as the machine cycle started. Irene came back in and stood quietly with her hands in front of her, looking at her mother for more instructions. For a moment I wondered if she had some kind of special needs, except that she'd been quick and clear when I'd had the accident. Maybe she'd had to bridle her tongue at first in patience as she ran after her injured mother, and had now got so used to her mother bossing her about from her chair that she no longer realised how extraordinary it was.

'Now,' Patsy said, 'we'll need a clean bowl o' hot water, and cotton wool and the plasters box.' Irene nodded, and went into a walk-in cupboard in the corner. 'Sit you here,' she added, and reached out a hand to drag a kitchen chair over to her. 'In the light.' She bent forward to inspect my head, still sitting in her chair. I closed my eyes. Her hands were assured as she moved mine away, washed the wound and inspected it. 'You're given yourself a fair dunt. I doubt it needs stitching. Irene, gie the surgery a phone and explain. You can easy run her along to Bixter to get it looked at.'

'We need to be out of here well before high water,' I said. 'Cribba Sound.' I wasn't negotiating the Icelanders and the Black Stane with this spinning head.

'Yea, yea, plenty o' time for that.'

She mopped away, then I heard the crackle of a plaster being unwrapped, and felt it being pressed to my scalp. 'There, that'll do you for ee now. Steri-strip. Great stuff.'

I opened my eyes again. 'Thanks. Thank you very much.'

She gestured towards the path. 'And here's your man back with your spare ganseys. Irene, keep him at the door while the lass gets dressed.'

'Forty-five minutes,' Irene said. 'The doctor can see you at quarter to two.' She went out to guard the door, and I got into the clothes she'd brought. The T-shirt was Patsy's, and hung off me; the pants and jeans were Irene's, and I just managed to squeeze into them.

'Three-quarters o' an hour. Then there's time for a bowl o' soup,' Patsy said. 'Irene, let the young man in, then gie Ertie a call for his lunch, and tell him we have visitors.' She rose, levering herself up from her chair, and grasped her stick. 'I was in an accident. You maybe kent.'

I nodded. 'I heard.' I wasn't sure what to say, and resorted to formality. 'I'm sorry for your loss.'

A wave of the former bitterness came back for a moment. 'I told him he was no' able to drive south, after all these years, but he widna listen.' She stood for a moment, brooding, mouth hard, then took a step towards the Rayburn and lifted the lid of the pan. A most beautiful smell of tattie soup washed out in a cloud of steam.

'I'm mending,' she said. She nodded towards a pair of crutches in the corner past her chair. 'I still need those occasionally. I'm mending slower than if I was your age, but I have the help o' me bairns.' A spasm crossed her face for a moment, as if she'd moved wrongly, and hurt something. 'I'm out o' the wheelchair, and mostly off the crutches.' She changed the subject. 'You're Cass from the Ladie.' She looked at Anders. 'But you're no' the policeman that wears a kilt even for going out in the boat.'

'Anders Johansen.' He leant forward to shake her hand. 'I was Cass's engineer on the longship for the film, three years back.'

'Aye, aye, we heard all about that. And I'm Patsy. Now, sit you both down at the table, and have some soup to warm you.' She gave her daughter a sudden malicious look from her green-brown eyes. 'Then you'll run Cass to the surgery, and I'll enjoy having a smart young Viking all to meself.'

It was a mild joke, but it threw Irene completely. She went white, then flushed red, her patient composure broken, and turned away from us. I could see her back move with her quickened breathing. When she turned back she hadn't quite mastered herself; there was still a red spot high on each cheekbone as she went over to the worktop and began buttering rolls. There was a long silence. I glanced at Patsy and thought there was malice in her eyes as she said in a completely ordinary voice, 'There's ham we can have with the rolls. Don't forget the mustard.'

Chapter Five

Kishie: *A woven basket for carrying burdens like groceries or peats. People carried it using a* **kishie-baand**, *a leather or rope strap that went around the shoulders or forehead; ponies brought home peats using kishies, one on each side.* [Old Norse, **kassi**, *a basket.*]

Irene was busy laying out plates on the table when there were steps outside, a shadow fell across the briggistane, and her brother Ertie came in. The first thing I noticed about him was how good-looking he was, classic tall, dark, handsome, and wearing an equally striking brown and white anchor-pattern gansey. His face was damp from a hasty wash, his hair raked in wet comb-streaks. The blast of antiperspirant almost drowned the smell of whisky. He had a strong look of his sister, the same dark hair and olive-brown eyes, except that her face was thin and his was rounded, with a dimple on his chin. He stood in the doorway a moment, and nodded at us. 'I watched you sailing in.' He spoke slowly, with a hint of a slur in his voice. 'Are you come from far?' His eyes were on Anders; there was a thread of envy in his voice. 'Norway?'

Anders shook his head. 'Not today. I came over with the *Swan* yesterday.' He gestured at me. 'Cass's boat lives in Brae, so we did only half a dozen miles.'

'Ertie,' his mother said, 'this is Cass from the Ladie.'

She didn't add *the policeman's girlfriend*, but I could see he knew from that who I was: Gavin's bidey-in, and Dermot Lynch's daughter. He held out his hand formally, and tried a smile. 'Ertie Arthurson.

I shoulda kent your boat, for I'm seen you out in her, back and fore, when I'm been after a mackerel or twa for supper.'

'Set dee doon, boy,' his mother said. Her voice was angry, as if she'd long ago lost patience with him. I half-expected him to obey, as Irene had, but instead he hesitated, looking in dismay at the five seats. Anders was beside Patsy, who was in what was obviously her usual place, leaving the chair nearest the cooker for Irene, and the empty one at the head of the table, the traditional father's place. Patsy gave an annoyed click of her tongue and gestured Ertie forwards. 'Sit down, his ghost is no' going to leap up and throw you off.'

Ertie looked unhappy, but did as he was bid. I could guess why he'd hesitated; when there had been only four of them, Patsy, Irene, Ertie and Keith, then the father's place would have been left empty, but now, with five of us, someone had to sit in it. It was the eldest son's right, and I had no doubt he was older than Keith by a good five or six years.

Irene brought the soup over in mugs, and followed it with a plateful of ham rolls. It was best Shetland soup, so thick with tatties and carrots that the spoon could stand up in it, and it did me the world of good.

'Has your head stopped spinning now?' Patsy asked.

I risked nodding, and found that yes, it mostly had. 'A lot better, thanks to you.'

She waved that away. 'I retired just before the accident, but it does me good to keep me hand in.'

There was an eating silence for a bit, then I decided to chance my arm. 'I'm blyde to see Ebony's taken no harm from his run out.'

There was a sudden silence as the spoons stilled. Irene gave me a quick, suspicious look, as if she'd remembered that I was the policeman's girlfriend.

'We helped round him up,' I explained. 'Keith was kind enough to stop by and let me know he'd taken no harm.'

The stiff poses relaxed. 'No, he took no harm from it,' Irene said. 'A bit tired out, that was all, and no wonder, running all the way to Eid.' Her voice was clipped, and she shot a hard glance at her brother.

If a gate had been left open, it was easy to see who was getting the blame.

His reply came out as a snarl. 'I told you a dozen times, I never touched the bloody gate!'

There was a fraught silence for a moment, then Patsy said, 'It was good o' Aidan to bring the trailer to him.'

'He's a bonny horse.'

'He widna a been my choice for a stallion,' Ertie said. His speech was clear now. If I hadn't smelt the whisky on him, I'd have taken him for sober. 'I dinna like blacks. We're aye had broken coloured ponies. That's what the Klaufister stud is kent for, no muckle blacks like for a funeral.'

I looked up at him quickly, and looked away again from the suppressed anger in his face. His fist was clenched on the table. His black gaze moved to his sister. 'I never left that gate open. And I'm the eldest. You shouldna have brought that whitteret here, wi' his fancy ways.' His fist slammed on the table. He rose abruptly and glowered at us for a moment, then took two rolls in his hand and headed out of the door.

There was a moment of embarrassed silence, while his footsteps clomped out, and Anders and I concentrated hard on our soup. Then Patsy gave a long sigh. 'You'll pay no heed to Ertie. It's been a hard time for the family.'

We nodded understanding, then Irene looked at the clock. 'Here, we'd need to be going.'

We left Anders to do the dishes, and scurried out. I was mortified to need the support of Irene's arm for the grassy track to the road, where the car was parked. A racket of barking from the grey pick-up behind it made me jump. 'Ertie'll take them out later,' Irene said. 'Or I will.'

I suspected it would be her job.

'You mustn't mind my brother,' Irene said, once we'd negotiated round the Clousta houses and were onto the wider road. 'He took Dad's death hard. They were very close. And he wasn't happy about me getting Keith home. But Mam was injured, she couldn't do anything at all when she first came back from the hospital, and me big sister, she's got two young ones, Noah's eight, and Taylor's just gone to the school, and Danielle, that's Ertie's wife, she's got two peerie things, so I was having to look to Mam, and do all the croft work mostly on my own.'

Da willing horse is aye tauld ta rin faster, Magnie would say. Folk who worked without complaint were given more and more to do until they snapped under the burden. I looked sideways at Irene's thin face and wondered how close she still was to snapping.

'I wasn't managing,' she said. 'Then Mam suggested getting Keith home. Well, I wasn't sure he'd come, he didn't bide after the funeral, but Mam aye thought the best o' him, and I was getting more and more exhausted, so I phoned him and laid it on him that he had to come. I was never thinking of him biding. I thought he'd just get compassionate leave or something, to tide me over till Ertie was more himself. It was a shock to find he'd given up his job and his flat, and was planning on staying in Shetland. He was always the one who wanted to live in the city. That's why he studied to be an accountant. He wrought in London for nearly a year, but it was all that expensive, and he moved north to Newcastle last hairst. Maybe he found he missed Shetland. I don't ken. And he was aye Mam's boy, so she was glad to see him.' She sighed. 'Do you hae brothers?'

'No.'

'They're worse as whelps in a litter. Aye squabbling about something. I shoulda kent that. I thought with it being an emergency and all, they'd forget the old rivalry and pull together, but it didn't happen. Instead o' shaking himself oot o' it and doing more about the croft, Ertie turned stubborn and said he wasn't taking orders from Keith, and wouldn't do anything at all, and he and Danielle were quarrelling all the time.' I slid a glance at Irene, and saw tears standing in her eyes. 'So it all seemed to be getting worse instead of better, but at least I could leave them to it and concentrate on Mam. Keith got a job in Lerwick, and Ertie started going to his work again, and he and Danielle were talking, and there was a bit of peace. Then round about Easter Keith said we needed a new stallion, and talked Mam round behind our backs, and next thing we kent he'd bought him, and that set it all off again. 'Danielle—' She flushed and closed her lips firmly for a moment, then spoke in a would-be positive voice. 'But Mam was starting to be on her feet, and I was feeling fitter. I'm aye at me worst in winter. Ertie looked to the sheep and I took over the kye, we have the start o' a dairy business, and Keith and I did the horses together, the way I used to with Dad. We hae some bonny foals this year, all from our old stallion.' Her voice sparked into enthusiasm. 'Waterloo Robbie, bay, with that charactistic shoulder flash. He's a bonny boy. We've had him since I was a bairn, but of course we couldn't keep two stallions.' Her face mingled regret with the practicality of a professional animal keeper. 'He's over in Skeld now. But his foals should do well at the sales. And here we are at Twatt already.'

I remained silent, letting her concentrate on the turn-off, and going down the brae. While she'd been talking I'd been looking out at the loch of Clousta and wondering again at the distance Ebony had run, with all these green verges to tempt him to stop and eat.

The doctor was ready for me. She agreed that I wasn't showing serious signs of concussion, put three stitches in, told me to wash my hair with a mild shampoo when I got home then keep it dry for a week, take it easy this evening and the next couple of days, and come back in a week to get the stitches taken out.

'What do you work at?' I asked Irene, once we were on our way again. 'Apart from the croft, I mean. Or are you full-time at Klaufister?'

'Slave labour,' she said. Her face hardened. 'In town. Eezi-eats. You ken, the new place where Mackie's was?'

I nodded. M&Co had been one of the few chain stores to get a toehold in central Lerwick. It had closed not so long ago, and the building had bought by the latest fast-food chain from America, the sort of place that sold skinny fries and fat burgers.

'The Press Gang had nothing on modern labour practices,' she said. 'They phone us as they need us, so that they never have anyone standing round doing nothing. It can be as little as an hour's notice.' She sighed. 'I never finished the school, you see. I had ME in upper primary, starting in the summer when I was ten. It was an awful thing. I was that tired all the time. Some days I could only manage to eat my breakfast in me PJs, and then I had to go back to bed again. Mam had to give up work to look after me. Then when I started to feel well enough to go to school, the jolting in the school bus made it worse, and Mam had to come and fetch me home again after a couple of hours. It was a nightmare. I managed me English and Maths exams, with a home tutor, and Art, because I could do that at home. That was all I could do, and I didn't do that well in any o' them. So I'm no' qualified for anything better. But it's a horrible place to work. Rigid. All run by computer from America. Even the manager has to do what it says.'

Life on the Navy fighting ships the pressed men had gone to had been rigid too, but at least there was a captain on the quarterdeck to make the decisions.

'What would you like to do?'

She shot me a sideways, wary look I couldn't quite account for. 'Oh, I don't ken. Something with animals, but it's over-late for me to start studying again now.'

I didn't believe her, but I was a stranger, and there was no reason she should tell me her secret dreams. She added, 'Maybe I'll manage to save enough from this job to get a holiday. I always wanted to see France.' She sighed. 'But I don't even have a passport.'

'It's a bonny country,' I said. 'You maybe don't ken, my mother's French. But how are you keeping now?'

'Mostly better. I hae more allergies than I used to have, strong smells o' things. I move fast through the supermarket washing powders aisle. I'm pretty wiped by the end of days like the Viking Show, or if I have a shift of several hours. And here we are.'

She turned the car around so that it was parked ready to go again, and I walked unaided down the track to the house. We found Patsy and Anders chatting away, and Patsy smiling.

'Are you sure,' Patsy said, once she'd inspected the stitching, and agreed with a flash of humour that I'd fit in with Frankenstein now, 'that you're safe to sail home?'

'Yes,' I said firmly. 'I can't leave *Khalida* at your pontoon overnight, there's not enough water, and Anders needs to be back at the boating club this evening. He's off to Unst on the *Swan* on Friday.'

'Well . . . if you're sure. Irene could easy run you back to the Ladie, if Anders could sail your boat home.'

'No. Not past the Icelanders or through Cribba Sound on his own. But thank you.' I turned my head cautiously to smile at her. 'You've been very kind. Thank you for everything, and I'll get your clothes back to you the first chance I get.'

I ignored Anders' offered arm along the pontoon, and clambered aboard under my own steam. Cat and Rat appeared from the cabin, Cat's tail raised in greeting, Rat's whiskers whiffling. Ertie came out of the original house and followed us to *Khalida*. 'You get aboard and get your engine started,' he said, 'and I'll untie your ropes and give you a push off.'

'Have we water enough to go in a circle, or do I need to back out?'

He didn't need to think about it; this was his home waters. 'Reverse to the point, then you'll have water to turn from there, but don't go too far from the line out. Are you going back by Cribba Sound?'

'Thinking to.'

'You'll have plenty of water. Just keep in the middle.' He gave a sudden, charming smile that transformed his face from matter-of-fact to magnetising. I understood how he'd managed to get away with drinking before work for so long. 'And the wind's behind you all the way. That's what sailing boats like, isn't it?' He laid his hand on the guard rail. The shake in it quivered through the whole boat. I undid the aft rope and coiled it up. Anders went forrard ready to take the bow rope, and we set off in good order. Patsy and Irene waved from the doorway, and I called a last thank you.

We backed out, then turned level with the point, as Ertie had said. He waited to make sure we got away safely, then raised a hand and went back into his house. I wondered where his wife, Danielle, had gone. Back to her parents, maybe. We negotiated round the island, then hoisted the geneker again, its crumpled nylon smoothing to a curve as the wind filled it, and set our nose between the mussel buoys for Cribba Sound.

The wind filled in as we came home. It was barely five o'clock when I dropped Anders off at Brae. I wished him luck, refused offers of help, persuaded Cat away from Rat, and puttered the *Deuk* home.

The shepherd's warning was coming true. There were waves running through the sound now, and dark clouds massing over Aith. I dealt with the outdoor animals before the rain came. The sheep were all present and correct, and the burn was still running; the ponies did their usual shoving and eating each other's food, but the foals got what was meant for them in their enclosure, and not too much of the older horses' mix; five of the hens and the cockerel went into their run good as gold, but the black one with the particularly wild topknot decided I was a mass murderer trying to lure her into a trap. It took ten minutes of creeping up on her before she finally flung herself in with the others in a flurry of flapping and squawking, as if I'd been keeping her away from them all the time. I doled out the grain and oyster shells for Lady Layers, clanged the door shut on them and bolted it. 'Hens!' I said to Cat, who'd been watching from the gatepost with what I thought might be a sympathetic expression.

That done, I took a cup of tea outside. The sun sinking through the clouds with that pre-rain yellowed light heightened the colours: the russet of the hills, the first red moor grass and spagnum moss in the marshy places. In the garden, the waxen orange rose hips shone as if they'd been polished. A salmon boat going home left a golden trail.

I sat there as the clouds rolled up towards me, with a curtain of rain sweeping up the voe below. Cat and Julie chased each other round the garden, Kitten watched from the wall, and we all raced for the door as the first heavy drops hit us. The sitootery roof sounded as if someone had turned a hose on it, and out of the window I could just make out the sheep huddled together in the shelter of the wall. I was glad I'd got the hens in.

I was about to re-warm the stew I hadn't eaten yesterday when my phone rang: Gavin. 'Hello, Cass.'

'Hiya! How's your mum?'

'She's fighting. She's still on the drip, and getting water from a sponge, but she's bright and communicating with nods and headshakes. The doctor's pleased with her.'

'Oh, Gavin, that's good!'

'What've you been up to today?'

'I fed everyone, then Anders and I took *Khalida* round to Clousta. I'd never been there, so I thought it was a good chance. Awkward place, but a bonny day.' I hesitated, realised that of course he'd find out anyway, and added, 'I fell in.'

'Not like you.'

'I let go of the geneker halyard and the top of the furler came down and hit me, then I overbalanced and there I was, swimming. But at least,' I added cheerfully, 'I'd already taken my lifejacket off, so I don't have to go to Lerwick to get it re-armed. And the folk at the house there were very kind – they dried me off, gave us soup, and ran me over for stitches. I'm glad you can't see me. I look like Frankenstein's daughter.'

There was silence for a moment. 'Which house in Clousta?'

'Klaufister. Where the loose stallion came from.'

'You were there today?' The unease in his voice unsettled me.

'At lunchtime, and a bit of the afternoon. We left just before three.' He was still silent. 'Gavin, what's wrong?'

'Cass . . . look, I can't tell you why, but I want you to write down what you did at Klaufister, just notes, to remind you. While it's fresh in your memory. What people said, how they looked, everything you noticed.'

'Yes.' I didn't ask the *why* that was burning on my lips. If he could have told me, he would. Something had gone very wrong at

Klaufister. I remembered Patsy's bitterness, Irene's exhaustion, Ertie's sudden display of anger. I took a deep breath and moved back to ordinary. 'Ketling Julie's not pleased at the catflap not working for her.'

'She'll have to wait till she's six months, and sorted. Keep an eye open for Cat seeing off strange toms, and whisk her straight indoors at the first yowl or back-roll.'

We spoke on for a few minutes, chatting nothings, until at last he sighed and said, 'I'd better go to Mother. I'll phone you at bedtime.'

We said goodbye, then I set Gavin's stew to heat while I washed my hair gently, as instructed, changed back into my own clothes and put the borrowed ones in the machine, then fed the cats and let Ketling Julie out for a last charge. The stew was slightly past its best, but I ate it anyway, with macaroni cooked in it, and beetroot slices to liven it up. A search for pudding found some yoghurt. I'd need to get to Eid Co-op tomorrow for interesting things to eat, rather than slipping into least-resistance mode.

By then it was half past seven. The shadows were starting to lengthen, the rain had stopped, and Venus was bright above the Clousta hills. I wondered again what was going on behind them, at Klaufister. Gavin had said to write down everything I could remember. I found paper and a pen, tried sitting on the bench outside again but was driven in by midges within seconds, and settled down in the sitootery. The cats came to join me: Cat on the back of the sofa, where he had a grandstand view of the shore, Kitten in Gavin's chair and Julie curled up in my lap.

I'd got as far as us eating soup when there was the sound of car wheels on the gravel on the other side of the hill, and the flash of headlights. I went to look, and saw a cream-coloured, old-fashioned sports car with a blonde woman at the wheel. Gavin's police sidekick, DS Freya Peterson, had come to call.

Hospitality meant I had to go and greet her, midges or not. I gave my hands a quick skoosh of Smidge, rubbed them on my face and bare feet and headed out. The midges zoomed in like fighter-pilots, straight for my ears. I rubbed them too and opened the gate.

DS Peterson was already out of the car, and moving at speed towards me.

'Come in quick,' I said, and held the door wide.

We dived into the house together, and I fielded Julie as she tried to escape. 'Tea?' I asked, over a fusillade of squawks.

'Yes, please.' DS Peterson laid her laptop bag on a chair, took off her black jacket and hung it over the back, casual, accustomed movements, as if she was used to visiting here. That was one reason I was glad to be home more. I had every faith in Gavin, but propinquity and shared work was a dangerous mixture. She hadn't, I noticed, asked after Gavin's mother, as if she was up to date with that news. 'Black coffee, no sugar.'

I was glad she didn't add, 'I'm sweet enough.' *Sweet* was the last adjective anyone would apply to DS Peterson. Handsome, with her regular features and blonde hair pulled back in a neat clasp, efficient, organised, but those green eyes of hers made me think of a mermaid looking dispassionately at the follies of human beings. My lifestyle of going where the wind took my boat would drive her round the bend.

We settled ourselves in the sitootery, and she opened her laptop and typed a couple of lines, then looked across at me. 'Gavin called me. He said he hadn't told you what had happened at Klaufister, but that you'd been there during the day.'

I nodded. There was a heavy feeling in my breast. 'Anders too.'

'I've sent Shona to talk to him.' Shona was her sidekick, and her echo.

She hesitated for a moment, frowning, then set her hands to the keyboard. 'Well, tell me what you were doing there, in as much length as you can.'

I used my notes so far to help me: my fall, Irene calling us over, Patsy, Ertie. DS Peterson typed away. I felt that I was betraying the Klaufister folk's kindness in speaking about the undercurrents within the household, but this was a police matter.

As I spoke, I became more and more anxious to find out what had gone wrong.

'Did you go up to the old house? The ruined one?' she asked, when I'd talked myself to a halt.

I shook my head, and was pleased to find the giddiness had gone.

'Did anyone mention it, or seem concerned about it?'

'No. I don't remember anyone even glancing at it, but then, they were helping me in and out of the house, and it was well above the path. It had a fence around it, and piles of rubble. I thought someone might be clearing it out to put animals in.'

'They store stuff there,' DS Peterson said. She tilted the screen of her laptop downwards. 'Not half an hour after you left, Ertie Arthurson went up there for some feed, and found his brother Keith. He was dead.'

Chapter Six

Klibber: *A wooden frame like a pony's saddle with a horn on each side for hooking a kishie over.* [Norse, **klyvbere**, from **klyv**, *a pack,* and **bera**, *to carry.*]

Dead! I'd expected something like this, from Gavin's reaction and DS Peterson's prompt visit, but it was still a shock. 'He wasn't there when I visited,' I said at last. 'They said he worked in Lerwick.'

'He did, but he wasn't there today. The last time he was seen alive was when he said goodnight to his mother the evening before, just before nine.'

'Nine? Was he going out?'

'She goes to bed early, since the accident. Irene was in her room, listening to an audiobook, and Ertie was in his house.'

'Where did Keith sleep?'

'In the main house. The room he and Ertie had shared as boys, before Ertie did up the old house for himself.'

'Irene didn't hear him getting ready for bed? Brushing his teeth?'

'She says not. It was a bonny evening. She had a notion he'd gone out for a walk. He'd been late home. He saw a client from five to five fifty. We've verified that. He left Lerwick at six, came home to the message about the loose horse, changed, collected their own trailer and Land Rover, and went up to Voe to get it.'

'He called in here,' I said. 'On his way back from Voe. That was a bit after seven, maybe nearly half past. To thank me for helping round it up.'

She raised her fair brows. 'Did he now? Well, well. A bit out of his way, with a rampaging stallion in the trailer.'

'I thought so too. I think he was hoping to ingratiate himself with Gavin.'

She nodded slowly. 'A social climber? Trying to get in with the right people?'

'It's what they do down south, isn't it?' Shetland didn't have that kind of social structure, or certainly not in the country. No man was a hero to his neighbours.

'Can you take me through that conversation?'

I did my best. 'I'll admit I was prejudiced against him,' I said, once I was finished. 'He was, oh, smarmy.' DS Peterson pulled an agreeing face. 'And a normal Shetland man fetching a horse would wear a boiler suit and rubber boots. Keith'd taken the time to dress up in horsey clothes, instead of jumping in the pick-up and fetching Ebony straight away.' I thought about that. 'Aidan, Rainbow's dad, he's fairly high up in Sullom Voe. Worth impressing as well as Gavin, I suppose. Or maybe he wanted to make it clear he was an experienced horse owner, not a mere crofter with messy fences. Maybe he wanted to get in with Gavin in case there was trouble about Ebony being loose on the road.'

'He went straight home from here. He was there just after eight. He and Irene checked the horse'd taken no harm, which it hadn't. Irene said he was preoccupied, as if he was thinking about something.'

'Did she know what?'

'She thought it might be about the horse getting out. She'd walked the fence herself when she found out he was missing, in case there was a gap, and found nothing. And the gate was shut.'

'Someone let him out?' *He widna a been my choice for a stallion,* Ertie had said, and both Irene and Patsy were blaming him for having left the gate open, in spite of his denials. They were family and knew him, but all the same, I thought I believed him. Irene hadn't seemed enthusiastic about Ebony either; she'd been fond of the stallion they'd had, and a black horse represented a change of direction for the stud. *Keith talked Mam round behind our backs*, she'd said. Keith imposing his will over theirs. Might she have disliked that enough to chase Ebony out of the field, in the hope he'd come to harm on the road? Given him enough of a fright to make him run all the way to Bixter, with the main road and school traffic? She obviously liked the horses, but she had that breeder's detachment too. Or maybe it was darker than that. She'd spoken as if the horses had been her herd, as the cows were Ertie's – then she'd been overruled. Maybe putting Ebony in harm's way was her silent revenge for being the family's beast of burden.

I'd been quiet too long. DS Peterson was looking at me, brows raised. I shook my head. 'Nothing.'

'Possibly he shoved the gate open, or possibly someone let him out, leaving the gate open, and then someone local walking their dog noticed the gate open and shut it again. Officers are doing the house-to-house right now. They'll ask about that.'

'So . . .' I said, since she seemed to be in a forthcoming mood. 'Keith brought the horse back at eight, checked it over, had something to eat?' She nodded. 'Then said goodnight to his mum, and wasn't seen again that evening. What about the morning?'

'He normally got up earlier than the rest, to e-bike to Bixter for the workers' bus, to get into town for nine. He wasn't on it, and he didn't turn up for his work, but nobody worried at first, because he said he might come in later, since he'd stayed late the night before.'

'So the home folk thought he'd gone to work, and the work folk thought he was still home.'

She nodded. 'Any thoughts about that?'

I shrugged. Right enough, it was odd that nobody'd been aware of him not getting up, so to speak, but the house might have thick walls, or quiet plumbing, or Patsy and Irene might be sound sleepers.

She went back to her laptop. 'What about this bitterness you sensed? What was causing it?'

'It was just an impression, and remember they were strangers to me.' I paused, trying to sort out the memories. 'Patsy was angry at her husband, for insisting on driving south. He was to blame for the accident.'

'How disabled was she?'

'She needed a staff to move about the room, and there was a pair of crutches by her chair.'

'Housebound?'

'I suppose so. If she needed the car, she'd have to walk a hundred and fifty metres on a grassy track to the road. She said she was out of the wheelchair, so she must have had one, but she'd maybe given it back to the hospital. I didn't notice one in the hall, but I wasn't looking for one either.'

'Able to walk the distance to the old house?'

I shook my head. 'I don't know. She was able to move about in the kitchen, but with a staff one side, and the other hand on a chair. It looked to me like she'd need her crutches or an arm to get to the car.'

'The daughter, Irene. What about her?'

'Tired out coping with everything. Helping her mam, running the croft, going to work at a moment's notice whenever they call her. Glad to have Keith home to help at first, but fed up with the brothers not getting on.'

'Why didn't they get on?'

'Town mouse and country mouse.'

'Ertie's the older brother.'

She didn't need to say any more. The oldest boy inherited the croft, everybody kent that. Ertie was the stay-at-home brother who'd worked on it, Keith had gone off to London. Yet here he was back, and set to stay, if buying a long-priced stallion was an expression of intent.

I remembered the confident way he'd said, *I've taken over the Klaufister stud*.

DS Peterson's hands hovered over the laptop. 'Anything else that you noticed that might be relevant?'

I shook my head. 'Do you know . . .?' I began, then remembered

Gavin saying time of death was always an estimate. 'Roughly, when do you think he might have died?'

She gave me a reproving look. 'Between nine last night and three thirty today.'

'Yeah.'

She relented. 'Not for repeating, but late yesterday evening or during the night is more likely than today.'

I felt a chill run shivering down my spine, followed by nausea.

'He was lying there dead while we were there?'

She nodded, and closed her laptop. I thought of that clean kitchen, the warm smell of soup, with Irene bustling about, and Patsy being competent with my head, and shuddered again. It hadn't exactly been normal, with undercurrents of anger and malice swirling round, but I found it hard to believe that one of them knew that Keith was lying dead in the ruined house just above us.

It was only after I'd shown DS Peterson out and was sitting in the sitootery in the last of the sun that I remembered Vaila's comment, *An insurance job*, and Rainbow's quick, suppressing look. I'd taken it for teenage cynicism, but now I wondered if they knew something, some rumour from the horsey world. I'd need to talk to them.

I was still mulling that over when the phone rang. I reached over to the sofa, where I'd left it, and realised a familiar yacht was nosing towards Magnie's pontoon: *Khalida*. She looked good, well-balanced under jib only, and the sail shone white against the green hill. Anders was going visiting. I hoped he wouldn't underestimate the distance she'd travel on sheer momentum when he came alongside.

It was Magnie on the phone. 'Now, then, lass,' he said by way of greeting. 'What's the latest word with Gavin?'

'Good news. She's alert, and managing to nod.'

'That's good to hear. He'll be relieved at that. He'll no' be coming home yet, though?'

'Not till Monday. He's got a week's leave.'

'Well, well.' Preliminaries over, he launched in. 'I'm got Anders on his way here, visiting. I wondered if you'd like to come over in that peerie boat o' yours to make sure we're up to speed for the North Isles on Friday.'

I knew as well as he did that that was just an excuse. In his days as a fishing skipper he'd been in and out of the North Isles as often as I'd raised an anchor. He'd seen DS Peterson's highly noticeable car parked above the house, and no doubt Anders was about to tell him about the interview with Shona. They wanted to compare notes. Ketling Julie was curled up on the couch, sleeping off a charge round the garden followed by a hearty meal; Kitten was on the wall, chittering her teeth at the sparrows on the roof. 'Cat'll be glad to see his pal,' I agreed. 'Be with you in ten.'

'I'll put the kettle on,' he said.

I caught up a warm jacket, my lifejacket and the battery, and headed down to the *Deuk*. Cat was at my heels within seconds, and we arrived at Magnie's pontoon in twelve minutes dead. I moored up alongside *Khalida* and left Cat to enlist Rat on anti-Tab duty. Tab was Magnie's rescued Siamese, and she and Cat had a running stand-off over who was allowed where on Tab's beach. She'd conceded the pontoon, but not an inch of the shingle beyond. She'd seen *Khalida* coming and was already on duty sitting on one of the fence strainers, tail and spine fur raised and blue eyes blazing. I hoped Cat bringing reinforcements wouldn't enrage her, and was relieved when he headed straight into *Khalida*'s cabin. A flash of a long tail in the window and a slight rock of the boat meant he and Rat were going back to Cat's kittenhood game of chasing each other around the cabin. Tab relaxed slightly, but stayed on her post, whiskers bristling.

I took off my lifejacket, gave *Khalida*'s mooring lines an unobtrusive checking glance, and headed at speed up the beach-stones path to the house, waving away midgies as I went.

I liked Magnie's kitchen. It was a warm, old-fashioned space that probably hadn't changed since his childhood: a cream-coloured Rayburn that radiated heat, with a couch beside it, and an armchair facing it at just the right distance for propping feet up on the chrome towel rail. The china sinks were below the window, and there was a wooden table half-covered with letters, seed catalogues and last week's *Shetland Times*, which he read cover to cover over Friday lunchtime. The two plain chairs had been his and his mother's while his father had been living, but now they were tucked in neatly, and Magnie sat in his late father's captain's chair. Anders was sitting on the couch with Tigger, Magnie's peaceable stripey, on his knee.

'Well, lass,' Magnie said by way of greeting, 'let's see the stitching then.'

Anders had been quick off the mark. I gave him a reproving look, and he flung up one hand. 'Hey, don't blame me! Magnie's nephew saw the whole thing.'

'Oh, yeah?'

'Great-nephew,' Magnie said. 'Me niece Susan's oldest boy, you mind Susan, at bides just by the bridge. Mattie, he's called. Mattie Harcus.'

The name rang a bell, but I couldn't instantly place it.

'He's maybe a couple of years younger as you, and no' married. He works on the ferries.' He paused as if he was going to say something more, then frowned and finished, 'He'll be crewing for you on Monday.' That explained the familiarity; I'd cast an eye over the crew list before leaving the ship, just to remind myself. Magnie paused for another swig of tea. 'Well, he bides in Clousta, in the peerie house down by the shore, on the other side o' the Klaufister headland, and it was his day off. He saw you coming in, but then you went behind the headland, so naturally he took a bit o' a walk up the hill ahint his house.'

Naturally. 'So he saw me fall in,' I said resignedly. I was never going to hear the end of this.

'The coloured sail came down on top of you, he said, and knocked you in.'

'I overbalanced.'

Magnie shook his head at me. 'You should be more careful, lass. Dip dee doon.' He put a mug of tea into my hands. 'So he saw you go over, and Anders help you out, and then he saw you were bleeding, and Irene coming out to help you.'

'She was very kind,' I said. 'They were all kind.' I glanced at Anders. 'I felt bad talking about them to DS Peterson.'

'I also,' Anders said. 'But the young policewoman, Shona, she said it was a case of murder.'

'It was that,' Magnie said. 'Mattie was just making his way down the hill when he heard Ertie shouting, and saw him running to the house from the old house above where he bides, the ruined one, and then Irene came running out with him, and he tried to stop her, and she pushed past him. She went into the ruins, wi' Ertie following her, and then he heard her screaming. Ertie brought her out o' there, and they went into the main house, and then not much over half an hour later the police came along wi' the blue lights and the sirens.'

Mattie had had a fair wait on top of the hill. I hoped he'd had time to take faerdie maet and a Thermos with him.

'And then,' Magnie continued serenely, 'there was all the usual stuff, a white tent around the body – at least the old walls'll protect that from the next gale – and yellow tape, and Freya Peterson arriving in her black suit and briefcase without a hair out of place, and going into the house, with a swarm of constables around her.'

'Could he see into the old house from up on the hill?'

Magnie shook his head. 'Barely. He could just see something that looked like a light-coloured jacket, on the ground among the ruins. He only had pocket spyglasses with him, not proper ones. He could make out that it was a body, but no details.'

'He'd be the nearest house to Klaufister,' I said. *Late yesterday evening or during the night*, DS Peterson had said. 'He didn't happen to hear anything in the night?'

'Not in the night, no,' Magnie said. He paused to take a long swig of tea, and reached for the biscuit tin to pass round. He liked keeping an audience in suspense. Anders and I took a gingernut each, and waited. 'But,' Magnie said, once he felt he'd got us worked up enough, 'he heard shouting during the evening. Yesterday evening. He was up checking on his sheep just before it got too dark to see, there was a lamb he wasn't happy about, and when he was on the top of the hill he heard Ertie and Keith arguing in the new house. It was a fine evening, and there was a kitchen window open. Well, he took it to be them, but when he thought about it he could only be sure about Keith's voice. That funny knapping way he has o' speaking.'

'Shetland rhythm, south vowels,' I agreed.

'And when I pushed him, well, he couldn't even be sure the other person was a man. It coulda been a wife. He couldna see them, and then when he came around the curve o' the hill, he thought the voices were coming from the new house. About nine, he thought, or maybe a peerie bit after. It was dark then, but the moon was up. And he said maybe the reason he thought it was Ertie was because both Patsy and Irene would be in bed by then.'

'He couldn't distinguish words?'

'Nothing clear. The only thing he thought he mighta heard was "You never left me." Something like that.'

'*You never left me*,' Anders repeated.

We sat in silence, thinking about that.

'And,' Magnie finished, 'he wondered if he should try and intervene, given Ertie's state, then he thought they'd both likely turn on him, so he got out of there, back to his own house. And once he got there he wasna sure if he'd done right, because of the shots.' His grey-green eyes danced; he was having fun dribbling out the information.

Anders sat upright. 'Shots?'

'That's more like it,' I agreed. 'So when did he hear shots?'

'Yesterday morning. He was woken at dawn by banging, and at first he'd taken it for someone scaring geese, but it was a bit early for that, and then he thought it must be some visitor in the hills after hares. He didn't look at the time, just cursed and went back to sleep, but when he thought about it, he thought it was mebbe around six. It was clear daylight, and the sun was just on his windowsill.'

'Shots,' I repeated. 'I wonder who round there has a gun.'

'Your man would ken that, for they need a licence, even for that cannon thing they use at regattas. Mattie didn't ken o' anyone.'

'DS Peterson didn't say how he'd died.' I glanced at Anders, and he shook his head. Looking at him reminded me. 'Magnie, you never heard anything about Irene from Klaufister having a boyfriend from Norway?'

'I noticed that too,' Anders said. 'Her reaction when her mother joked about being left with a Viking.'

Magnie frowned. 'You ken, I think it rings a bell, but from a good way back. What age would she be, this Irene?'

'Twenty-six or -seven.'

Magnie shook his head. 'This was longer ago as that. I'll keep thinking.' He looked at me. 'Your man won't be back to take over the case?'

'No. I don't think it, anyway. He's got a week with his mother and Kenny. It's DS Peterson in charge, till the Major Investigation Team gets up from south.'

Magnie sighed. 'I'm vexed to hear that. I'd a liked him to be here. Well, you tell him what Mattie said, and he can pass it on.' He set his cup down and stood to check out of the window. I peered past him. Cat and Rat were now sitting side by side on *Khalida*'s cabin roof; Tab had moved to one of the posts at the end of the pontoon, tail swishing. 'I think there might be warfare brewing. You'd mebbe better get the enemy out o' here.'

Cat's fur was fluffed out too. Threatening him was one thing, but he wasn't having a strange-looking cat with blue eyes threatening his friend. 'I think I'd better,' I said.

We went out into the midgies. Anders lifted Rat onto his shoulder, and I got Cat's lifejacket on and coaxed him back onto the *Deuk*, still grumbling menaces. It was only once I was well on the way home that I began to wonder about why Magnie was so keen that Gavin would come home. He knew as well as I did that a Major Incident Team would be sent up from south, and Gavin's degree of involvement depended entirely on their good will.

Both Kitten and Julie sniffed dubiously at Cat when we got in; Kitten went so far as to hiss, and take herself off to a high worktop. I made soothing noises, then sat down to think about tomorrow. There was a shopping list on the table notepad, scribbled in Gavin's neat, cramped hand, and unfortunately I'd need to go into town, as it ended with *layers' mash*. There was also a mysterious *oilcloth*, and dimensions, which sounded like the kitchen table. I went out to the shed for a tape measure, to check.

It was strange going into Gavin's shed when he wasn't there. Naturally the cats came out with me, and took the chance to poke around in a normally forbidden zone. He'd transformed it into a working space that I'd be glad to have onboard the *Swan*, if we had room: white walls with painted shadows of the tool that lived on each hook, lengths of wood strung from rope in the ceiling, a workbench with a vice at each corner, a bin with offcuts for the fire, and a line of containers along the windowsill. It smelt of woodshavings and oil. I closed my eyes for a moment and breathed in, pretending he was there. Then I took up the steel tape measure from the bench, rounded up the cats and stopped trespassing. He'd be home on Monday, if his family could manage without him.

I kept thinking about what Magnie's nephew had overheard. *You never left me.* It didn't make sense, in the context of a quarrel – I couldn't see why any of the Klaufister folk would complain that Keith hadn't left them. I tried to think of it as part of another phrase. *You never left me alone . . .* If Ertie had been as critical of Keith to his face as he was behind his back, and I had no doubt he would have been, Keith might have said that to Ertie. I'd see what Gavin thought.

I was reading in bed when he phoned. 'Hiya! How's your mum doing?'

'Still good. There's colour in her face. She's doing the physio, and there's definitely movement in her left hand.'

'Oh, that's good news.'

'How are things up there? Freya said she'd been to see you.'

'I didn't have much to tell her. Gavin, are you allowed to say how he died?'

He made a non-commital sound, and I explained about Magnie's great-nephew who'd heard shots the morning before, and a quarrel that evening. 'I don't think he's said anything to the police. Magnie was vexed to hear you weren't racing home to take over.'

'I'll phone him,' Gavin said. 'Shots in the morning, and a quarrel around nine, between Keith and possibly Ertie. *You never left me.*'

'I was wondering about that. It didn't seem to make sense. How about Keith saying to Ertie, "You never left me alone." Always on his back, criticising, not wanting him there.'

'A good possible.' He paused, and changed tack. 'How're things at home? Cats, foals, hens, sheep?'

'Exhausting, but all well, as far as I can see. I found your shopping list. Where do you get the hen food from?'

'Voe.'

'Oh, that's easy enough. Is the oilcloth for the kitchen table?'

'I'm used to it, do you mind?'

'I'm used to it too.' It was a bit old-fashioned in the UK, but every French country table had a brightly coloured tablecloth, bought at the local market. 'I'll have a look in Home Furnishing.'

We chatted for a bit longer, but Gavin sounded like he was ready to drop, and I felt knackered myself. It had been a busy day: negotiating into Clousta, a swim in the sea, stitches, being interviewed, Magnie's nephew hearing shots . . .

I turned over and went out like a light.

III
Mines

Thursday 25th August

Tides at Brae

HW 01.22 (2.2m)
LW 07.34 (0.5m)
HW 13.58 (1.9m)
LW 19.47 (0.7m)

Sunrise 05.43; moonset 14.01; moonrise 20.07; sunset 20.29.

Waning gibbous moon.

Chapter Seven

Der aye a grain o' water whaar da staig smores: *There's no smoke without fire.* [Literally, *There's always a bit of water where the young horse drowns.*]

I woke up to the bonniest of days: a light wind from the west, and a clear, pale sky hazed over with wisps of mares' tails. The sea was fretted over with ripples; the hills were auburn, with hummocks of moss like jade rocks among the heather. Below the house, the iris swords by the burn glistened in the morning dew.

When I got up, my stitched head ached only a little; nothing a paracetamol wouldn't sort, and it was too fine a day to waste. Oilcloths and hen food could wait. I'd go to Aith, to make plans with my crew for the second and third days of three school trips in *Swan*. He was Trevor Mullay, and he was the second coxswain for the lifeboat. The coxswain had a day off, he'd said on the phone, so he'd be down in the lifeboat station, covering for him.

I was sorry to be taking the *Deuk* instead of *Khalida*, but at least the electric engine was as near silent as made no difference. We slipped away from the pontoon with barely a ripple to disturb the seals on the Blade, and headed south towards Aith. The sheep-cropped grass on the hills showed the contours of the land, the rectangular outlines of long-overgrown lazybeds. The mussel floats gleamed with the sun's reflection in their black plastic.

I left Cat aboard in the marina and headed along to the Eid Co-op for some interesting food. I was in luck; the meat cabinet was full.

I got a foil tray of Chinese shredded beef and another of Italian mince balls, added bacon and two Sandwick bakery ready-made desserts, then went round the shop putting bits and pieces into the basket: vegetables, milk, cheese, bread, some chocolate biscuits for onboard and a sympathy card to take to Patsy at Klaufister, when I returned her clothes.

Last night's Radio Shetland would only have had the barest of reports on the death at Klaufister, but naturally the queue in the shop was discussing it with interest. A man in a boiler suit and yellow wellies said that he'd heard there had been shots in the hill, and they had a couple of moments speculation over the best place to shoot into the ruined house from: from the hill above Mattie Harcus's house was the conclusion, with a bit of sage nodding. 'He's on day shifts on the Yell ferries,' said a stout woman in a parka. 'He'd have been home all evening. Surely he'd have heard if there'd been shots then, or during the night.'

I wasn't quite sure if she was implying that Mattie might have shot Keith.

'Though if he was going to shoot a Klaufister man it wouldna be that one,' she added. The others nodded, as if they knew exactly what she was talking about. I remembered Magnie's hesitation the night before, as if there was something he wasn't telling us – some kind of bad blood between Mattie and Ertie, it sounded like. I wished I'd met him before he came sailing with us on *Swan* on Monday.

The man in the boiler suit shook his head, and reverted to the previous remark. 'He coulda used one of these silencers they have in the films. That sounds like a popping cork.'

The stout woman wasn't convinced. 'And the old house o' Klaufister was right nearby, with Ertie in it, and Patsy and Irene no' much further away. You're no' saying Ertie wouldn't have heard something, from twenty metres away. You'd hear a popped cork at that distance.'

'Depends on the state he was in,' the man said bluntly.

I'd wondered about that myself. Clousta was a quiet place, where a shot would echo round the hills. Surely Patsy and Irene would have heard it, even if Ertie had been too drunk to notice. Of course maybe they had heard, and told DS Peterson already. That could fix the time of death more precisely than she'd admitted to me.

'Or it coulda been muffled by the walls o' the old house. Solid built, it was.'

'Mebbe,' the man said, unconvinced, and paid for his errands.

'Your man'll likely ken more,' the stout woman said to me.

'He's away right now. His mother had a stroke, so he's gone down to be with her.'

That produced a volley of sympathetic tutting and good wishes. I paid for my two bagfuls and lugged them down to the marina, checked on Cat, who was sunbathing peacefully on the warmed fibreglass of the cabin roof, and headed for the lifeboat station.

It was a new, white building on the shore end of the pier, harled outside, wood-lined inside, with the workshop and crew's outdoor gear downstairs, and a big picture window in the upper storey overlooking the voe. I glanced out as I came up into the main room, and saw that they had a grandstand view of anything I might get up to out there. I supposed it was a reassuring thought.

Trevor was in the office, hunched over a computer. I remembered him from the *Swan* training weekend we'd done back in April, not long after I'd been appointed as mate. He was in his late twenties, medium height, but almost as wide as he was tall, shoulders developed from his day job on one of the big fishing boats, and impressively strong; he'd hauled our 70-kilo replica man-overboard casualty, Dead Fred, up from the water as if he was a blow-up toy. He had midbrown hair and a square, tanned face. He owned a smaller boat in the Aith marina, two berths along from the hammerhead where I'd moored *Khalida*, and I'd occasionally seen him accompanied by two boys of the younger primary age. Usually he radiated good humour, but today he was frowning at the screen, one hand tapping the desk impatiently.

He turned a relieved face as I came in. 'Forms,' he explained. We exchanged a rolled-eye look. 'Can't put out on the water without filling in a folderful afterwards.'

'On the *Swan* too – but that'll be my job, not yours.'

'Coffee?' His smile was strained, and there were lines on his forehead and dark circles under his eyes, as if he hadn't slept well.

'Please.'

We moved through into the main room and sat down on the squashy chairs overlooking the voe. Three scarfs were swimming just off the pier, glistening dark green in the sun, necks raised like periscopes.

'The usual sort of trip?' Trevor said. It sounded like he was making an effort to sound everyday. 'No more as twelve, including teachers. Bairns onboard, safety brief, motor out, mainsail up, round Papa Little, lower mainsail, back to pier?'

'Twice each day,' I agreed. 'Primary bairns on Monday, I have Mattie Harcus crewing for that.' I glanced over at him as I said that, but he didn't react as the shop folk had. 'Same again with secondary bairns on Tuesday, and then bairns from the oldest class of Aith, Walls and Sandness together on Wednesday, for sailing round to Walls.'

'Then a day with the Walls bairns: out the south mouth and into Gruting, then back, three times.'

I nodded. 'And Anders is the engineer for the whole week – have you met him?'

Trevor considered for a moment. 'I think I mebbe have, when you were working wi' the longship, three years ago. Fair-headed – you'd spot him for a Norsky at sixty paces.'

I nodded. 'He'll likely sleep onboard, but I'd need to get home, for the animals. I was wondering if I could maybe get a lift back with you from Walls on Wednesday, and a lift both ways on Thursday. I don't drive, and Gavin's away.'

'It's the Ladie you bide at, isn't it?'

I could see him calculating the extra time that would add to his journey. 'Yes, but I'll bring the boat down to Aith and meet you here.'

There was quickly suppressed relief in his light-blue eyes. 'That'd be no bother. I can get you from the marina. We can work out times come Wednesday. When d'you want me onboard on Tuesday?'

'We'll be here for eight, but there's no need for you to be that early. We'll prep her after the trip on Monday.'

Business organised, I relaxed, looking out across the fretted water. Trevor sighed, rubbed a hand over his eyes and set his mug down. 'I'm no' quite together. This is an awful business, over at Klaufister.'

I nodded agreement.

'Did I hear you were there when they found him?'

I shook my head. 'We were there earlier. I got a bump on the head from a block, and they invited us in to clean me up and run me to the surgery for stitches. They were all kind. It was only after we'd gone that Ertie went up to the old house, for feed, and found . . .' I hesitated and went for the Shetland circumlocution. 'Him that's away.'

Trevor was silent for a moment; his face darkened. 'Him and me didna get on. I ken you're no' supposed to speak ill o' the dead, but he set my hackles up. There was something about him. It was the way he boasted about how well he'd done south and the exciting life he led down there. I didn't believe he'd done well down south at all. If he really had, he wouldn't have been back up here playing at being a crofter.'

It was an odd way of putting it. 'Playing?'

'He kent nothing about it.' He flushed. 'See, I was at the school wi' him. The Eid school. Well, wi' them all, but Ertie was two years above me.' His face softened, relaxed into a reminiscent smile. 'I was in Allison's year. We were childhood sweethearts.' He glanced at me. 'You ken I'm married to Allison, Keith's sister?'

I shook my head. 'I didn't ken.'

'Him that's gone was me brother-in-law. Irene was two years below us, and Keith was two more. He started the school when I was in P4, and came into the secondary when I was getting ready to go to the Anderson. So I kent him. He had absolutely no interest in the croft, and once he got into secondary and thought he was no small cheese, he sneered at those of us who had. He went on all the time about how he was going to make it big in London and earn a million times what we'd get from staying on Shetland. It was Ertie who took his sheep and kye to the Waas Show, and the lasses helped their dad and granddad wi' the horses. Their grandfather was the one who began the Klaufister stud, and he and their dad built it up. Klaufister horses have a good name in the Shetland pony world.'

'Broken coloureds,' I said, so as not to be a total ignoramus.

'Yea, mostly red and white. Even when there was no market for horses, they got good prices for them. Still do.' He paused to consider. 'I'm no' sure getting that black stallion was a good move. It's fashionable right now, but when you've built up a name for one thing, it's no' always a good idea to change. Irene'll need to think about it.'

'There are fashions in horses?' I asked.

'Yea, yea.' He turned his head to smile at me. 'You're no' had much to do wi' beasts, have you?'

'I'm learning,' I said. 'While Gavin's away, I'm in charge of three horses and two foals, a park of sheep and lambs and a hutchful of tappit hens. And the cats.'

'A croftful,' he agreed gravely. Now he was more like himself; the gleam in his eye told me I was being teased. 'Yea, there are fashions. I didna come from a horsey family, but I learned about it from Allison. You could ask Irene, when you have a couple of hours to spare.' His voice was affectionate; whatever he felt about the late Keith, he got on well with his sister-in-law. 'For a while it was all broken coloureds. In the eighties, when most of them were going for meat. The colours made bonny rugs. Then it was miniatures, as lawn ornaments, and then, in the recession, when folk were cutting back, the standards came back in, for children riding, or for pulling carts. They ate the same amount, but they were more use.'

I nodded.

'Right now, according to Allison, standards are still in, and black's the popular colour. Well, down south the colours are mostly black and red anyway. So I suppose he might get better sales south with black foals, but that's not what folk associate with Klaufister, so folk looking for that wouldn't look there, and folk looking for traditional Klaufister foals will be disappointed.' He set his mug aside with a shrug. 'But that's a problem for next year's foals. It'll be up to Irene and Ertie to decide if they want to keep the black stallion or send him to the sale in October.' He sighed and finished, 'I was glad it was nothing serious between him and Emma. He wasn't at all what I'd want for her, no matter how much he got round our mam.'

He glanced at me, and saw I was looking blank.

'Emma, that's my peerie sister. He took her out for a drink, back and fore. Nothing serious. She's a bonny young lass, and he was wanting the company – it's no' exactly a wild life out at Klaufister, with Ertie on the drink and the women going to bed before nine. He wasn't what I wanted for Emma, but she was dazzled by his stories, and the townie air.' *Dazzled* made it sound more serious than Trevor was giving out. 'He seemed to be telling her that they'd go back south and get a flat in town, live the life, go to the concerts and parties.'

I remembered my years in Edinburgh, working to get qualifications to return to sea. Concerts and parties hadn't featured. 'It's not all it's cracked up to be.'

'I ken that, and she had the sense to ken it too, but she's only nineteen, and never been further than Glasgow. London's the city of Oz for her. When I tried to inject a bit o' reality, pointed out he'd no' lasted long there, she said I'd never been to London either.' He sighed. 'Which was true. And then, buying that stallion. He might be telling Emma he was just here to tide things over, and they'd be going back south any moment, but you don't put money like that on a horse if you're not staying.' His jaw hardened. 'I could see Emma being like Irene, stuck out at Klaufister drudging on the croft, or like Danielle.' He stopped abruptly, as if this was dirty washing not to be aired. 'And then trapped in a minimum wage job wi' our mam babysitting for her when he took off with someone else – because although she wouldn't see it, he was just the type to do that.'

I wasn't sure of that. 'He was a creep, but there are a lot of men who are all over other women, but still stick wi' their wives.'

Trevor shook his head. 'If he couldn't stick to her afore they married, he definitely wouldn't stick afterwards. And it's an ill bird who fouls his own nest. No, she's well rid o' him.' He rose and picked up both mugs. 'But that's no' what she's thinking right now.' He seemed to realise that what he was saying about Emma now contradicted what he'd said earlier about her not being serious about Keith, and finished hastily, 'It was all an awful shock. Anyway, I'll see you on Tuesday morning.' He paused, mugs in hand. 'I don't suppose you ran across the Clousta witch while you were there in the voe?'

I stared at him. 'The Clousta witch?' I repeated.

'Mary Nicolson. She bides on her own just over the hill from the North Voe o' Clousta. The first house as you go in from the sea, down by the shore. She used to work south, then she came back here. She bides in a peerie hoose wi' a cat that's black all over, and follows her everywhere, like a dog. Even in the boat, when she's off for a piltick or two. That's what got her the name o' a witch, that and that there's a story she bides in the same place that Maggie Black did, her that was put on the Black Stane and left to die. You might no' have seen her, but she'd most certainly have seen you.'

'Mary Nicolson,' I said. It rang a faint bell, but it was a common enough name in Shetland.

'Her family came from near you. One of the ruined houses, I canna mind which. Come to think o' it, you might even ken her, for she's of your communion. Roman. Onyway, if there was anything to have seen, she'd have seen it. She likely sent the police away wi' a flea in their ear, she keeps herself to herself, but she might talk to you, if you went over to her.' He paused, and reddened. 'I want this pinned on the right person. I don't want any cloud to rest on Emma. I want her to move on from him that's away, and find someen better.' He nodded at me. 'It's a fine day to take your peerie motorboat into Clousta. You go and talk to Mary. Tell her I sent you, and why. Then you can pass anything she kens on to your man.'

'I'll do that,' I said.

I headed back to the marina, mulling that over. I'd never heard of the Witch of Clousta, but if she lived on the north side of the voe she had a grandstand view of Klaufister. Trevor was right about the day too; it was a great day for a motorboat excursion through Cribba Sound. I could meet Mary Nicolson and put the borrowed clothes back while I was at it. I glanced at my watch. It was barely half past ten, so I had plenty of time to go and check on the animals then head out again. I could have a picnic on a beach on the way, then go and find Mary Nicolson.

I thought about Trevor's sister Emma as well. I didn't know her, but it was a common thing for young folk in Shetland to undervalue what we had here, and think that everything south had to be better: better schools, better cinemas, better nightlife. I was sure it wasn't true, but telling that to a nineteen-year-old who thought she'd found love and a ticket to a better life was a waste of breath. His urgency that she shouldn't be blamed was odd too. Surely she was the last one to want him dead – unless she'd discovered something about him that had disillusioned her completely, like that she wasn't the only girl he was promising the moon to. *If he couldn't stick to her afore they married*, Trevor had said. *It's an ill bird that fouls his own nest*. That sounded like an affair with a woman in Clousta. I'd ask Magnie about that later.

I headed back north, and paused at the cottage to offload and stow the shopping, and check up on the animals. I meant to keep going into Clousta after that, but Julie was so pleased to see me, and so keen to go outside, that I felt I couldn't. There was no sign of strange toms, so I let her out. I'd have lunch in the garden before I shut her back indoors.

Gavin phoned when I was at the cup-of-tea stage. 'Mother's doing well. She squeezed my hand with her good one, and managed to waggle the fingers of the other one. They're letting her drink juice by the teaspoonful. The doctor says she's going to be okay.'

'Oh, that's great! Are you still in Fort William?'

'Just. Kenny's going to come over this afternoon, to drive me back to the loch, then he'll take over with Mother for tonight, and I'll be on farm duty. Tomorrow will be dealing with horses who've done their best to forget anything they ever knew about stalking. What's the news with you?'

'Not much. I went to the Aith shop, and caught up with Trevor of the lifeboat – he's crew for Tuesday and Wednesday. It turned out he's married to Allison of Klaufister, the other sister, and on top of that his sister is the late Keith's girlfriend. He didn't like him. He said I was to talk to . . .' I gave the name its most sinister twist, '. . . the Witch o' Clousta. She won't talk to the police, he said, but she might talk to me, to pass on to you. She's a Catholic. Well, a Roman, he called it.'

'Ah, the church freemasonry. Mary Nicolson, of Clousta?'

'So he said. Her main crime seems to be she has a black cat which goes out in the boat with her.'

He laughed. 'I can see why he thinks she might talk to you. Give her my greetings. I ken her. She's not a professed nun, but she lives like one. She has a wee chapel in her house, and Father David says Mass there once a month. Ask her from me to help you, and let me ken what you find out.'

'Will do. Are you allowed to tell me the police station news?'

'None yet. The Major Incident Team arrived this morning, and they're all busy out at Klaufister. What's the word on the street?'

'I was trying to think about it and ended up feeling I was lost in a labyrinth, with tunnels everywhere. Ertie hated him because they'd always feuded, and Irene was mad about the stallion, and he was apparently seeing someone else behind his girlfriend's back. Maybe a neighbour's wife? Oh, and the gossip in the shop was that he was shot.'

'No,' Gavin said positively. 'I ken that much. But don't share that. Why do they think he was shot? Because of Mattie Harcus hearing shots the day before?'

'I suppose so. Other Clousta folk would have heard them as well.'

Gavin hesitated for a moment. 'This is absolutely for your ears only. He was wearing a sort of fancy scarf, a cravat thing. Someone grabbed the two ends and strangled him.'

Chapter Eight

Mirk: *Darkness.* [Old Norse, **myrkr**, *dark.*]

I set off again in the *Deuk* after I'd finished speaking to Gavin. I'd do a foray into Clousta, seek out the Witch, and take the clothes to Patsy. Gavin didn't usually get home much before six, and the animals had had their morning feed. They'd all be fine.

Gavin's voice echoed in my head. *Someone grabbed the two ends and strangled him.* The bitterness I'd felt in the house became a horrid picture of hatred that could look a man in the eye and hold tight as he struggled for breath. I didn't want to think about it; I couldn't help it. Ertie was strong enough. Irene looked fragile, but she could control a stallion.

A fulmar glided in a circle around me and settled on the water, black eyes watching me. It was high water now, slack tide. I slipped smoothly through Cribba Sound, with the black and white Vementry House on port and the hill leading up to the chambered cairn on starboard, and carried on past the V-lines of mussel floats around the next headland. It was a good kilometre through the narrow part, then another to the mouth of the South Voe of Clousta.

The wind must funnel through the west sound in winter gales, for the hill above me was worn to the bones, with long straight lines of rock protruding through the grass. There was a ball on the height of it to lead mariners in, maybe half of a meid for avoiding the Icelanders. It looked a big, metal thing, red with rust; I wondered if it was a disarmed mine from the first war. There was no sloping shore here as there was in our sheltered anchorage; the sea had taken mouthfuls from the land, leaving a three-metre drop of red soil held up by rocks.

I spotted Mary Nicolson's house straight away. It had been the last in a row of crofthouses, a hundred metres up from the sea, protected from the north by being tucked into the lee of the ribbed cliff behind it, and with the slope down to the seaweed-fringed shore below it enclosed in a waist-high wall. There was fresh whitewash on the walls, and a blue-painted door was hospitably open in the porch. A flare of salmon red suggested geraniums. The three skylights in the roof reflected the sunlight. Past it was the remains of the community who'd left Maggie Black on the stone to die, two long houses reduced to crumbling walls. A double-ended skiff lay on the beach. The landing path had been cleared of weed, and a line of rocks let sailors get out dry-shod. I nodded in approval, and slid the *Deuk* in alongside Mary's boat.

She had seen me coming. There was a movement in the porch, then she walked down the path to meet me.

The name 'witch' gave totally the wrong impression. She was forty-five at most, tall with an upright build. She wore brown trousers, jumper and sandals, and her dark hair was caught back in a plait. As she came near enough for me to see her face, the idea of witch fell away. In a world filled with people rushing from one place to another, she radiated serenity. This was her place, and she'd found . . . no, happiness was too uncertain a word. Her brown eyes were filled with a deep contentment that was above the vagaries of the world. A black cat followed her, elegant and aloof as a statue from an Egyptian tomb. It stopped at the beach edge and sat upright on a flat rock, ears pricked forward, surveying us.

She waited as I tethered the *Deuk*, then came forward, hand held out. 'Cass. Welcome.' Even her voice was hushed, as if she didn't want to disturb the quiet of the afternoon. From her accent, she'd worked south for a good part of her life. 'I've been wanting to meet you. How's your head?'

'Fine now.' I changed my tone to more formal. 'Gavin asked me to greet you from him. He's away in the Highlands – his mother had a stroke.' I added, off my own bat, 'She's called Morag. Will you keep her in your prayers?'

'I will, most surely.' She gave me a long, thoughtful look. 'So Gavin's sent you to ask me police questions?'

'Trevor, Allison of Klaufister's man, and the brother of Emma, who was going out with the late Keith. He said you'd have seen anything there was to be seen. He wants the blame fixed on the right person.'

'Well, then, you'd better come in.'

She gestured upwards, and I preceded her through the garden: potatoes and green vegetables first, then rows of fruit bushes, and at the end, by the door, pots of herbs and what looked like a beehive. There was a cow on a long tether on the other side of the wall, with a calf frisking around it. If she had sheep too she must be not far off self-sufficient.

The cottage breathed peace. It was the loveliest house I'd seen, completely free of land clutter. The porch door opened onto a staircase made of white-painted wood with black rubber treads on each step, and on each side was a small room: the kitchen on one side, and a glimpse of white wall with a crucifix on it on the other, the chapel Gavin had mentioned. Mary motioned me into the kitchen. I felt at home straight away: this was what I was used to, the minimum of items kept in absolute order. The wood-lined walls were painted white. There was a Rayburn in the chimney breast, with a kettle steaming on it, and a wooden worktop beside it, made from an old fishbox, with a white-painted shelf below. A pan and a frying pan hung above it, and one wooden spoon; two plates, two bowls and two mugs and a row of jam jars were arranged on the shelf. There was a china sink below the window. A table and two chairs stood at the stair wall, and there was an old-fashioned resting bench at the back wall with a fawn wool blanket on it. The blue rag rug in front of it was the only touch of colour in the room. The cat leapt onto the settee and continued to watch us. It had old-gold eyes and the most intelligent face I'd ever seen in a cat, like something from a fairy tale; you expected it to speak at any moment.

'Have a seat,' Mary said. She held up a handful of green leaves that she'd bent to pick as we came in. 'Can I make you herb tea?'

I nodded, and watched as she crushed the stems together, put them in a pot, and added water. I could smell rosemary: for remembrance. *Pray, love, remember.* We sat in silence while it infused. I had no feeling of needing to rush into speech. If this was witchcraft, it was white magic that medieval folk would have called sanctity. I could imagine her as an anchoress in a room beside the church, like Julian of Norwich, with all the village coming to tell her their troubles.

She poured the tea in one graceful movement, added a spoonful of honey, and handed me one cup. I sat for a moment enjoying the warmth of it in my hands, the smell that rose from it, then sipped. Immediately I felt a sense of space filling me, the world's perspective on our petty troubles, and sat up straight, fighting against it. From an eternal point of view, a murder might be one more in a string from the beginning of time, but for us, here and now, it was a calamity to everyone involved.

Mary smiled, a slow, still warmth. 'Perspective,' she said. 'Not dismissing, just giving the emotional space to think before rushing in.'

'Are you a . . . what do they call it, a tertiary?'

'In a way. I live as an oblate, following the Benedictine rule of work and prayer. Father David comes to say Mass for me once a month. It's advertised in the newsletter. You're welcome to join us.' She smiled again, but this smile brought her back into the world. 'You're a cradle-Catholic, aren't you?'

I nodded.

'I'm a late convert, like my three-times great-grandmother, who lived next door to you at the Ladie. Have you heard her story?' I shook my head.

She set her teacup down. 'Our family goes way back,' she said. 'Right back to a Nichol Olasson on Papa Little, in the early 1600s.

He had three sons, Nichol, Anders and Erasmus, and that's where the three families that lived around Houbansetter came from. The Mary Nicolson I'm named after came from Millburn, the old house by the pier.' She smiled. 'My grandmother was a great one for stories of the old days, and she told me this one. Mary Nicolson was the sister o' one of the early Methodist ministers in Shetland, John Nicolson. Her folk were from Quiensetter, the ruined house nearest to Aith, and Mary was the third child o' that name. That was an odd thing from the start, for there were no other Marys in the family. After the Mother of God, Granny told me. Mary married Adam Nicolson – his father was from Clousta, and they bade at Millburn, just below you.' She sighed. 'It must've been a busy place then. I'm talking the time of the Napoleonic wars. There were Mary's parents, at Quiensetter, along with her oldest brother, Christopher, he had a dozen children, and then there were Mary and Adam at Millburn, along with their three bairns, and Adam's sister Jane, when she got too old to be a servant in Gonfirth.'

I thought of our quiet road-end, and imagined thatched roofs on the ruined houses, the smell of peat smoke, boats drawn up on the beach, and the air filled with children's voices.

'Their oldest, Elizabeth, was my three-times great-grandmother.' Her smile was reminiscent, almost as if she was telling me something she remembered herself. 'Maybe Mary's parents, though they were kirk-goers, still had a respect for the old faith. There were Irish pedlers came round, and so Mary might have heard about her namesake the Queen of Heaven from them. She had this belief that she was meant to be a Catholic, Granny told me, and God had promised her that she would be baptised in the Catholic faith and receive the sacraments before she died. She must have repeated that to others, for it was known enough for one of the first priests to say Mass here after the Reformation to find out about her. This was in 1860, and she was seriously ill, so they sent a woman ahead to find out if she was able to receive them, then Father Bernard went, along with a guide and a companion who could act as interpreter, for Mary would have spoken old Shetland. Father Bernard himself wrote an account of what happened. They found Mary almost paralysed, but when she was told "a priest is here, he is here beside you", her senses and speech returned, and to the astonishment of her family, she clearly stated that she wished to die in the faith of the Catholic Church. She was baptised and also received the last rites. She showed great joy, and asked to hold the hand of the priest God had sent to her.' This Mary must have told the story often, but her eyes shone with tears. 'Her family were black-affronted, and refused to have the priest and his companions in the house overnight. I'm the first in the family to follow my namesake into the old faith.' She gestured around her at the plain white walls. 'And so here I am.'

'What do you do all day?'

'Pray, and work. I follow the Benedictine Hours.' A glance at my face showed I didn't know what they were. 'Vigils, Lauds, Terce, and then the morning's spent working until Sext, at one, then my main meal, followed by None. I'd just finished that when I saw you arriving. This is my recreation time until Adoration, at five, then Vespers, my evening meal, and finally Compline, the night prayer of the church, at half past seven.' Her face shone, and her voice lingered over the ancient names. She smiled at me. 'It's not a life for everyone, but it suits me.' She paused, then added, very simply, 'I had not long finished Lauds when I heard shots, the day before yesterday. Tuesday. Was that one of the things Gavin would want you to ask me about?'

I nodded. 'What time would that be?'

'Quarter past six.'

'You didn't look to see who was shooting?'

'No. But I heard a clatter of hooves, as if the horses were reacting to it.'

'You didn't go and look?'

She shook her head. I wondered if what had frightened Ebony had been someone shooting at him, except that I didn't feel that someone like Irene or Ertie, who'd worked with animals all their life, would try to kill a bonny, healthy stallion. If they had succeeded, though, I wondered if it would be an offence. He was their own animal; if there was no cruelty involved, the law would probably say they were entitled to do that. Or perhaps he'd been frightened along the road by pellets from an air-rifle. I remembered the smooth black haunches, and shook my head. There'd been no sign of injury. 'Would you know,' I asked tentatively, 'what sort of a gun?'

She shook her head. 'We never had one at home. After the war, my father would never touch a gun.'

'You didn't see anything in the evening?' Keith had said goodnight to his mother at nine. 'After nine o'clock? Lights in the ruined house, or anyone moving about? Or heard people arguing?'

'From eight, I'm in my room, upstairs. I don't leave it until Vigils, at four. There are so often people moving about, dog walkers with head torches.' A shadow crossed her face, but her lips tightened on what she might have said. I waited, and she sighed. 'It's hard to know what to say. How much to say. But your man has an honest face. I trust him to use judgement. You'll tell him what I say, as close to my words as you can?'

'Yes.'

She nodded and took a deep breath. 'Well, Ertie's wife, Danielle. You've not met her?'

I shook my head.

'A bonny lass, but young, very young. They should never have married each other. She had no idea what she was taking on. He eased up on the drink for a bit – they say, don't they, that the only two things that'll get a man off drink are love and the Bible.' She shook her head. 'It's too simple. Well, love made him try, but he didn't believe he had a problem. Things got difficult, with two children in three years, and then there was his father's death. When he took to drinking more heavily, she made allowances for a bit, then the quarrels began, and ended up with them parting. That was back in June. She stayed in their house with the peerie things, and he moved back to the old house. He's there yet, too stubborn to give way.'

She paused, then continued, her voice heavy with reluctance. 'I think I would tell Gavin this. Sometimes Keith would go and visit Danielle in the evenings, after Ertie had gone into his house and slammed the door. When it was light nights, I saw him, and as it got darker I'd see the light of his torch going up the drive from Klaufister to the road and round the bay.' She didn't make protests about it possibly being an innocent visit for a cup of tea; she spent her days looking truth in the face. *It's an ill bird who fouls his own nest*, Trevor had said. Not any neighbour's wife, but his own brother's. Was this what he'd wanted me to hear from Mary? 'He'd be there about an hour.' She raised her eyes to mine, and said with the utmost calmness, 'I'm in recovery from alcoholism. Five years ago, I was in a state worse than Ertie's. He came over here on Tuesday afternoon, and asked me to help him. I told him I'd been there, and described what his life had come to. I told him I knew about the belief that you're still in control. That you could give it up any time, that you're not that bad. After all, you haven't lost your licence yet, or woken up in a police cell yet, or hurt anyone. The yets. I told him that it wasn't normal to wake up in a bed stinking of urine, and not know what you did last night.' I stared at her, so serene, so posed, and couldn't think of anything to say. She smiled, understanding my confusion. 'I told him,' she said softly, 'that I knew what it felt like to go to bed praying that I'd never wake up more, then waking up after all, and going straight to the bottle for a drink – not a dram, a mugful. His drink is whisky; mine was gin. I described what his life had come to, and I told him how I knew. I'd lost my job, my husband, my chance of children. I didn't feel I was worth anything. I was in a pit, and I didn't believe I'd ever climb out.' She shook her head, remembering that younger self. 'Then I met someone, a nurse, a well-dressed, efficient nurse, who told me all I'd just told him. She'd been there too, and she convinced me recovery was possible. Now I was telling him. "How?" he asked, and I said it had to start with surrendering to belief in a higher power. He could call it God, Buddha, Jedi life force, whatever he saw it as, but he had to trust it to govern his life. Only then could I help him.'

'What did he say?'

'He was afraid. I hoped he'd come back – then he found Keith's body the next day.' She looked across at the old house. 'I'm still hoping.'

We sat in silence for a moment, then she lifted her head. 'There's one other person who knew of Keith's visits. You ken Mattie, who lives over the hill from Klaufister, just on the other side of the headland Danielle lives on?'

I nodded. 'Magnie's great-nephew,' I said. 'Mattie Harcus. He's crewing for the *Swan* on Monday.'

Mary looked across the voe. 'Mattie knew. I'd see him going up the hill in the evening and watching over at Klaufister – checking on Keith going about. But, see, he was concerned about Danielle.' She paused, shook her head, and said bluntly, 'He loves her. Mattie works on the ferries, and his first job was on the Whalsay ferry. That was how he met Danielle. Well, they were courting, until she met Ertie, and he charmed her away.' She shot me a frowning glance. 'Do you find it hard to believe how charming Ertie can be when he puts his mind to it?'

'No,' I said. 'I've seen it switched on.'

'Well, Danielle married Ertie, and they had the bairns. It seemed like they were getting on well enough. Then Mattie came to bide here. He's mostly on the Papa ferry for the summer schedule, but they move him around as they need him, so one day he can be on Papa, and the next on Bluemull Sound. This cottage halves his travelling times for Papa. The idea was he'd get a house in Yell for winter, and bide here in summer, but that didn't happen last winter.' She sighed, and went back to the murder. 'Mattie's been watching. He's Danielle's good neighbour, fixing things for her, taking her a palette he's chopped up, taking her and the bairns out in his boat. Waiting, I thought, until things got so bad that he could talk her back to him. I don't know how that'll end.'

I'd thought that Mattie's surveillance of us was extreme, even for a nosy neighbour. His interest in anything happening at Klaufister was explained now. So was the gossip in the shop, and Magnie's anxiety for Gavin to come home. His great-nephew was too close to the Klaufister folk for comfort.

'Did Keith go to Danielle's on the night he died?'

'Not with a torch. That night I sat by the window, watching the stars. It was a beautiful clear night.' She smiled at me. *'The heavens declare the glory of God, the skies proclaim the work of His hands.* The least light would have shone like a searchlight.'

'If you'd had the patience to wait for your night vision,' I said thoughtfully, 'you wouldn't have needed a torch. There was a bright moon too.' Mattie had been out on the hill in the dark.

'Yes,' she agreed.

'But Keith didn't strike me as having much patience,' I said. 'And he'd lived south for years. He'd have got used to streetlights.'

Mary nodded. 'You understand, all I can see from here is a moving light in the dark. I can't see who's carrying it. The only reason I thought it was Keith visiting Danielle was because I'd seen him go there in daylight. The evening before yesterday, Tuesday evening, nobody took a torch along the road from Klaufister. Someone went as far as the gate and back down. Tomorrow's bin day, so I took it to be Keith taking a bin bag up to the store by the gate. That might have been not long before nine.' She smiled. 'The wonders of technology. I don't have a clock in any of the rooms, just my phone set up to ring a bell ten minutes before each set of prayers.'

'But not having a watch makes you a good judge of time.'

'Yes.' She reflected. 'Say ten to nine.'

'Were there still lights on inside the house?'

'The kitchen one. That would be for Keith. Patsy's was out, and Irene's bedside lamp was lit. She usually goes straight to bed after she's got Patsy down. She told you she'd had ME for many years?'

'Yes, she said.'

'She still tires easily, and she's one who wants an active life, out on the croft, working with the horses. She and her dad built up that stud over the years. Then there's her work too, being called out at the last moment like that. When she's tired she can't read, her eyes blur, but she listens on headphones.'

'So,' I said, 'from nine o'clock, both of them would have been in bed, Patsy sound asleep and Irene shutting out the world with a book.'

'Yes.'

'And everyone in Clousta would know that.' When you lived in a peerie place, you soon learned all about your neighbour's habits. A pair of unopened curtains in an old person's house would have someone on their doorstep within half an hour.

Mary nodded.

'How about Keith's room, and Ertie's?'

'Keith's windows are on the far side of the house from me. Ertie's house was lit up, the TV light flickering away. That's what he usually does, after mirknen, watches football.'

Neighbours would know that too. If you'd arranged to meet up with Keith in the old house after dark, you wouldn't have to worry about keeping the noise down.

'There were no lights in the older house? The ruined one?' I thought of the walls casting a dark shadow, the rubble-covered floor of most old crofthouses, stones from the tumbled walls. 'You'd need one there.'

She shook her head. 'I saw nothing.'

I thought of the skylights that had shone in the sun, facing across the voe. 'No reflected light, crossing your window?'

'No.'

'You didn't see anyone moving about?'

She shook her head, and answered simply, 'Not at Klaufister. I saw Mattie up on the hill checking sheep, but that was earlier, at dusk. There was nobody moving about with a torch.'

Even as negative evidence, I reflected, it was useful. Keith hadn't gone along to see Ertie's wife earlier that night. It was more likely to be Keith than Ertie taking up the bin bag to the road; Ertie, who'd lived in Klaufister all his life, wouldn't have needed a torch on a bonny moonlit night. Keith had still been alive then, and he'd gone back into the house while Ertie'd been watching the footie.

'When did you go to sleep?'

'Around ten.' She added, in explanation, 'Vigils is at four.' She spread her hands. 'I'm afraid that's all I have to tell you.' She rose, and I stood too. Then she glanced out of the window, and her face filled with bright joy. 'He's coming back!'

I looked out, and saw Ertie's metal salmon dory nosing into the slip.

Chapter Nine

Chromite: *Shetland's largest mineral workings were the iron chromate pits near Baltasound, Unst, dug between the 1870s and 1920s. The Hagdale mine was the largest chromite mine in Britain.*

I rose to go, but Mary waved me back into my chair. 'No, no, don't rush away. Ertie would have seen your boat. He'd no' have come over if he wanted to avoid you.'

It was true. I subsided into my chair again, and watched through the window as she went down to greet him, intrigued. Her voice as she spoke of Ertie had been the first sign that she hadn't managed to completely detach herself from the world. She moved down to meet him as smoothly as she'd come to greet me, her black cat at her heels, but there was a joy in her walk that hadn't been there before. She leant forward to kiss his cheek, and took his arm as they walked back up the slope to the cottage.

'Aye, aye, Cass,' Ertie said. His voice sounded like it was an effort to speak. He slumped down on the resting chair as if it was his usual place, and the black cat jumped up on his lap. Mary made a new pot of tea, and brought out little oatcakes and a pat of butter – real butter, her own make, by the rich colour. She didn't take any herself, but pressed them on us both.

Ertie looked dreadful. The outdoor colour had drained from his face, leaving shadows like bruises under his eyes. His mouth was pulled down as if it could never smile again, and there was a nick on his chin, with a wisp of cotton wool clinging to it. He rubbed a trembling hand up over his face, then stretched it out to his tea and brought the mug to him, clasping the warmth. He looked across at Mary. 'We're had the police aside us aa day. I'm exhausted wi' it. Questions and questions, and them writing down what you say.' I remembered my experience of being a suspect, when Gavin and I had first met, and wished he was here. Gavin would have sat opposite him, voice calm, hands busy on tying a miniature fish-hook with invisible line, just as if he was chatting over a cup of tea. Suspects might go away realising they'd said far more than they meant, but I didn't think they'd be this drained and hollow-eyed.

Ertie looked at me. 'They kept asking what we'd each been like at breakfast, and then at lunch, and all I could say was, just as usual. And they seemed to think it was suspicious that none of us had seen him in the morning, or kent that he hadn't gone, but we wouldn't have. He's a grown man. He got up and got himself out of a morning, off on his bike to meet the bus at Bixter. He'd be out of the house at half past seven, earlier if it was a bad day, and he had wind to cycle against. He'd have been gone long before I roused. Irene helpit Mam to shower and dress, round about eight, then they'd have breakfast together. So they'd no ken whether he'd been there that morning or not either. He'd usually be long gone.'

I still thought they'd have noticed signs of Keith not having got up before them: no lingering steam and a soap smell in the shower, or damp footprints on the bath mat; no abandoned cereal bowl and mug in the kitchen sink.

'That blonde Peterson wife,' Ertie added, 'you can tell she's never had a day's illness in her life. She doesn't understand how tired it can make you. Both Irene and Mam sleep early and sleep sound, and then start the day gently. Then, at lunchtime, there was no sign, none, that any o' us knew anything about it. You could tell them that.'

'I told them that,' I said. 'A kindly family who'd welcomed me and helped me.'

There was a flash of something I couldn't quite catch in his eyes before he nodded. 'We were glad to do it. That was a nasty bump you took, and a swim too.'

'I'll never live that one down,' I said ruefully. 'My pal Magnie had heard all about it long before I got home.' Too late, I realised that it maybe wasn't tactful to mention Mattie's great-uncle, but Ertie gave a half-smile.

'Our neighbour Mattie wi' the spyglasses? Right enough, he's Magnie's sister's lass's boy. There's no' muckle goes on hereabouts that he doesna ken about. Hit's a pity he didna see wha it was killed me brother. If it wasna . . .' Mary raised a hand in a shushing movement, and he shot her a quick, guilty look, and stopped. I wondered how he meant to end the sentence. *If it wasna him?* Local gossip had been suspicious of Mattie too, and now I knew why; he loved Ertie's wife. He'd been about that evening; he'd heard an argument between Keith and someone else using the words 'You never left me.' But what reason did Mattie have to kill Keith? *He loves her.* Jealousy that he seemed to be succeeding with Danielle, or shock at the realisation that she'd thrown Ertie out, not for him, but to have an affair with his brother.

I'd been quiet too long. Ertie was looking at me. 'It was you who found him,' I said gently.

Ertie nodded. 'Not long after you left. It was time to feed the lambs, so I went up to the old house wi' me bucket – we have a couple of metal bins there, to store the feed in – and I saw him straight off. He was lying on the ground kinda crumpled over, as if someen had picked him up and dropped him. That fancy scarf he aye wore to dress up was tight round his neck.' He shuddered. 'He was stiffened in that position. When I touched his hand it was like wood. I didn't touch him any more. I kent he was dead.' He took a deep breath. 'I've taken enough dead animals off the hill. I shoulda expected it. But I—' He stopped, and buried his face in his hands.

'And you heard nothing in the night?' I asked. 'The night before you found him, I mean.'

He shook his head. 'I was watching the TV.' He paused, hesitated. A shadow of uncertainty passed over his face. 'Maybe . . . after

I turned the TV off, I thought there were sheep got in there. I thought I heard something moving around. But the feed was in bins, so even if they'd got in they wouldn't get at it. All they'd do was eat the grass, and save me strimming it. So I left them to it and went to bed.' His face had a startled look. 'I'd forgotten that till now. They asked me, this morning, but I'd forgotten.'

I took that as meaning he'd been hungover. 'Any idea of the time?'

He shook his head.

Mary leant towards him. 'You do know,' she said softly. 'You were watching football. I heard the cheering.'

His face brightened. 'Yea. The police went through all that. Premier League. It was Wolves against Everton, at home, and the kick-off was eight o'clock. Wolves won, five–three, and I watched the commentary and the replays at the end as well. It must have been getting on for half past ten before I switched the telly off. And the noise I heard, thought I heard, that was just after. Half past ten.'

Mattie had heard the argument about nine fifteen.

'But you didn't look to see what it was,' Mary said.

'No.' Ertie drank the last of his tea, swirling it round in the mug between his clasped hands. His face reddened, and he opened his mouth as if he was about to speak, then hesitated, looked across at Mary, and took a deep breath. This was what he'd come to say. 'Only . . . see, when I said to the police about the match, I'm no' sure if it was true or no'. Well, it kinda was. I was on the couch, right enough, watching it. I sat down to watch it, but I'd had a long day, and I was tired. I was thinking about what you told me. So I thought I'd just have a beer as I watched. It was me first that day. So I set meself down, wi' . . .' He flushed and stopped again, then took another breath and told the truth. 'It was me first beer that day. But I'd had a dram earlier. More as one. The bottle was empty, so I said, well, I'll have a beer rather as open another bottle. Everything was all getting difficult, with Keith home, and I wasna coping. So I sat, and I remember opening a second can and drinking it, then opening the second bottle after all, and I musta dozed off, because the next thing I remember was waking up and finding the match had only fifteen minutes to go. So I watched the end of it, and then the replays o' the goals, and that's how I kent enough to make it sound as if I'd seen the whole thing. Only . . .' He came to a halt. Mary rose and refilled his mug, and he clutched it gratefully and took a gulp before resuming. 'Only when I woke I had this impression that I'd been outside. I didn't remember it, but I felt cold, and I had a confused kind of feeling.' He raised his eyes to Mary. 'I'm that afraid that I might have killed him and no' remember it.'

He fell silent, and Mary let the silence linger around us for a long while before she asked, as gently as a falling swan's feather, 'Did they tell you how your brother died?'

He shook his head. 'They didn't need to. I found him, remember. I saw the way that fancy scarf he always wore was pulled round his neck.' He shuddered, his eyes bleak with the memory. 'And the way he was lying, as if someone standing facing him had grabbed the ends o' it, and pulled tight, near lifted him off his feet, then dropped him.' He spread his hands and looked at them. 'I'm strong enough to have done that.'

'But do you think you really would have?' Mary asked. 'However little you got on, would you, could you have choked the life from him?'

He shuddered again even as she was saying it, but answered honestly. 'I don't ken. In my sane senses, no, but when I'd had a drink in me, if he'd annoyed me, I couldn't say. He coulda said something, and I coulda grabbed him, and . . .' He made a twisting movement with his hands. 'But you can see why I said nothing to the police.'

'Surely,' I said, 'he'd have had the sense not to come annoying you when you were watching the footie. One glance through the window would have shown him you had a can in your hand. He'd have known it wasn't a good time to come and annoy you.' I thought a bit more. 'And why would you go outside when you were happily ensconced on the sofa?'

His bleak look lightened. 'If I'd heard something outside?'

I shook my head. 'You'd have done just as you did later: thought it was sheep, and ignored it. No, it doesn't work. If he came in and annoyed you, even if you killed him and passed out, you'd have found him dead there. Conversely, if he was up to something in the old house, he'd have taken pains to be quiet, and you wouldn't have heard him over the footie.'

'You don't think I killed him?'

I wasn't sure how to answer. Mary looked him straight in the eyes. 'Do you think you did?'

He couldn't meet her gaze. He turned his face away, and muttered to his feet. 'I'm afraid that I might have. I don't ken. I was in me slippers, and they were soakit through, as if I'd been outside.' He turned on me, fiercely. 'You're no' to tell your man about this. I'd be too easy a suspect.'

He was right. The Major Incident Team might be delighted to have an easy suspect handed to them on a plate. 'Gavin's not part of the investigating team,' I said. 'He wouldn't go for an obvious suspect. But I think you should let me tell him. Or tell them yourself, about the noise you heard in the old house, but not the rest.'

He looked at me for a long moment, then smiled, the charm turned on once more. 'Okay. I'll tell them. But if they arrest me, I expect to see you visiting with a cake that has a file baked into it.'

'Deal.' I rose. I wanted to sort all this out in my head. 'I'll go now. Thank you for the tea, Mary.' I looked at Ertie. 'Take care.'

Mary saw me down to the boat and helped me shove her back into the water. She was as strong as I was. We didn't speak; didn't mention Ertie. I thanked her again and sculled into deeper water, then waved a hand, started the engine and headed across the bay to Klaufister. It was later than I'd meant; I'd keep the visit short, and head home afterwards. I could go up to *Khalida* in the evening, or even tomorrow morning.

I wished I was going straight home. I needed time and space. I wasn't sure what to make of it all. I felt there was a thread I wasn't seeing, a streak of colour running through it all that I couldn't grasp.

The police were busy at Klaufister. There was yellow tape strung along electric fence poles, a white tent visible through the doorway of the ruined house and people everywhere: white suits, black jackets. Radio conversations crackled in the air.

I putted towards the jetty and was met by an officer. 'Sorry, miss,' she said. 'I'm afraid you can't land here. A police investigation is under way.'

'I know the family,' I said. 'They were very kind to me when I fell in yesterday, and I wanted to return the clothes they lent me.' I could see she knew the story. Her face was uncertain for a moment, then she shook her head. I lifted the carrier bag, and fished out the card. 'Could you give these to Patsy, please?'

'Yes, I can do that.' She took them, and I was just about to back away from the pontoon when there was a shout from up above, and a waved black arm. The gesture looked like someone was beckoning.

'Yes, she can come up,' the other officer called. 'Patsy wants to see her.'

'I won't stay long,' I said reassuringly, and flung my bow rope around the pontoon's plastic handrail.

Patsy looked as if her world had collapsed. Keith had been her darling, the peerie boy she'd shown off to her pals even when the others had deserted her for the animals. Her pride, who'd made it big south. The black she wore had drained all the colour from her face, adding ten years to her age. Her eyes were lost in dark shadows, and her cheeks had sunk to gauntness. She tried to smile as I came in, but her mouth wavered, and she put up a hand to hide it. I saw her chest heave with the effort of taking enough breath to speak. 'I said to them to bring you up,' she managed, in a flat, cracked voice. 'I wanted to check your stitches. How are you feeling?'

I was shaken by a wave of distress. I dumped the clothes and card on the nearest chair, and went over to kneel by her chair. I put my hand over hers. 'I'm so very sorry.'

Her paper-dry hand turned in mine and gripped for a moment. Her eyes were bleak, empty, as if she couldn't see anything outside her loss of her son.

'I won't disturb you,' I said. 'Can I make a cup of tea?'

She looked for a moment as if she couldn't remember what tea was, then nodded. 'Don't run away. It's fine to have someone to speak to. Dip dee doon. Irene'll make the tea.'

'It's no bother to make it,' I said. I stood up and went over to the kettle. The mugs were standing ready, and the box of teabags. Patsy didn't argue, but sat in silence, her empty gaze towards the window. I glanced where she was looking and saw a huddle of officers and white suits with a stretcher on wheels. They were about to move the body. For a moment I wasn't sure if I should say anything, then I knew she had the right to know. 'I think they're going to take him now,' I said softly.

For a moment I thought she hadn't heard, then she grasped her staff. 'Give me your arm. I'll see my boy away.'

She leant on my arm as far as the door, and we stood there, as if we were waiting for a funeral procession to pass, eyes staring at the hill in front of us. Irene was up there, working with a line of ponies tied to the fence. She looked down, swung herself over the fence and came quickly towards us, glancing down towards the old house as she came. She must have seen what was going on, for she didn't say anything, simply came to stand on the other side of her mother, one hand tucked under her arm. A WPO came to stand on Irene's other side; the family liaison officer.

It seemed a long wait, then at last they came up, disconcertingly silent, the shrouded trolley running on smooth wheels up the grassy path to the house. The stiffness Ertie had spoken of must have worn off, for they had him straight as if he was in his coffin, with the jut of feet and face visible under the white cloth. Patsy gave a mew like a kitten as they came level with us, and took a sudden step forward, one hand stretched out to stop them. 'Let me see my boy.'

The stretcher-pullers paused, looking uncertainly at each other, then the WPO beside us nodded. One of them put the brake on, and they stood back to let Patsy come forward. She walked by herself, pulling her arm from Irene's hold, eyes fixed on the shrouded figure, and steadied herself with one hand on the trolley as she drew the sheet back. I looked away as her hand moved, but not quickly enough. Keith was there, but his features were smoothed to blankness, like a waxen dummy. The person he had been was gone. Beside me, Irene gave a stifled cry and clutched my arm.

It seemed a long time that Patsy stood there, looking down. At last she touched his face in a last caress, then drew the sheet up over him and stepped back. Irene and the WPO darted forward to help her. She made it as far as the door before her legs collapsed under her, and two sturdy police officers came forward to help them carry her into the bedroom, and lie her down.

'What can I do?' I asked Irene.

'A hot water bottle,' she said, 'and tea, with milk and a couple of spoons of sugar. I'll get her into bed.'

I organised that, and added a couple of plain biscuits. By the time I brought them in, Irene had Patsy lying under a cover with shoes and jumper off. There was still a stunned look on her face, as if she didn't believe what she had just seen. A tear slid from under her closed eyelids and began to roll down her cheek.

I gave Irene the bottle and set the tea and biscuits on the chest by the door. 'I'll go now,' I said softly, 'unless there's anything else I can do.'

Irene shook her head. I heard the WPO's soothing voice behind me as I slipped away, and then Irene's footsteps. She caught my arm. 'Thank you, Cass. It was good of you to come.'

I looked at her white, tired face and haunted eyes. 'You need more help,' I said bluntly. 'You can't manage all this on your own.'

She gave a vague wave of one hand, and shook her head. 'I'll manage. I have to manage.'

I looked across the voe, and was visited by an inspiration. 'Do you ken Mary? Could you ask her to come and help you for a day or two, until your mother's got over the shock?'

'No,' Irene said, shrinking back. 'No, I can't ask her.' It was almost a cry. 'I can't ask anyone! Please.' She looked me in the face and repeated it. '*Please.* We just need to be on our own.'

I could see she was near losing control. I couldn't persist. 'Okay,' I said.

She nodded thanks, and turned away, walking slowly at first, then almost stumbling upwards back to the house. I watched her go, then continued to the pontoon.

I hoped the WPO would worry about Irene as well as Patsy.

It all echoed in my head as I motored homewards. Shots heard early in the morning; Keith's visits to Danielle. Mattie, watching over her in love. Patsy's desperate face, and Irene's exhaustion. Ertie's bleak look as he said *I'm afraid that I might have killed him.* Mary's unexpected confession that she understood Ertie's drinking, because she'd been there. *I'd lost my job, my husband, my chance of children.* That struck home. I could take or leave alcohol, but I needed the sea like a drug, like a lover, except that I couldn't have the sea and Gavin, a home, children. But I'd be only thirty-two in November: I had time to think about it yet. I looked west as I came out of Cribba Sound, past the Atlantic swell rolling in from the sea road leading to where there was nothing in the world but your ship poised on a saucer of shining water under a great arch of sky, and felt my heart ache for it.

I made good time getting home. The cats were very pleased to see me. I let Julie out for a run round the garden while I checked the rest of the animals: hens, horses, sheep, lambs, all present and correct. After that I sat for a bit on the seat at the back of the house, looking out over the sound. It was only five o'clock, but the light was already mellowing to tints of evening, the hills dusted with gold, the moorgrass stems glistening. The yellow buttons of tansy by the gate were translucent above their fresh green leaves.

The flowers reminded me that I needed to think about Gavin's entries for the Aith Harvest Festival. I'd spotted a catalogue on the kitchen table, with a cartoon picture of a basket of vegetables and a vase of flowers. I needed to ring the possibles and write labels for them, then pick them at the last minute before I took them down.

There was no shortage of categories. The flowers, pot plants and floral decoration came first. I absolutely couldn't do a vase of flowers, but I might just manage a couple of jamjars of *Three of a kind, Outdoor-grown*. There was a long list of fruit and vegetable classes, and I found Gavin had already ringed the ones he thought he could enter: apples, plums, carrots, cauliflower, mangetout, runner beans, potatoes. I went out to look. I could identify all of them, except that as the potatoes and carrots were busily growing underground, I wasn't sure how I could tell which were good ones. I supposed I dug up a flourishing leaf-clump and looked.

After that I did the animals: fed horses, counted sheep, rounded up and fed hens. Work over, I headed indoors, shutting the door firmly to keep midges out and Ketling Julie in. I wasn't particularly hungry, but I surveyed this morning's haul and went for the stir-fry beef. I'd washed my plate and the frying pan, and was busy persuading the last touches of red sauce off the china sink when the phone rang. I leapt for it. 'Hello?'

A female voice I didn't recognise said uncertainly, 'Is that Cass?'

'Yes,' I said, 'I'm Cass. Who's that?'

There was a long pause. It had been a young woman speaking, early twenties, I'd guess, and she had the unmistakable Whalsay accent. 'I'm Danielle,' she said at last. 'Ertie's wife.' There was another pause. 'You dinna ken me, though I saw you the other day, coming into Clousta and visiting Klaufister.'

'Yes,' I said, when she stopped again. 'I was there again today.'

'I saw you. Irene said you were kind. See, I wanted . . .' Another pause, then the words came out in a rush. 'I feel I have a right cheek asking, when you don't ken me, but I wanted to speak to you. I was wondering if we could meet up. No' at the house – I'm no' there today, and there's never peace, wi' the bairns there. I was thinking you maybe come into town from time to time.'

I thought about my boat, up at Brae waiting for me, and how Anders would be back on the *Swan* tomorrow, and the bonny sailing forecast, and how busy I'd be for the days after that, and took a silent resolute breath. This was more important. 'I could come in tomorrow. I don't have a car, so it would be by bus.' I leant forward to my bus timetable on the pinboard. There were buses going in at 12.42

and 14.52. I'd have to see how long Caedoc's examination took. 'I have stuff to do in the morning, so I don't know if I'll be on the lunchtime bus or the mid-afternoon one.'

She gave a sigh of relief. 'Tomorrow would be fantastic. I work in the Home Furnishing, but I get breaks. I'll save mine till you come, and we can nip next door for a coffee.'

'I can do that,' I said, 'but listen, I can't promise not to tell the police things you tell me. I can't keep things from Gavin.'

'I ken that,' she said. 'That's why I wanted to speak to you.'

'And you do understand he's not on this investigation? But if you tell me, he'll make sure it's passed on to the investigating team. And if you have information about the murder—'

She cut me off. 'No, no, it's no' that. Well, it kinda is, but it's not that I saw anything, or ken who the murderer is. It's nothing like that.'

'If it was, you need to tell the police,' I said.

She didn't answer that, but rushed on. 'Thank you! I'll see you tomorrow afternoon. I'm in the haberdashery department, you ken, the fabrics, on the ground floor. You'll really come?'

'I'll come,' I said.

There was no point in speculating what Ertie's wife might know that she wanted to tell Gavin. I could tell him she'd called me.

It was a good bit later when Gavin rang. His voice came over the miles muffled, distorted, as if he was underwater.

'Gavin! Are you at the loch?'

'Just.' His voice sounded as if he was out in a high wind. 'We have no idea, in Shetland, how bad roads are getting in the . . . last twenty miles is more pothole than . . .' His voice wavered and cut out, as if he was underwater. '. . . deluge storms last winter, and . . . serious difference . . . hire car . . .'

'You keep cutting out,' I said.

'Say that aga— . . . barely hear you.'

'Bad line,' I said clearly. 'I keep losing you.'

'Kenny's . . . with Mother tonight . . . off to his show . . . in charge.'

'Good luck.'

'You're going again . . . goodnight. I'll . . . Invergarry tomorrow.'

'Goodnight, sleep well.' The call cut out, leaving me feeling suddenly alone.

I sighed, and went to find my book, for a quiet evening in, but I couldn't concentrate. The faces of the Klaufister folk were spinning round in my head. In the end I gave it up, ran myself a bath, and lay for nearly an hour in the soothing water, making my mind a blank. I'd tell Gavin everything I'd learned when we spoke tomorrow.

It relaxed me, but I still lay and looked through the window at the stars for a long while before I finally fell asleep.

IV
Children's Ponies

Friday 26th August

Tides at Brae

HW 02.15 (2.0m)
LW 08.25 (0.8m)
HW 14.49 (1.8m)
LW 20.50 (0.85m)

Sunrise 05.46; moonset 15.52; moonrise 20.03; sunset 20.26.

Third quarter moon.

Chapter Ten

Traawirt: *Self-willed, stubborn, awkward.* [Old Scots, **trawirt**, *obstinate*.]

I woke to grey clouds, lit white from above, and racing westwards across the skylight. I got up to look out. There was a good breeze waving the tree branches and sending white horses scudding through the sound, but nothing the *Deuk* couldn't handle between here and Voe, and the forecast was for it to fall. I had young Caedoc's VVE appointment at 10.30. I hoped he'd behave. After that, I had to go into town to meet Danielle. I lay for a bit, contemplating the moving clouds with gloomy foreboding, then got up. Yesterday's slight headache had gone, but there was an itch where the stitches were beginning to tighten. I showered, keeping my head dry, brushed my hair carefully, and began the day.

It took nearly an hour to deal with the animals. I put my own porridge on to simmer, then fed the cats, trying to make sure that Julie ate only her kitten food, and didn't dash to her parents' bowls to scoff theirs too. While they were eating, I phoned Gavin and left a message that I was remembering about Caedoc. I let Julie into the garden while I got the hens out of their hutch with only the usual amount of fluffing up and mock panic, as if they'd forgotten overnight what a human was, and put their mash in their run. I collected the eggs and promised myself an omelette for tea. When I moved on to the sheep, the burn was running and there were sixteen ewes, but one lamb short. I counted twice and still got twenty-six, until I spotted the one right down at the shore, running up and down on the wrong side of the fence, and getting towards the panic stage about being separated from its mam. Mind their feet, Rainbow had said. I walked slowly down the fence towards him and picked him up in both hands, as if he was a cat. He was surprisingly heavy for his size, and I nearly dropped him as he kicked out, grazing my jeans with one sharp hoof. I lifted him over the fence and set him down on his own side. 'And stay there,' I told him. He raced to his mother and began sucking vigorously, stumpy tail waggling. I shook my head at him, and went up to the ponies.

The foals were lying sleeping; the adult ponies were standing with their heads over the gate, and Fergus did his impatient pawing at the fence, which ended in him getting one hoof between the wires and on the wrong side. He didn't seem to be able to get it out himself, so I climbed over into the field and stood with my back to his head, as I'd seen Gavin doing, leaning my shoulder against his to take the weight off the hoof. He was surprisingly solid, and not being able to see his face made me uneasy. 'You bite my bum,' I warned him, 'and you'll regret it.' I leant back against his shoulder, and after a bit of a struggle, where he made his leg rigid, finally managed to fold it up, the way Gavin did, and ease it out between the wires. 'Good boy,' I said, patting him. 'Don't do that again.'

He made a snorting noise in reply, and I fetched Caedoc's head-collar. It seemed a good time to get it on him, ready for later. He was remarkably amenable about it, even though I got it the wrong way up first go. I stood for a minute looking at him. He'd grown since I last saw him, but he was still well below my waist height, and very much a baby, with his out-of-proportion head, short curly tail and lanky legs, made longer by the white stockings which ended in neat pink hooves. His head and backside were black, with a white stripe round his middle, like a guinea pig, and he had his mother's white blotch on his forehead. His brown eyes were big and friendly, and he had impossibly long lashes. He looked good to me, satisfying to the eye, as if he'd grow into a bonny horse. The other foal, Caitlin, was red and white, and slightly smaller. She was obviously used to a headcollar too, for when she saw Caedoc getting his on, she came over and tried to shove in for a mint. I doled her one, then left them in peace.

Right. My breakfast, at last. The porridge was within seconds of being burned. I took it through to the sitootery, so that I could look out over the sound while I ate. The mist on the hills was thinning, as if the sun was trying to break through above, and the racing clouds had slowed to an amble. It was a shame to waste the afternoon in town, especially as I could take *Khalida* back now Anders was going aboard *Swan*, but I'd said to Danielle I'd be there, and Home Furnishing, where she worked, meant I could get Gavin's oilcloth and the hens' meat from Voe. I checked the timetable again: buses home at 15.40 and the usual 17.10. If I couldn't get in till the mid-afternoon one, I'd have no time to do anything other than Danielle and the oilcloth. I'd just have to see when the vet came, and how long the examination took.

It was well after nine now. I wondered how on earth Gavin managed to get to work on time when he was here on his own. There was extra work now with the young animals, but then in winter there were nets of hay for the ponies and bales for the sheep, and locking the hens in early. He'd have to come home after work, and not go to the pub with the others in his squad, if they did that. Maybe they couldn't, here in Shetland, where everyone would ken exactly who they were, and what they did for a living. A table of police officers in the corner would soon empty the rest of the bar.

It was only 10.25 when there was the sound of gravel scrunching under wheels, and I looked out to see a grey van coming over the hill. It stopped beside Gavin's Land Rover, and a young woman in a dark-green boiler suit jumped out. She had fair hair cut in short curls, and a cheerful, open face with an always-outdoors tan.

'Hello!' she called. 'Annie the vet, for Caedoc's VVE.'

'I'm Cass,' I said. 'Gavin's partner. Gavin was called away. His mother had a stroke.'

She strode forward and gave me a sympathetic look from unexpected brown eyes. 'Bad?'

'Middling. She seems to be coming on well, given her age.'

'So you're deputising. Know anything about horses?'

'Nothing,' I said cheerfully. 'I'm a sailor.'

'Magnie's lass. I ken.' She jerked her chin towards Aith. 'I grew up in Eid. Me dad was one of Magnie's fishing cronies.'

'Everybody kens Magnie,' I agreed.

'I'll send Gavin a formal report, but I can give you the gist, for you to tell him when you speak.'

'That'd be grand.' I was going to lead her towards the gate, but she already had one leg over the wire fence and was giving Fergus's chin a rub.

'Tell Gavin this boy's putting on too much weight. He might need to live on a tether till the grass stops growing.'

'He won't like that.'

'He won't like laminitis either. Do you have an electric fence?'

I gave a *don't know* shrug.

'A tether then. He needs to be coralled in half this area, and no extra feed. I mean it. No pony nuts, no mix, just the grass in the field. Feed the others separately. Okay, you can give him veg scraps, but green veg only, not potato peelings. Nothing that might block his windpipe – chop things like carrots smaller, longieways.'

'Okay,' I said. Carrots didn't sound like green veg to me, but I got the drift.

Annie shook her head at Fergus, and said in Shetlan, 'Whin da coo taks her fit oot o' da mire, da mare puts her ane in.'

I gave her a blank look.

'Haven't you heard that one? You never get a rest with animals. When you've got the work over with one lot, another lot starts. You've got all the lambs, foals and calves born and out in the park, and you expect peace, but Shetlands need an eye kept on them through the summer. If you see Fergus walking as if he's on tiptoe, put him on a five-metre tether on the shortest grass you can find, soft earth but not damp, and come and get powders for him straight away.'

It seemed there was no end of things to remember about animals.

I looked across at the simplicity of white-slashed water racing through the sound.

'Well, let's have a look at you, boy.' She caught hold of Caedoc's chin strap and crouched down beside him, murmuring soothingly as she checked inside his ears, looked in his eyes, felt his jaw bone and opened his mouth to look at his teeth. He bore it surprisingly well, with only an indignant toss of his head when she let his mouth close again. Annie unwrapped a stethoscope from her neck. 'Hold him a moment, will you? Just keep him standing here. That's a good boy.' Her speech to me was abrupt, but she was sure and unhurried in her movements with him, patting his chest before running a hand down each leg and lifting each hoof, then listening to his body in several places. Heart and lungs, I supposed. Once she'd done that she stood up. 'Can you walk him up and down for me? Up to that knowe and back again.'

'Come on, Caedoc,' I said, and set off. I'd learned enough to walk beside him, and he came willingly, head up, as if he thought something interesting might be going to happen. I still had the mints in my pocket, so I gave him one at the hill. Going back stopped being a walk halfway, and he pulled his way back to Annie in a series of leaps.

'Hmmm,' she said, and took the halter. 'Come on then, boy.' Naturally he walked and ran perfectly for her. She got him to stand squarely and gave me the headcollar while she walked round him, feeling and stroking, used the stethoscope again, then nodded decisively and put it away. 'I'll just take a couple of hairs to check for dwarfism.' She tugged several hairs from his mane and glanced over at me. 'That he's not a carrier. Skeletal atavism.' It didn't sound good. I gave her an enquiring look. 'Dwarfism,' she repeated. 'Bone abnormalities, and often respiratory problems, or alimentary ones. A horse who inherits the gene from one parent can be fine, but the gene can be passed on down the generations, and if both parents have it, the foal could well present with it, and have to be put down.' She slipped the headcollar off and handed it to me. 'You can go back to your pal, boy.' Caedoc charged off, kicking up exuberantly, as if he'd been in durance vile for a month, and he and Caitlin did two circuits of the park, short tails flying.

Annie watched him go, then turned to me. 'You can tell Gavin he's a nice little horse, and if his genes are fine there's no reason at present why he shouldn't make a stallion. Legs straight, chest sound, nice head, proportions good. He's a bonny boy, and good-natured with it. Keep going with him for another couple of years, and we'll see how he turns out. You won't be moving south before then?'

I gave her a startled look.

'Gavin was telling me about your cottage,' she said. 'I ken the West Highlands a bit. We used to go caravanning there, though not at Gavin's loch. Even my dad wouldn't have taken a caravan down that hill with the hairpin bends.'

'I've seen it from up on the hill,' I said, 'and photos of the inside, but not made it there yet. September, Gavin was thinking.' It was the Highland version of our cottage at the Ladie, two rooms downstairs, two up, and a little bedroom downstairs converted into a bathroom with a calor gas hot water tank. There was running water when there was enough in the burn, but no electricity. I rather liked the look of it, and hoped we would manage to spend a week there in the autumn.

'I'll send the bill to Gavin,' Annie said. She put up a foot to the step of her van and paused. 'I wish he was here, in charge. This is an awful thing at Klaufister.'

'Yes,' I agreed.

'Did I hear you were there when they found him?'

'No, just before. I had a misanter with a block hitting me on the head, and Patsy patched me up. Ertie found him not long after I'd gone.'

She pulled a wry face. 'He'd feel it, and the more since they didn't get along. They had totally different interests, always, from when they were peerie. But they were brothers, for all that.'

'Were you at the school together?' I asked.

'Not with Ertie. He's the oldest o' the family. He'll be thirty soon.' She gave a wry smile, put the stepped-up foot back on the ground and turned to lean against the van, facing me. 'The make o' his father, even down to the traawirt streak. Patsy should have kent better than to try to persuade Arthur not to drive south. Just suggesting he couldn't was enough to make him determined.' She gave Fergus a pat. 'Ertie's spent too much time with horses. Stubborn and perverse. He wouldn't even consider the agricultural college in Orkney. Wouldn't leave the croft.' Her face saddened. 'I was fond of Arthur. I don't suppose I'd have become a vet if it hadn't been for him. He let Irene and me follow him round like a pair of puppies, and showed us what he and Ertie were doing with the animals. We had it all planned out: Ertie would be the crofter, and Irene would be the vet, and I'd be her assistant.' She had fair skin under the tan; to my surprise, she blushed. Maybe she'd had a childhood crush on Irene's handsome elder brother. She added, 'When she started wi' the ME, that was in upper primary, then the teachers would send her work with me. I'd go home on her school bus and help her with it, then Patsy would run me home for my tea. I'd tell her all the gossip from the day so that she wouldn't feel left out when she came back. It was a hard time for her.' She gave me a fierce look. 'I used to get right mad at other bairns who said she was just being lazy, or wished out loud that their parents would let them lie in bed all day. For a bit, maybe as long as four or five months after she first started with it, it was as much as she could do to shower and dress. She had to take her breakfast back to bed, because she was too tired to sit at the table. She was that miserable with it. I hated to see her like that. She'd always been such a live wire, working with the horses. My dad only had sheep, and I loved horses, so Arthur let me borrow one of theirs. Sukey, she was called. I'd ride over to Clousta on Saturday so Irene and I could be together all day.'

She'd mentioned Ertie and Irene, but not the others. 'Was Allison interested in the croft?'

Annie shook her head. 'When she was younger, a bit, but she preferred Barbie dolls, and as soon as she hit ten she went all teenager and thought about boyfriends and marrying, and having a fancy house in a town. And Keith wasn't interested. He went the opposite way – stubbornly not interested. He was going to be a big man in the city. He didn't even get excited on show days. All day before Waas and Cunningsburgh, Irene and I would be brushing the ponies till they shone, and polishing the tack in the evening, Allison would work with the dogs, and Ertie would hose down the kye. I'd stay overnight, and we'd get up at the crack of dawn to load the animals into the truck, and get our show clothes on, with a boiler suit and rubber boots on top, and pile into the car. There'd be a whole bunch of us there, folk we kent from school. We'd unload the animals and get them settled in their place, and give them a last brush, and oil their hooves.' She smiled, shaking her head at their younger selves. 'We'd even spray Pledge on their backs, to give a shine, and volumising hairspray into their tails. I tell you, they looked gorgeous. There were riding classes first, and Irene and I would both enter.' Her face was soft, reminiscent. 'We didn't mind which of us got the red rosette, so long as one of us did. Then showing went on all morning. After that we'd get sandwiches or chips in the hall, whatever was going, and take it to eat outside, near the animals, and fetch them more water, all that. Then we'd go round the show in a bunch, looking at all the exhibits.'

It sounded fun. I remembered the excitement of regatta days, Dad and I getting up at dawn to tow the boat to Mid Yell, Aith, Walls, Scalloway, the chatter as we got our boats ready, then the intent silence as we launched and headed for the start line. 'But Keith didn't get involved?'

She shook her head. 'He didn't arrive till late morning, with Patsy, in the kind of clothes he'd wear for school, and he'd spend the day hanging round with her and the old folk.' She paused to think. 'It was kinda sad, looking back. He must've felt left out, lonely maybe, but he never let on, if he did. He'd smirk at the grannies and they'd all tell us what a fine well-behaved boy he was.' She grinned. 'You can imagine what we thought of that. But he didn't seem interested in the land or beasts at all.' Her face stilled, reflective. 'Maybe it was like there was no place for him, with Ertie being keen on the kye, Allison petting the dogs, and Irene loving the ponies. They got all of Arthur's attention. Maybe there was none left for Keith.' She sighed. 'And now Irene's working for that place in Lerwick, and Ertie's taken to the drink again.' She shook her head. 'I hoped love might get him out of it, but, well, he and Danielle . . . she was far too young when they married.' She gave me a swift look and went back to abrupt mode. 'Wasn't it you who helped catch the stallion when he got loose?'

I nodded.

'How did that happen? No sign of a broken tether, or something like that?'

'Not on him. He didn't have a headcollar at all. A gate left open, maybe?'

She gave me a sceptical glance. 'Maybe. He didn't seem too distressed, when you caught him?'

'He was pretty upset. He'd got himself so worked up he didn't know what he wanted. Or at least, he did, he wanted his own field, and water, and peace, but he was too high to let someone catch him and take him there.'

'Out of breath distressed?'

'Yes, a bit.'

'Or lame?'

I shook my head.

'Yes, well, he's back where he belongs now. Irene'll take good care of him.' She hesitated on the step for a moment, as if she wanted to say more, then mastered herself and swung herself into the driving seat. 'Tell Gavin I was asking after him. I hope his mother comes along fine.' She shut the door, swerved backwards into the turning space with a beautiful economy of movement, and drove off up the hill.

The hazy start had cleared to a bonny summer day by the time I unhitched the *Deuk*'s mooring lines and shoved her away from the pontoon. It was about the same time as the *Swan* was setting off from Lerwick, only eighteen miles away across Shetland. I could imagine her dark-green hull backing away from her berth beside Albert

Buildings, with the trainees busy taking in the fenders, and shut the image off. My job was to support Gavin, as he'd supported me this last year, staying at home with the animals while I sailed the world. I went round the back of the house on the lake and continued diagonally across to the entrance to Olnafirth. A starboard turn brought the *Deuk*'s nose towards Voe: the large, white Voe House on the hill above the darker low buildings of the former weaving sheds and the pub/restaurant, and the marina and Sail Loft, now a camping böd. The sun shone on the ruins of the old kirk, just above the water's edge to port. The hill was a bonny russet colour, and two scarfs dived as I approached.

I was well early; it was only a quarter to twelve now. I'd easily have time to get my hennie-maet at the shop, stow it aboard and have a much-needed cup of tea and something to eat before the 12.42 bus.

I moored the *Deuk* to the outside of the marina pontoon and walked up the hill to the shop, thinking about what Annie had said about the Klaufister family. What seemed oddest to me was the sudden change in Keith. He wasn't into the croft, and never had been. I wondered a bit about that. Young children usually fell in with what pleased their parents. Gavin had been a farm child, not as passionate about the Highland cattle as his brother, but keen on animals and well able to do his share of work. When he'd been working in Inverness he'd gone back each weekend to help out. I tried to imagine the Arthurson family. Two boys, two girls, with two years between each, enough to make a difference in strength and usefulness between the two boys, especially with Ertie the oldest and Keith the youngest. Maybe he'd felt inadequate because he couldn't do the things Ertie did. Perhaps he'd been afraid of the huge cows Ertie walked among so confidently, just as I was unsure of going among horses. He'd changed his fear and inferiority into an 'I don't want to' and become the one left out at shows, sticking with his mother when everyone else had charged round in a bunch. I tried to imagine the adult I'd briefly met as a ten-year-old. Yes, I could imagine him being his mother's good boy, lapping up the praise from her friends, since his father and brother didn't want him. There'd been resentment of Mam's boy in Ertie's comments about the stallion.

I was seeing that little boy now. He'd gone to the Anderson High School and been clever there. He'd escaped south, gone to London. I wondered how he'd got on there, whether he'd been a smart city-slicker, or despised as a country hick with jumped-up notions. He was in his mid-twenties. If he'd fitted in, surely he'd have found a girlfriend, maybe been eyeing up a house. He wouldn't have been free to drop everything. Perhaps Irene's call asking for his help was the reason he'd been waiting for to come home. He'd found his mother in a wheelchair, his brother hitting the bottle, his oldest sister busy with her own household and his frail sister Irene holding the fort. He'd stepped up to the mark and taken it on. I thought well of him for that. He'd committed himself to the croft to the extent of taking over the stud and buying the stallion, but I wondered how much he'd consulted Irene over that. Maybe his taking over had felt like usurpation. There had been distress in her face, and concern for her mother, but no grief for her brother.

The shop was quiet. I got myself a pack of cheese bannocks for lunch, spreadable butter and an apple, then lugged the bag of hens' mash to the boat and sat in the *Deuk*'s cockpit eating and looking out over the water until bus time.

Chapter Eleven

Sometime or idder Brinkie has been as weel saddled: *Comment on someone who has seen better days and come down in the world.*

The sun shone on the east-side water, the North Sea, as we set off towards Lerwick. Coming down the long Kames was my first chance to see the turbine columns on the hills close up: slender grey towers, with a crane beside them, lifting up each section. At this distance it looked like a child's game, or maybe the ruins of a Greek temple, but each tube that the crane was manoeuvring was fifty metres long. At Catfirth, a salmon boat heading for Whalsay was outlined like a cut-out against the silver water.

I stayed on the bus till the Esplanade and watched for a moment as *Swan* raised her mainsail in the north mouth, then turned my back on her forging through the water and strode to Home Furnishing as if I was trying to chase the sight away.

When I arrived, I stood for a moment, steadying my breathing. I was rarely in there, because it sold all the kind of household stuff a boat owner didn't need: fancy lampshades, floppy-haired bath mats, paintings, china ornaments. I realised as I walked in that I hadn't known the half of it. What could anyone possibly want with chest-high artificial poppies as big as a dinner plate, or resin toilet seats apparently filled with real shells?

I looked around for Danielle, but there was nobody visible at the moment. It was only half past one; maybe she wasn't expecting me yet. I could have a look at oilcloth. I headed towards the rainbow swathes of material. In French markets the fabrics were heaped in bales on tables, but the oilcloth was usually on a roll, and it was like that here, a pyramid of bright colours and patterns which transported me back to Easter with my French grandparents, and carrying Mamy's basket at the Lencloître fair. I could almost smell grilling eels in the air. There was a jaunty pattern of cocks and hens, a riot of cabbage-sized pink roses, and a convoy of VW camping vans; there were cherries and pots of herbs, spots and stripes and checks. I felt my brain scrambling with the choice. Something simple we could live with on weekdays, but that would set off our best china on Sundays. The sober black and white check was front-runner until I spotted a lively lemon trees pattern which would be a pool of sunshine on a dark winter morning. Mamy would have liked it, and a white cloth could go over it on best-china days.

I was digging out the bit of paper with the measurements when the assistant came out from the door between upright rolls of glittery fabric. She was a bonny blonde lass of the upright Viking build I associated with Whalsay, from childhood years of playing netball against them. Everyone had emphasised how young she'd been when they married, but living with an alcoholic had aged her. If I hadn't known she must be twenty-three or four, I'd have taken her for nearer thirty. She came straight over to me. 'Cass?'

'Danielle? Hi.'

'Thanks for coming.' She gave a tentative smile, and gestured at the cloth. 'Can I sell you something?'

'Yes, please.' I looked at my measurements and put a hand on the lemons roll. 'Two metres of this one, please,' I said.

She nodded, and began to unhook the roll from its rod, struggling a little with the weight of it. I took one end and we carried it over to the wide table.

'Thanks,' she said. 'They're heavy, these rolls.' She unrolled it and smoothed it along the brass measuring bar. 'Two metres. Right.'

She bent over the cloth, cutting slowly and evenly, and I had a chance to study her. Close to, she didn't look well. Her fair hair was cut in feathery curls round her shoulders, but it hung limp over her tall forehead as if all the life had been drained out of it. She'd made up her pale-blue eyes carefully, but the thick swathe of mascara didn't hide the redness of the eyelids, or draw attention away from the darker shadows under her eyes. When she stopped smiling, the corners of her mouth dragged down. Cutting finished, she folded the oilcloth into a bag and gestured towards the till, where she scanned the barcode on the roll and typed in the length. 'That's £15.98.'

I flashed my credit card at the machine. Danielle gave me my receipt, then glanced up at the clock. 'I can take a break now. Shall we go to the café next door?'

'A cup of tea'd be fine,' I said.

'I'll just tell them I'm going.'

I nodded, collected my oilcloth and went out, vaguely apprehensive; I had the feeling that I might be drawn into something dodgy, even though she'd said on the phone she wanted her information given to Gavin. I liked the way everyone trusted him.

I hadn't been in the café she'd indicated before. It was a refurbished extension to the Home Furnishing building, and it had home-baked fancies. I wasn't sure if Danielle would want anything, so I passed on the bright green mint tiffin, got myself a mug of tea and sat down. Danielle was only a couple of minutes behind me, still in her shop overall. She gave the clock a hurried look as she brought her mug over. 'I only have twenty minutes,' she explained, then paused, suddenly uncertain. 'This must seem a right cheek. You don't ken me. But, see, I'm heard about you, on your tall ship, and on the *Swan*, and Irene told me about you going over yesterday. She said you were kind. And I needed to speak to someone about all this, and get your advice about what I should do. And I ken as well what they're saying.' She gave me a quick look, then began drawing a butterfly in the rim of coffee spilled from her mug. 'About me, I mean. Me and him that's awa'. That we were over-friendly.' She lifted her head to look directly at me. I nodded.

She took a deep breath. 'It's no' true. It really isn't. We werena going to bed together. It wasna like that at all.' Her hands gestured in the air for a moment, as she searched for the right words. 'You like living at the end of the road at the Ladie, don't you? You're settled there, you and your man.'

'Yes,' I said, feeling suddenly as though I was committing to something. 'I feel settled there.'

'I canna be doing with it.' Her voice rose, and she checked it to a murmur. 'You'd think that I'd be used wi' it, coming from Whalsay, but it's no like that at all, living on an island. I grew up in Symbister, wi' me and my brothers and sister in our house, and my aunt lived next door, and my uncle was just outside Symbister in their new house, so there were loads of cousins to go round in a gang with. There were dances and weddings and foys at the hall, and the regatta – there was aye something going on.' She flushed. 'And I don't want to sound as if all I think about is money. It's no' that. But Dad was a fisherman, and so we had enough money that we took it for granted. A Christmas gathering o' the family in Tenerife each year, and special presents for birthdays, and trips to Aberdeen to see the big pantomime. Now . . .' Her fair skin went scarlet. One finger began to add spots to the coffee butterfly's wings. 'See, I kent when I met Ertie that he was a crofter man, right to his bones. I kent I'd have to live on the croft, though I put my foot down about living wi' Patsy.'

For a moment she sounded worldly-wise. 'I did at least ken that living with the mother-in-law aye ends in tears. Then the croft next door came up for sale. That doesn't happen often, you ken, and it had a house too. So we grabbed it. It took all our savings, and then of course we realised that because we owned it, it counted as a farm, not a croft, and so we couldn't get all the grants that crofters get, though Arthur helped us with that a bit. He put in for new fences for us, and said it was for Klaufister, but you can't do that more than once. Then, oh, last autumn, Ertie decided to start a dairy, selling Klaufister butter and cheese, so he and Arthur applied for start-up grants, but we still had to borrow for the rest of the cost. It's lucky he'd barely started with it, because now that's on Irene's shoulders too. The house needs all kind of things done to it. I've done my best to make it bonny inside.' She gestured towards Home Furnishing. 'I'm good wi' my hands, and I've painted and papered, and made bonny curtains, but it's an old house.' Her mouth twisted. 'And tiny. Two rooms upstairs, two down, same as you have at the Ladie, and a bathroom in the extension. My dad built the house I grew up in, all new and spacious, with a toilet and shower on each floor. The kids love it.'

She gave the clock a harried glance. 'I'm talking too much, but I wanted to let you see. I'm a fisherman's lass.' She gave me a rueful smile. 'A sea woman, like you. I'm no' cut out for a crofter's wife. The cows are over big, I'm no' at ease wi' them. I used to help more, but I can't with the bairns hanging round me. A byre's no place for toddlers. So a lot of the time I'm stuck inside with them, or at best around the garden – and you are stuck, too, be warned, because it's such a work getting them into the car to go anywhere, even to mother and toddlers. It's an expedition. Clean clothes, nappies, snacks. If it wasn't that I can leave them wi' Mam while I'm working here, I'd never get out at all.'

The frustration of it rang in her voice. I thought of being stuck at the Ladie with children too small to bundle into a boat, and wasn't sure how I'd cope.

'And Ertie and I are split up, and he's no' . . .' She made the wry face again. 'No' fit for taking care of them ee now. So I pack up the entire car wi' all they need for three days, and head over to Whalsay for the weekend, so Mam can babysit while I work Fridays and Saturdays.' She flushed. 'I went on Wednesday this week, because of the Walls Show. Mam's meeting me here wi' the bairns at the end of today, and we'll go out to Klaufister.'

I wasn't quite sure how to ask this. 'Is it no' awkward still biding next door to Ertie?'

She made a wry face. 'It is, but then he's the bairns' dad, and he loves them.' Her voice hardened. 'Or he used to love them. Now all he cares about is his next drink.' Her voice softened to regret. 'Peerie Arthur, that's our oldest, he's four now, and he's a crofter's boy to his bones. He was helping Ertie drive the tractor practically before he could walk, and he followed him round like a pony on a lead-rein.' A flash of what looked like guilt crossed her face, quickly suppressed, but leaving a red flush lingering under her fair skin. 'Peerie Meggie, she's only just two, but she loves helping Patsy wi' the hens, and Irene has her up on the old mare already. And besides . . .' She trailed off, face turned down, then raised it, cheeks red. 'I still love him too, but I canna live wi' the drink. I thought, when we married, that he loved me enough to come off it, but an alcoholic, their world's skewed. They don't see they have a problem. Won't see it. I won't say he kept the drinking within limits, but he kept it within his limits.' Tears stood in her eyes. She shook her head. 'If it wasn't that it brought me the bairns I'd say I never should have married him. Mam did her best to warn me, and Dad absolutely wasn't keen on him, but I wouldn't listen. Then Arthur's death was an awful shock and distress, and it spiralled down from there. I did my best to help him get out of it, but it's like an illness that's gripped him. He can fight it no more than he can fight away a temperature. Dinna get me wrong, he's never laid a finger on me, however much he's had, but there's a lot of slamming about and arguments.' She looked down at the table again and blinked to keep the tears back. 'I suppose he didn't love me enough to stay sober. Then Irene went behind his back and got Keith home, and Ertie got ten times worse until I couldn't bear it. He'd have a dram for the road first thing before going off to his work – no, not a dram, half a mugful of gin, because whisky made him feel sick in the morning.' Her face filled with bleak distress. 'He'd drop a vitamin tablet in it and say it was fine him having no breakfast, he'd had his vitamins. His work put him to day shifts only, they could see the problem, but now he was heading off to his work with a half-bottle in his pocket, and he'd buy another on his way home, and if he'd ever met the police he'd have been banned straight off. And it was good o' his work to do that, but no late shifts made a huge difference to his pay packet, and I started to worry about money. Then he lay about the house, drinking all evening. You have no idea how awful that was. He'd rouse himself and make an effort wi' the bairns, and usually he was an amiable enough drunk, but he was so unpredictable that Peerie Arthur got scared o' him and clung to me. And we didn't have the money for a bottle of whisky a day. I hoped if I said that I just couldn't keep going any longer unless he gave it up, that'd give him a shock to make him stop.' She paused for a moment, eyes closed, mouth working. 'But he just got mad as the devil and slammed out, and the next I kent he'd moved back into the old house and was making sure I kent how uncomfortable he was. And his work sacked him, so he had nothing to do but lie about watching TV.'

'Not that uncomfortable,' I said. 'His peerie sister feeding him home-made soup, and a TV big enough to light up the whole voe.'

She managed a wavering smile at that. 'And I saw the slamming,' I added. 'When I was there. He was mad at being blamed for leaving the gate open when the stallion escaped.'

'Yea, all that.' She frowned. 'That was an odd thing. I suppose Ertie could have done it, but it's an auto thing, shutting gates. I think he'd have made sure it was closed even if he'd had a dram. And he wouldn't be working with the horses anyway, they're Irene's babies, so why would he be in that park? And if you're going to say it was for spite at Keith, well, he was mad at him right enough, and mad about the stallion too, but he wouldn't put it in harm's way like that. No matter how drunk he was. He'd never put a beast at risk of being injured or killed on the road.' She shook her head. 'No.'

I still wasn't quite sure why she'd asked me here. 'Was he murder-mad at Keith?' I asked. I took a deep breath. 'Because of you?'

She started, then gave a slow, determined shake of her head. 'It wasn't like that. Keith.' She came out with the name defiantly. 'That was the first thing I wanted to tell you. We weren't at all the way everyone thought.' She sighed. 'Look, I'd met him at our wedding, but not again since. Ertie insisted he wasn't going to Sunday lunch with Patsy and Irene as usual, not if he had to sit at table with Keith, and Keith was out at work when I went over to see Patsy.' Her mouth turned down. 'Which I did as little as possible. Then one day Keith called at the house, to meet his nephew and niece, he said, and

I gave him a cup of tea, and he sat and talked. I was sorry for him. He was kinda lonely, disillusioned. When he went south he thought he'd escaped the croft and all that lifestyle, except that it hadn't worked out as he'd hoped. No' that he ever said that to me, but I could tell. He thought he'd come home as the chief executive of a fancy London firm, but when he went down to London, he found he couldn't speak the way they did, and he didn't have the posh background. He went from being the clever one of the family to being one in a sea of people streaming in and out of the Tube, and Newcastle was no better. He said he came back because his sister asked for his help, but I think he was homesick.' She smiled, and came out with one of Magnie's proverbs. 'He was looking for a hair to make a tether. It was an excuse to do what he wanted to do, deep down. He was homesick the way I miss Whalsay – somewhere where everyone kens who I am and where I belong. But he didn't want to come back a failure, so he was trying to make himself someone here, taking over the stud and getting that expensive stallion.'

I remembered what Annie'd said about him being odd man out at the shows as a child. 'Was it working, d'you think?'

Danielle shook her head. 'I'd never have said so to Keith, but no.' Her face was sad. 'You should have heard Ertie speak about him. He was just getting it all wrong. Instead of keeping quiet and easing his way in, he was coming across like he was rubbishing the Shetland ways. As if he was trying to show them how much better the south ways were, where things were done properly.'

I thought of the clothes he'd worn to come and collect a stallion from a neighbour, and nodded.

'He used to come and talk. That was all.' She lifted her head and stared straight at me. 'It really was. That was one of the things Ertie and I had the big row about. He said he wouldn't have him in the house, and I said it was time he made a bit of an effort since Keith had come to help them. Then we had the row and I said I'd had enough. It was me or the drink. Ertie stormed out, but he still didn't speak to Keith. He stayed in his own house, unless he came out to do a bit of croft work, and had lunch on weekdays with Patsy and

Irene. So Keith was left with nobody, especially when Patsy and Irene went off to bed in the middle of the evening, and I was lonely too. I'd been lonely already with Ertie there, because he wasn't there for me. He was out on the croft, or at his work. He'd eat his tea then slump in front of the footie with his bottle. I kent he was working for us, me and the bairns, and he drank a bit less when he was busy with the animals, but I felt like I'd become a nothing. Like I'd stopped being me. I made his meat and raised the bairns and cleaned the house, and I felt like I was dying inside.'

She paused to drink the last of her coffee, then looked uncertainly at me. 'You don't have bairns, do you?'

I shook my head. 'No.'

She gave me a quick flash of a look that said I'd need to get on with it if I wanted them. 'I must sound awful. But I bet there are so many mothers that think like that. You post the happy smiling photos on Facebook, and don't talk about the days that start with Meggie being sick all down the front of your last clean T-shirt, and Peerie Arthur having a touch of a feerie, and clinging to your leg all morning, wanting you to sit and read stories when you have a heap of housework things to do, and your man expecting his tea when he comes in.'

'It sounds grim,' I said.

She nodded. 'It's not that I don't love them. I'd walk through fire for them without even thinking about it. But you don't realise until you have them that your life's going to be pretty tough until you can pack them off to school and let them be the teacher's problem for a few wonderful hours.' She sighed, and returned to her point. 'And Keith was really sympathetic about all that. Ertie never had time to ask me how my day had been. Keith always asked that first, and listened when I told him.' She gave a wry smile. 'Told him all the things I should have been telling Ertie. Sometimes we didn't talk much at all. I'd get out my knitting or my sewing, and he sat with a mug of tea. Then, when he'd drunk it, he went home to go to bed, ready for getting up early in the morning, and I did a last tidy up and went to bed too. And that really was all. And of course I should have thought that it would start gossip, but somehow I didn't. I was so glad of someone treating me like an adult that though I kent, I didn't want to ken.' She sighed. 'But I wanted to tell you all that, so that your man would understand.' She swept the butterfly away, dried her hand on her napkin and spoke determinedly, face set. 'That was the first thing. And the second is this. I want to make sure Ertie's no' arrested for murder. See, the evening of the night Keith was killed, he was with me, and after that he was out cold.'

I looked at her in surprise, and she met my gaze defiantly.

'That's not what he says,' I said slowly. 'He said he'd been watching the footie.'

'He was, but at home. At our house, I mean. He'd been drinking, and he came over. I'm not surprised he doesn't remember. Drunks don't. The match wasn't long started, and he was half watching it, and half talking.' She shrugged. 'It was rambling, like he barely knew he was talking. He said he'd been speaking to Mary, you ken Mary, the nun wife. She'd been an alcoholic like him, he said. I hadn't kent that. And she'd recovered, and she said he could too. He wanted to try.' Tears filled her eyes for a minute, and she blinked them away. 'Mary'd prayed with him. He said he missed me and the bairns and he wanted to start again. He was thinking of joining her church, and would I come too? And I said that if it'd get him off the drink, then I would. I didn't ken how much he meant it, or if it was just the drink talking. So I listened, and agreed to everything, and then he got up to go. He was sleep-walking by then, you ken the way, and so I walked home with him to make sure he didn't fall over the banks or come too sleepy and curl up on a heather tussock for the night.' She smiled. 'It was like leading a pony. I took his arm and steered him home.'

DS Peterson wasn't going to like this story. 'What time was this?'

She made a considering face. 'Maybe not long after half past nine. Maybe twenty to ten, by the time we got there.'

'You didn't see anyone about at Klaufister, or hear anyone?'

Her face stilled. 'No . . . no . . . but I had a horrid feeling, as if I was being watched. It was all bright moonlight and dark shadows, and the house was in darkness.' She shuddered. 'I got him onto his sofa. The TV was still going. The match was nearly finished. I kent he'd sleep there, or if he woke up, he'd stagger up to bed. And then I hared it homewards, still with that uneasy feeling, and checked the bairns, then keyed the door and went to bed myself.' She finished defiantly, 'And he may no' remember, but it's God's own truth. He was with me, then out cold. And that's why I went off to Whalsay on Wednesday, instead of yesterday. I panicked. He was talking about getting back together, but I wasn't being sucked back in.'

I wasn't sure whether I believed her or not. That last sentence had rung true, and her account of what Ertie had said fitted with what Mary had told me about how she'd talked to him. Then there was his visit yesterday. He'd thought he'd slept through the match, but he also thought he'd been outside. If he'd visited Danielle as she said, and talked reconciliation, could he really have no memory of it?

Her voice hardened. 'He was in no state to start a quarrel with Keith. I'd swear to that.' Her pale-blue eyes sparked a challenge. 'Do you believe me?'

I hesitated, spreading my hands. 'I don't know. When Ertie spoke about it yesterday, at Mary's, he didn't mention you. He thought he'd fallen asleep in front of the telly.'

'That's what I said. He was in the state he wouldn't remember. But I'll tell the police he was with me.'

I didn't know what to say. I wanted to warn her not to try lying to the police. It would only make them sure Ertie had done it. 'It'll look really suspicious if you come forward brandishing an alibi he's already contradicted.'

'Just tell the truth.' Her voice had a bitter edge. Then she glanced up at the clock and rose, shoving her chair back with a scrape. 'Have to go.' She froze to give me one last look and a murmured, 'Thanks', then scurried out of the café.

I gathered up my bags and headed north to Bolt's, thinking as I went. I had believed her about Keith; that had the ring of truth, though I suspected there had been an unacknowledged attraction between them, for him to visit so often, and her to accept his visits.

She was upset and shaken by Keith's death, but not torn apart. I wouldn't have believed her story of Ertie coming over in such a state that he'd remember nothing about it, except that it fitted Mary's.

I was almost at the Legion and about to cross the road when I glanced back at Home Furnishing. Two dark backs were just turning into the doorway. I recognised DS Peterson's constable, Shona, with her shining dark hair clipped back in the same way as her boss's.

I wondered if Danielle'd tell the police the same story she'd told me, and if they'd believe it.

Chapter Twelve

Shetland Pony Grand National: *A regular event at Olympia, with the pony riders dressed as jockeys.*

I caught the 15.40 bus by the skin of my teeth, and was duly dropped off at Voe. I dumped my shopping into the *Deuk*'s cuddy and paused, thinking things through. I could be at Brae by twenty to five; half an hour for messing about, then back out with *Khalida*, towing the *Deuk* behind me. I'd be moored up at the Ladie by six, feed all those animals again, have some tea myself – no, take my tea onboard, and go straight out again once everyone was fed – at which point my phone pinged. It was Vaila, reminding me they'd see me soon for pony washing. I wouldn't have time to get my boat now. A wave of bleakness swept over me. I wanted my normal life back again, with my boat under me, and the open sea ahead, and Gavin to come home to.

Right. I braced myself. I couldn't have my druthers, so I'd need to get on with life as it was. *Khalida* would be fine in her berth at Brae, and I'd get her home another day. For now, I needed to get back and wash horses.

The *Deuk* sped silently westwards between the mussel rafts and salmon farms of Olna Firth, and came smoothly around Linga. The sea was shining further west, the road to the wide Atlantic. I turned my head away from it and focused on the narrowing of the headlands into Houbansetter sound.

Cat had been on the lookout for someone coming home. He came bounding down from the gatepost as I turned into the pontoon, a grey blur against the green grass of the verge, with Kitten following behind. I made a fuss of them both, then began shifting the shopping: the heavy hens' mash first, then the other stuff. Julie charged out as soon as the cottage door was opened, squawking with indignation at being left behind. The kitchen clock said ten to five. I put the kettle on, then did a quick survey of everyone: hens pottering contentedly round the garden, sheep and lambs all present and correct, Fergus on his hillock, surveying two grazing mares and two foals stretched flat on the grass, sleeping. Nobody in a hurry to be fed or shut in. I could have a cup of tea before the lasses arrived.

I'd just taken my first sip when I heard a car approaching. Mug still in hand, I went to the doorway and watched as Aidan's pick-up scrunched down the gravel and stopped at the gate. Vaila and Rainbow tumbled out, wearing old jeans and T-shirts bright as jockey silks. They went straight for the back of it and fished out a selection of buckets, tethers, brushes and bottles. Aidan rolled down his window and leant out of it. 'Hi, Cass. I'll come back for them in about an hour and a half. They need a decent night's sleep before tomorrow's big day.'

'Dad!' Rainbow protested. 'We won't be going to sleep at half past six.'

'No, but I know you pair. You'll be cleaning tack and ironing shirts all evening.' His voice was firm. 'Tea's at seven. I'll be back at six thirty.'

'Oh well,' Rainbow said philosophically, standing clear to let him turn. 'They were done last week for the Viking Show, so it shouldn't take too long.'

'Right,' I said. I swallowed the last of my tea and put the mug on the windowsill. 'What do I do?'

Vaila gave me two buckets. 'Fill these up with comfortably warm water.'

'Two minutes.' I hurried into old jeans and a T-shirt, then filled the buckets as requested. When I carried them out again, the two mares and two foals were lined up at the fence, each one tied to a separate post, and Vaila and Rainbow were already at work brushing.

'That's good,' Rainbow said. 'Okay, first we have to rinse manes and tails and shampoo them, then rinse again, conditioner and comb out. Then we'll sort the rest of them, then do a final rinse. You start with Milla.'

Milla was Caedoc's mother, a generally peaceable red and white beast who moved round the park like a galleon dipping through the tropics. She also had enough blonde mane for three Hollywood starlets. Vaila handed me a plastic brush like a hairbrush and a two-litre jug. 'Pour the water on with this, and cup your hand around her eyes so the water doesn't go in them.'

'Watch your feet,' Rainbow advised. 'She'll probably plunge about a bit.'

I watched Vaila working on the other mare for a moment: a careful pour along the top of the mane which had the pony pulling backwards on her tether with a snort of disgust, then a skoosh of shampoo which Vaila massaged in, adding a bit more water to make a lather. She chatted cheerfully to the mare as she worked. Past her, Rainbow was crouching down to reassure Caedoc, who was struggling to get free from the fence.

I murmured reassuring nonsense to Milla as I cupped my hand round her eye, brushed her bush of blonde fringe backwards and poured the first half-litre of water over it. It ran straight off in glossy droplets. I tried again, and some of it stayed on, darkening the red fur under the blonde hairs. I added shampoo, still nattering away about what fun she'd have at the show, and scrunched it in with my hands. Vaila had been right about getting wet; my T-shirt was dripping already, with the light wind turning the warm water to cold, and as I began lathering Milla leant against me, soaking the upper half of my jeans as well. The smell of wet horse was overlaid by light floral. I kept lathering and the suds turned from white to mud-brown. The rinse washed them down her sides and left her mane shining blonde once more. I put on conditioner, combed it through, then rinsed it all again. It would be bonny once it dried, and it felt silky-smooth.

Vaila had moved on to the other mare's tail. She simply lifted it up and dunked it in a oner into the bucket of water, then got on with the lathering. The mare sighed and stood there.

I told Milla she was a good girl, gave her a polo mint and went for more water, then stroked my hand along her damp back and tried lifting her tail. It was surprisingly rigid; I'd forgotten about the bone running through it. Milla snorted and tilted one back foot warningly. I moved in and lifted the bucket up her tail from below, watching that hoof. She gave a resigned snort and set it flat again.

The water in the bucket went black the moment I swirled the tail around in it. I swittled as well as I could, then did the soaping, and rinsed with another bucket of warm water, hoping the household supply would hold out. Her tail clung together in a wet rope, but it would fluff out when it dried.

Body next. Milla was only my waist height, but there was a good deal of her when you started washing, and a lot of it was white, speckled now with bits of grit brought up by the water. Vaila was putting the shampoo on a large sponge and rubbing it in with circular movements. I followed suit, and Milla stood patiently while I worked my way round her, even down to her white feet, which had long hair covering her ankles and needed several lots of rinse before they came clean. By the time I'd finished all that her mane and tail were starting to dry, and I was right; they did look bonny in the last of the sunshine.

'Dock,' Rainbow said, looking up from a wriggling Caitlin. She hadn't got Caedoc particularly wet, just brushed his still-woolly baby coat until it shone. His sticky-up mane was damp, the white bits bright, and his tail curled in white ringlets.

I looked down at the pontoon, hoping for enlightenment. 'Her backside,' Vaila said. 'Lift her tail and wash it.'

I lifted her tail as instructed, but the minute I started washing, she lifted it of her own accord, and a stream of glistening poo slid out. 'Thanks, Milla,' I said, jumping clear. 'No, don't stand in it.'

'Move her and wash that foot again,' Vaila said.

'We'd need to find a clean bit of park for them overnight,' Rainbow said. 'We can tether the mares and Fergus, but leave the foals running loose.' She stood up and stretched. 'Looking good. D'you want to do Fergus next?'

I did Fergus. The amount of mud and grit that came out of his coat was nothing moderate, and his thick mane took three bucketfuls just to get it wet. By the time I'd finished him my arms and back were aching. I stretched them as the lasses walked the field for cleanliness, twirled stakes into the grass and made sure the end of the ropes could reach the burn but not another horse. 'If they possibly can,' Vaila said, 'they'll tie themselves in knots. Okay, ponies.'

I untied Fergus and managed to walk him to his tether, then went back for Milla. Behind me, Rainbow gave a yell of mingled annoyance and resignation. I turned round to see Fergus rolling on his clean back, short legs waving in the air. He clambered to his feet with several grass stains on his white bits. 'They always do that,' Rainbow said. 'We'll get them out in the morning.'

I looked round at us. We were all dripping wet, with soap stains down our fronts, dishevelled hair and wrinkled hands from the water. 'Thanks, guys. I wouldn't have done that at all without you.'

'You're welcome,' Rainbow said. 'We enjoy working with horses. And it'll be a fun day, you'll see.' She glanced over at the sun, poised above the Clousta hills. 'Dad'll be here any minute.' They began to gather up the brushes and buckets.

'Tomorrow,' Vaila said rapidly, as she stretched over the fence to retrieve a brush that had been dropped there, 'you'll need, like, your officer clothes, for the ring, or a white shirt, black breeks and a tie.'

'One of Gavin's tweed jackets,' Rainbow suggested. 'A shame he's not here. He looked really good in his kilt at the Viking Show, leading Caedoc round.'

'I'm definitely not qualified to lead anyone round,' I protested.

'You'll have to,' Vaila said. 'We'll be leading Rainbow's lot. And you'll need strong shoes, or wellies, and a boiler suit to put over the good clothes, for when we arrive and do all the brushing.'

'Okay.' I had one of those, for engine and paint work.

Vaila read my expression. 'Not something that's going to put boat oil all over their white bits.' She tilted her head, listening. 'That's Aidan now.'

'Message me if you think of anything else.'

'Faerdie-maet for breakfast,' Rainbow said. She lifted the bucketful of brushes and began speed-speaking. 'Their best headcollars. Gavin got leather ones with coloured browbands, and lead ropes. He'll have a box of stuff somewhere, just bring it. Extra buckets and brushes. Chopped carrots and polos for bribery.'

'What time's the truck coming?'

'Half six at ours. With you before seven, if nobody objects to going aboard.' She glanced round at the still-loose hens as we walked through the garden, and piled her armful of gear onto Vaila. 'Shall I give you a hand to round the hens up for the night?'

It was so much easier with two of us. Even the wild-topknot one seemed to feel it was bedtime. I wondered how many hours Gavin had spent chasing the last stray from under bushes on his own.

Aidan's pick-up was at the gate now. He tooted. 'See you tomorrow,' Rainbow said, and the pair of them scrambled aboard in a flurry of elbows and sticking-out buckets.

'Thanks,' I called after them, and stood watching as Aidan spun round with a wave and headed off over the hill.

I took a moment to look at the horses. The foals were by their mothers, sucking as if they'd been deprived of food for a week, tails waggling furiously. The white patches shone against the green grass.

It was quarter to seven now, and the shadows were lengthening on the grass, the clear air thickening. I counted the sheep: all present and correct. I got the hens' mash and put it in their run. Tethers made it easier to feed the mares and foals separately, and not feed Fergus, to his disgust. By the time I got back into the house, I was feeling wrung out. I unpacked the shopping, made a cheese omelette, and ate it curled up on the sofa. I had half of the Sandwick trifle, which livened me up, then I made myself another cup of tea and took up my laptop. I wasn't sure when Gavin might get a phone message, but the farm did have a dial-up internet, so I could let him know about Caedoc and what Danielle had said. I was just in the middle of an email when my phone rang. I leapt for it. Gavin's voice came out against a background of muffled voices: Invergarry pub, I guessed. 'Cass, hello.'

'Gavin! I was writing to you. How's Morag?'

'Doing very well.' His voice was light with relief. 'I phoned the hospital. She drank a whole cup of tea, and she's got feeling in her hand. They're keeping up the exercises, and they're going to start her walking on Monday, with a view to sending her home at the end of the week.'

'Oh, that's good news!'

'I'm in Invergarry now. The nearest reliable phone signal. Kenny comes back on Sunday, but he'll go straight to Fort William, spend the night there and see Mother, and then he'll come back here and I'll visit Mother in the morning, then head for the airport. I've got an Aberdeen flight, 16.45. Good news for the farm. Kenny met our second cousin Callum, who came and worked at the farm last summer, and persuaded him to come and lend a hand for a bit.' He paused to change gear. 'How are things with you?'

'Good. Oh, Gavin, I never realised how much work you have to do for all the animals. How do you ever get to work on time?'

He laughed. 'Get up early to allow for it. You wait till the cow arrives. A native Shetland breed, not very big, and mostly black, with long horns.'

'A cow!' His voice teased, but I remembered Trevor, yesterday, speaking of his sister, *stuck out at Klaufister, drudging on the croft*, and of all the animal work I'd done today, and of Danielle speaking about her bairns, and felt a sudden panic fill me.

Gavin spoke cheerfully over it. 'How d'you fancy learning to make butter and cheese? Mother can teach you. I do miss having fresh dairy. We always have it at home.'

I took a deep breath and spoke normally. 'Fresh-made butter would be nice. And what was that wonderful soft cheese she made, crowdie? Is it hard to do?'

'She always said not, but I suspect that was a lifetime of practice. Are you okay?'

'Tired. It's been a long day, beginning with Caedoc's VVE.'

'How did it go?'

'Well. It was Annie who came and did it. She said she'd send you a report and the bill, but he's a nice little horse, and nothing to stop him being a stallion, so long as his genes are okay. She took hairs to check for dwarfism.'

'Yes, that can be a problem with Shetlands. And he behaved?'

'Mostly for me, and impeccably for her. We'll see how he does tomorrow.'

'Tomorrow?' He sounded blank.

'The Walls Show.'

'Creator Lord, so it is. I'd forgotten all about it. Is Rainbow taking them?'

'She and Vaila came round, and we spent part of the evening washing them all. Where do you keep their showing halters and brushes and things like that?'

'In a cardboard box in the shed, under my workbench.'

'Can I borrow one of your tweed jackets, and a shirt and tie?'

I could hear he was smiling. 'You're going to show them?'

'Vaila said she and Rainbow would have their hands full with Rainbow's ones.'

'My black tie's in the top drawer, rolled up, and yes, to the jacket and shirt. White shirt, black or fawn trousers.'

'I only have black. And black wellies.' I remembered Fergus. 'Fergus is to eat less, or go on a tether.'

'I was thinking that myself. He's a solid little horse.'

'With a lot of white bits,' I said feelingly. 'Which he rolled on.'

Gavin laughed. 'But they'll look gorgeous at the show.'

'Did you get into town?'

'In the afternoon.' I hesitated. 'I met up with Danielle, Ertie's wife. You haven't spoken to DS Peterson?'

'I phoned you first.'

'Good answer. Well . . .' I did my best to describe Danielle and the situation with Ertie. 'And she says there was nothing between her and Keith. They were both lonely, and he used to come round to her house for a cup of tea and a chat, and that was all.'

'Mmm. A dangerous thing, shared loneliness.'

'And she wants to give Ertie an alibi. She says he came to the house, drunk enough that he was only just standing, and said he'd been talking to Mary – oh, I haven't told you about that.' I explained yesterday afternoon, and Mary's revelation of her past.

'Yes, I kent about that,' Gavin said.

'Ertie told Danielle he was going to give up the drink and join the church, and would she join it with him? She said he was nearly flaked out, and she steadied him home and got him on the sofa and left him. Could he have done all that and totally forgotten it?'

'Oh, yes, that's perfectly possible. A drunken blackout isn't what a lot of folk think. An alcoholic can lose great chunks of time when he's been out and about, and do all sorts of things which he has no recollection of afterwards. He may not even have appeared that drunk to other people. Did you believe her?'

'I don't know. For Keith, yes, I think so. She was eloquent about being trapped by small children.'

'Yes,' Gavin said seriously. 'It's a genuine problem. And it's easy to say, "Fight it," but it's no' so easy to do. It's a lot of work getting you and two toddlers in a fit state to jump in the car and go, and the more you neglect yourself the more work it is and the less you feel able to do it. And then you get really conscious of how scruffy you look compared to the women your husband's working with, but the children have you too worn out to do something about that, and it turns into a downward cycle of nappies and washing machines and mother and toddler group if you're lucky.'

'I'll resist,' I said. 'I'll greet you at the door with a freshly washed face and my sailing clothes on and hand you a grubby, smelly child from each hip as I head for *Khalida*.'

'Deal.'

'But for Ertie, I'm not sure,' I said, moving swiftly on, before the conversation got too near the bone. 'Yes, I think so, if you say the forgetting's possible. It fitted with what Mary said.'

'I'll get someone to take a statement from Mary. Shona, maybe. How're things at home?'

'The cats are fine. The hens are a bit panicky but laying well. An egg each, most days. I've been gathering them up. What do you do with them all? I made omelette for tea just now.'

'I've been having scrambled eggs for breakfast, instead of porridge, and omelette for tea one night a week. I take the rest into the station, for a donation to the charity box.'

'I could take them to Inga. She doesn't have hens.'

'And get the gossip at the same time. She'll ken Danielle from the pre-school children network.'

He was teasing me again. 'Or netball,' I agreed cheerfully. 'Danielle's from Whalsay, they're great netball players. They always beat us. That tall build.'

We chatted for a bit more, then he said reluctantly, 'I'd need to check on what's going on at the station. Sleep well, *mo chridhe*, and I'll speak to you again tomorrow.'

'Sleep well. Goodnight.' The phone blinked off, and I stared at it for a moment, suddenly bleak. The house felt very quiet. Then I shook myself, and got going with all that I needed for tomorrow. The box of headcollars first. I felt the blues wash over me as I went into Gavin's shed, and focused on what I was doing. The box was there, as he'd said. I took it into the house and opened it. He'd taken the hairs from the brushes, but they were still grey with pony-dust. I slooshed them in a bucket of hot water and washing-up liquid, then set them on the step to drip. The headcollars were leather, with one decorative band going across the pony's forehead, made of plaited ribbon, two in red, black and white and three in brown, gold and white, with a little froosh of ribbons at each end, and with matching lead ropes of thick cord. They all looked clean, but I gave the leather an extra rub. Faerdie-maet. I had the Yell cherry scones, and apples. I set the flask ready to fill in the morning. Money, for a catalogue and lunch.

Clothes. I put on my black jeans and found one of Gavin's white shirts. It was too big, but the jacket would cover that, and though the jacket was also too big, it wasn't ridiculous, and it was a soft green that would look good with the bright horses. Tie. Rubber boots. I looked at myself in the bathroom mirror and thought I looked suitably horsey, or at least that I'd get away with it.

I hung the jacket and shirt up, put the jeans and tie on the chair, and stowed the rest of it inside the clean buckets by the front door. Boiler suit over the top, ready to put on.

Bedtime. I put the kettle on for my hot water bottle and went to stand at the door. The very last gasp of light was still lingering in the west, over the Clousta hills, but the rest of the sky was midnight blue, and filled with glorious stars.

I wished Gavin was here to share them with me.

V
Breeding and Showing

Saturday 27th August

Tides at Brae

HW 03.18 (1.8m)
LW 09.36 (1.0m)
HW 15.52 (1.7m)
LW 22.35 (0.9m)

Sunrise 05.48; moonset 17.34; sunset 20.23; moonrise 20.31.

Waning quarter moon.

Chapter Thirteen

Laek til a laek: an aald horse til a faelly dyke. *Comment on tendency for people to seek familiar situations where they feel at home.* [Literally, *Like to like: an old horse to a wall with turfs laid on the top.*]

I'd set the alarm for half past five, but I woke slightly before it, and padded to the window for a look out before I made my first cup of tea. The sun wasn't yet risen, but it was light enough to show the makings of a bonny day: the sky was cloudless, the trees round the cottage stood up straight and still, and the sea in the sound was like polished glass. The sheep were still asleep, black, brown and grey rocks on green grass, with the lambs cuddled in to their mothers.

I showered, bundled my hair unbrushed in a band, sprayed myself generously with anti-midge stuff and opened the cottage door. Within seconds, the midgies had zoomed in like fighter pilots. The spray stopped them biting, but they crawled over my face and ears as I fed the sheep and put the hens' mash in their run. They'd have to stay in there all day. The cats came out with me, shaking their ears and stopping to scratch every couple of minutes, and seemed relieved when I went back inside. I gave them extra food, ate my own breakfast, and dressed with care: Gavin's shirt, tie and jacket, black jeans, hair plaited, boiler suit on top. I set my buckets on the briggistanes, made sure Ketling Julie was indoors, then got rubber boots on and began carting everything to the gate, ready to go.

The horses must have been obedient, for I heard the clatter of an approaching truck at bang on quarter to seven. It turned out to be a very large truck, the sort used for transporting cattle, ponies or two levels of sheep south on the ferry. The driver stopped precisely at the field gate, and Vaila and Rainbow tumbled out of the passenger side. They headed straight for the horses, and I followed.

Loading was surprisingly straightforward. Fergus looked almost enthusiastic as he clattered up the ramp, the mares stomped up with a resigned air, and the foals followed in a series of leaps. There were already half a dozen horses inside. I helped attach ours, and Vaila and Rainbow scrambled up into the high cab. There wasn't a lot of room, as the floor space was already filled with buckets. I clambered after them and swung the heavy door shut.

'Good-good,' the driver said cheerfully. 'Seatbelts on? Off we go.'

It felt like a long journey, with the truck going at a sober thirty all the way. If I craned my head right round I could see the horses standing, heads down to balance as they swayed. Once we reached the Walls road we became part of a traffic jam of trucks, horse-boxes, trailers and vans, and turned in at last to the showfield itself. There was a chaos of beasts being unloaded: cows, sheep, ponies, dogs, along with cats and small pets in cages, children clutching vases of flowers and mothers with trays of baking or plastic bags of knitting. 'We'll be over in the far corner, up behind the council houses,' Rainbow said. 'I'll find out which pens we're in while you start unloading.'

I abseiled down to let her out; the driver leapt down with practised ease and began taking down the tailgate. Milla followed me down the ramp, head high, ears pricked as she looked around. Vaila and Caedoc came after her, and we set off. Rainbow was walking along the line of metal hurdle cages around the showing ring, checking the labels, then she turned and looked for us, and waved enthusiastically. *Dalesgarth, Mrs L. Gardner*, the card read, when we reached them: Rainbow's granny, who nominally owned the horses.

'These four pens,' Rainbow said. We put Milla and Caedoc in, then spent the next half-hour getting the rest of them. Fergus walked over with several excited bounces and ringing neighs at all these other horses; the red mare Vaila had ridden the other day stomped beside me with a 'seen it before' air, and Yahbini progressed to the pen in a series of leaps and made a spirited attempt to climb out of it the minute he realised his neighbour was another stallion.

'Telegraph poles,' the other owner yelled at Rainbow as he made an attempt to control his, a thigh-high red one with a lot of mane. He forced the rearing beast down by sheer muscle-power and dragged it off to the Hydro pole a hundred metres away. Rainbow got Yahbini to the one behind the pens, and attached him with a loose bowline. Immediately he started going round and round, neighing defiance at this other horse that had dared to look at his mares.

'He'll soon calm down,' Rainbow said nonchalantly. 'Buckets.'

We retrieved the buckets, stored them behind our pens and began brushing, ignoring the bustle of ponies arriving all around us. Milla's tail was a glorious waterfall of fine gold, and her mane had recovered its bounce. Both her socks and Caedoc's needed to be re-washed, and Caedoc rivalled Fergus in the green patches on white back competition. I kept brushing out manes and tails, surprising myself by how sanguine I'd got about stepping behind back legs, while the lasses did technical stuff: re-washing docks, spraying Pledge onto cloths to wipe over rounded haunches, dosing the brushed-out tails with hairspray, and painting oil on hooves. I found I was rather enjoying myself: the sun rising warm on my face, the bustle of ponies and children getting ready, the air of excitement among the ponies as they looked around.

I was straightening my back after my last tail when a familiar voice yelled, 'Dass!' and Peerie Charlie, Vaila's little brother, came charging over. For a moment I didn't recognise him. He'd just started school, and had turned from a big toddler into a little boy overnight. His gold curls had been clipped to a boy cut, and he was dressed in riding clothes which were roomy in the body and long in the arms. A round riding helmet dangled from one hand. His sister Dawn was behind, equally horsemanlike.

'Wow!' I said. 'You look impressive.'

'I'm riding,' he said. 'Scarlet.' He pointed to the red mare Vaila had ridden, patiently getting her saddle put on her, and fished in his jacket pocket. 'I brought her some carrot, but I'll only give it to her if she behaves. Are you riding?'

I shook my head. 'I can't ride. You're one up on me there.'

'I could let you lead me,' he offered.

'No, I'm not any good at that either.'

'You're good at sailing,' he said kindly, gave a yell and a wave across the show ring and charged off to talk to another riding-clad small child. Dawn nodded a hello and went over to stroke a grey horse whose dapples shone in the sun.

'What's the time?' Rainbow said. She looked at her phone. 'Twenty-five past eight. Breakfast.'

We shared our faerdie-maet and tea sitting on upturned buckets, watching what was going on around us. There were still four empty pens, and a late horsebox was just arriving. As it turned sideways on to us, I saw the name painted on its panel: *Klaufister Shetland Pony Stud*. 'They've come after all, then,' Vaila said. 'Mam wasn't sure if they would.'

'Gives Yabbi a chance to beat Ebony this time round,' Rainbow said. The Klaufister truck opened its tailgate. Several coloured ponies clattered out at speed and were whisked into their pens by Irene, Ertie and another woman I took to be their sister, Allison.

'No Ebony,' said Vaila, watching them. She and Rainbow exchanged a quick look I couldn't read. Satisfaction? But Rainbow had sounded quite confident about Yabbi beating him, and I wouldn't have thought she'd want to win by default. I was surprised that the Klaufister folk were here, so soon after Keith's death, and with police all round the house still, but then, I reflected, this was Irene's business. These ponies needed a list of prizes to go with their pictures on the stud website.

Rainbow rose and stretched. 'Okay, water.' We filled our buckets at the tap, and tied them in a corner of each pen, then the girls dropped their boiler suits to show black jackets brushed within an inch of their lives, fawn jodhpurs and polished boots. Peerie Charlie charged back to join us, bouncing with importance at being included among the competitors. Rainbow opened her programme, and nodded to him. 'Best turned-out pony and rider. Cass'll lead you for that, on Milla.'

I gave her an appalled look.

'It's only a looks class. If the judge asks you to trot, shake your head and let the others pass you. It'll mostly be standing there.' She gave Charlie a sympathetic look. 'You won't do very well, Charlie, because you don't have a proper saddle, but give the judge a good impression for your own classes. After that it's riding classes. Best ridden, that's us, then lead rein, you're in that, then junior handler. Helmet on.' She glanced at me. 'Then stallions. You can relax for a bit.' She reddened. 'You're done a great job. Thanks.'

'You're welcome.' I added truthfully, 'I'm enjoying myself.'

'It's a shame Gavin's not here,' Rainbow said. 'He was looking forward to it.'

'I'll send him some photos.' I reached for my phone and set it ready.

'Here they come,' Vaila said. A group of three was coming towards us: a man in black cloth breeks and all-over gansey sporting a *Steward* rosette, a crofter-style woman in gansey and jeans with a catalogue, clipboard and plastic bag of rosettes, and a woman in a long waxed raincoat with shirt, tie and breeches underneath, and a fedora-style black hat. She nodded to the others, and she and the man went to stand in the middle of the ring. The crofter woman obviously knew everyone, for she came around the pens, speaking to individuals, with a nod towards the ring.

'That's us,' Rainbow said. 'Up you go, Charlie.' She lifted him up. He took a tight hold of Milla's mane and I clipped on her lead rope and braced myself. Rainbow caught up her helmet and went over to Yahbini, still snorting angrily at the other stallion, but now saddled and bridled. He looked magnificent. 'Leg up,' Rainbow said to Vaila, and landed in his saddle lightly as sea-foam settling. 'Good luck.'

'And to you.' Vaila turned to Dawn. 'All set? Just follow me, and keep watching what the other competitors are doing. Cass, you follow Dawn. Good luck.'

We walked one sedate round of the ring, then turned into the centre of the circle and stood in a line. Irene was in the ring too, impeccably professional in black, with her hair in a net under her bowler hat. Her pony was red and white, and polished so that its chestnut flanks glinted with sunlight. There was no sign of the stress I'd seen on Thursday; she was calm and purposeful in her own element. The judge inspected each horse, checking under the mane, picking up a hoof, running a finger under the saddle. Charlie sat mast-straight and Milla stood to attention, with only a sigh as the judge lifted her tail, then came back to Charlie and patted Milla's neck. 'Well done. She's beautifully clean.'

Charlie hesitated, then honesty took over. 'Cass washed her,' he admitted. 'I wanted to help,' he added, 'but Mam said I needed an early night to make it through today.'

The judge smiled. 'Well done, Cass,' she said, and moved on. After she'd checked us all, she stood back and took a long look at each of us, then beckoned the woman with the rosettes bag. She indicated the winners, and they were called forward: Rainbow, Irene, Vaila, Dawn. Charlie made a philosophical face. 'Rainbow said we wouldn't win.'

'But you sat up really straight,' I said. 'You gave the judge a good impression.'

The winners did a victory walk round the ring, then we all came out. Rainbow's freckled face was flushed with pride. 'Best ridden. Good luck, lasses.'

Vaila and Dawn adjusted their reins then they all went forward into the ring, Scarlet sedately, the grey pony plodding behind, and Yahbini with a suggestion of sideways. Irene's red and white arched its neck and walked delicately behind him, nostrils flared.

They lined up, then walked and ran around the ring together, then individually. My schoolfriend Inga, Vaila and Dawn's mum, appeared beside me as they began. 'How're they doing?'

'Good so far.'

'The others all got a rosette each,' Charlie said. 'I need a saddle next year.'

'You get one in the next class,' Inga said.

Vaila's Scarlet behaved well, and Dawn's grey looked bonny, but Yahbini was magnificent, with his froosh of mane and tail flying, and Rainbow was in her element, her thin face mask-like with concentration. I wasn't surprised when he was called in first at the final line up, and awarded the red rosette. Irene came second, a middle-primary-age boy on one of the Klaufister ponies came third, and Dawn was fourth.

'Well done,' I said, as they reappeared.

'Grey Shetlands are unusual enough to be showy,' Vaila said philosophically. She realised that might sound sour-grapes and smiled at her sister. 'She went really well for you.'

'He behaved beautifully,' Rainbow said. She tied Yabbi up again, and took the saddle off. 'Now you, peerie-breeks. Leading-rein class. Up you go.'

I took several photos as they went round. Vaila was obviously controlling Scarlet, but Charlie sat up straight with his hands clenched on the reins and his legs stretched downwards in the stirrups. Irene was leading the pony she'd ridden with a small boy onboard, and Allison was leading another Klaufister red and white with a small girl. I thought Peerie Charlie was going to be done for when the judge ordered a trot, for he bounced about for the first couple of steps while the others were rising and falling perfectly, but then he seemed to catch the rhythm of it. I realised why as they came round past us. 'Stand . . . sit . . . stand . . . sit,' Vaila was chanting softly as she ran round with him.

'He hasn't fallen off yet,' Inga said cheerfully.

The judge lined them up again for their individual rounds. This time Peerie Charlie was prepared, and he and the horse went round nicely together. There was a long moment of suspense once everyone had gone round, then she beckoned them in, with Peerie Charlie first. I grinned.

'There'll be no living with him now,' Dawn said, but her eyes were shining as she photographed him receiving the red rosette.

The next class was something called First Ridden, where the

riders were on their own. There was a Klaufister boy in it, who took the red rosette.

'That'll be you next year,' Rainbow told Charlie.

'We should have found someone to borrow,' Vaila said. She shrugged. 'Oh, well, there are plenty of classes.'

'Junior Handlers,' Rainbow said. 'Good luck, Charlie.' He grabbed Scarlet's lead rein with a determined look on his face and headed for the ring, towing her behind him.

'Walk beside her head!' Vaila hissed after him.

'Under ten years,' Inga read from her catalogue, 'judged on standing, leading, trotting and child's ability to control pony.'

'She's having a good day,' Rainbow said. 'She might do most of it.'

'No,' Vaila said, 'don't head for the front.' Charlie hadn't heard. He'd hauled Scarlet straight to the head of the column.

'She's walking not too badly,' Rainbow said.

Inga cast an amused look at them both, leaning forward in their eagerness. 'Keep her head up,' Vaila hissed.

It didn't look to me as if Peerie Charlie was in control exactly, but his determination was transferring itself to Scarlet, and she walked and trotted on the judge's command, and went back to standing. Peerie Charlie had a grip of iron on the lead-rope, right by her nose; she wasn't going to snatch so much as a blade of grass. They watched as the others did the walking and trotting, then the judge came back to the line-up, and bent over Peerie Charlie. She must have asked him to pick up a hoof, for he bent down and lifted one of Scarlet's front legs, then he gave the judge the lead rope. Vaila groaned, and Rainbow hid her face in her hands. Charlie went to Scarlet's hind legs and picked up one of her back hooves. I was impressed. Then he came back to the judge, and she asked him something else. He nodded vigorously, took the lead rope back, and stood square in front of Scarlet. 'Back up,' he said loudly, then, when she didn't move, he repeated 'Back' and put one hand on her chest. To my astonishment, Scarlet took three steps backwards. Peerie Charlie gave her an *about time too* nod and turned to the judge. She was smiling as she moved to the next one, the older boy from Klaufister. He was obviously more competent, but the judge must have made allowances for age, or just liked Peerie Charlie's style, for he got the red rosette.

'Phew!' Dawn said as he led Scarlet out of the ring, beaming. 'Us next.'

'Well done,' Vaila said to Charlie. 'Hand her here.'

This time the judge watched with narrowed eyes as the riders made their ponies walk, trot, go across the ring to turn in the other direction, keep the pony standing, lift feet and make it back up. On the ground, Rainbow looked slight beside Yahbini's muscled neck and haunches, but there was no doubt she had him under perfect control, and we all cheered when she came in first, with Vaila second and Dawn third. 'Well deserved,' Vaila said to her, as they brought the ponies back. 'What's next?'

What was next turned out to be Fergus, in the gelding class, and under Rainbow's handling he was more awake than I'd ever seen him: a striding walk, a neat trot, short legs going like speeded-up clockwork, and standing like a statue with his head up and ears pricked for the judge's inspection. He came second. Vaila was waiting by the gate and grabbed him from Rainbow so that she could run for Yabbi, and the stallion class. The crofter who'd shifted his to a telegraph pole went first, holding his snorting, head-shaking beast in a firm grip. Yabbi and Rainbow came next, with another couple after them. They went down in size from Yahbini through the crofter's one, still dancing sideways trying to see who was behind him, down to a black and white one that didn't come up to the waist of the woman leading him. The judge spent a long time deliberating, getting the miniature stallion and Yahbini running out in front of her, and checking them close to.

An older woman had come up to sit beside Inga. She had a programme, folded open at the horse classes. I turned my head to look down at it: right enough, third on the list was Minstead Ebony, Klaufister Stud. She saw me looking and nodded. 'Irene's not brought the black stallion, the one that beat our Yabbi.'

It seemed odd not to have brought him, since he'd been entered.

'Maybe he injured himself when he got loose,' I said tentatively.

The woman shook her head. 'No' he. I asked Irene, when I saw he wasn't in the pen, and she said she thought she'd leave him at home and concentrate on the mares. Wished me luck with Yabbi. She even said he ought to have won at the Viking Show, which I thought was good o' her, though I wasn't sure I agreed. Ebony's a bonny horse.'

'But so's Yabbi,' I said. I added tentatively, 'Are you Rainbow's granny?'

'Lorraine,' she said. 'And you're Cass. Rainbow said you were a great help yesterday and this morning. Thanks to you.'

'I enjoyed it,' I said, and broke off. The judge had finally decided; she was talking to the clerk with the clipboard, who nodded and brought out the rosettes. Yabbi and Rainbow were called in first, and we all clapped enthusiastically.

'And how's Gavin's mum doing?' Lorraine asked.

I explained, still watching the ring. The judge said something to Rainbow as she handed her the rosette which made her flush with pleasure as she replied.

'What did she say?' Vaila demanded, as Rainbow brought him back.

'That he was a good stallion, and I should show him south,' Rainbow said. She didn't take time to savour the compliment. 'Year-olds next.'

She, Vaila and Dawn each grabbed a pony and led them out and round, and Dawn's came in first, to her delight. After that the morning turned into a blur. There was class after class, starting with the youngsters, then mares without a foal and mares with one, then at last it was the foals, a rodeo of them in the ring together. 'You take Caedoc,' Rainbow said, handing me his headcollar. 'Don't go between him and the judge, and just follow what the others do.' Some were tired enough from their exciting day to behave reasonably sedately; others, Caedoc included, wanted to charge round, and one, who'd obviously not been handled much, treated us to a bucking bronco display. I grasped Caedoc's lead rope firmly, did my best to restrain him, and was gratified when he was called in first.

'Hang on to him,' Rainbow said. 'He'll be back. Caitlin next.' She already had her out and ready to go. I stopped Caedoc from following, and kept him there through the classes of filly foals. Rainbow took Caedoc back to be judged against the other winning male youngsters, and when he won that, against the winning filly. This got him an extra-large rosette with *Junior Champion* blazed across it, and, Rainbow said, I'd have to go back in the ring to be judged again for overall champion. There were three of us: Rainbow with Yabbi, Irene with one of her mares, and Caedoc. Pleased as Gavin would have been to have Caedoc the overall champion, it was Yabbi's day, and Rainbow's face shone like the morning star as she took the Best in Show rosette from the judge. That made Irene's mare the 'best of opposite sex to champion'.

I thought that was it all over, but suddenly Peerie Charlie reappeared, grinning, with coloured stripes on his face, a painted sacking tunic and a feathered headdress. He did a war whoop. 'Are you dressing up, Cass?'

'No,' Inga said, appearing with an armload of costumes. 'Vaila – Rainbow – Dawn.' She dished out tunics, feather headbands and wooden hatchets with coloured wool wound round the handles. 'Facepaints.' The girls drew stripes across their cheeks, then belted coloured blankets around the grey pony, Fergus and Milla, added a bunch of scarlet pompoms to each bridle, vaulted on, and headed for the ring, with Peerie Charlie and Scarlet towed on a lead rein behind Rainbow and Milla. Peerie Charlie let out another war whoop which had Yabbi dancing sideways on his telegraph pole. Inga and I followed, phones at the ready. The older boy from Klaufister was a clown, the younger one was a spaceman, the older girl was a Viking princess in blue velvet, and the little girl looked sweet in a flower-girl outfit. Leading her, Irene was riding side-saddle in a long black skirt below her jacket, and an Edwardian-style top hat with a veil. Lorraine tut-tutted, and Inga gave a little shake of her head before she concentrated on getting a photo of the bairns and horses in all their war finery. They weren't being judged as a group though, the judge had to go for one of them, and ended up choosing Peerie Charlie, to his delight.

'Not bad,' Vaila said, as we brought the horses back to their pens, took off the headcollars and left them in peace to tackle haynets. 'Several trophies too.'

I took a last photo of our rosettes tied to the fence, added *Caedoc junior champion !!! xxx* and sent it to Gavin, then looked across at the hall. 'Is it lunchtime now?'

Chapter Fourteen

Da njuggel is grippet it! *Said when mechanical apparatus stops for no apparent reason, or when things or events are brought to a sudden halt, not easily explained.*

Lunch was good, a buffet of sandwiches, filled rolls and fancies eaten in a squashed hubbub of show-goers. Inga and I found two seats at the end of a table, and the youngsters headed for a corner with a dozen others. I nodded to the woman beside me, and realised it was our landlady, Kayleigh. She'd been at school with Inga and me, and she was a crofter lass even then, with muscles that could see off any of the boys daft enough to challenge her to arm-wrestling, and her dark hair cut short for ease of keeping. Her teeth gleamed in her tanned face as she smiled in greeting. 'Aye, aye, Cass, Inga. How're you both doing?' She looked at me. 'How's Gavin's mum?'

'Good,' I said. 'Really good. They're going to start her walking on Monday, and hope to send her home at the end of the week.'

'Ah, that's good news,' Kayleigh said. 'Tell him I'm glad to hear it.' She turned to Inga. 'And your three'll be involved wi' Rainbow's horses, I hae nae doubt.'

Inga gestured towards the corner of youngsters. 'Having a great time.'

'That's good,' Kayleigh said. 'In the money?'

'Various rosettes.' She added cheerfully, 'Charlie got the lead rein, junior handler and fancy dress, so he'll be impossible for a week.'

Kayleigh looked at me. 'How're you coping all on your lone, wi' the animals?'

'I'm fine,' I said. 'Rainbow showed me what to do, and I'm doing it.'

'Grand.' She paused to take a mouthful of cheese roll. 'I'm no' had a look at your foal for a while, but he had bonny markings. What did you call him, Caedoc? Is Gavin still thinking to buy him to keep as a stallion?'

'He spoke about it, and Caedoc got his first VVE examination.'

'Junior Champion too,' Inga said.

'Boys a boys, that's great! They're serious breeders out here on the westside, so he must be good.'

'How are your croft plans going?' I asked. 'Gavin was talking about a cow.'

Kayleigh pulled a face. 'Red tape, you ken. You've no idea the forms you have to fill in to do anything wi' the public. But I'm getting there. We're hoping to start next April. No' for the cruise ships, we couldn't cope wi' a busload, but we can welcome small parties, and schoolbairns, while you're out, so it doesn't disturb your privacy, and not in your garden. Gavin and I were thinking to bring the cow over once he's got the byre repaired and a stall for her, and then she can calve at the Ladie. She's a bonny beast, and very amiable.' She smiled. 'You could set up a sideline in home-made crowdie, while you spend the winter ashore.'

Inga shook her head at me, laughing. 'Who'd a thought in Home Ec that you'd end up selling food to the public?'

I pulled a face. 'Not sure about that.'

Kayleigh finished her roll, drank her tea, then looked at me. 'Are you heading out again? I'll maybe come with you. There was something I wanted to talk to you about.'

I felt a sudden panicky sinking of the heart. I hoped she wasn't going to say that she wanted her cottage back, now I'd committed to life ashore. I'd grown to love the Ladie, the sound below us, alive with passing wildlife, and Brae and Aith in the distance. I finished my tea and stood up.

'Go you,' Inga said. 'I'll have another cup of tea, and wait for the bairns. They won't want Charlie tagged on to them all afternoon.'

We went out into the fresh air. I'd thought it was busy before, but this morning had been only exhibitors, and now the crowds were arriving. The car park was full, vehicles were parked all along the road in both directions and there were groups of chattering people in summer clothes everywhere. We dodged around them and headed for the relative quiet of the pony pens. The buckets were in use now, but there was a fine grassy knowe to sit on.

'It's for you to pass on to Gavin,' Kayleigh said, once we were comfortably settled.

It seemed the entire world wanted me to liaise with Gavin for them. I nodded. Kayleigh gave a deep sigh, and gazed into the distance for a moment.

'It's about Klaufister,' she said at last. A wave of relief came over me. 'About the croft. He maybe kens already, but in case no' . . . see, I'm on the Grazings Committee.'

The Grazings Committee was the group of crofters in charge of organising anything to do with crofting for its particular area.

'Patsy phoned me,' she said. 'Oh, maybe six weeks back. She wanted my advice about assigning the croft. Giving it over to someone else during her lifetime, now she's not so able, and saving a bit o' red tape once she's dead. Now that's no' in the Grazings Committee's remit, it has to be done through the Crofting Commission, but it's good for us to ken about, if a croft is going to change hands, and of course it's fine if someone's willing to think ahead like that, and not let the croft get run down. So I explained that to her, and told her where she'd find the forms, and then we spoke a bit about de-crofting the house if she wanted to keep that, or renting it from the new crofter. I didn't see that as a problem, as Ertie has his own house anyway.' She hesitated. 'Well, depending on what happens with Danielle. And if they were to de-croft the house Patsy and Irene have, then he'd be able to get grants to re-refurbish the old one, if things don't work out between him and Danielle, or even build a new one, given the age of it.' She paused again, her face distressed.

'Except that it wasn't Ertie she was wanting to assign it to, nor Irene. She wanted to give the croft over to Keith.'

I stared at her. 'Keith?'

Kayleigh nodded. 'Keith, that's lived south the maist o' his life, and never took any interest as a bairn. I didn't really ken him, wi' him no' being at the Brae school, but I saw him at the shows.' She echoed Annie. 'He never paid any heed to the animals. There'd be a bunch of us charging round together, working with them, but he just stuck with his mam. Kinda sad.' She sighed, and paused for a moment. 'Anyway, be that as it may, Patsy said he's taking an interest now. He bought the stallion to bring new blood in, and he has ideas for taking the stud forward, and she wants him to have it. I tried to say to her how Ertie's wrocht there all his life, and how Irene helped her dad build up the horse stud, but she wasn't having it. It was all to go to Keith, house and all. He'd never turn his mother out from her home, she said, and brushed it aside when I said that if he got a wife she might no' be so keen to have his sister and mother camped on her.'

Ertie hadn't said why he might have gone out and killed Keith, but here was the kind of motive the police would love: finding out that his mother was planning to hand the croft he'd worked all his life over to his detested little brother.

'And did she actually go ahead with it?' I asked.

Kayleigh nodded. 'It was in the paper two Fridays ago. I thought maybe Gavin might no' have seen it. Well, the njuggel's grippit that one now.'

She saw the blank look I gave her. I knew that the njuggel was the Shetland water-horse, but I didn't see what it had to do with this.

'You're no heard that een? It means something's come to a dead stop, like the mill-wheel when the njuggel took hold of it.' She reddened. 'I feel like I'm betraying a confidence, but, well, you remember we had murder in our family. I ken how it feels, the suspicion. It needs to be sorted right, and it won't be until the police have all the information.' She nodded and rose. 'You tell Gavin about it.'

I sat quietly for a few moments, thinking about that. Klaufister was to be given to the one person who'd never shown any signs of caring about it, over the heads of two who passionately loved it, and one of them the older son. If Ertie had known this, he had a double motive for killing Keith: Danielle and the croft. I wondered if that was why Danielle had come forward with an alibi for him.

Opposite me, the Klaufister folk hadn't gone to the hall for lunch; they'd brought sandwiches and folding chairs, and were having a quiet picnic in the corner behind the pony pens, out of the way of people passing. The mourning air of their black clothes gave them a detached air. I noticed that nobody went over to them. There were several of them: Irene, Ertie, Trevor, Allison and their two children, the boy who'd won the first ridden class and the Viking princess. Beside them was a tall fair woman that I took to be Danielle's mother, over to mind the bairns and take them to the show while Danielle worked: the dark not-quite-school spaceman boy who'd been in the leading rein class, Peerie Arthur, and the golden ringlets little flowergirl, Meggie. Patsy wasn't there. It would have been a long day for someone on crutches.

I didn't want to think about Keith's death here. I got up and checked the water buckets, then took one over to refill for topping up the rest. The ponies were getting bored now; Caedoc and Caitlin were lying flat, sleeping, and the others were standing, noses drooping. Even Yabbi was rubbing his chin meditatively against his telegraph pole, ignoring all the other horses. I took him more water, and he came over to slurp it about, including over me, then moved to the length of his tether to watch the people traipsing round the showfield. I left him to it and went for a quick wander myself.

The showfield was spread over a fair area. I began at the pens of cows, and spent a moment looking at them. The pure-bred Shetland cows were smaller than the others, but still startlingly large this close, with shiny black and white coats, and long, sharp-tipped horns. I wondered if one of them was the one Kayleigh had bought. Ertie was there with them, filling up buckets and scratching their foreheads. I watched him for a moment, noticing the lines on his face and dark rings under his eyes, but also seeing the way he moved around them, calm and professional, like Irene with the horses. The light wind blowing the smell of kye from him to me held no hint of drink, just cigarette smoke. There were pigs too, though not native Shetland *grice*, which were something like a wild boar, according to the replica in the Museum; the last one of them was eaten during the First World War. I had no doubt that if they were still about, Kayleigh would want a pen of those too, and I was squeamish about that. I could eat an anonymous cow from somewhere else, but I wasn't sure I could swallow a creature I'd spent months feeding. There was a whole field of tethered rams with impressively curled horns; the winners had rosettes tied to their backs. The pens of ewes and lambs were backed onto the first side of pony pens. Like the foals, the lambs had had enough, and were sleeping close to their mothers, who chewed the cud and watched the passing people with incurious eyes.

There was a spread of marquees as well as the agricultural shed and various fast-food vans which filled the air with the smell of burgers: three large ones, a fancy one with windows in the sides, and, next to the Mr Whippy van, a gazebo selling hot dogs. The nearest tent was probably pets, as it had a pack of fed-up dogs tethered to separate stakes in front of it, as well as a pen of miniature spotted goats and a rabbit hutch, which turned out to hold a black hen and five half-grown chicks. Inside the tent was a variety of ducks and hens, though no tappit hens, and cages with all kinds of pets: budgies, canaries, rabbits with hanging-down ears and a ruff round their necks, guinea pigs, a grey squirrel-like creature that I thought might be a chinchilla, and, on the bottom layer of cages, a pair of kittens huddled into their blanket, peering out with scared eyes at the parade of stomping feet, and an adult stripey who had turned his back to it all and was trying to sleep till it was over.

The agricultural shed was beautifully cool after the warmth of the tent, and the trestle tables along each side sagged under the weight of magnificent baking. I'd come in at the children's end, an impressive display of pizza, paper plates with three brownies or glitter-frosted cupcakes and some imaginative decorated novelty sponges. There was a panda in a bamboo forest, a golden-haired sleeping princess on six differently coloured mattresses and covered with a bedcover woven in two colours of icing; there was a cheeseburger, pink pigs in a chocolate-fingers pen and a wonderful blue VW Beetle which had won first prize.

Peerie Charlie suddenly appeared beside me. 'I like that one,' he said, pointing to one I hadn't spotted, a tan and white guinea pig on a yellow ground. It was beautifully done, and had a bright, lively eye.

'Yea, really good,' I agreed, 'but I'm no' sure I'd want to eat it. Eating a guinea pig, yuck.'

'They used to eat them,' Peerie Charlie said. 'Somewhere. It was the job of the boys to herd them. My teacher said so. She said I'd be good at it.' He stood on tiptoe to check out the card by the Beetle. 'One – s – t. First. I can read now I'm at school.'

'But you know from the red card that it's first,' I pointed out.

He pulled a face and pointed to the green card by the pigs. 'Wuh – lll – d – one. Well done. See?'

'You're a genius, after only two weeks at school.'

'My teacher says I'm very clever.' His face clouded. 'But she says that to everyone, even when they get things wrong.' He brightened again. 'Except I don't get them wrong. What else is in here?'

I looked along the table. 'Cake and more cake.' There was some very nice fruit cake ahead, cut in half to show the texture. I betted some were Baked by a Gentleman. Gavin had been joking about entering that. I had a sharp pang of wishing he was here, and suppressed it. The one with the trophy label was an iced carrot cake, with little marzipan carrots round its edge, and a sprinkling of ginger lumps in the middle. 'Shortbread. Jam. A cake-stand of assorted fancies.'

Peerie Charlie sighed, and I echoed the sound. Apart from fancy cakes, it wasn't much fun looking at food you weren't allowed to sample. 'There are children's models and paintings round the other side.' I glanced up at the pinboards. 'And poems.'

Peerie Charlie gave a sigh that came right up from his toes, and slid his hand into mine, temporarily forgetting he was a schoolboy now. 'How about we go back to the horses? I'm tired. I could go to sleep on your jacket.'

'Okay,' I said. 'Does your mam know where you are?'

'I told her I was going to look for you at the horses. Then I was on my way when we saw you coming in here, so she watched me coming to find you, then went to see what the lasses were up to.' He smiled suddenly and reached into his pocket for a five-pound note. 'She said I was to buy us an ice cream each. The ones with the pointy top, from the van.'

I liked that idea. We headed over to Mr Whippy, queued for about half an hour, and at last came away licking an outrageously sugary pyramid topped with a rivulet of green and red sauce, and with a flake sticking out of it. We strolled slowly, licking, and by the time we'd got to the horses, and Charlie had shared the cone bit with Scarlet, we were both so sticky that we had to go to the water tap to clean our hands.

We were just wandering back when Peerie Charlie let out a shriek and ran up to the small dark spaceman. 'Aye aye,' he said. 'You were in the riding class I won, and the fancy dress, but not the leading the pony one.'

The boy nodded, clutching his granny's hand. I could see he wasn't at school yet, and so maybe hadn't met someone as ebullient as Charlie. The granny had a strong resemblance to Danielle, and was carrying the flowergirl on one hip.

'My pony's called Scarlet,' Charlie said. 'She's over there. Come and see.' He noticed the boy was still holding his granny's hand, and held out his own nearly clean one. 'I'm Charlie.'

The boy hesitated, but his granny urged him to go and look. 'And then you can show Charlie your pony. We'll just bide here.'

I smiled at her as the boys ran off, Peerie Charlie chattering nineteen to the dozen. 'I think you must be Danielle's mam. I'm Cass.'

'She said she'd spoken to you.' The little flowergirl on her hip was struggling to get down. 'Yea, Meggie, we'll go too.' She put the toddler down, holding on to one hand, and said over her curly head, 'I'm Laura Poulson. Is that your peerie man?'

I shook my head. 'My best school pal's youngest. Inga Anderson, from Brae.'

'A dark lass. Yea, yea, I ken her from the netball. I'm in the veteran's league, and she's still in the women's, like Danielle, but I ken her. A determined player.'

That sounded like Inga. 'I borrow him from time to time.'

Laura gave a sudden smile that made her seem my own age. 'Then give him back quick. I ken. I feel like doing that meself sometimes. Are you sitting here?'

I nodded at the knowe where we'd left our stuff. 'Just there, by the saddles.' We strolled over, and Laura put Meggie down. 'Go you, Meggie. We'll bide here. Mind not to let the horse eat your frock.'

The little girl ran over to her brother. We sat down and watched as Charlie led them to Scarlet's pen and demonstrated stroking her nose. 'He's not at school yet, Arthur, is he?'

She shook her head. 'Another year to go.' She looked over to where he was standing silently beside Charlie, who was still chattering nineteen to the dozen. 'He'll be five and a half when he goes, but that's a good thing. He's kinda shy.'

I nodded. Neither of us said that his subdued, nervous manner could be due to an alcoholic in the house.

'But the chalet's nearly ready,' his granny added, as if she was following that thought. 'Willie, that's my man, he's been working hard at it all summer, getting the flooring in and the plasterboard up, and Danielle chose the colours for the walls the last time she was over, so he went to Frank Williamson's last week, and he's all set to start on painting. I came to her this weekend, instead of her coming to me, because of the show. Ertie didn't want the bairns to miss it. They'd all kinds of things to put to it, you ken, collections of wild flowers, and paintings, and Peerie Arthur baked a batch of brownies. He got a second with them, and his rosette for the ponies, so he was brawly pleased.'

I was struggling to think what to say. *The chalet's nearly ready. Danielle's chosen the colours.* The granny's next words clinched it.

'They've been going to the nursery in Whalsay on Fridays ever since Danielle started coming over, well, Peerie Arthur was in the nursery, and I took Meggie to the playgroup, just so's they'd ken the other bairns and not feel too strange.'

I managed to sound casual. 'When're they moving in?'

'Next month. Willie's determined to have it ready before he goes back to sea.' She shook her head. 'He wants his peerie lass out of there.'

Next month! – and here we were almost at the end of this one. Nothing that Danielle had said suggested that she was moving away from Klaufister within a couple of weeks. The guilty look that had crossed her face as she'd talked about how much Peerie Arthur loved the croft was explained now. *I wasn't being sucked back in.* I wondered if Ertie knew that there was no reconciliation on the cards; instead, he was about to lose his bairns.

Laura hadn't noticed my silence. 'I'm keeping an eye on the charity shop for furniture and curtains, and we've ordered rugs from the place in town. Next visit they might be able to stay in there, though I'll miss having the bairns jumping into bed wi' me first thing. But it'll be that fine to have them close by, and Danielle can work another couple of days a week, to make ends meet. I'll gladly babysit until she manages work nearer home. We have an old spare car, so she can leave hers at the other end of the ferry.'

'It'll be fine to have them near,' I agreed. I was still feeling poleaxed. 'Will Ertie want them at weekends?'

Her eyes sparked. 'He may want, but he'll not get till he's capable o' taking care of them. I'll put my foot down about that. Patsy's no' able for a toddler like Meggie, and won't be for a while yet, and Peerie Arthur needs to get a bit more confidence.' She shook her head. 'No, I'll be granny in charge for a bit.' She gave me a quick, sideways look, then another longer one, assessing my expression. 'Danielle didn't mention to you that she's moving out?'

I shook my head.

Laura looked taken aback. 'I didn't realise. I thought, from what she said about you having a good chat together – listen, you'll no'' tell the Klaufister folk, will you? Please don't say a word. Danielle'll tell Ertie herself, once they're safely away. I'm taking a load of stuff this weekend, so that when they're ready Danielle can put what they need in the car during the night, then set off the next morning. That'll spare the bairns the shouting there might be. They need stability now, you ken.'

'Yes,' I agreed. I wasn't sure that going like that was the best way to keep the peace, but Danielle knew Ertie better than I did, and the width of Mainland, with its spine of the Kames separating west from east, and a stretch of water between Mainland and Whalsay, was a good barrier. Furthermore, everyone on Whalsay would know the score. If Ertie turned up blind-drunk at the ferry terminal, they'd refuse to let him onboard.

Charlie had finished showing Scarlet and all her rosettes to Peerie Arthur and Meggie. He came back to us now, towing Peerie Arthur beside him and with Meggie in the other hand, and stopped in front of Laura. 'Me and Arthur would like to see his pony now. And Meggie's too.'

Peerie Arthur didn't speak, but he nodded, eyes big and dark in his thin face, and his granny rose. 'Come on then, the three of you. Let's go and have a look.' I made to rise, but Laura waved me back. 'No, no, you take a bit of a rest. You were likely up at dawn loading ponies, and you've another couple of hours to go before the show's over.'

I didn't like to bother her with Charlie, but I thought of the way the other horsey folk had kept away from the Klaufister pen, not intruding on their trouble. I didn't want to push myself in. 'Thanks. But you be sure and send him back if he's getting under Irene's feet.' I looked at Charlie and Peerie Arthur. 'I'll bide here, if you want to go back and forward between us.'

'Yes!' Charlie said, and took Arthur's hand. The two boys charged off across the empty show-ring, with Meggie running after them, curls flying. 'Don't frighten the horses by rushing up to them,' Laura called after them. She smiled at me. 'Your Charlie's a fine, confident, peerie boy. He'll squeeze a word out of our Arthur yet. Bye.'

She headed off after them. They'd stopped exaggeratedly three metres short of the pen and tiptoed forwards, still hand-in-hand when they got to the Klaufister pen. Irene rose from her chair to meet them, and Danielle's mum explained who Charlie was. Irene looked across at me and waved, then retreated to the shadow of their box.

I made myself comfortable on the knowe and watched the boys. Peerie Charlie was still talking away, but it seemed to me that every so often he asked a question, waited for an answer, and got one. Maybe Peerie Arthur's granny was right; peace, school and an encouraging friend would work wonders. Yet I liked Ertie. I watched him stand up from his chair and go over to the children, crouching down by them to talk to them. Drink was an illness, Danielle had said, but all the same, she was taking her children away from him as if he was infectious. And how did that fit in with her story of agreeing to a reconciliation?

'He's not bothering the Klaufister folk, is he?' Inga asked, coming suddenly out of the crowds.

I shook my head. 'Talking to the boy. Danielle and Ertie's boy.'

'Peerie Arthur. I see him. Ah well.' She sat down on the grass and reached into one of the bags for a flask. 'More tea?'

'Yes, please.'

She found a second cup and poured it out.

'Inga,' I said after the first couple of sips, 'is Danielle moving back to Whalsay one of those things that everyone kens except the Klaufister folk?'

'Did her mam mention it?'

I nodded. Inga shook her head, smiling. 'All o' Whalsay certainly kens. Danielle's dad might have said he was building the chalet for holidaymakers, and maybe that's how it started out, but once Laura began taking Danielle into the charity shop at weekends to help choose furniture, of course folk put two and two together. I ken about that because there's a lass from Whalsay on the netball committee, and she mentioned it to me. Not before everybody – it was at one of those pre-meeting meetings, where you sort out the agenda, and the decisions you want, and who you have to talk round beforehand. So I think it maybe is generally kent, but I don't know whether the Klaufister folk have heard about it. Nobody'd mention it to Ertie, of course, and Patsy's no' able to go out and about much right now, but Irene might have heard at her work. Not that it sounds like she'd have much time to talk, from what I've heard about her working conditions, called in at the last minute when they have a press of impatient folk.' She looked around the crowded showground. 'And anyone who didn't ken will now. There's nothing like a sunny show day for letting folk stop and have a chat, and catch up on the news.' She sighed. 'It's a sad thing for them, but you can see how it's affecting the boy. He's like one of those Victorian photos of a street child, all big eyes in a white face. If Ertie really can't give up the drink, she's better getting the bairns a clean start.' She made a regretful face. 'It's strange how folk make all the fuss about drugs when alcohol's the worst one of them all, and ruins far more lives here in Shetland.'

'It's the devil you know,' I agreed. 'Just a dram, that'll never hurt you.'

'Ah well.' Inga rose. 'I'd better take those bairns off from under the Klaufister folk's feet. I'll leave you to your rest.'

Chapter Fifteen

Progeny: *A class in which three ponies who are blood-relations are exhibited as a group.*

I half sat, half lay in the sun, ignoring the bustle around me. The heat and crowds were making my head ache again. It was getting on for three, and the crowd was starting to thin out; folk had gone round the animals, admired the baking and hosiery and now the hall would be chock-a-block with people wanting a cup of tea. Beside me, the ponies drowsed in the sun. I could feel that they wanted to be home too. The *Swan* would be moored at Baltasound pier, the water ripples shining on her mallard-green hull. She'd have gone there in her fishing life, in the days of the great herring boom, part of a fleet that might be six hundred vessels strong, all packed into the bay of Baltasound, with the men living onboard the boats, and the gutting women living in cabins along the shore.

I shook the thought away. I'd be skipper for the school trips on Monday. Magnie would be enjoying a yarn with his Unst cronies and cousins, and Anders would be inspecting the advertised display of old engines, and talking enginese to their owner.

There was a thump beside me: Rainbow and Vaila sitting down. 'Cass?' Rainbow said.

I opened my eyes. Vaila was her usual insouciant self, but Rainbow had a worried frown, and she was white under her freckles, as if she'd had a shock. 'Can we speak to you a moment?' she asked.

I pulled myself to a sitting position. 'What's wrong?'

Vaila reached for the tea flask and beakers and poured out. She put one into Rainbow's hands, then found an ice-cream tub. 'Biscuits. Mam's millionaire shortbread.'

Rainbow took one, and sipped her tea. A bit of colour stole back into her cheeks.

'So?' I said.

Vaila pulled a face at Rainbow which I read as 'Your story.' Rainbow sighed, and leant forward towards me. 'It all started ages ago, back when I was doing my work experience. April. You ken, wi' the school. Vaila was with a law firm in Lerwick, and I was with Shetland Vets. I was right pleased to get that, because I kent there were several folk wanting to go there.' Her face lit up. 'It was a really interesting week. I was shadowing Annie. She only qualified last summer, and she was really good at explaining everything, and she told me all about vet school, and what she did there, and what I'd need to do to have a chance of getting in. We did all sorts of things.' She caught Vaila's eye, cut off a recital of examples and got to the point. 'I went out on her rounds with her, to crofts. One of the visits was to Klaufister, to check Ebony. See, you remember the stallion scheme I was telling you about? VVE?'

'Yes.' I rolled my eyes. 'Young Caedoc had his examination yesterday, remember.'

It showed how worried she was that she'd forgotten it. 'Did he behave?'

'For Annie, yes. Not so much for me. Anyway, he passed.'

'Good.'

'So, the VVE, and Ebony.'

'Yea. Well, the thing is, it's voluntary, and because Ebony was bred south, he hadn't had it done. But folk up here set great store by it.' The frown disappeared for a moment as her thin face sparked with enthusiasm. 'It's like, Shetland ponies from Shetland is a big thing. It's a quality brand.' She swept a hand round the pens. 'The stallions and mares are all checked and only the good ones get the accreditation. Folk come from all over the world to our pony sales. So it matters, and Keith Arthurson kent that, so he had to get Ebony registered for it.' She grimaced, and the frown returned. 'See, I shouldn't be telling you any of this. It's confidential to the vets, and I only ken because I was there, accompanying Annie.' She took a deep breath. 'He didn't pass. Annie examined him from teeth to tail, and he was fine, but she also took hairs for skeletal atavism. It's a dwarfism gene.'

I nodded. 'She took them from Caedoc too.'

'The results came back the next day. "That's a right shame," Annie said, and then she phoned Keith and said he was a carrier for it, and he absolutely shouldn't be bred from.'

I nodded understanding. Keith Arthurson's expensive stallion that he bought to show to his neighbours he was up to running a stud had turned out to be a dud. Now I understood Vaila's murmur of *insurance fraud*, and why Annie had been asking about how he'd been after his wild run on the roads. 'So he paid a fortune for a horse that he couldn't breed from.'

Rainbow shook her head. 'It's worse than that.' Her hands clenched on the mug. She looked across at me, face taut with distress. 'Like, folk come from all over Shetland to the shows outwith their area, to see the horses in the other studs. I was chatting ee now to a lass from the Watlee stud, that's one of the big ones in Unst, with more than twenty mares. She's the daughter of the owners, and I ken her to speak to from going round the shows. We were discussing breeding, and I was telling her about Yabbi. She said they'd have a chance of black foals next year. They'd got a stallion up from Clousta to cover the mares. Ebony.' Her voice shook. 'Keith kent. He'd been told back in April that he wasn't to breed from Ebony, and yet he'd sent him up to cover those mares in June. Twenty mares, and every one of those might have a foal that could be deformed, or pass the gene on, and have deformed foals down the line.' Her voice rose; she reddened, and softened it. 'It's a dreadful, wicked thing to have done. And there are his own mares, the Klaufister ones. They're all likely in foal to Ebony.' She stopped for breath, then added, 'I don't ken what to do about it. I don't think Annie can say anything, because it's like a doctor confidentiality, that's what they told me. She can't tell the stud book folk about it – at least, I don't think so, though maybe because of the potential damage to future foals, then she should. But Ebony escaped like that, and I wondered at the time if that was maybe deliberate.' She glanced at Vaila, and repeated her words. 'An insurance job.'

I put it into words. 'You think Keith might have chased him onto the road in the hope that he'd drop dead of a heart attack, and then he'd not only be out of a hole, but he'd get the money for him too.'

Rainbow nodded unhappily. 'I ken accidents happen, but I don't believe in Irene allowing a gap in her park fence that a stallion could get out of. I'm not even sure about Ertie leaving a gate open, however drunk he was. But now Keith's dead. I thought I needed to tell someone. I thought you could tell Gavin. He'd ken what to do about it.'

'On the telly, you can get medical records if it's a murder,' Vaila said.

'Gavin'll know if you can get vet records too,' I said. 'But if you hadn't come forward with this, he wouldn't have known what to look for, so you've done the right thing.' Rainbow's face lightened. I kept thinking. 'Apart from Keith and the vet, would anyone else know about Ebony's condition? Was Irene there, or Ertie, when Ebony was being examined?'

Rainbow shook her head. 'Ertie wasn't. Irene came back from her work just as we were leaving, but Annie hadn't got the test results yet. But Keith couldn't have told Irene. She'd never have allowed him to cover the Klaufister mares or put Ebony up to Unst if she'd known. And if he hadn't put Ebony to the Klaufister mares she'd have asked why, and made sure the Unst folk knew, if he'd told her.'

I didn't see Keith admitting to his lifelong-crofter little sister that he'd been sold a pup. 'There's no other way she could have found out? Is she friendly with the vet, for example? It might have come out in casual conversation. *What've you decided to do with your stallion?* kind of thing.'

'She does ken Annie,' Rainbow said. 'You could see they were friends, when she arrived. But I don't know if Irene meets up with folk after work, like that. She doesn't keep well. She never goes to the show dances, unless it's the prize-giving too, and then she only stays till the trophies are handed out. She had ME as a teenager.'

'And if it's like a doctor,' Vaila put in, 'then they'd be trained not to talk about it. I think Annie'd have kept quiet, even to a friend.'

'Unless she found out that Keith had used him,' Rainbow said. 'If she was up in Unst for something, and they told her who the mares were in foal to, or at the Viking Show. Maybe then she'd have a word with Irene, to try and make sure he wasn't bred from again.' She looked across at the Klaufister pen. 'And Irene didn't bring him today, though he'd been entered. He was in the catalogue to be here. And she told Granny that Yabbi should have won at the Viking Show. She wasn't just being polite, like I thought. She knew.'

'Gavin can ask the vet about records. And what was wrong with him was that he's a carrier for this dwarfism condition?'

The girls nodded. I thought about that for a moment. Keith knew his stallion was no good, yet he'd put him to the Klaufister mares and sent him up to Unst all the same. Irene wouldn't have sent him if she'd known; Rainbow was certain of that, and I was inclined to agree, which meant she didn't know at the time, and I thought from her telling Rainbow that Yabbi should have won meant she wouldn't have shown Ebony at the Viking Show if she'd known he'd be disqualified as a stallion. It seemed more likely that sometime between the Viking Show, a week ago, and yesterday, she'd discovered the truth. I wasn't sure it would have been through Annie, even if they'd been at school together. As Vaila said, it was like a doctor's confidentiality.

Irene, who spent most time with their mother, making her most likely to know earlier that Patsy had decided to transfer the croft to Keith. They were handing me murder motives by the shovelful.

'How does it work, the breeding?' I asked. 'Is there a stud fee per mare?'

'Sometimes you just do a stallion swap,' Rainbow said, 'but if you don't ken the person, you pay a stinting fee. No foal, no fee – except that there would have been a foal, so I'm not sure what they'd do then.'

'And if the Unst stud found out there'd be a serious stushie?'

Rainbow nodded. 'He'd never be trusted here again, if he'd done that. It's . . . it's . . . ' Her voice rose. She said passionately, 'You don't do that! Horse breeding up here, folk trust each other. They trust that the beasts are who the owner says they are.' She paused and added, reluctantly, 'Well, likely no' in selling them. It's up to the buyer at the Marts to check the horse is sound. But for things like hiring a stallion. You'd never, ever think that someone would deliberately hire out one that shouldn't be bred from. South, of course, you get blood tests done, all that, check the passport with the picture, but up here it all runs on good faith. If you betray that, you're through.'

I loved her vehement innocence, and wished she'd keep it.

'Mostly you ken them, though,' Vaila put in. 'The good ones. You've seen them winning prizes as foals, at the shows, and then at the sales, and you ken who's bought what.' She looked at me. 'She does! Show her a horse and she'll give you its pedigree back four generations.'

'It's no' a clever trick,' Rainbow said. 'It's just 'cause I'm interested.' She shook her head. 'If Irene finds out about the Unst stud, she'll be so mortified. She and her dad built up Klaufister. And I don't see how she can keep from finding out, because it needs to be known. Those foals are tainted. They should never be bred from, so that's a serious loss to the breeder. Twenty mares . . . well, say it was a good year at the sales, next year's sales, and they got two hundred pounds for each colt and fifteen hundred pounds for the fillies. That'd be . . . ' There was a pause while she worked it out.

'Ten colts at two hundred pounds each, two grand,' Vaila said helpfully.

'I ken,' Rainbow retorted. 'And ten fillies, fifteen grand. Seventeen thousand, if you had ten of each.'

'Do they mostly sell for breeding from?'

'The fillies, yeah. The colts, you never know if they'll make the stallion grade, only one in a hundred gets through, so they can go for riding, or driving – you ken, dressage, and cone-driving, and obstacle courses. They're great at nipping round hay bales and tyres while the bigger horses are still sorting their feet out. Ebony might be good at that, if he was gelded. Or riding, but you'd need to know what you were doing, to be able to handle him.'

'So,' I said, 'if the Unst folk found out that he was no good, they might not lose so much on the colts, but they'd make a serious loss on the fillies.'

Rainbow nodded. Behind us, Yabbi gave a shrill neigh and began winding himself round the telegraph pole. The girls stayed sitting upright, looking at me.

'You'll tell Gavin?' Vaila asked.

I nodded, and they subsided back onto the grass. We sat in subdued silence until the peace was broken by a tannoy announcement: 'Good afternoon, folk. If you'll make your way to the south end of the green shed we'll start the prize-giving in five minutes.'

There was a moment of stillness, then all the folk on the showfield turned, like a shoal of fish. Rainbow and Vaila stood up and brushed the grass off themselves, and I followed suit. We joined the moving crowd, and ended up in a circle round the show chair, who was doing the announcements. The rosettes had already been handed out; this was for the trophies, a tableful of polished silver cups which were distributed with speed. I sent Peerie Charlie forward for Caedoc's, he had one of his own for Junior Handler, and Rainbow had an armful for Yabbi. We posed for photos afterwards, and then rattling and clanking at the back of the showfield meant that the trucks were arriving to take everyone home. There was no hesitation from any of the ponies about going back up the ramp; they'd had a long day, and wanted their own field. 'Me too,' I said to Caedoc as he towed me upwards.

Rainbow and Vaila came out of the cab to help turn them into their park. They were so tired they didn't bother even to graze, just lay down and put their noses on the grass. The foals stretched out flat. I waved goodbye, lugged the pony stuff box into the kitchen and automatically put the kettle on, then switched it off again. I was awash with tea.

It was half past five, and I was dog-tired, but I wasn't hungry, after a day spent eating faerdie-maet. I wanted my boat home. It'd be coming dark by eight. There was a soft westerly wind on the water, a smooth reach south from Brae to the Ladie. I was just about to reach for the *Deuk*'s batteries when I remembered the Harvest Festival tomorrow. I knew Gavin wanted to enter things, just to support them, and Maman would be singing there too. Very well, it'd be a longer sail than I'd thought. My heart leapt at that. I'd left the catalogue and my list on the kitchen table. I'd go out into the yard and see what I could do. I'd set it ready at the pontoon, take it aboard *Khalida* when I stopped to drop the *Deuk* off, sail down to Aith and take it up to the hall, then sail home in the last of the light and the first of the stars.

Collecting items didn't take long. The cats charged around me as I picked three stems of montbretia, splashed in red, yellow and orange, three intact marguerites, and three wiry stems of the scarlet humming-bird ones. I picked the three biggest apples I could see, the three biggest plums and the largest cauliflower. They'd look small beside the Polycrub ones, but I could label them *outdoor grown*. I got the spade from the shed and dug under the most withered tattie shaw. I'd forgotten the thrill of tilting the spade back to see the pale earth-apples gleaming in the soil. I picked out the four best and brushed the earth off them, then tackled the green fronds of carrot. The earth parted with a most beautiful raw carrot smell. I'd got a handful of various sizes, so I did the three best again, then created a bonny plate with peas, carrots, a small cauliflower, mange-tout and runner beans, and covered it with clingfilm to keep them in place. There was a handy box in the front porch, and I packed all the entries into it, and added a folded piece of paper with each entry, as per instructions, with the class on the outside and Gavin's name inside. Then I fed the cats and hens, dressed in warmer clothes, caught up my jacket and the *Deuk*'s batteries, shut Ketling Julie in, and headed for the pontoon with Cat and Kitten bounding behind me. Twenty past six.

It was a bonny run up towards Brae. The water was silver-blue, patterned with darker ripples, and the houses along the road cast long shadows down the soft green parks. Cat crouched in his usual corner; Kitten went below to snuggle into her basket. We purred past Linga, past the humped back of the Burgastoo, past the lit windows of Busta House and rounded into the marina. I tied the *Deuk* up behing *Khalida*, swung myself aboard and stood for a moment in my own cockpit, feeling home flooding over me, feeling like myself again. This was where I belonged, aboard my own boat, which I'd bought with the money I'd earned teaching holiday children to sail around the Med. She might be small, as yachts went, but she was big enough to keep me safe, small enough to handle on my own. I looked with satisfaction at the smart blue cover on the new mainsail, the taut lines of halyards, the rolled jib, then opened the washboards and went below. Cat was right behind me; he knew his own boat. He jumped straight into my berth; Kitten sniffed suspiciously along the wooden fiddles where Rat had been, then settled down beside him.

Anders had left everything immaculately tidy: the chart table with only the local chart and log book on the varnished wood, the stainless steel cooker and round sink gleaming, and, on the opposite side, the prop-legged table set down so that there was a long line of navy cushions. The light-airs sails had been returned to their place. There was a stronger smell of oil than usual, as if he'd been busy with the engine. I snicked the start battery on, and went back into the cockpit to turn the key. The engine started first go, and it sounded smoother than when I'd last used it. I sent a silent *thank you* north.

I was itching to take her out. I'd thought I was becoming a landswoman, but the sea was calling me. I secured the *Deuk* to *Khalida*'s stern cleats then threw off the mooring lines and backed *Khalida* from her berth. Once we'd cleared the marina I hoisted the main, and got her sailing, then unrolled the jib and glanced at the speed reading. 3.7 knots . . . 4.0 . . . 5.1 . . . 5.8. That was better than she'd do under engine. I sat back, savouring the sea noises. The waves trickled under *Khalida*'s forefoot, shushed along her sides and spread in a widening V of foam from her stern. Little *Deuk* bounced behind us. I smiled and turned my face to the last rays of sun, almost touching the western hills now, going down in a glory of amber light that spilled over onto the water. Cat came up from below and sat by my side. A wave of happiness washed over me. These were my home waters. The brown curve of Linga was to port, and the Røna gradually opened up to starboard, the shining road to the Atlantic, with Vementry Isle as its sentinel, and Papa Stour long and low on the horizon. I waved to the house I'd grown up in, in case Maman or Dad was watching, then focused on avoiding lobster pot buoys and the lines of mussel floats to dodge into the sound, and moor up at the Ladie. I had the engine ticking over, but I didn't need it. I turned her nose to wind, dropped the main, turned her back to the jetty and let her get up speed again, then rolled the jib up and let her own momentum take her to the pontoon. It took only two minutes to free the *Deuk* and clip her in her usual place, stow the box of produce aboard and set off again.

The streetlights were flickering into life when I arrived in Aith. I moored up at the hammerhead, hefted the box out of the boat and strode up to the hall, where there were already folk bustling about, laying tables in the Rankin Lounge and making sandwiches in the kitchen. I popped my head around the door. 'I have some entries. Where should I leave them?'

'The tables are all labelled,' one woman answered. 'If you could put them with their classes, that'd save us time in the morning.'

'No problem,' I said, and went off to search for labels. It was easily done; I left my smaller exhibits beside the remarkably large Polycrub ones, and returned to *Khalida* for a bonny sail back. The sun had gone down now, but the western sky was creamy-blue, and the thin clouds hovering above the Clousta hills were lit translucent white from below. The air was cooling, but not yet cold, and there was still plenty of light on the water. It took us only three-quarters of an hour to get back to the Ladie. I stowed my sails and double-checked *Khalida*'s ropes, then headed up to the house.

Tomorrow would be a restful day by comparison, and I'd have time to sort out what I needed for it in the morning. I made myself a boiled egg and ate it in the kitchen, with the Rayburn taking off the chill and heating up the water for the bath I'd promised myself. I kept my phone at my hand in case Gavin rang, but he must have been still in charge at the farm. He might manage an email later, or maybe I could send him one, with the day's developments. Now the bustle had subsided I felt I had almost too much to think about. I'd been handed a whole new heap of motives. There was Kayleigh's account of Patsy wanting to hand over the croft to Keith. For Irene and Ertie that meant the loss of the croft they'd worked on all their days to the prodigal son returned, the brother who'd always despised crofting. I wondered if the fact that his accountancy job could pay the bills was a twist of the knife to Irene, who wasn't strong enough to work full-time; to Ertie, who couldn't conquer his demons. Then there was Danielle's plan to move to Whalsay, taking Ertie's bairns away from him. Might Ertie have blamed Keith for that, and decided in his drink-twisted mind that if Keith was gone, he'd conquer the drink and Danielle would stay? Finally there was what Rainbow had told me about Ebony. If Irene hadn't known about him before, it seemed from her not having brought him to Walls that she'd found out now. The stud in Unst could have a case for suing, and Klaufister would take a loss too, with their next year foals being tainted. Then there was the fraud aspect; as Rainbow had said, up here folk worked on a sort of informed trust. It would be a serious blow to Klaufister's reputation as a stud, even though everyone would blame Keith for it, knowing that Irene would never perpetrate something like that.

I was just about to fetch my laptop and try to write it all down when the phone rang, making me jump. I snatched it up. 'Gavin?'

'Cass, *mo chridhe*, how did your day go?'

'Fun but exhausting. What's the word on your mother?'

'I just phoned the hospital. She's doing fine, and managed to swallow some soup, and move her fingers.'

'Ah, that's great. She'll be back to herself in no time.'

'The nurse said that too. She even said they were talking of letting her home at the end of next week, if she keeps doing well.'

'Oh, that would be great! And all your animals?'

'Cows fine, milking tiring, hens fine, dogs missing Kenny, cats ignoring me, ponies pretending they've forgotten anything they ever knew about stalking. I'll be glad to be home.' He paused and changed gear. 'I only got the photos of the show five minutes ago, when I got to Invergarry. I sat in the car to look through them. Caedoc looked like a right little stallion. I liked the one of you all, holding all the trophies. Rainbow was in the money. Oh, and the one of the Native Americans on their coloured ponies. That was great.'

'Yes, they had fun with that. You should have heard Peerie Charlie's war whoop.' I told him a bit more about the showing, then ended, 'The Klaufister folk were there too, but in mourning. They wore black in the ring, and stayed by their box the rest of the time. I've got a whole load of new information for you.'

'Ah, the local show's the place to be for hearing what's going on. One moment, while I get my notebook and pen out.'

I told him as clearly as I could, and there was a long pause after I'd finished. 'Gavin?' I said, thinking we'd been cut off.

'Still here. So: Patsy was going to assign the croft to Keith, but Ertie and Irene might not have known that till a fortnight ago. Danielle's set to move out, and everybody kens but Ertie and his family. And Rainbow's story about Ebony, the skeletal atavism gene. I can follow that up too. I have Annie's number in my phone. Thanks, Cass.' There was another pause, then he spoke again, his voice warm. 'So tell me everything else that's going on at home. I'm missing you. How are the cats, and what did you pick for the Harvest Festival? Have you managed to get your boat back to the pontoon?'

VI
Driving

Sunday 28th August

Tides at Brae

HW 04.45 (1.7m)
LW 11.24 (1.1m)
HW 17.21 (1.7m)
LW 00.12 (0.9m)

Sunrise 05.53; moonset 19.06; sunset 20.17; moonrise 22.56.

Waning quarter moon.

Chapter Sixteen

Pair in hand: *Two horses being led or driven side by side.*

It was a grey morning, chilly, but pleasant enough, and still with a good sailing breeze from the west. It would have been ideal for a sail, except that this morning was Mass in Lerwick, followed by full Sunday lunch with Maman and Dad, followed by the Aith Harvest Festival Show, with Maman singing. I'd be lucky to get home before dark. I looked down at *Khalida*, neat and trim by the pontoon with her mast reaching skywards, and was glad all the same that I had her home.

I'd decided to take the *Deuk* over to their house first thing, so that they didn't have to detour to pick me up. I was used to being independent, even if not driving made things complicated at times. The cats could come too, and have a restful morning at my parents' house. After lunch we'd come back with the *Deuk* and I'd have a couple of hours at home, and then my parents would pick me up as they passed on their way to Aith and drop me off again on their way home. My next worry was whether I should let the hens loose, since Cat wouldn't be there to watch out for polecats. I wished I could phone Gavin and ask him. They might be safer confined to their run, even though they'd been in it yesterday. Goodness, animals were a lot of work.

I sighed, and got up to get on with my day. I was getting slicker at doling out feed, and not letting the hens out helped. I collected the eggs and put two boxfuls by my Mass book to take to Maman, along with a bag of mangetout. Sheep last, and then I showered and changed into church-going clothes, rounded up the cats, collected the electric motor's battery from the charger and lugged everything down to the *Deuk*, with Cat and Kitten bounding exuberantly round me and doing their best to trip me up.

It would have been a bonny morning for a sail. I admired my boat's lines as she lay at the pier: the curve of her bow, the gleam on her white sides. Tomorrow. I'd take her down to join *Swan*. Meantime, it was a bonny morning to go for a motor. I got everything aboard, put Julie's basket below, ignoring the squawked protests, and clipped the others on. It took us less than fifteen minutes to go round the back of Papa Little and nose into the beach where I'd kept my childhood sailing dinghy, *Osprey*. Low water was at half past eleven, and high wouldn't be till half five, so I could leave the *Deuk* beached, and the tide would just be getting back to her when we were ready to go. I tied her on as tight a line as I could to a boulder at the top of the beach, added an extra rope to be sure, then followed the cats up to the house.

It had been a good few weeks since I'd managed a Sunday Mass. I was trying to calculate how many as Dad drove us between the Kames and through Girlsta to Lerwick. I'd managed to get to Mass somewhere most weeks during the summer, including one in Gaelic in the Western Isles, and one in Norwegian in Bergen, but it wasn't the same as Mass at home, with Gavin.

It was strange arriving at the church door without him. I followed Maman and Dad to their usual pew, near enough to the front for Maman to swell the singing, far enough for Dad to doze during the sermon. We arranged ourselves in the pew: Maman in her swirling white wool coat with a lace mantilla over her dark chignon, Dad in suit trousers and a dark-blue jumper, me in my officer navy. It turned out to be the twenty-first Sunday of the year: Joshua giving the Israelites the choice whether to serve the Lord, the psalm about the Lord's help to those in distress, then St Paul on the duties of wives and husbands to each other. At least he insisted that husbands should love their wives in return for the wife being subordinate in everything. I was glad Gavin didn't expect that of me. Even as trad a Catholic as Dad didn't expect Maman to do as he said. I suppressed a smile as the Gospel started with 'This saying is hard; who can accept it?' but it went on to echo the first reading in a choice of commitment: 'Master, to whom shall we go? You have the words of eternal life.' Once they'd made their choice, Father David said, there was no going back.

I was in the process of making my choice, I argued. I'd come halfway. I'd left my beautiful tall ship heading for Australia, and come home to be mate of the *Swan*. I'd be home all winter, supporting Gavin by looking after the animals, and trying for a land job to keep up my share of the household expenses – except that I suspected Gavin would prefer me doing volunteer work I enjoyed, like *Swan* maintenance, to having me stuck on a checkout at Brae Co-op. He had a good salary, he'd say, and he'd rather spend it on me being happy. Well, of course, I'd prefer being happy too, but I'd always earned for myself. At the moment we each paid half of the normal expenses of the household, and Gavin bought the extras, like car fuel, the horse, sheep and hen feed, and the real tree at Christmas. I was aware that he was probably slipping in more than was strictly his due, but not admitting to that saved my pride, and I was grateful.

I would need to think about the winter. *Swan*'s last trip would be mid-October, then she'd be out of the water for a major forepeak refit. More and more countries were insisting on a black-water tank, which she didn't have, and the Swan Trust was taking the chance to upgrade the galley too. I could see if the trustees would pay me to go round the schools talking about the *Swan* to older pupils and drumming up interest in coming aboard. I left my thoughts with a start as Maman rose to her feet for the creed, and tried to atone by staying focused for the rest of the Mass. The exit hymn was 'Follow me, follow me': commitment again. '*Leave your fishing nets and boats upon the shore.*' There were times when Holy Writ was a bit too apt.

On the way out, I noticed a head of red hair halfway up the aisle, that lovely Scottish shade like autumn bracken with dapples of sunlight on it. I wished I could see her face, because I thought I knew who it was, and if I was right, the investigation into Keith's death couldn't be in better hands. Morag, who'd been a rookie cop with Gavin way back when, and had headed the last Major Incident Team here in Shetland. Instead of Gavin being elbowed out, the pair of them had shared an office, and Gavin had brought her out to the Ladie for dinner. We'd taken to each other.

The aisle was too crowded for me to nip forward and say hello. I waited till she turned towards the door, for a better look. Yes, I was sure it was Morag. If she'd been behind us, she'd have spotted me with Maman and Dad. I hoped she'd wait at the end of the church, but she greeted Father David, then disappeared out of sight.

Father David gave me a shrewd look as I tried not to crane past him into the doorway. 'Well, Dermot, Eugénie, Cass, good to see you all again. And how is Gavin's mother doing, Cass?'

'Coming at,' I said. 'They're hoping she might get home at the end of the week.' I'd noticed her name on the 'pray for' list. Gavin would have thought of that, or Dad. Hospital, then priest.

We came out onto the pavement. 'Coffee or not?' Maman asked.

There was no sign of Morag outside the church. 'A quick one?' I suggested, and explained. 'There was someone in the church I was hoping to meet up with. The head of the investigation team. Can I see if she's gone round for coffee?' I looked, but there was no sign of her in the parish rooms either. Ah well. She knew where I lived, if she wanted to catch up with me.

We arrived back at Maman and Dad's to find the cats installed in front of the fire and a wonderful smell of casserole filling the house. It turned out to be duck with orange sauce, preceded by slices of sausage and pickled guerkins with bread warm from the oven, and followed by a lemon tart. Dad said he was saving the bottle of bubbly for when Gavin got back, but I accepted a half glass of a velvety red. The coffee afterwards cleared my head. I coaxed the cats away from their fire and headed down to the beach, where the *Deuk* was floating nicely on the rising tide. I got everyone aboard, then poled out with the end of an oar, started the engine and drove us home.

It wasn't quite three o'clock by the time we arrived back at the Ladie. Cat went for a quick patrol, to check nothing had happened in his territory while he'd been away; Kitten and Julie charged round the garden for a bit, tails fluffed, then disappeared into the house. I let the hens out for a foray and collapsed with a cup of tea in the sitootery. I'd get half an hour's rest before I had to go again. I spent it looking out at the grey water in the sound, the milky-grey sky with darker wisps of cloud moving across it, and not thinking of anything much, just enjoying the silence. I felt I'd done my chatting for the day, and wasn't sure, as the clock ticked towards half past three, that I wanted more socialising, but I'd said I'd go, and Maman singing was always a treat. Besides, I needed to collect our fruit and veg and find out if we'd won anything, so that I could tell Gavin this evening.

I was ready at the door when Dad's car came down the drive. Cat was on guard on the gatepost, Kitten was up a tree, and Ketling Julie was sleeping off her exciting day in the laundry basket. I had cash money for buying teas, though I wasn't sure I could fit even a small fancy in, and my phone to send photos of the produce to Gavin. Dad had changed into more casual clothes, but Maman was still dressed in her Sunday best.

'What're you going to sing?' I asked.

She shrugged. 'It was difficult to choose. I thought I would need to do one in English, so I'll do 'The Shepherd's Plain Life', with a simple accompaniment from their pianist, and then a French folk song about the wine harvest. I thought that would be both enjoyable for the audience and appropriate, and one of the North Ness boys is going to accompany me on the guitar for that. Then of course I will join in the community hymns.' She sounded as if she was nervous.

'It's just a local hall,' Dad said reassuringly.

Maman sat up straight, and her eyes sparked. 'I do not care if it is a bus stop with three muttons in it. It is an engagement. I will sing as if they were the Royal Box at La Scala.' She swept one hand backwards towards me. 'You would not expect Cass to sail badly just because it was a local regatta.'

From which, I gathered, Dad was not quite forgiven for having let her in for it in the first place, but there was no sign of prima donna affront when we arrived at the hall. She came in with a warm greeting for the kirk ladies at the door, and was swept off into the lounge at the back for tea before the service started. Dad went with her; I gestured towards the main hall. 'I'll just check on how Gavin's entries did.'

The hall was filled with tables of produce, scented with flowers, and busy with folk admiring. I'd been pondering about growing fruit and vegetables for self-sufficiency: my answer was here. Almost every entry in the fruit section had been grown in a Polycrub, those half-cylinder greenhouses made locally from recycled salmon cage tubes covered with extra-tough polycarbonate glass. From the first few, they'd mushroomed up, and now nearly every rural house had one beside it. I looked along the fruit table: purple damsons with a velvet bloom on them, plump apples and pears easily the size of supermarket ones, a bowl of strawberries, raspberries and blackcurrants, a sheaf of glossy scarlet tomatoes, a plate of black grapes. People who were putting serious work into their Polycrubs wouldn't need to visit the supermarket fruit shelves. The outdoor vegetables included peas, leeks, fist-sized onions, bright carrots lippering over the paper plate, turnips in several sizes and colours, cauliflowers and even some of the broccoli with pointy bits. I was pleased to see Gavin had taken several prizes; a third for his apples, a first for the cauliflower, a third for the mixed basket and a second for the bunch of carrots. I took several photos and sent them off.

I'd just done that when a voice behind me said, 'Hi.' I turned, and it was Irene. There was no sign of yesterday's smart professional woman; maybe show day had been too much for her. She was looking ill: drained and thin, with slumped shoulders and a dragging way to all her movements. 'How's the head?' she said.

'Fine.' I tilted my head and parted my hair to show her. 'I just need to watch where I'm combing of a morning. Thanks to you for all your help.' I paused then asked tentatively, 'How's your Mam doing?'

Her eyes filled with tears. She shook her head and answered obliquely. 'It was an awful shock. Keith was her favourite.'

'And all the worry of the investigation on top,' I said.

She nodded, and wiped her eyes. 'But the police need to do their job. You have to look away and let them get on with it. Try not to think about it.' She took a deep breath and straightened her face. 'Do you ken my sister?' She gestured at the woman behind the gardening books and bric-a-brac stall at the end of the hall, and raised her voice slightly. 'Allison? Have you met Cass? She went for a swim in front of our house the other day.'

'I'm never going to live that one down,' I said. 'It was the first thing my pal Magnie mentioned that same evening.'

Allison came out from behind her stall with a friendly smile. 'Hi, Cass. We've no' met before, but I saw you at the show, and of course I've seen your boat in the voe. You ken my man, Trevor – he's sailing wi' you on the *Swan* next week.'

'We're very glad to have him.'

As children, she and Irene must have been very alike. They had the same colouring and face shape, and probably the same wiry build, but now Allison had the curves of someone who'd spent several years finishing toast crusts for toddlers, and cooked a good meal for her man every day. Town mouse, country mouse, I'd said of the brothers, and the sisters were the same. Irene was workmanlike in a plain white blouse with her hair plaited back, but Allison had a flowered top over dark trousers, and shoulder-length hair swept back in two wings that I suspected took serious work of a morning. Her face was made up with fashionable eyeliner pointed from the ends of her eyes and frosty pink lipstick.

The one who'd escaped Klaufister. 'And how's Gavin's mum doing?'

'Coming at. They're hoping she'll be home this week.' I

wondered where she'd come across Gavin. She must have read the surprise in my face, for she explained, 'I work at the school. I used to teach, before we had the bairns. I didn't want to go back full-time, but I go into the nursery and early years as an assistant three mornings a week, and I was there when Gavin and another officer came out to talk to them about police work. He was great with them. Took all their questions seriously, even the one about what he wore under his kilt.'

'Someone had to ask that,' Irene said.

'Bound to,' I agreed.

'That's good to hear his mother's coming home.' She hesitated, then asked, 'So might he be able to get back here himself?'

I nodded. 'He'll be home tomorrow.'

Her face brightened. 'That's good to hear.' She made a vague gesture in the direction of Klaufister. 'All this. The investigation. It needs to be cleared up, and fast.'

'There's a good woman in charge, from south,' I said. 'Morag. She's a pal of Gavin's from way back when they were constables.'

'I don't think we've seen a Morag,' Irene said. 'It was Shona Webster talking to me. She was fine. It didn't feel like the third-degree at all.' Her face crumpled for a moment, as if she was going to cry. 'It's just . . . all of it. The horridness.'

Her sister put an arm around her. 'Tell you what, Reenie, why don't you go and get a cup of tea and a piece of shortbread, you ken you can eat a small bit, and have a rest before the singing. On you go. It's no good you upsetting yourself.' She smiled. 'We need to give the performance of our lives in front of Cass's mother.' Irene looked uncertain for a moment.

'If there's shortbread, save me a piece,' I said. 'I'm coming for a cuppa in a minute.'

Irene gave her sister an uncertain look, then nodded and headed off towards the lounge.

'She's not strong,' Allison said. She motioned me to behind her stall, where we could lean against the stage and talk quietly while still keeping an eye on the hall and potential customers. 'She's mostly recovered from the ME, but it never quite goes. She still has allergies that give her a couple of tired days. Then Keith's passing... well, it's taken it out of her emotionally and that hits the physical too. She blames herself. Keith'd never have come back up here if she hadn't asked him to help out. She didn't mean him to stay.' She gave me a swift, sideways glance. 'And she definitely didn't mean him to cut Ertie out with the croft. They neither of them saw that coming, and it was a dreadful shock when Irene saw it in the paper.'

'You kent about that then,' I said.

She nodded, taking it for granted that I knew too, and added quickly, 'Not before Keith's death.' She averted her head, looking at her feet like a child caught in wrongdoing. 'I feel bad too. I should have helped more. I ken I have the bairns, but I could have taken them over and done the housework for Mam, or got Irene to get them to help her gather eggs or feed the horses while I dealt with the other animals. I helped more at first, immediately after Dad's death, but there was school, and it was winter, and bad roads, and somehow I went less and less. I didn't realise how little Ertie was doing.' Another quick look to check I understood about Ertie. I nodded. 'I should have expected it,' she said. Her voice echoed Patsy's bitterness. 'It's the way it goes. He's no' able to cope wi' things, and the drink's his crutch. But whiles you feel he's attention-seeking by hitting the drink when the going gets tough, and everyone else could do with him supporting them for once. I don't blame Danielle for having had enough.'

'When did he start drinking?' I asked.

'Oh, back in his teens, at the discos. See, he never quite fitted in wi' the other bairns. Well, he kinda did, they liked him fine, but when we were growing up, well, I had a best pal my age, up at the Clousta Manse, and Irene had Annie over at Aith, the pair of them charging about on ponies like mad things, but there were no boys his age, so he spent his time wi' Dad, helping around the croft. Dad had him driving the tractor from his lap when he was just a toddler. The croft was all he was interested in. School was just to be endured until he could get back home. When he started going to the discos he took a drink to ease his nerves and then it got that the fewer social things he went to, the more he needed it.' She paused, shaking her head. 'We all hoped that when he met Danielle, and they had the bairns, that he'd cut down on the drink, and he did seem better for a bit. But when Dad died, and all the responsibility was on his shoulders, he crumpled. I don't blame Irene for calling Keith, since both Ertie and I were failing her, but I didn't expect him to come home for good. I'd have talked to Mam if I'd known what she was doing, tried to talk her out of it. Ertie and Irene have worked for the croft all their lives. It wasn't right.'

'Have you talked to her about it now? I mean, about what she's going to do now Keith's gone?'

Allison made a helpless gesture. 'She's in the right of it that she inherited from Dad, but I don't agree with her that she has the right to assign it where she wants.' She gave me an awkward, sideways look. 'She asked me if I'd want it, for my boy to inherit. No, I told her. That croft's a full-time job, and Trevor's busy with the boat and the lifeboat. Noah and Taylor are happy in Marthastoon with other bairns around them, and charging round Eid on bonny summer evenings. They wouldn't want to be stuck out at the end of a single-track road that's one o' the first to be blocked in winter.' She paused for breath, and finished, 'And neither would I. Oh, sometimes I miss the peace and quiet of being out in the country, no lawnmowers all round you, and seeing the stars at night, but not to go back and live there. No.'

Aith was hardly a metropolis, but I understood what she meant. Mary's peace and quiet was a trap to Allison, as it was to Danielle.

'But if you don't want it . . . won't she re-think Ertie and Irene, to assign it to? For Ertie's boy?'

Allison shook her head. 'I tried to argue with her. It should go to Ertie and Irene between them, and to Peerie Arthur after them, and I told her so.' She pulled a face. 'We had a bit of a row over it. I tried to say that Ertie was drinking from shock and grief, and he'd get over it if he had to keep the croft going, and she flung back a dozen examples of other local men to say that wasn't the case. And it wasn't fair that Irene's not being able to work full-time should stop her inheriting when she helped Dad build up the stud. But the thing is, Mam's right about needing money. Nobody makes money from a croft. It just about kept a family, a century ago, when there was a cow for milk, sheep to slaughter, hens for eggs, a taatie rig and hay for the beasts, so long as there was a boat too and piltocks were plentiful, and the women and children were at home to do all the work while the men were at sea. Not now. If you have several crofts together, and sheep on them, maybe. The kye are beef cattle, and Dad made a fair bit per beast when they went to be slaughtered, but cattle need fed up here, and the price of feed is just going up and up, so he barely broke even.' She might not want the croft, but she'd grown up with it. 'The sheep are a bit better, the hill sheep, he made a bit there, but the bigger sheep, the black-face, they need extra feed in the winter, and shelter for lambing. The price he got per lamb barely paid the lorry to transport them to the marts.'

'We bought a couple of lambs last September, for the freezer,' I said. 'Ninety pounds each.'

She nodded. 'Hill lambs. And from that, transport and the man who slaughters them had to be paid.' She shook her head. 'Then you go into the supermarket and see Shetland lamb costing thirty-five pounds for a joint. Somebody's raking it in, but it's not the crofters.'

'I've been thinking about self-sufficiency,' I said. I gestured at the tables filled with produce. 'These Polycrubs, an apple tree in one of those, and you'd never need to buy apples again.'

'Nor tatties, if you had a rig, nor any other kind of vegetable if you had a well-dug yaird wi' seaweed spread on it every year. But folk don't have the time to do that kind of work these days. It's easier to earn the money and take it to the supermarket.'

'So,' I said, summing up, 'a man in possession of a good croft needs a wife with a good income to support him.'

She smiled. 'That's about the size of it.' Her face transformed to adoration, looking over my shoulder. I turned and saw her children forging through the folk towards us. They skidded to a halt and spoke in chorus, looking at me, with the boy's voice winning out over his sister's shriller tones. 'I got a prize for my dinosaur.' He had a spiky haircut, a Super Mario T-shirt and the over-confident air of a child who has his mother twisted round his little finger. 'Did you see it?'

I shook my head.

'Yes, go and show Cass, Noah,' Allison said, taking it for granted that I'd want to see it.

'It's over there.' Noah pointed to the corner I'd not yet got to. 'It's made of vegetables. Come and see.'

I followed, and found a table of children's vegetable creations. Noah's dinosaur was an ingenious 3D blend of potato body, parsnip neck and courgette head, tail and spines, stuck together with cocktail sticks. 'It's a masterpiece,' I said, genuinely impressed.

His little sister tugged my sleeve. 'That's mine,' she said, pointing to a courgette caterpillar on a plate. I admired it, then the girl charged off, shrieking at one of her friends, and Noah turned to me again.

'You're the wife that investigates murders, aren't you?' He looked behind him, checking nobody was within earshot. 'Because that was my uncle Keith that was murdered. Are you going to find out who killed him?'

'No,' I said firmly. 'The police are finding out. I'm busy sailing *Swan*.'

'I think you should investigate,' he said. 'Mam's really worried about it all.' Suddenly there was a bleakness about him under the bounce. 'And she was really mad about Uncle Keith getting the croft, and I bet Uncle Ertie was even madder. Even Dad was mad about it. There was an awful row one Sunday dinner. It's traumatic when folk are mad. I think you should do something.'

'Yes, it is,' I agreed. 'But I really can't investigate.' His face fell. 'My man's a policeman though. He's doing his best to make it right. I'll tell him to hurry up.'

Noah's face brightened. He looked at me to make sure I meant it, then nodded. 'Good.' He turned, poised to run off, then added a thanks before charging towards the hall door.

I didn't like to take notice of what a child had let fall, but I was sure that Allison had just done her best to convince me that she'd neither known nor cared about Keith getting the croft.

I looked over towards her. One of the kirk women was asking her cheerfully, 'How's your afternoon gone, Allison?' She glanced at the clock. 'Time to cloo up now?'

'Getting that way,' Allison agreed, and began piling up books. I remembered that I'd asked Irene to keep me a piece of shortbread. I'd better go and join her.

Irene had kept me a seat beside her, with a piece of shortbread on a plate, and a clean cup and saucer. A woman in a pinnie came straight over with a tea-kettle in each hand as soon as I sat down. 'Tea, coffee?'

'Tea, please.'

She poured me a cupful. 'The milk's on the table.'

'I must go,' Irene said. 'We'll have a quick bit of a warm-up.' I held out one hand to stop her.

'Irene,' I said, and hesitated, not sure what to say, then launched in. 'You need help. You're running yourself ragged. It's more than six months since your mam's accident, and she's surely able to do more for herself than she's letting you think.' She gave me a startled look, and I hurried on before the feeling I was making a fool of myself took over. 'If you didn't have to do for your mam, that would be one less burden.'

She froze for a moment, staring at me, then said, 'I need to go,' and hurried off, leaving me not quite sure what I'd said wrong. I sighed, and took my tea and shortbread over to Maman and Dad.

'Well?' Dad said. 'What did you win?'

I gave him chapter and verse. The clattering of people moving chairs and tables floated through from the hall, and people around us began to stir. Maman rose. 'I will go look where I will sing.'

'Coming,' I said.

It was a fun service. The congregation got to sing all the harvest hymns I remembered from the school end-of-term services, and the North Ness boys took us into Gospel mode with two fast-strumming yee-haar-style hymns. Her accompanist looked nervous, but Maman sang 'The Shepherd's Plain Life' beautifully, then moved into fun mode with a jaunty folk song which I remembered Mamy singing to me when I was a child, 'Plantons la vigne'. I found myself humming along; Dad, beside me, was tapping his feet.

In among it was the Westside Churches Choir, who filed on in white blouses and red neckerchiefs. Irene was with them, looking nervous. The woman beside her gave her hand a reassuring squeeze. It was Annie, the vet, and they sang like that, hand-fast: first a bonny creation hymn, then a fun one which began with 'All Things Bright and Beautiful', then transformed into a gardener's list of creatures they'd prefer had been left out of Eden. '*I had my best pal,*' Allison had said, '*and Irene had Annie, over at Aith. The pair of them charged about on ponies like mad things.*' Best pals from their schooldays. Annie had described how she'd taken work and gossip back after school. When the song ended, as they bowed during the applause, they moved apart.

I wondered if Annie had after all broken her confidentiality rule to tell Irene the truth about Ebony.

Then there was Allison and her children. She'd been very quick to dismiss any interest in Klaufister, but I thought she was one who'd take anything going if it was for her bairns. Keith was out of the running now. If Danielle took Ertie's children away to Whalsay, the croft could well be up for grabs, and she might have heard of the chalet being prepared, through gossip in the staffroom.

I wondered what she'd really said to Patsy on the subject.

Chapter Seventeen

Viking Show: *A Shetland ponies show, usually held on the third weekend of August, which includes agility classes and cone-driving.*

Naturally I hadn't forgotten the *Swan*, who'd spent her day sailing down from Baltasound to Aith. Her ETA was six thirty, so the minute the service finished I gave Dad the box with Gavin's produce and 'winner' cards and hurried down to the pier. I was just in time: *Swan* was two hundred metres from the head of the voe, gliding towards the pier with Magnie at the wheel and Anders in the bows, ready to throw up ropes. I took a moment to admire her, the red mainsail rolled neatly on the boom, the dark-green hull reflecting the ripples on the water.

Anders saw me waiting and raised a hand. I could see from the faces around him, flushed with enjoyment, that it had been a good trip. Magnie manoeuvred *Swan* alongside, I caught the rope Anders threw and put it round a bollard, then went back for the stern rope. By that time several folk were on shore with me, adjusting lines, while others hauled in from onboard. In less time than it would take to tell, she was fast at the pierhead. Magnie nodded up at me. 'Come to check I'm no' damaged your ship?'

'No fear o' that. I bet you had a good passage.'

'Not bad. The wind was a peerie thing light, but we had a fine westerly to let us reach all the way. It was only later on it turned south-east, and we had to get the engine going.' He glanced at the marina. 'Have you the motorboat here?'

'Dad's car. Maman was singing at the Harvest Festival.' I glanced back at the hall. 'I can't stay long. Do you have your car here?'

Magnie shook his head. 'Boat.'

'I'll need to go, but why not stop off at ours for a bite to eat? You can tell me all about it.'

'I'll stay aboard,' Anders said. 'Rat and I are comfortably settled here.'

'I'll maybe stop for a cuppa and a debrief,' Magnie said. 'I'm no' hungry, wi' a weekend of *Swan* meals inside me. But thanks to you, Cass.' He glanced up at the scrum of departing cars up at the hall. 'You get back to your folk, and I'll tend to mine. I'll see you in an hour or so.'

I left them handing bags up to the pier, and returned to the hall. The light was thickening now, and by the time we got to the Ladie it was dusk outside, the last brightness choked by a grey mist lying on the Ward of Papa Little and hazing the sound. It was dark enough indoors to need a light on in the kitchen. I dumped the box of Gavin's produce on the table, then went back out to feed horses, set the hens' maet in the run and round them up. It began to rain while I was still trying to catch the last of them, and my shirt was soon soaked through. I made a dive for the wretched fowl and managed to grab her, shoved her into the hutch, then ran for the cottage.

The dark made it feel cold and sinister. I switched the light on in the sitootery, but that made the black outside the big picture window blacker, so I switched it off again and lit the Rayburn. The warmth would soon fill the whole house. I left it to take up while I changed into dry clothes, added a jumper and came back down to feed the cats.

It felt like it had been a long day. I slid the kettle over onto the hotplate. Magnie might be full of *Swan* breakfast and lunch, but he'd want a cup of tea, and muckle biscuits and cheese always went down well. I prepared a plateful, then went to check out of the window. The mist was still powdering the sound, but thinner now, patchy, and Magnie's steaming light gleamed through it, making a circle of window raindrops glitter. A clatter at the catflap, and Cat charged in, shook himself, then sat in his box by the Rayburn to wash. I pulled on my sailing jacket and Gavin's rubber boots, and headed down to the pontoon to take Magnie's lines.

'I'll no' bide long,' he said, as he came into the kitchen. He nodded at the Rayburn. 'Yea, yea, it's getting that time of year. Another thing for you to tend.' He hung his jacket up and sat down at the table. 'That all went off well. Fine weather, folk who all got on well together, and a good passage.'

'That's what we like.' I set the mug of extra-strong tea and the plate of muckle biscuits and cheese to his hand and sat down myself. Cat jumped onto my knee. 'How was Unst show?'

'Fine too. Anders had a lot of fun among the old engines. Me, I sat in the tay tent and yarned wi' me Unst cousins, and took a foray out every so often to check on our folk.' He took a swig of tea. 'Ah, you're learned to make a right cup o' tay at last. Yea, there was a lock o' speaking back and forward, and there was one thing I thought you could maybe tell Gavin about. Have you heard o' the Viking Gene project?'

It rang a vague bell. 'Some university was testing folk who had Shetland great-grandparents? There was something in the paper recently – some cancer gene found in Whalsay folk.'

'That's the one. No' as far back as great, it was two Shetland grandparents, and of course there was no difficulty in finding that. It's been going for a good while now. Edinburgh University. Maybe twenty years in Orkney, and then they rolled it up to Shetland a dozen years ago. Just recently they expanded it to the Western Isles as well. What they were doing was looking at various genes common to folk o' Viking descent, wi' the hope of isolating genes causing particular diseases.' He reached for a biscuit, and I followed suit. 'Well, no' causing them, but making folk more likely to get them. Things like diabetes and heart disease. So I thought, well, it sounds interesting, and signed up. There was a great long questionnaire about my health, and they took blood, and did a twa-hour medical. The late Arthur Arthurson was on it, I ken that, because we spoke about it one time, and he enrolled the boys as well. Forewarned is forearmed, he said. Him that's gone, Keith, he was home then, and Ertie definitely signed up, for he was waiting to go in for his medical when I came out.'

He paused and I nodded understanding.

'So, one o' the genes they were looking at was one which means folk who have it are more likely to get a particular type of cancer. It seems a good few Whalsay folk have this gene. They've been working on it for a while, but it's only recently they've been sure enough to notify the folk affected. There was a bit about it in the paper just a couple of months ago, because there was a man who got the letter and when he started to feel unwell, he thought he'd better have it checked out, instead of blaming his age. Turned out it was this cancer.'

I wasn't sure where this was leading, but if Magnie thought Gavin ought to ken, then it wouldn't be nothing.

'Well, one of the folk I was yarning wi' was a fisherman who does relief work as a postie. He's on the project too, so when they sent out these letters while he was working, he kent what they looked like. He told me about it because he was worried. See, he delivered one of these letters to the late Keith, at Klaufister. A week ago.' He paused, and I waited.

'To Keith,' Magnie repeated. 'No' to his father, though I'm sure they don't ken he's dead, because notifying the project would be the last thing anyone would be bothering about, in the circumstances. No' to Ertie.'

I frowned. 'But wouldn't they all have the gene?'

'Not,' Magnie said, 'if Keith wasn't his father's son.'

There was a long silence.

'Is there any idea that he mightn't be?' I said, at last.

'I was still at sea then, but my pal said there was a bit of talk at the time,' Magnie said. 'I'm never heard any mention of it. But my pal said that Patsy was over-friendly with a man who bade in Clousta for a bit. I forget which house – one of the ones in the long line up above the voe. The man was from Whalsay, and he was working on the wastside. A piece younger as Patsy, my pal said, and that tall, fair, Norse look.'

I remembered Keith's looks: sandy hair, as tall as Ertie but lighter built. 'Keith didn't look like Ertie or the lasses, but that happens sometimes in families. Was Patsy fair when she was young?'

Magnie shook his head. 'Dark mouse, like her mother. Arthur was dark. Ertie and Irene get their colouring from him. And Arthur's from Clousta pretty far back, and Patsy came from Walls. No Whalsay blood in either of them, that I ken. Well, there could be, way back, but I don't ken how long these genes keep passing down. The Uni folk only wanted grandparents.'

'So,' I said, 'if it was an old long-forgotten story, is it likely that Keith would ken? Or that Ertie would?'

Magnie shook his head. 'Likely he wouldn't. The man went back to Whalsay to work to his father on the boat after a couple of months. There was never any suggestion that Arthur didn't think Keith was his, and never any sign o' the Whalsay man taking an interest in him, so the talk died down.'

'So if a letter came to Keith announcing he had Whalsay genes when nobody else had . . .' I made a wry face. 'Somebody'd be asking questions.'

'He might've kept it to himself.'

I thought about that for a moment, imagining the letter on the table when he came home from his work. He'd open it, with his mother and maybe his sister there. Maybe say, "Oh, it's from the Viking Genes people. I'd forgotten all about that." A frown. "They say I have this gene that predisposes me to such and such." Then there'd be a bit of chat about it. That would be far more natural than him taking the letter to his room and reading it there. I looked across at Magnie. 'Not if he didn't know. He wouldn't think there was anything odd about it. The postie would have arrived while he was at work, so he might assume they'd already had their letters. Except that they knew they hadn't.'

Suddenly I remembered Patsy's odd joke about a fine young Viking, and Irene's embarrassment. She'd known what her mother was referring to: not a romance of Irene's, as I'd thought, but Patsy's own long-ago affair with Keith's father.

'And I asked the man's name,' Magnie said.

I looked at him, waiting.

'Poulson. George Poulson. He married Laura Sinclair on Whalsay, and he's the father of the lass that's married to Ertie.'

My mouth fell open. 'Danielle's father? Danielle and the late Keith were half-brother and -sister?'

'So it seems.' Magnie rose.

I sat in silence for a moment, thinking about that. '*He wants his peerie lass out of there,*' Danielle's mother had said, and I could see why, if her man knew he could be Keith's father, and if the gossip about her and Keith had made it as far as Whalsay. On the other hand, the relationship Danielle had described was more like brother and sister. 'Might they have known?'

Magnie shook his head. 'Not unless the parents told them, and I canna see why they would. There was no reason why he shouldn't be Arthur's child – well, in law he was, even if he wasn't in blood. And it's no' likely the young man would mention it abroad either – he'd be feared Arthur would kick Patsy out, if he got to hear o' it, and leave him obliged to keep her.' He rose. 'Well, I'll be getting home. You'll let Gavin ken about it.'

'I'll do that.'

He paused, one hand on the door handle. 'Oh, Mattie came along the *Swan* just as we were clooing up. He was hoping to meet you before the bairns arrived, so I told him to join you and Anders for breakfast.'

'Sounds good.'

I went down with him to help him shove off from among the cluster of boats at the pier. The rain had stopped; the mist lay in patches on the water and trapped sound, so that as Magnie set off towards his house there was an echo from Papa Little, as if there was another boat there. It was only once he was as far as Cole Deep that I realised the sound was still murmuring in the background. I moved softly off the pontoon and stood on the shore, listening. Nobody'd be working salmon or mussels this late, yet there was another boat out there. Then the faint rumble cut out, and the silence filled my ears again. I heard a flicked scratch, magnified by the mist, and for a moment a tiny light flared in the darkness. In this deadened world with all my senses on the alert, for a moment I thought I caught the smell of smoke. Another moment later I was sure of it. Someone out there in the darkness had lit a cigarette. I watched and saw the glow as he, she, took a draw of it.

I was being watched. Well, two could play at that game. I went up the hill to the cottage, walking in the light spilling from the windows to make sure I was seen, and went upstairs to turn a light on there. Then I swapped my hi-vis sailing jacket for Gavin's dark-green oilskin one. He had night vision binoculars too. I hung them round my neck. Taking care to make no noise, I slipped out again and went up the track until I could cross it in shadow, then walked softly on the dark grass verge back down to the shore and sat down on a rock at the side of the pier.

A scuffle behind me made me jump and whirl around, but it turned out only to be Cat and Kitten, delighted at someone doing something interesting at night. 'Shhh,' I breathed at them, and turned back seawards. Gavin's binoculars were surprisingly effective, even in these conditions. The boat hovering on the edge of the mist was a metal salmon workboat with one person in it. I kept watching, and after a few more drags there was a red arc in the darkness as the cigarette was flung into the water. Then the person bent forward, and I heard the motor again. The boat edged out of the mist and pointed its nose towards the pier. He, she, was coming visiting. I put the spyglasses away and walked over to the pontoon. It might not be sensible to confront them head on, but I wasn't having anyone mooring a metal boat against *Khalida*'s swan-white sides. I hung out a couple of fenders and waited.

The motor cut out ten yards from the pontoon. 'Aye, aye!' I called into the silence.

I could see who it was now: Ertie, and what on earth he thought he was doing coming through Cribba Sound in the half-dark, with mist on the water, goodness only knew. I leant over to take his lines, my heart sinking. I almost wished I'd stayed in the cottage, locked the door, switched the lights off and pretended to be asleep. The last thing I felt like right now was negotiating with a drunk.

However, I couldn't smell whisky, just cigarettes, and he seemed sober enough. 'I was wanting to come and have a word wi' you,' he said. 'Well, wi' your man. It's about Keith.'

'Gavin's not here right now,' I said. I couldn't be bothered explaining again about it not being his case. 'But if you tell me, I'll pass it on to him.'

'Yea,' he said. 'They always say, *Don't hang on to secrets. Tell the police.* Otherwise you get murdered too.'

I wasn't taking him up to the house. I gestured towards *Khalida*. 'Come aboard, and I'll put the kettle on.'

He followed obediently. I was pleased to see he had no difficulty in swinging himself from the metal boat to *Khalida*. Maybe he wasn't going to conk out on me. If he did, I'd cover him with a blanket, and leave him to sleep it off. I gestured him towards the furthest corner of the cabin, and put the prop-leg table up. If he was more drunk than he seemed, and the situation turned sticky, he was behind it, and I would be on my perch on the engine box, with the door at my back and the darkness beyond. Gavin would have approved.

I made a strong coffee, and set it in front of him. Biscuit stocks were running low, but there were a couple of mint Clubs in the tub. I tipped them on the table. 'I'm needing a Co-op trip for supplies. Do you take milk?'

'This is fine. Thanks.' He cupped his hands round the mug and stared into the dark brew for a moment, brows drawn together, took a sip, then went back to staring.

'You were going to tell me something about Keith,' I said.

'Yea.' He nodded, then turned his face to me, eyes unfocused. 'Keith.' Then his eyes sharpened. 'Yea. It's no' easy. It's all family stuff. I never kent till, what, a week ago. You take things for granted. You never ask . . .'

It could be a long night. I took one of the Clubs, to encourage me, and began unwrapping it. 'How about you begin at the beginning?'

His eyes went back to staring into the distance. 'The beginning... I'm no' sure I ken when it began. Keith was aye different. He didna fit in wi' me and Dad, working round the croft, and he was aye Mam's favourite. I don't ken now which way round that happened. Whether we resented him because he was closer to her, or whether he resented me because I was Dad's boy and Mam made more of him to compensate.' His brows drew together, and his mouth twisted. 'I never liked him.' He shot me an angry look. 'I ken I should have. He was me brother. But I didna. He was aye being superior, showing off how clever he was at the school, and being dismissive about everything I cared about.' His voice mimicked. '*Stupid cows, only stupid people like you would want anything to do with them*. And I wasn't clever enough to answer back, so I'd thump him instead, and then I'd get telt off by Mam for picking on him. The older I got the harder it was. I was well grown by the time I was thirteen, any First World War recruiting sergeant would have taken me, and he was a weedy object, going to the height, and wi' no muscles to speak o', but his tongue was nastier than ever. I did my best to ignore him. It was round about then that Irene got ill, and she was my special peerie sister, so I was helping support her. Then in S1 he wanted to go to the Lerwick school, instead of Aith like the rest of us, and Dad said that was a load of nonsense, but Mam talked Dad round, and I was that relieved. He'd be home at night, so I started doing up the old house, so I didn't have to share a room wi' him any more. Dad showed me what to do, then left me to get on with it in me own time. I had a fair bit of that, once I'd left the school. So I got the roof re-felted, and re-glassed the front windows, and put plasterboard up in the downstairs rooms. There was electricity in, and we cleaned out the old Rayburn and got it going. As soon as I could, I moved in there.' He shrugged. 'That all made things easier. Besides, I kent Keith'd be out of Klaufister for good the minute he could be. He'd bide in the Lerwick hostel during the week for his fifth year, then he'd be off to university. The clever one of the family, while all I could do was drive diggers and tend kye. I didn't care. It's what I wanted to do.'

His voice was defiant. He'd chosen the path he wanted, but he'd been made to feel inferior for choosing it.

'I only ever wanted to sail,' I said. 'Sail the world.'

His face lightened. 'And you did.'

I nodded. 'So Keith was a pain and picked on you when you were children, and you were glad when he went off south,' I prompted.

'That was I. Mam missed him, she kinda mooched about for a bit, but then things settled down again. He didn't come home much, but she went down to see him while he was at Aberdeen, two or three times a term, Friday night boat, then Sunday night home. She'd come home looking all lit up, and spend the next week telling us every detail. She never seemed as interested in what we were doing. But he was gone, that was the main thing, and I didn't think he'd ever be back. When he went down to London it was harder on Mam. She only managed one visit in the year he was there, soon after he moved. She couldn't nip up and down, the way she had to Aberdeen, it would cost too much, between boat and train fares. She tried to be cheerful about that, saying they'd FaceTime, but somehow when she phoned him, he was on his way out, and he'd promise to phone back, but he never did. Then after a bit he moved to a flat which didn't have room for her, or so he said, though what they'd done before was that she slept in his bed and he slept on the couch for the weekend, so I don't ken why they didn't keep doing that. But he said there wasn't room, and she accepted that.' There was a look of pity on his face. 'I felt sorry for her then. You could see how it hurt her.' He paused again, swirling his coffee round between his crofter's hands, nails battered with work, a smear of oil on one thumb. His face softened. 'Meanwhile I'd met Danielle, and we'd had the bairns. Then there was the accident. Mam and Dad went down to do the New Year sales, to get a new boiler for the house, and a lorry came out of a side turning, and Dad didn't stop quickly enough. Mam blamed Dad, but it wasn't his fault. Drivers south, they've no consideration, no' like Shetland folk who drive at a reasonable speed and look out for each other.'

That was the opposite way from how my father had told the story, but I didn't interrupt.

Ertie set his coffee cup down and glared at it. 'It was an awful shock. Awful. We'd waved them off to head for the boat, and then Mam phoned to tell us what the B&B was like, and I spoke to Dad. We had a sick cow, and he wanted to check how she was doing. I told him she'd eaten a bit, and was brighter, and he said, "That's fine. See you on Tuesday, boy." That was the last . . .' His voice choked up; he ducked his head away from me. I took the mugs and got up to wash them.

'We'd been that close,' he said, when I'd washed, dried and stowed away. 'More pals than he and Mam were. She wasn't interested in the croft. Dad and I, we worked together. I couldn't cope without him. Partly the amount of work, and partly how much I missed him. I hadn't been drinking that much, but now I started again. I did try to take less, but somehow I couldn't stop myself.' He looked across at me, pupils huge in the dim light. 'It's the first drink that's the dangerous one, Mary said. The one you have to give up. The one you take to relax in an awkward situation, or to give you confidence for another bad day ahead. It triggers a chemical reaction in the body, almost like an allergic reaction. Mary called it a progressive illness. Once it grips you, you need more alcohol, and more.' He ran a shaking hand through his dark hair, and I realised with a shock that he was sober. He'd resisted that first drink all day. He looked up at me, as if he'd read my thoughts. 'That's three days now. Since I thought I'd killed my brother. Can I smoke?' I nodded, and fetched a saucer for an ashtray, and he lit up. 'So Irene phoned for Keith to come home.' His eyes blazed. It was plain there'd been a fierce row about that. 'But she didn't expect him to bide either. It was just to tide us over. And Mam was that pleased to see him. So I kept my mouth shut and put up with him showing off all over the place. Then he bought that stallion.' His voice raged. 'He never said a word to Irene or me. He got the authority from Mam to use croft money, and went off down and bought the beast. He was lucky it was a good one, for I ken fine he didn't have the knowledge to tell good from bad. And the money came from the croft account, which could ill afford it.' He looked at me. 'You'll ken how hand-to-mouth crofting is. You can't just take three grand without discussing it. Dad and I had been thinking of upgrading our slaughter area. So when he appeared with this stallion I was that mad, and I said so. I was working the croft, no' him, and Mam should have consulted me before authorising it.'

I wasn't sure if I was throwing petrol on a fire, but I asked anyway. 'Did you ken your Mam had made the croft over to him, before he died?'

'Did I ken!' He was so angry I expected the hair on his head to spark with it. 'He told me, ee day when I was working wi' the sheep. Two or three weeks ago. I was bent over a yowe clipping her toe-nails when he strolled over in his English clothes and asked in his sneeriest voice if I knew that Mam had applied to the Commission to assign the croft to him. Said he'd let me stay in the old house and use the pier for me bits of mussels and fishing, though we'd maybe need to talk about me paying him rent. I was frozen for a moment, then I managed to take a breath and keep clipping the yowe's feet, cool as he was. When I could trust my voice I said that we'd need to discuss it all. I had some idea the Crofting Commission might uphold me over him, if I applied direct to them. I'd worked the place all these years. Then I let that yowe go, and got another one and began working on it, even though once I'd got it I realised it barely needed it, and he went off.' He reddened. 'But I told Mam what I thought, when Keith was off at work, and Irene had a go at her too. Waste of time . . . and then the notice came in the paper. She'd gone and done it over our heads. Then a week ago we discovered why Keith was so different from the rest of us. You ken about the Viking Genes project?'

I nodded.

'Well, there's this gene that's more common in Whalsay folk, as if there's one way-back Viking ancestor that had it, and it turned out that Keith had it. Well, that didn't make sense. Neither Dad nor Mam was from Whalsay. "Must be a mistake," I said to Mam, while Keith wasn't about – well, I wasn't in the room with him if I could help it – and she went a bit red and said, as if it was totally normal, "Oh, Keith's father was from Whalsay." And I stared at her, stupid-way, and Irene said, "What d'you mean, Mam?" And Mam said... she said—' He broke off completely, shaking his head as if he couldn't bear to go on. I was glad Magnie had warned me.

'She said,' I said gently, 'that Keith's father was someone different from your dad.'

He nodded. 'She didn't even try to explain.' His voice was hard. 'She just said she had a right to leave the croft to any of us. Irene wasn't well enough to work to keep it, and I was always in the drink. Keith was the only reliable one.' His voice rose to a wail of anguish. 'Giving Dad's croft to a man who wasn't even his son.'

'Do you think the Crofting Commission would have supported you?'

His face was bleak. 'They might have . . . I don't ken. It would have been worth a try, even if it meant washing our dirty linen in public – oh, no' about Keith's ancestry. Just about Mam assigning it to him behind our backs, without even talking about it.'

'So your mam told you about Keith's father when he wasn't there.' He nodded. 'Do you think he knew?'

His mouth fell open. There was a startled look in his eyes, and he was silent for a moment. 'I'm no' sure,' he said at last. 'He said about the croft, but he never mentioned not being Dad's son. He maybe didn't.' He looked at me frowning. 'It would have been something else to throw in my face, and I think he'd have said, if he'd known. Might that matter?'

'It might. Your mam didn't say who his father was?'

He shook his head. 'I didn't want to ken. I didn't want to think about it.' His face lightened. 'But if someone else kent . . . might that be a motive for his murder? Someone from his other family? Should I try and find out from Mam who his father was?'

'No,' I said, firmly. There was no need for Ertie to know that Danielle and Keith were half-brother and -sister. 'Absolutely not. But you want me to tell Gavin about it?' I didn't understand why he was handing himself a prime motive for the police to consider.

'Yea.' He hesitated, reddening. 'I ken I'm the prime suspect. The way he was killed, someone grabbing his scarf and pulling it – that had to be someone with a bit o' strength, and someone that wasn't afraid to face him. And Mam giving him the croft, that's my motive. Well, I ken your man. He'd be straight wi' me, and I want to be straight wi' him. I don't think he'll stitch me up. He'll want it to be sorted right.' He stubbed out his cigarette, rose, and leant forward to give me a clumsy pat on the shoulder. His hand reeked of cigarette smoke. 'You're as straight as he is. I'll trust you too.'

I got out of the cabin doorway to let him pass me, wondering whether I should be letting him go. Even if he was sober, it was late to be driving about in this mist.

'You tell him,' he repeated, once he was in the cockpit. 'It looks bad, but I've come forward with it, instead of making them dig it all up. That'll surely count for something.' He clambered over into his boat. I undid his lines and held up one hand as he motored off.

Chapter Eighteen

Obstacle race: *A driving event where the pony and cart have to thread their way around hay bales and stacks of tyres, to time.*

I'd not even reached the cottage door when I realised I'd got another visitor. A slanted flash of car headlights lit the mist lying on the hill behind the cottage. I sighed, and waited by the gate to see who on earth was calling now. The place was like Piccadilly Circus, and on a Sunday evening too.

A Bolt's Car Hire red Fiesta came down the track and skidded to a halt by the gate, scattering gravel from under its wheels. The woman who came out of it was medium height, medium build, and wearing a black suit enlivened by a flowered scarf. She had a head of glorious red hair. Morag had come to see me.

'Hello, Cass!' she said. 'I had to race back to the station after Mass, and I knew you'd be heading for lunch with your parents. Gavin's told me about your mother's Sunday lunches. But I thought I'd catch you in this evening, for a news exchange. How are you doing, and what's the latest on Gavin's mum?'

'Yesterday evening's was that she was getting along well. She'd even managed some soup, and moved her fingers in the paralysed arm. They're hoping to get her home at the end of the week.'

'But he's still coming back tomorrow?'

I nodded. 'He only has the one week.'

'So Freya said.'

I showed her into the sitootery and made us both a cup of tea.

When I brought it through she was standing by the window, looking out into the dark. 'You've got your boat here? I can just make out a mast.'

'Yesterday,' I said. 'After the show. I spent most of the day leading horses about, starting at seven a.m.'

Her mouth twitched. 'The local agricultural show? Gavin would have been sorry to miss that.'

'He was,' I agreed. 'The lasses were sorry too. They said his kilt looked good in the show ring.'

She laughed out loud at that, and bent down to pick up Ketling Julie and sit down with her on her lap. 'So,' she said, 'this is all highly irregular, as usual, but then Shetland's an irregular sort of place. I ken you don't know the people this time, but at least you met them before Keith's death.'

'They were very kind,' I said. 'Gave me dry clothes and bandaged me up.'

Morag nodded. 'And you'll be returning those clothes.'

'I've done that. I was over on Thursday.' It seemed a long time ago.

'It'd be interesting to know how different the atmosphere of the house is, without Keith Arthurson. Freya said you felt there was tension there. Bitterness. Did you feel that had changed?'

I thought about that for a moment, then shook my head. 'It's hard to say. It wasn't the same, but I'd barely arrived when I saw they were taking Keith's body away. We went outside and stood, like folk at a funeral, and then Patsy collapsed. Intense grief. Keith was her favourite. She wasn't at the Walls Show yesterday, but Irene was, with the Klaufister ponies, and her sister, Allison, and Ertie with the cows, all very businesslike, but dressed for a funeral, and not mixing much with other folk.' I remembered his gentleness with the cows. 'Trying to forget his own problems.'

She leant forward. 'Yes. The drink. And he was afraid he'd killed his brother in a drunken blackout.'

I nodded.

'And he told you that when you visited the woman they call the Witch.'

'She's an oblate, living a monastic life, but outwith a convent.'

'Genuine piety or running away from the world?' She shot the question at me, and I gave her a startled look, then shook my head.

'It felt genuine. She follows the hours, and her house is as basic as you can get. I was rather envious actually – a simple, settled life, with everything she needs to hand. Everything she wants.' I remembered her face when Ertie arrived, and couldn't bring myself to betray the crack in her armour, her weakness in the world. 'She'd been in the world. Now she's a recovered alcoholic, and she's using that to help Ertie.'

'Danielle's story. He wanted to give up drink and go for religion instead.'

'I think it might be true.' I nodded towards the dark water. 'There was no smell of drink about him at the show, and he came over here earlier. He was smoking like a chimney, but he said he hadn't had a drink for three days.' I made an awkward face, thinking that Ertie'd trusted me to tell Gavin, not the other police. Then I realised that Magnie had told me first, and straightened up. 'He was confirming something Magnie'd told me earlier.'

I explained the Viking Genes project and Magnie's pal the postman, and she nodded, and summarised. 'The three Arthurson men joined it, and only Keith got the letter, because his father wasn't Arthur Arthurson, but a man from Whalsay.'

'Yes.'

'And his father was Danielle's father too. They were half-siblings?'

I nodded again, and she was silent for a long moment. 'There was a rumour that Danielle and Keith were having an affair, but she denied it. I wonder if the rumour fits anywhere into our murder. Someone who knew about Keith might have thought they were committing incest.' She brooded over that for a moment, then came back to Mary Nicolson. 'The Witch wasn't forthcoming with our officers. Saw nothing, heard nothing. But Gavin said she told you she'd heard shots, the morning before Keith's death. Just after – Lauds, was it? About six?'

'Yes. And Mattie heard them too, the neighbour who's keen on Danielle.'

'He didn't mention that to us, nor that Keith was visiting her. Wanting to keep her out of it.' She grimaced. 'Several other neighbours did, along with Mattie being keen on her, and a hint or two about Keith not looking like the others. Almost made me long for an Edinburgh street when people don't know anything about their neighbours, and don't want to. Gavin told me you heard Danielle's take on Keith and her – just friends. Believe it?'

'Yes, I think I did.'

'Unlikely as it sounds, so did I.' She made a wry face. 'Stuck at the end of nowhere with two toddlers, and a man too busy to do anything other than eat the food she puts down in front of him, and with a drink problem on top. Crofting's not an easy life.'

'No,' I said, with fervour. 'I'm realising how much Gavin does while I'm away. Horses, sheep, hens, the garden. It's never-ending. I don't know how he manages to fit work in.'

'You need to be a special kind of person to do it. You have to love it, to feel the land in your bones.' She gave me a sharp look. 'Do you think you can become that, for Gavin's sake?'

'I don't know,' I said slowly. 'If I have the sea at my doorstep, so that I can look at it and breathe, yes, maybe. I helped set up the vegetable patch, and I'm really pleased with how it's all turned out. I like having fresh eggs, and I don't mind mucking hens out. A cow's on its way. We'll see how I get on with that. I think the hardest thing will be having to be Gavin's pensioner. We need to talk about that.'

She smiled. 'I hope you make it.' A pause, then she went back to Klaufister. 'That was a good shout, about the re-assignation of the croft. Shona tackled Patsy on that.'

She paused, evidently sorting the facts out in her mind. 'Like you, she felt a lot of tension in her. Anger. She blamed her husband for the accident, said she'd told him he couldn't drive south. She was angry about his death, leaving her with all the croft work on their shoulders. She was defensive about the re-assignment – insisted that Keith was the only possible person to take the croft over. Irene wasn't strong enough to do the croft work and earn the money to support it, Ertie got lost in the drink after his father's death and was no use for anything. Keith had come home from south to support her, he was taking an interest in the horses, and giving him the croft was the least she could do. Now she had the problem all over again. She said to Shona that their neighbour, Mattie, was a hard-working man. Maybe he could do with the extra land.'

I gave her a horrified look. 'She'd assign the croft away from her own children?'

'Maybe you do have the makings of a landswoman. Yes, that's what she said. Or, she added, there was her daughter Allison and her man. Maybe they'd fancy moving out to the country, and bringing the two peerie things up as crofter children.'

'I saw Allison today. She said she wasn't interested, and her reasons were plausible, the isolation of the place, but there was something about the way she spoke. I thought she was protesting too much. I wonder . . .' I thought for a moment. 'Danielle and Ertie have split up, and Mattie's keen on Danielle. I wonder if Patsy was thinking Mattie taking it over might secure it for Ertie's children.'

'Except that Danielle's off to Whalsay.'

'Inga didn't think the Klaufister folk knew that. It's never been mentioned by anyone.'

'Hmmm.'

'I'll be seeing Trevor, Allison's husband, on Tuesday. I could get his take on whether he and Allison'd be interested in taking it over. See if it matches hers.'

'If you can work it in casually. Everyone kens you're Gavin's partner. So that's one thread: inheriting the croft. They found out two weeks ago, when it came in the paper.'

I shook my head. 'Ertie and Irene knew sooner. Two or three weeks ago, he said. Keith came and gloated at him. They tackled their mother, but she wasn't budging.'

'A bit longer for a grievance to fester. What else?' She checked a list on her phone. 'Oh, yes, finances. A PC went to talk to Keith's office about him. He was reasonably well liked, competent at his job, but he didn't quite fit in with the others. "A bit fond of talking about what he did in London," one of them said, and the others agreed. With his work no better than competent, one of them looked at his references, and it definitely wasn't a high-flying City firm. "The way he talked you'd think it was Goldman Sachs." After that we talked to his bank manager. He'd paid a huge rent in London, and there was a lot of eating out and wine-bar lunches. Half of next month's salary was spent by the end of each month, and when he moved to Newcastle he wasn't much better off, for though the rent was lower, so was his salary. There still wasn't much left at the end of the month, and we've found no sign of a savings account. So naturally we wondered where the money for the stallion came from. Taken out of the croft bank account, Patsy said, and why shouldn't it have been? He was an asset to the stud. No answer to that, but Shona thought there was more than a touch of defensiveness, as if either Ertie or Irene had objected, and been over-ruled.'

'Ertie was angry about that too. And it turned out he wasn't an asset,' I said.

'Yes. Last night's information, about the stallion. Gavin knows the vet, so he'll talk to her, and persuade her to break the seal of privacy, under the circumstances. A quick phone call to the Unst stud this morning sorted that one: yes, they had Minstead Ebony over in June, a bonny stallion, and they're hoping he covered most of the mares. They'll see come spring. The PC didn't say why we were asking, of course. Just matters arising. Then there are the Klaufister mares. Ebony covered them too. Irene was away at the time, she said, there was a course near Perth on pony driving, but Keith had said he was going to use Ebony, and there's no reason why he shouldn't have. She made on she was surprised at being asked, but Davie, the PC I'd assigned to Irene, wasn't convinced. She has a right poker face, he said, likely from selling horses. Gavin said you'd told him she didn't take him to the show yesterday, though he was entered.'

'I think she knew,' I said. 'She said to Rainbow that Yabbi, that's Rainbow's black stallion, should have won best stallion at the

Viking Show. Do you know ... if it came to light about Ebony, that Keith knew he could pass on this disease, and still bred from him, could the owners of those mares and foals sue the croft, since he belongs to the croft? After all, it's a serious financial loss to the Unst stud. The lasses reckoned seventeen grand, and then the loss of the foals they'd have had from any filly foals they'd planned to keep on top of that.'

She made another note. 'I'll check up on that.'

An insurance job. 'And if there's any insurance on the stallion, and what the small print is.'

'I think they'd certainly not pay out under those circumstances. They might, if Keith had been deceived in some way at the time he bought the stallion, but if he could have done a vet check and didn't, then it's probably lack of due diligence, and his own fault.'

'And Irene found out about it in the last week,' I said. 'Between the Viking Show, when she showed him, and Walls, when she didn't.'

'A murder motive?'

I made a dubious face. 'Maybe. She wouldn't be happy about the foals, and the stud's reputation.'

'And the stallion getting loose and the timing of his death fits her finding out.'

'I suppose,' I conceded. I was sorry for Irene. I didn't want to see her as a murderer. 'Do you have a timeline for the evening of his death?'

'Partially. You saw him about half past seven, he got home at eight, had a meal. Patsy and Irene had eaten, but Patsy sat with him while Irene put the stallion into the field. While they were doing that, Ertie went over to Danielle's, if we believe her story, sometime after eight, when the footie started. Irene helped Patsy to bed and Keith said goodnight to her, then he took the bins up to the road, about nine. Then there's Mattie's story of a quarrel between Keith and someone else, about quarter past.' She spoke the words softly. '*You never left me.* Then we have Danielle's story of bringing Ertie back, around fifteen minutes later, and feeling she was being watched. Finally, Ertie heard noises in the old house about half past ten.'

'So,' I said, 'there was the quarrel, Keith was killed, the killer was going to move the body when he or she realised Danielle and Ertie were there. They waited till Danielle had gone, then moved it.'

'That's our current suggested scenario.'

'Irene, Ertie, Danielle, Mattie, all there on the spot.'

She nodded. 'Ertie, first. Let's assume Danielle's lying. She doesn't want her children to be a murderer's bairns. Behaviour suspicious, claiming he might have killed his brother in a blackout. Most people would have the sense to keep quiet about that. Motives: dislike of his mother's golden boy. Anger about the croft. Jealousy over his visits to Danielle. I'll add annoyance about croft money for the stallion as a make-weight, and the croft's reputation if Irene told him about the dwarfism gene. Opportunity: best chance, living alone right by where the body was found. Ability: strong enough to kill Keith and shift the body.'

I nodded.

'Suspect two: Irene. Behaviour: giving nothing away. Too controlled, running her mother's errands. You don't know what's going on under the surface. No boyfriend, seems never to have had one.' I thought of two women's hands clasping in the back row of singers, but said nothing. 'Motive: the croft. Her only chance to have a croft, unless she marries one. She asked Keith up to help, and he ended up stealing it from her.'

'Other motive: the stud,' I said. 'If she knew about the stallion, she'd be furious at the damage that would do to the stud's reputation, deliberately using a dud stallion. There was also the financial loss, of fillies that couldn't be bred from.'

'Yes,' Morag agreed. 'Opportunity: yes, after her mother was in bed. She'd know the kind of state Ertie would be in. She could have asked Keith to shift a bag of feed for her from the old house, something like that. Something to soothe the stallion down. Ability: yes, if she was quick. A tourniquet like that round his neck, if it was grabbed and pulled hard, he'd lose consciousness in seconds. She's strong in the arms from handling horses.'

My heart sank. It was all plausible, particularly as Keith'd trust Irene more than he'd trust Ertie.

'She wasn't obviously on the spot, but I'd put Allison in as suspect 3,' Morag said. 'Or her husband, Trevor. Motive: Keith taking the croft from her son; to be investigated further. Opportunity: harder. She could have done the same as Irene, asked him to come out and talk, so as not to disturb Patsy and Irene, but she'd have had to come by car, and nobody heard one. Ability: if Irene could do it, so could she. Trevor, even more so. He's a fisherman used to hauling creels. Opportunity: nobody saw a car, but she could bicycle, or even walk over the hills from Aith.'

'Yes,' I said thoughtfully. 'Bike, someone would have passed her on the road. Walking, maybe, but she doesn't look like a five-mile walker.'

'No,' Morag agreed, 'but I like her better as a suspect than number four: Danielle. Motive: not obvious. Ertie didn't know it, but she was getting clear of Ertie, Klaufister and all they stood for. She didn't want the croft. No obvious opportunity.'

'Yes,' I said. 'According to Mary, he didn't go over that night. And if he had, what reason could Danielle possibly have given for leaving the children in bed and walking to Klaufister with Keith?'

'You're assuming the story about Ertie coming over wasn't true.'

'I think we have to, don't we, for her to have killed Keith? If it was true, Mattie heard the quarrel before she brought him home. And even if she'd phoned Keith and said she needed to speak to him urgently, he'd have come to her, so why would she be quarrelling with him in Klaufister?'

'Yes,' Morag agreed, 'and while she's trying to sell us the idea of Ertie being out cold, she'd had five years to learn that the one predictable thing about drunks is their unpredictability. She couldn't have counted on him not hearing her. Ability: yes. She'd just done four years of gradual weight-training.' She spotted my *oh really?* expression before I'd realised I'd made it, and smiled. 'I have nephews. Four years, starting with lifting a seven-pound baby and ending with a two-and-a-half-stone four-year-old.'

'It's a pity her account of what he said to her chimes so well with Mary's,' I said. 'Otherwise I'd be wondering if she knew something to Ertie's discredit, that she was coming forward flourishing an alibi for him.'

'And herself.'

'Yes. This is maybe too Agatha Christie, but I don't suppose she killed Keith to throw suspicion on Ertie? Motive: then she can leave him knowing he's safely behind bars. There've been too many cases of revenge killings of women by ex-partners in the last while.'

'Yes,' Morag agreed. 'With the added motive of having grown to loathe him over the drink. She may have said she still loved him to you, but hate is more likely. Who have we missed? Mattie. In love with Danielle. Angry with Keith, and jealous. Physically strong, right on the spot. In that case, Danielle's story is true. Mattie quarrelled with Keith, killed him, heard Danielle and Ertie coming, waited till they'd gone, then dumped the body. And if Ertie was taken up for killing Keith, they'd both be out of his way.' She rose. 'I'd better let you get on. Let Gavin ken if anything crops up, and he can pass it on.' She smiled. 'Have a good day sailing tomorrow. I wish I was coming with you.'

'Maybe once the case is done and dusted,' I said.

'I'll hold you to that,' she said, and headed out into the dark.

I looked at the clock, and felt a sharp pang of disappointment. It was almost ten o'clock now. Gavin wouldn't go to Invergarry to phone this late. I might as well go to bed.

I went up to brush my teeth, thinking about what Morag had said. *Do you think you can become that, for Gavin's sake?* I'd been a sea woman all my life, with the beach on my doorstep. I'd got *Osprey* when I was ten, and spent my life messing about on boats ever since. It still felt strange to sleep on land, with no water noises coming through the hull at my ear. Yet I knew it was a choice I'd have to make, eventually: Gavin and land life; or the sea, and losing all the possibilities of a land life and children. If I was to commit to Gavin it had to be a free choice with my whole heart. I knew what that choice would entail: a wedding with the bishop presiding, if Dad had any say, and no children before it. Being a policeman's wife, staying at home with an expanding family. Teaching them to sail as soon as they were old enough, my hopeful self added. A crofter's wife, as Morag had said.

Looking at the shining horizon from on land.

I sighed, and went off to prepare my sailing clothes for tomorrow.

VII
Advertising

Monday 29th August

Tides at Brae

HW 06.31 (1.7m)
LW 12.43 (1.1m)
HW 18.45 (1.8m)

Sunrise 05.53; moonset 19.06; sunset 20.17; moonrise 22.56.

Crescent moon.

Chapter Nineteen

My Little Pony: *The pastel-coloured Shetland pony.*

It wasn't going to be a super-long day, because the pupils had to be back at the school for three thirty p.m., so I expected to be home by five. I got up at six and fed everyone, let the hens out and told Cat he was in charge, then headed off. I'd meant to take the *Deuk*, but it was pretty breezy, with white-crested rollers racing through the sound, and a forecast of gusts of 29 knots, so I wrapped up warmly and took *Khalida* instead. The wind was still from the south-east, so I unrolled the jib, and we fought our way down to the pier and into the marina. I secured *Khalida* to the hammerhead and walked briskly round to the *Swan*.

A pleasing smell of frying bacon hit me as I came to the main hatch. Anders was up; three mugs, the toaster, a loaf and assorted jars of jam were set on the table, under guard from Rat sitting on the back of the long bench.

'Aye aye!' I called down. 'That smells wonderful.'

Anders' fair head appeared round the galley door. 'Aye aye, Cass. I saw you coming down. The bacon's nearly done, and I'll put the eggs on now.'

'Is Mattie joining us?'

'Yes. He came in last night to say hello. We can talk strategy over bacon and eggs. This is my first time with children, remember.' He frowned. 'There's too much wind now, but the forecast is for it to fall.'

'Yes, we can put two reefs in the mainsail before we head out. The airt of wind is good.' I came down into the cabin, divested myself of some of my layers and hung my jacket up. '*Halo, Røt.* How's it going?'

He whiffled back at me, and I stroked him. Once the visitors arrived he'd need to go into the aft cabin, in case someone was afraid or allergic, but maybe Anders could take small groups of children who wanted to meet him down to say hello.

I felt a movement on deck and went up. A stranger was standing in the gangway: late twenties, with an outdoors tan, dark hair and blue eyes, and a tired, careworn face, as if he spent his nights worrying. He wore a hi-viz ferry-issue jacket, black waterproof trousers and yellow rubber boots. He turned as I came up the steps and nodded a greeting. 'Aye aye. I'm Mattie Harcus. I don't think we're met afore, but I'm Magnie's nephew that bides in Clousta.'

Working onboard *Sørlandet* had got me much better at dealing with meeting folk. I smiled at him and made with the words. 'It's fine to meet you. Thank you for coming to give a hand aboard. *Swan* couldn't work without you volunteers.'

He made a *you're welcome* gesture and turned to hang his jacket up, then slid behind the table. 'And this lad has our breakfast all ready for us.'

'I'm glad of it,' I said. 'I spent the morning feeding animals and dealing with hens. I didn't have time to make anything for myself. And we won't have time for lunch, between trips.'

We sat down round the table. Today was Middle Primary pupils, half of the class on each trip, as we could only take ten of them at once, along with their teacher and another adult. 'I ken you've crewed aboard the *Swan* before,' I said to Mattie. 'It's a touch windy now, so we can put two reefs in, go up to the end of the voe with the wind behind us, tack her round in the bay of Quiensetter and come back close-hauled on a slant – they'll like that. We can do a couple of tacks, see how far we can get into Aith voe.' *Swan* didn't point to windward like a yacht, that was for sure. 'We'll be lucky if we get her into the bay below Braewick. Then motor on, drop the sail well short of the pier, stow it and bring them in, ready to swap them for the second lot. Do it again.'

They both nodded.

'Once the sails are up, they've got sheets to fill in.' I took out the worksheets with the drawing of *Swan* and spaces to fill in names and put them ready on the chart table, along with a pack of pencils and a sharpener. 'We can give them juice and biscuits too. The main thing is constant supervision. We'll start with a safety briefing, get lifejackets on, then take them to rope stations and get going.' I looked over at Anders. 'Shall we use the capstan?' The capstan was our mechanical winch, and very handy for heavy hauling when we were short-handed.

He nodded. 'I'll work it, if you keep all the children hauling up at the other end.'

I looked at Mattie. 'Leaving you at the helm?'

'I'm fine wi' that.'

We heard our trainees before we saw them, a stomping of feet and babble of voices along the pier. They'd gone for eleven pupils and only one teacher, an elderly man who looked like he stood no nonsense. 'Martin Georgeson,' he said, introducing himself. 'We had eleven keen ones, and we didn't want to leave one out. Two of them are sons of fishermen, so they're good hands aboard a boat already.'

'Good hands are always welcome,' I said. I gathered them all around me, showed them how to go down backwards into the cabin, and did the safety briefing. I kept it short, then we got them all fitted with lifejackets and spread out around the deck to help with taking in ropes and stowing fenders. Once that was done I looked around at them. 'Well, shall we do some sail hauling?'

They all nodded, so I got them to the foredeck and explained about how we were going to pull the uppermost bit of telegraph pole, which would bring the sail with it. I lined them up to haul on the peak halyard, with the teacher and I reaching up the halyard to sweat it, and one of the fishermen's boys leading the tailing. Anders started the capstan going for the throat, the heaviest end, and gradually the red sail slipped up the mast and settled into a bonny curve. There were a few 'oooh' noises as they looked up at it, way above their heads. I nodded to Anders and he went below to cut the engine. The exhaust skoosh, snuffle, skoosh stopped, and we could hear the creaking of the rigging over the waves again. I set the pupils to tidying up ropes, showing them how to coil them in neat circles, then put them to work on the explorer sheet with the names to fill in, and stood among them like Gulliver in Lilliput, answering questions and directing them to nameplates they'd missed.

I couldn't help but be proud of the bonny sight we'd be giving Aith folk as we sailed up the voe, like a visitor from the past to gladden the hearts of the older folk who remembered the days when Lerwick harbour was filled with boats like these.

We sailed smoothly up the voe and into Houbansetter, then sat everyone down for tacking round. Once she was settled on her new course, it was time to put the kettle on. I was about to go below when the teacher came up to me with a glooming face, looked around to see who was nearby and asked for a private word.

My heart sank. I gestured towards the cabin and followed him down the steps.

'I'm not happy that that man should be aboard, in the circumstances,' he said, the moment my foot had touched the cabin sole. 'Can you get someone else for the other trip?'

For a moment I didn't know what man he meant. Was Anders too good-looking to be allowed near impressionable eight-year-olds? I'd noticed the lasses noticing him. Or was it because, being Norwegian, he didn't have his child protection certificate? Then I realised the teacher must be meaning Mattie. The murder was casting its shadow over everyone connected with it. Well, he could want. Mattie was the last on Morag's list, and in law he was innocent until proved guilty. Anyway, I didn't have a magic wand to summon someone else up. It was hard enough finding crew on a working day. I sat down at the table, not hurrying, and gestured him to a seat.

'Mr Georgeson, you'll need to explain,' I said calmly. 'Who are you talking about, and why?'

He looked at me as if I was stupid. 'Mattie Harcus. He's a serious suspect in a murder case. He shouldn't be aboard with young people.' A shadow darkened the hatch. Georgeson glanced upward, reddened and fell silent. I gave a quick glance over my shoulder and saw a yellow boot moving away. Mattie had heard what was being said.

I took a moment to think then a deep breath before replying. 'The crew list was made up back in April, and we're very grateful to our volunteers. We're not going to mess them about without good reason, either by suddenly asking one to leave or by asking another one to turn out at a moment's notice, especially on a working day. None of them is ever alone with a passenger at any time.' I gestured upwards. 'As you can see for yourself. Everyone's on deck. If it'll set your mind at ease, I'll make sure that it's either Anders or I who come below to make teas and get biscuits, keeping Mattie on deck.'

'He shouldn't be onboard at all,' Georgeson repeated.

I kept the calm, but added the steeliest look I had, the one that stopped even Peerie Charlie in his tracks. 'Mattie is a suspect only in popular gossip. I'm sure the school rises above that. Like all the people in Clousta, he's been interviewed by the police for any relevant information. He's not been charged or arrested, and even if he had been, a person is innocent until proved guilty in court.' I paused to let that sink in, and finished, 'We need three people to manage *Swan*. If you wish to cancel the other trip for this reason, then I think the school might well lay itself open to a charge of slander. As well as being liable for the full cost of the day, of course.' I smiled sweetly at him and rose. 'I'll offer tea, coffee and juice round. Can you tell me if any of your pupils is lactose intolerant?'

I could see him brooding over it all the trip, and I suspected he might have phoned the school while he was below, but nothing more was said, and when we got into the pier and waved those children off, the next group was watching us come in. This time we had the right number of ten pupils and two teachers, and all of them greeted us all cheerfully enough, though I noticed a couple of sideways glances at Mattie and a whispered comment from one boy to another. He heard it too, and a look of disbelief washed over his face, then he mastered it, and gave a smile and a greeting.

'Hiya,' the teacher in the bright green jacket said cheerfully. 'I'm Shelley Henderson, and this is our classroom assistant, Emma Mullay.'

I managed not to jump. This had to be Trevor's sister, who'd been going out with Keith. She was a bonny lass in her early twenties, with that fashionable make-up of perfect skin and brows and a long sweep of eyeliner. Her hair was smartly cut and streaked with blonde over a reddish-brown tint which I wasn't sure was natural either. She was dressed practically, in jeans and a waterproof jacket over a warm jumper, and she had a pair of waterproof trousers slung over her handbag. The jumper and jeans were black, and there was a puffiness about her eyelids. She gave me a tentative smile. 'Hi.'

I smiled back. 'Hi, Shelley! Emma, you're Trevor's sister, aren't you? He's crewing for us tomorrow and Wednesday. I'm Cass, the skipper. Welcome aboard. We'll just get the children below for a briefing, then we can get lifejackets on and head out.'

It was turning out a much bonnier day than I'd expected. By the time we'd got these kids kitted up the clouds had cleared to leave the sky half-blue, and every so often the sun danced out from behind the clouds, lighting the water and turning *Swan*'s tar-dark decks to mahogany red. The wind had fallen as promised, from 30 knots down to a much more manageable 23, and we got them to help shake out the second reef in the big red mainsail. This lot of children were slightly younger, seven-year-olds, rather solemn at being aboard, and staring up at the mast with round eyes. 'Have you climbed up there?' one asked me.

I nodded. 'We have a special climbing harness to wear for going up the mast, but I didn't climb. One of the other crew pulled me up on a halyard – these ropes that pull the sails up.'

'You're heavier than a sail,' he objected. 'It's only cloth.'

'That's true,' I agreed, 'but *Swan*'s sails are made of specially heavy cloth. You'll see.'

We got the sail up and the bairns spread round the boat, chatting and looking about them, with Shelley and Emma moving round the groups and encouraging them to sit down on the cabin roof rather than stand at the rails. I went over to her. 'We have some worksheets, for the children to find the names written around the boat. Shall I bring them up?'

'That'd be good,' she said.

'Can I make you a cup of tea while I'm down?'

She gave me a grateful look. 'Ooh, yes, please! We didn't have time at break, because we had to round up the bairns and get their gear on.'

'Milk? Sugar? What about Shelley?'

'Just milk for us both, please. Ta.'

I told Anders I was off to boil the kettle, and came back five minutes later with a basin holding a jug of juice, ten plastic beakers and the biscuit tin, then returned for mugs and the teapot. Emma was pouring juice and Shelley was distributing it, so I followed her with biscuits. Soon everyone was munching cheerfully. I gave them five minutes, then went round, chatting and pointing out names on the boat for them to copy to their sheet. I ended up beside Emma, who was standing up in the prow, turned away from us all, back rigid. 'You okay?' I asked softly.

She nodded, and turned so that she was sideways on to me, still looking seawards. 'Just things catching up on me.' Her eyes were glassy with tears. 'You ken. Keith.' Her breath caught on the name. 'I was okay for a bit, watching the bairns, and everything being new, and then suddenly I remembered he'd passed, and it felt awful that I could have forgotten, even for a moment.' She took a deep breath. 'I'll be fine. I will.' Her shoulders squared. 'You met him, didn't you? He telt me about it, on the phone. It was the last time we spoke.' Her voice wavered. 'He'd come to get the horse back.' She gave me an appraising look. 'He said you were in a dress, and far bonnier than he'd expected a sailor lass to be.'

'I was glad to be of help,' I said politely. *Swan*'s skipper didn't say exactly what she thought. My brain caught up with what she'd just said. *The last time we spoke.* I tried to think of an alternative to a blunt, *What time was that?* 'Did you do a goodnight call?'

She nodded. 'We couldn't meet up every evening, because he didn't always have the car, if Irene was out on shift, but we aye phoned, sometime around ten. This time he was earlier, not long after he'd got back there with the horse and had his tea, because, see, he wanted to tell them. He said he'd had enough. He was heading back south.'

She turned fully and looked at me. 'We spoke about you because of the stallion. He was angry about it getting out. He said he came up because Irene asked him, and he thought that maybe if he came to help they'd all think better o' him. But he said it hadn't worked out like that. Ertie hated him as much as ever.' She glanced around and lowered her voice. 'He said Ertie was a drunken bastard. He thought if he took an interest in the stud that would please Irene, but she was mad about him bringing in the new stallion without consulting her, and they neither o' them spoke to him if they could help it. They weren't like he'd imagined a family being, and he wasn't putting up with it any longer. He said . . .' She broke off and turned away. There was a moment while she took control of herself again. 'He said he'd be off on tomorrow night's boat, and I could come and join him once he was settled, if I liked.' She faltered to silence, and ended, 'I think telling me was him kinda psyching himself up to tell his mother. He kent how much it would upset her. Except by tomorrow's boat he was gone.' Her voice hardened. 'One of them killed him.' Her chest heaved. 'I'd need to get back to the bairns,' she said abruptly, and passed me, walking unsteadily towards them.

I turned to watch the deck automatically, thinking. It didn't make sense. If he'd told Ertie or Irene he was going, they'd have cheered and offered to drive him to the boat. Only Patsy would have minded. *Not long after he'd got there with the horse and had his tea.* Half past eight, maybe, between having his tea and saying goodnight to Patsy – except that nobody had mentioned him saying he was leaving. I wondered if he'd chickened out.

We were nearing the end of the voe. It was time we turned. I nodded to Mattie and made sure all the bairns were sitting down, well out of the way of the boom, and there was the bustle of tacking the main and refastening the gybe preventer before I had peace again.

On the boat tomorrow. I kept thinking about it as we sailed back; as I walked round the children and answered a million questions. Something had happened that day to make him feel he'd had enough. The stallion getting loose? I'd been thinking about an insurance job, but maybe it'd been malice, the stallion being damaged for Keith. Ertie, warning his brother his time at Klaufister was up. Irene, furious at him taking the croft, trying to eliminate his contribution to the stud. Mattie's revenge on his rival for Danielle. A message saying, *You next*.

If Danielle's story was true, she'd been there shepherding Ertie home about the time Mattie heard a quarrel. *You never left me alone . . . you never left me . . .* I imagined the words spoken. *You never loved me?* Danielle had said there was nothing between them, but perhaps Keith had thought there was. Or perhaps there had been something. Maybe he'd thought she'd go with him south. He'd tried to ask her, they'd moved to the old house so as not to wake anyone with their talk, it had turned from discussion into quarrel, he wouldn't take no for an answer, maybe threatened to tell Ertie they'd been having an affair, and she'd killed him.

I wasn't sure I believed any of it.

I kept an eye on Mattie through the afternoon, and though he was cheerful enough while he was chatting to the bairns, or showing them how something was done, when he was alone for a moment the stunned look came back to his face.

He didn't speak of it until we'd waved them all off, tidied up on deck and were below with a recovery-aid cup of tea. Then he looked at me. 'Thanks, Cass. For sticking up for me.' He shook his head. 'It's all—' He made a pushing-away gesture with his hands. 'It's nasty. It's bad enough losing a neighbour like that, but to have folk speaking, and that teacher thinking I shouldn't be allowed near bairns – that was a shock. I kent there would be a bit o' speak, but I wasn't expecting that.' He paused, shaking his head. 'But you told him just right. A person's innocent till proved guilty in court. I'm no' been charged nor arrested, and there's no reason I would be. I had every reason to keep him alive.' He paused for a moment, to emphasise the words, looking at me, then Anders, then finished clearly, 'He was going to make Klaufister croft over to me.'

I stared at him. He looked perfectly serious. He nodded, and took a mouthful of his tea.

'Give you Klaufister?' I repeated, when I'd caught my breath. I thought of Patsy, having her gift thrown back in her face; of Ertie and Irene, who wanted it more than anything on earth, seeing it given to a stranger.

'His mam had made it over to him, and he was going to pass it on to me.' He set his mug away from him and leant towards me. 'It's God's own truth. I ken it's hard to believe, but . . . see, you likely ken all about him visiting Danielle.' His eyes were staring into mine. I nodded. 'He'd got fond of her. He told me that. He said Ertie was no good for her, he was busy drinking himself to death. She'd told him that she and I used to be courting, and he said I'd be good for her, if she'd marry me, and good for the bairns. He didn't want the croft, and he thought it should go to Peerie Arthur in the end, if I'd run it for him in the meantime.' His face calmed. 'This was the night he died. I was out checking lambs, and I saw the torch coming up to the bin store. It was Keith, and he said he wanted to speak to me. He told me that his mother had made it over to him – well, I kent that, from the paper. She'd told him he was the only one of her bairns who'd ever cared about her. Ertie and Irene only bothered about following their father round, and Allison was taken up with her pals. She was only there to make the food and wash their clothes, she'd said. The croft had come to her when his father died, except—' He stopped suddenly.

'I ken about that,' I said. 'Arthur wasn't Keith's father. So Keith did know about that.'

Mattie shook his head. 'No, no, he didna mention it.' He gave me a glance, then looked at the table, drawing a circle on it with one forefinger. 'I heard talk about it, working on the ferry. When he came back to Klaufister.' He was silent for a moment, then he said, 'I wondered about telling Danielle about it. That she and Keith were maybe related. But she swore there was nothing like that between them, and I kent she was going back to Whalsay as soon as her father could get the house ready. Well, that made me feel it wasn't my place to say anything. Her father, Keith's father too, was getting her out of that situation, and if he wanted to tell her, he would. And now Keith said he was going, I was glad I hadn't said anything.' He echoed Emma. 'Keith said he'd been asked to come up and help out, and he'd done that, and they were treating him like dirt. He wasn't giving the croft to them. Danielle had been kind to him, he said, she was the only one who made him feel he'd come home, and she had two bairns. But he didn't want Ertie getting his hands on it. He'd assign it to me, in trust for Peerie Arthur. I promised I'd do that for him.' He stopped as if he'd run out of words, and there was a long silence as we digested the information.

'Do you think he'd told anyone about that?' I asked, at last. Emma hadn't mentioned it.

Mattie shook his head, slowly. 'I dinna think it.' He finished, 'So you see, I had no reason to wish him dead. I don't ken if he'd managed to do anything more about it. I suppose it'll be assigned to Ertie and Irene now, or to Patsy again, for her to re-think.' He shrugged. 'Well, Danielle's going back to Whalsay, and I'll no' bide in Clousta without her. I'll leave them to go to hell in their own way.' He rose, reddening as if he was embarrassed at having said so much. 'Well, if that's us all clooed up now, I'd best be getting home.'

'Thanks for all your help,' I said.

'It's been a fine day on the water. Get the folk in the office to ask me again, now.'

He headed off up the companionway. I gathered up the mugs and took them through to the galley to wash, feeling like my brain was buzzing.

'Leave those,' Anders said. 'I'll do them with my dinner dishes, later. Off you go home and get some rest before tomorrow.'

'Thanks,' I said. I was glad I'd brought *Khalida*. All I had to do was walk round to the marina, cast off the ropes, unroll the jib and head home. It might only be half past four, but I was shattered. My head was throbbing with shrill voices asking questions. Delightful children, all of them, but it was time their parents got them back. I stumbled back to *Khalida*, fell aboard and sat down on the couch. I couldn't sail her in this state. I put the kettle on, and had just made myself a cup of coffee when the phone rang. I reached for it. 'Gavin?'

His voice came cheerfully over the miles between us. 'Good news here – Mother spoke. Only a couple of words, but she spoke.'

I forgot my tiredness. 'Oh, that's great! What did she say?'

'She asked for a cup of tea.'

'Well done her! Was she allowed it?'

'Carefully. I'm in Aberdeen now. No delays. I'll be at the cottage not long after you, about seven.'

Joy rushed through me. 'It'll be good to have you home.'

'I'm looking forward to seeing you too. How's your day gone?'

'It all went really well. Two good trips, the bairns enjoyed themselves, but goodness, I'm done for. Watching them all the time, and answering endless questions.'

'I got the produce photos. I liked the courgette dinosaur.'

'It was by Allison of Klaufister's boy. Noah. I met her. She assured me they didn't want the croft, and kent nothing about Keith getting it till after his death, but Noah told me he was worried about the murder. He wanted me to solve it. There's friction at home. He said his mam and dad were both really mad about Keith being given the croft.'

'A truthful child, or trying to be important?'

'He was a bit show-off earlier, but when he spoke about that he went almost shy. I could see it had upset him. Oh, and Irene looks dreadful. It's getting to her. Then today, I'll tell you properly when we're together, but I got a couple of bits of information. For a start, we had Mattie crewing – you remember, Magnie's nephew – and one teacher was a bit horrid about that. Listen, Mattie said that Keith was going to make the croft over to him.'

'To Mattie? Over Ertie and Irene's heads?'

'That's what he said. Keith told him he was going back south, and he wanted Mattie to marry Danielle, and for Peerie Arthur, that's Ertie's boy, to inherit the croft.'

'Interesting,' Gavin said.

'And Emma was onboard this afternoon. Keith's girlfriend. He told her he was going too.' I told him what she'd said, and my conjectures: not *You never left me*, but *You never loved me*.

'*You never loved me*,' he repeated thoughtfully. 'I'll get back to Morag with all this.'

'Is there,' I asked tentatively, 'any more news on it all?'

'Forensics. Obviously, keep it to yourself. Hang on, I'll move.' I heard his footsteps; the bustle and chat around him died away. 'That's better. I was going to save it for when I got home, but I don't like the way you're mixing with all the suspects like this. We got some of the forensic results from Aberdeen. Arthurson was definitely killed by strangulation, but the professor's not convinced it was by someone in front of him grabbing the ends of his scarf. He said the marks were faint, and almost covered by the marks from Keith's own scarf, but he was certain in his own mind that the actual murder was committed by someone with another length of cloth, like a dishtowel. He's still working on the threads from under Keith's nails. He reckons the murderer got him from behind, when he was sitting, flung the cloth over his head, crossed the ends and pulled tight. Then, straight away, they got his own scarf, wrapped it round his neck and tightened it, the way he was found, thinking that would make the police think he'd been killed by someone strong in front of him.'

'And outside. You wouldn't wear a scarf indoors.' I thought about that for a moment. *I'm getting the blame*, Ertie had said. 'Someone trying to make it look like Ertie? A strong man with a drink problem losing his temper?'

'That's how it looks to me too.'

249

'If you were standing, and Keith was sitting down, you'd need to be quick and determined, but not necessarily strong – or would you?'

'Not if he was relaxed, and you were fast enough. He'd lose consciousness almost straight away.'

'But if he didn't die in the old house, you'd have to move him to where he was found, and lift him enough to make him look as if he'd fallen from standing.'

'They have a trolley for moving shopping and feed bags from where they park the car down to the old house. A bit like a cartie – did you have one when you were a child?'

'I had a boat,' I said. 'With a launching trolley.'

He laughed. 'Kenny made our cartie. It was a wooden fishbox with two old pram wheels on the back and two scooter ones on a swivel axle at the front, and you steered it with a rope. We had a lot of fun with it. Morag said this one had four broad, lightweight wheels attached to a large fishbox, with a taller handle like on a supermarket trolley at one end.'

'Oh, yes, I remember seeing it by the door as I came out of the house. Big enough to get a person's torso into, even if the legs swung over the end.'

'She reckoned so. They kept it either by the house or by the passing place where they park the car. And it's downhill all the way from the road to the old house. Our murderer just needed to get him on it, and they'd have no difficulty moving him about. There were marks of the trolley in the old house, but that's not surprising. No traces in the house, say of mud from the wheels, but Irene said she'd hoovered the kitchen floor in the morning, and then she mopped it after you left.'

I made an apologetic face. 'Yeah, I did drip a bit. To get him off it, though . . .' I tried to visualise it. 'If you put his legs over, as if he was standing, yanked him up hard from under the oxters, then grabbed the ends of his scarf to lower him by?'

'I'm never sure whether it's the sailor in you, or your natural way of thinking, but I like the way you go straight for practical. Yes, I think that's how it was done. Could you do it?'

'I think so, with the trolley still taking most of his weight. And the adrenalin of having killed him, and fear of being caught. No chance of anything on the trolley? Prints or DNA?'

'It's been dusted for prints. Plenty on it, which they're busy sorting out, but unless he was killed by someone outwith Klaufister, there'd be nothing odd about that. Irene and Ertie both used it. They'd buy half a dozen bags of feed at a time and store them in the old house.' He paused, for emphasis. 'The last person to use it wore gloves.'

'Significant?'

'Maybe. Ertie doesn't wear them for hauling stuff, but Irene does, to give her a better grip, she told Morag. It helps with something that's at the limit of her strength. She thought she might well have had gloves on the last time she used it, and they both thought she was the last person they remembered using it, to bring a big load of shopping from the car.' He changed tone. 'So, please, be careful. Don't rule out the women because they didn't appear to have the strength.'

Irene. Danielle. *Four years of gradual weight-training*.

Gavin broke into my thoughts. 'That's my flight come up. I'll see you at home in a couple of hours. Around seven.'

Gavin coming home had woken me up. I went along the pontoon to the toilet, and was coming out when there was a movement in the doorway, and a rough blanket was flung over me. I felt a rope going round my arms, then I was picked up and dumped into a car. The hatch door slammed over me; the driver got in, turned the key, and drove off.

Chapter Twenty

Moonwalking: *Milday Socks, a miniature Shetland stallion, became world famous when he moonwalked near Eshaness Cliffs for an advert for a mobile phone provider.*

The blanket smelt of horses, and it was stifling. I lay still on the floor of the car and breathed steadily for a moment until my heart had stopped racing, then set my mind to thinking. I was in a hatchback which had been parked just around the corner from the toilets. The horse-blanket suggested it was the Klaufister car. It had been flung over me, and something was buckled or tied round me to hold it in place just above my elbows. I wriggled them experimentally. It felt broad and flat, like strapping rather than a rope, and it was too tight for me to move my upper arms.

The car went up the hill leading out of Aith and swung to the right, then went downhill: the Twatt road, towards Clousta. I'd been grabbed and shoved, rather than lifted, staggering on my own feet, then toppled into the boot. Irene could have done that; Ertie was strong enough to have lifted me in.

I tried again, but couldn't shift the strap. I wriggled over, and felt a hard square lump under my back – a ratchet fastening. We used them often enough on boats to tell me I needn't bother trying to loosen it. Though my elbows were rigid, I had the use of my hands. I couldn't reach round to the buckle, but I lifted one hand up forwards and felt the strap: 2cm-wide webbing, tight around my chest. I could cut the blanket beside it and pull it loose, then I might get my hands free – except, I realised, I didn't have my trusty penknife in my pocket, because I'd taken my jacket off to lie down. It was on *Khalida*'s couch, and a fat lot of good it was doing me there. I gave the folds of the blanket an experimental tug with both hands. It was an awkward angle, but if I kept pulling it upwards, that might get it loose enough to work the strap off. I'd have to hurry; the car was going along a straight piece of road, past Greenmeadow and Clousta Loch. Another five minutes.

I tugged as hard as I could, but as I pulled the blanket up the extra folds made it too thick to pull through. The car slowed, then turned off to the left, towards Klaufister. We must be nearly there. The car kept going, another mile or maybe two, then turned to the right and bumped along a rough hill track, stones for a few minutes, then smooth grass. We stopped at last, and reversed a few metres. The driver's door opened, then the rear door. There was rustling, like a plastic bag, half a dozen footsteps, then the mechanical clanking of some sort of door lever. Footsteps back, then the hatch opened above me, I was lifted up by the arms and set on my feet, then hustled across uneven ground and steadied as I stumbled on a step. The person took their hand off my right arm and snicked open the ratchet, then gave me a push forward. There was a gust of air and a heavy metal door slammed behind me. A handle turned, bolts shot home. A few seconds later the car started up and drove away.

The ratchet strap fell to the floor as I wrestled the horse-blanket over my head. The meadow-sweet smell of hay tickled my nose and rustled in my windpipe. I was looking at a dimly lit wall of hay bales with a rust-red roof above them. For a hopeful moment I thought the light came from a window, but it was too low down: an LED lantern was set just inside the door, with a sleeping bag, a lidded plastic bucket and the bag that had rustled beside it. I investigated that first: a packet of teabags, a pint of milk and a small packet of sugar, two Sandwick pies, a selection of four iced sponge squares, and a two-pack of toilet roll. The bucket contained a large Thermos and a bottle of water.

I sat back on a hay bale, feeling reassured. Unless the water in the flask was poisoned, I wasn't to be left to die, and my body dumped later. I had time to think through what I was going to do now. I poured some of the boiling water into the cup, sniffed it, then sipped it. It tasted fine: good country water. A cup of tea first, while I looked around me. The pattern of the rust-red walls was unmistakeable. I was shut inside a container, one of the ex-shipping metal boxes that crofters bought up to store hay or sheep feed somewhere convenient for winter-feeding hill animals. I knew sheep and cattle could eat the common home-produced silage, but ponies had to have expensive hay. Either Klaufister cured its own hay or they'd bought it in as soon as it was harvested south, for the container was almost filled with it, stacked four bales high. In this case, going by the journey here, the feed container was about two miles west of Clousta, up a track running south into the middle of a field. I tried to remember the geography of Clousta as we'd seen it from the sea, and the thought gave me a sudden surge of hope. Whoever had grabbed me didn't know about Anders, aboard the *Swan*. He was going to tidy up, then I betted he'd go up on deck for fresh air, or to the shop to buy dinner or a couple of tins of beer. He'd have to do that before six, when it closed, and he'd pass the marina gate. He'd see *Khalida*'s mast still in the marina, and investigate. He'd find my jacket and lifejacket on the seat, my phone on the table, and no sign of me. He'd phone Magnie, Magnie'd phone Gavin, and if he didn't get him, he'd phone the police, and the hunt would be on. They might be looking for me already, and Klaufister was the first place they'd look . . . except that they wouldn't find me there. I was in a container far enough from a house that it wouldn't matter if I hammered the side of it with something metal, like the Thermos, because nobody would hear me. The Coastguard helicopter's thermal imager would spot me, even inside a steel container, but I'd never hear the end of it if the chopper had to be called out for me. I took a chocolate fancy to go with the tea, and ate it slowly, thinking.

This considerate kidnapper who'd even left me a light and toilet paper was simply keeping me out of the way until they'd done something they needed time for. The obvious something was escaping off Shetland. It was Monday, so the ferry to Aberdeen was at five. I checked my watch: ten to. Unless it was someone other than the grabber, they'd missed the boat. There'd be the last Aberdeen plane, sometime around half past seven. The timing was good for that: an hour's drive away, check in at 6.30. The sleeping bag and food-and-water stash suggested I wasn't going to be let out till tomorrow, by which time they'd be far away, phoning in my whereabouts from Scotland or even Europe, if they'd booked a double flight, Shetland–Aberdeen, then Aberdeen to Paris or Amsterdam or Rome. I'd better get busy on getting out by myself.

The doors were solid. I gave each a good shove with my shoulder, and neither one budged an inch. I glared at them for a moment, trying to remember what containers looked like from the outside. There were three down at the pier below our house. Each door had two steel bars running up the outside of it, with a latch for each one. The bolts holding the bars had the nuts on the inside: four top and bottom and two in the middle for each rod. Twenty nuts to undo without a spanner, and I wasn't sure how much better off I'd be after all that effort, because the rods swivelled on a hook, so even if I could undo them, the rod would stay put. There were only two for each latch, though. If the latch fell off, the leverage holding the bolt might relax. I logged it as a possible idea.

Walls next. I leant forward and picked up the lantern, then switched it off, closed my eyes and counted to a hundred, then opened them again. Blackness. I waited, looking round. There was a grey smudge of light coming round the edges of the door, and pinpricks coming through the floor, but that was no good. Even if I could get a section of the wood up, these things sat solid to the ground, except for a couple of vent holes where the feral cats we'd finally managed to re-home used to get in and out of their lair in the space underneath. Cats could get out; I couldn't. I turned slowly around, looking at the hay bales. I'd almost come the full circle back to where I was when I realised I was actually seeing them, rectangular outlines stacked below the roof, and it wasn't just the dim light seeping in around the doors, or my eyes adjusting to the dark. There was a source of light behind the bales in the far corner. Glory be, was this one of the containers which had a person-sized door in one wall? I breathed a mingled entreaty and thank you upwards, snicked the lantern back on, and set it on the ground while I moved bales to give me steps up to the top of the stack. My estimate of Irene's strength went up. A bale wasn't heavy exactly, but it was too wide to hold in my arms, so I had to lift it using the twine that bound it, thin plastic twine that dug into my palms. I kept shifting, then clambered up and crawled along the top of the bales, shoving the lantern in front of me. They'd been well-stacked, and felt solid beneath me, but the smell and hay-dust was making my nose sting and my eyes were watering. Maybe I had a hay allergy. All the more reason to get out.

I got to where the light had been and angled the lantern so that I could see down the crack behind the bales. My luck was in. There was a door there. The top of the frame was just visible, and way down there was the glint of a metal handle. All I had to do was get to it. I wriggled back and had a good look at the bales between me and it: seven bales back, four high. Twenty-eight bales to move, and a small space to put them in. I pulled down the sleeves of my *Swan* sweatshirt, wrapping them round my palms, then got going, setting the bales as methodically as I could. After the first four, I realised that there wasn't going to be space to put them all in, and changed to getting the top two of each column down and stacked away.

It was exhausting work. I had to crawl along the lower two bales, get the top one down and drag it back out after me, stow it, go back for the next one. My arms were aching by the time I'd done the first seven. Halfway, I told myself, and kept going. At last, with six pairs of bales shifted, I was rewarded with the nearest upright of the door frame. I hauled the last two with a boost of energy and stood contemplating it: a beautiful wooden door with a Yale lock, keyhole on the outside, knob on my side. I turned it and shoved and a blast of fresh air came in. I opened it a foot and sat there on the bales, taking great gulps of hay-free air, then jumped out onto the grass and looked around.

I was on the ridge of the hill, looking down into the Voe of Clousta. Behind me was the common grazing scattald, miles of heather hill scattered with grazing sheep and ponies; before me, the hills, sea and houses were spread like a map, smooth green parks with a hint of gold in the long grass, silvery water ruffled in the centre and stilled at the edges. The sun was almost setting behind the West Burrafirth hills, and the crescent moon that had followed it all day hung over the Clousta hill and reflected in the water as a pale glimmer. Mattie's house was down and to the right, and Klaufister was hidden behind the headland. Both Klaufister cars were by the road, the hatchback and the grey pick-up. Danielle's house was the next one along, and then there was another half-mile to the houses at the head of the voe, with the road visible from Klaufister all the way. That was no good if someone decided to chase me in a car.

My breathing was still wheezy from the hay. I took off my sweatshirt, gave it a good shake out and tied it round my waist, then did my best to get rid of the seeds and dust from my T-shirt and trousers. I fetched the bottle of water and used most of it to give my face and hands a good wash, drank the rest, then sat down on the grass to consider what I could do next. I needed a phone, but the three houses below me were out. I'd liked Mattie, and being Magnie's nephew should be a guarantee of innocence, but love made otherwise sensible people do strange things. I wasn't risking my safety on him, nor on Danielle, and I absolutely wasn't going near Klaufister, or walking past along the road in full view. I needed to get to someone I trusted. I looked across the voe at Mary Nicolson's whitewashed cottage, with the cow grazing placidly on its tether, and the bushes in dark rows down the path. She had a phone. If I only had a boat.

I looked at Mattie's cottage. He wasn't home yet, for there was no car there, and there was a boat pulled up on the shore, just past the tide line, with the tide lapping not so very far below it. I could get to that unobserved, and there was nobody to hear me shifting it.

I took one of the pies to eat on the way and set off down the hill to the road, keeping below the ridge of the headland. If I couldn't see Klaufister's chimneys they couldn't see me. As I swung over the fence, I noticed a black patch in the long grass at the roadside, and crouched down to stare at it: the remains of some sort of firework, a line of half-burned cardboard tubes in a centre of charred grass. Bangers. Lower in the ditch was a damp cardboard box. I fished it out. There was writing in Chinese, and a picture of birds flying upwards. I'd noticed all the geese around when we'd come into Clousta from the sea. A flock of geese could destroy grazing land. This was a firework to sound like shots, to scare them away. *Mattie'd taken it for someone scaring geese*, Magnie had said.

I lifted my head to look at where I was. Before me was the road leading to Clousta and Twatt and Aith, with all the school traffic; behind me, an open hill where one black stallion could easily get lost. I sat there for a moment, thinking about that. Keith was going. He was on the boat tomorrow night, Emma had said; the day after Ebony had got loose. The stallion he'd bought with such high hopes of demonstrating he knew what he was doing in the Shetland pony world had turned out to be an expensive dud, and now Irene knew it too. He could have got up early, well before anyone else was up, caught Ebony and brought him up here. He could have taken off his headcollar, then set the bangers off, expecting Ebony to run off into the hill, to turn into a wild stallion who might be glimpsed at round-up time. To run so far that Irene could reasonably say he was lost, and claim the insurance.

It had to be Keith who'd done that. Irene, who knew and loved horses, would never have thought of it even for a moment. Even I could see what a dreadful idea it was. Ebony hadn't grown up on the scattald, as ponies in Shetland had, so it was alien territory to him. His environment had been green fields and show rings. He'd have as much difficulty surviving as a house cat dumped out to fend for itself, with only instinct to guide him away from cliffs and peat bogs. He was far more likely to end up breaking a leg and dying a miserable death. If he'd survived, he'd have teamed up with mares and caused havoc in the next generation of foals. But Keith knew nothing about animals. Maybe seeing a packet of goose-scarers in the byre had given him the idea, or maybe he was only thinking of getting out of the difficulty he'd created, getting rid of the stallion that couldn't be bred from, and letting Irene get the money for him – except that Ebony had gone the wrong way. Roads were familiar, and so instead of heading into the hill, he'd gone charging down the road. After the fright of bangers going off under his nose, he wouldn't let anyone near him, particularly not Keith, who'd caused them. Keith had had to leave him, and get off to work as usual. Maybe it was that last stupid failure that had made Keith decide to leave.

I left the bangers and packet lying, crossed the road and went down Mattie's track to his house. All was quiet; no barking dog, no cluster of panicking hens. I slipped past it, and kept going to the boat, my heart sinking as I got closer to it, and saw its neglected state. It wasn't in use, and hadn't been for some time. It was a fibreglass dinghy, but it had been lying with a slant of green-scummed water in it for long enough to leave several rings of slime on the inner hull. The oar blades were cracked, and the wooden trim had rotted. There was no way I was trusting my life to it.

I was almost at the end of Mattie's headland. If I kept going, walking softly on the grass and wilted seaweed under the shadow of the banks, the Klaufister pontoon was only two hundred metres away, with Ertie's metal salmon boat moored to it. With everyone in the house, I could slip aboard and go over to Mary's. I knew its engine ran, and I thought it likely he'd have left the key aboard, but you never knew; he might have the habit of taking it out and dropping it in his pocket. There'd been a light blue skiff as well, with oars. I might be as quick with that, on a bonny night like this, and silent too. It would depend on what I found when I got round there. I realised, with a leap of hope, that the police might still be there – communication and backup all in one.

I was out of luck for that one. I glimpsed a neon and white flash going round the corner of the road towards Twatt, and as soon as I edged my nose round the corner of the headland I saw that they'd gone, leaving only a line of yellow police tape across the entrance to the old house as a reminder of their presence. I'd missed them by minutes.

Very well, I'd go to Mary's. I looked across, but there was no sign of her in the garden. I tried to remember her times: Vespers at five, followed by Adoration, then her evening meal. I glanced at my watch. It was almost half past five. The kitchen window was too dark for me to see inside. Though I couldn't see her, she might see me. I waved with both arms, then did the classic SOS: arms spread for three longs, three shorts, three longs, and waited, eyes strained towards the still cottage. There was no sign of movement.

The pontoon was only two hundred metres away. I slid along with my back pressed against the banks, placing my feet on grass tufts instead of betraying stones or treacherous seaweed, and made it to Ertie's cottage. There was no sound from it, and the only lights darkening the dusk were the square windows in the new house. I slipped round the front of the old house as far as the porch, crouching down underneath the window, just in case, and straightened cautiously in the shadows. The barking dogs must live up in the pick-up. I paused, listening, and heard the trickle of a burn behind me, the waves mouthing the shore and tapping on the metal hull, voices from the house. The lights indoors would blind the Klaufister folk to the outside. Now I'd stopped moving the midgies were something fierce. I waved a hand across my face, then peered around the porch corner. The untidy jumble in front of the cottage would be a great help. The pile of blue plastic drums in the hollow of the burn were right beside the pontoon's shore end.

I could see people moving in the kitchen: Ertie, in a boiler suit; Irene. Patsy would be in her chair. I could hear the voices but not distinguish words. There was something flat about the tones, as if everything emotional had been said, and all that was left was practicalities. I risked oozing behind the drums, keeping in the shadows, leaning forward to see what I could.

Irene brought something to the table: a suitcase. She opened it, and began moving around, out of the room and back in, packing garments, every movement suggesting hurry. She shook one out to re-fold it: a woman's short-sleeved blouse. It was Irene who was going. With a jolt of sorrow, I realised I hadn't wanted Irene to have killed Keith; I'd liked her, and been sorry for her. I thought I knew where she'd be going, too. I remembered her saying wistfully, *I always wanted to see France*. If she went now, she'd get the last flight to Aberdeen, and there'd be flights after it arrived, including to Paris. I heard Patsy's voice in the background, giving instructions. The suitcase lid partly blocked the window. If I went for the pontoon while Irene was fetching something, I'd have a good chance of not being seen.

The blue skiff was moored on one side of it and the metal salmon boat on the other, both sideways on to the house. I could lie between them until I got a chance to check out the key situation for the salmon boat, and clamber aboard whichever one seemed the best bet. I watched Irene, and slithered out from behind the drums as soon as she turned away, then slipped onto the pontoon and lay down on the wooden boards. There was a wonderful smell of salt and seaweed, and I felt my heart reassured. I was in my own element now, with a boat at my hand. I checked my feet were drawn up into the shadow of the skiff, and waited. Silence; Irene's footsteps moving to and fro, and Patsy's voice. The snick of the suitcase catch, a scrape of a chair, then the door opened.

They came out together, Patsy leaning on Irene's arm, and Ertie behind, carrying a wheelie-suitcase and a white bag. Patsy and Irene were both wearing dark town clothes, and all three faces were grave as a funeral. They didn't speak as they moved slowly up to the car, but Patsy paused for a moment beside it, giving Ertie a long look, then they got into the car, Irene driving, Patsy in the passenger seat. Ertie put the bags in the boot, then stood by the roadside as they drove off. I put my head up to see inside the salmon boat while his back was turned. It had the usual wheel steering and throttle lever, but there was no key in the keyhole, nor any sign of a box where it might be kept: no storage space under the seat, no containers. It was an empty steel shell, and no good to me.

Ertie came slowly down the track, and went into the house. Quickly, I moved back onto the pontoon and undid the ropes of both boats. It went to my conscience to deliberately set a boat loose, but it'd come to no harm on this still night, and I'd make sure it was retrieved as soon as I'd contacted help. Both Gavin's number and Anders' were stored in my phone rather than my memory, but I knew Magnie's. I could phone him from Mary's and get Irene stopped at the airport. I checked Ertie wasn't looking out, then reached into the skiff to get the oars ready.

Time to go. I took a deep breath, shoved the salmon boat backwards from the pontoon as hard as I could, then leapt into the blue skiff, snatched up one oar and pushed off, then reached for the other, sat down and began rowing.

There was a shout from the cottage, and running feet. I looked up and saw Ertie pelting for the jetty, leaping easily over the burn, his haste shaking the pontoon. He had one hand grabbing towards the water. I realised I had a trailing rope and did an extra stroke, then reached over the side to pull it in. He caught the end of it, and I gave a yank that almost had him overbalancing into the water. Another tug, and I was free, and rowing with fast, smooth strokes.

'Stop!' he yelled after me. 'Stop and listen to me, at least.'

I didn't stop. He danced with impatience on the pontoon, then realised that the waves he was making were sending the salmon boat further away from the jetty. It was two metres from the jetty now, too far to reach. Without pausing to think he jumped from the pontoon into the water, landing with a resounding splash an arms-length from it, and managed to grab the gunwale.

I watched him as I rowed, putting my back into every stroke. If I had to go back for him I would. He was clinging on to the boat's side. It was too high for him to climb into from the water, but he knew that, and didn't try. He was swimming it back to the pontoon. In a minute he'd be after me, with all the power of a 90hp engine. I kept rowing, glancing over my shoulder to make sure I was still going direct to Mary's pontoon.

She'd heard the splash, and come out onto her briggistane. She was watching us: me rowing arrow-straight towards her, and Ertie clambering out onto the pontoon, looping the boat's rope round a cleat, running to his house, grabbing the key, running back and leaping into the boat, throwing the rope off. The noise of the engine cut into the silence.

I glanced over my shoulder again. I was past halfway now, with maybe two hundred metres to go. The engine noise increased to a roar, and Ertie started the boat towards me in two plumes of white wave. I kept rowing, not looking round again. He was coming closer – closer – then I realised disbelievingly that he really was going to ram me. I stood up and dived clear, just in time as the boat rocked under me. There was a bang, and a horrible splintering, tearing noise, and the skiff broke in pieces as the steel boat crashed into it.

The water was freezing, particularly on my head as it went under. I remembered not to gasp as the shock of it hit me, and began swimming, away from the steel boat's propeller. I came up, gasping now, and struck out for the shore, vaguely thinking that I must give Clousta Voe a wide berth in future, since every time I came here I ended up in the water. Behind me, the engine roar had diminished to idle. It sounded like Ertie was disentangling his boat from the remains of the skiff – which, I thought regretfully, had been a nice little boat. I could see the pebbles below me, red, yellow, white, and waving strands of weed. Not much further before I could put my feet down. My heart was thudding as if I was about to have a seizure. I put my feet down, groping, and went under again, fought back to the surface and kept swimming, stroke after stroke, each one slower than the last, until my feet touched bottom. I put my hands down, and felt the smooth pebbles, then shoved myself to my feet, swaying as if I was drunk. Mary was striding down her path towards me. She held out both hands to help me stagger ashore, dripping and shivering, and looked over my shoulder to Ertie. This was the moment, I thought suddenly, with a spurt of alarm, where she'd turn out to be in league with Ertie, and our murderer after all. Her first words reassured me.

'Ertie, what on earth do you think you're doing?' I wondered for a moment if she'd been a teacher. Her voice would have stopped a classful of unruly pupils in their tracks.

'Cass!' Ertie replied. 'You need to stop her. She wants to talk to the police, and stop Mam getting on the plane.'

There was a long pause. We both turned our heads to look at him. 'Stop Mam?' I repeated slowly.

'Patsy?' Mary said.

Ertie looked at me. 'I thought you kent. It was me mother that killed Keith.'

Chapter Twenty-one

All-overs: *Shetland ponies Vitamin and Fivla modelled pony-sized Shetland all-over jumpers for a Visit Scotland photo shoot.*

It was me mother that killed Keith. The silence lasted so long that I felt I'd gone deaf, as if the water had clogged my ears.

'She's going,' Ertie said at last. 'She has it all worked out. She'll vanish. She says none of us will ever hear from her more, so that the police can't track her.' His face was still. 'She never cared much for us anyway. Keith was the only one she loved.' His cheeks crumpled as if he was going to cry. 'We just wanted to help her.'

Mary took my arm. 'Cass, you'll freeze standing here. Come and get dried. I have a shower, and I can give you a dressing gown. Ertie, I don't want your sunk boat fouling my landing stage. Go and retrieve it, and drag it ashore, so I can use it for firewood, then come and talk to us. I've got a boiler suit you can change into.'

He nodded, and turned towards his boat. I thought that now his passion was spent, he was glad to hand the whole mess over to her.

'Best to give him something to do,' Mary said, keeping her arm around me as she steered me up the path. 'Otherwise he'll be back to Klaufister, and to the bottle.'

'They'll be looking for me,' I said. 'Anders, on the *Swan*. He'd have seen my boat still in the marina. Gavin's on his way from Aberdeen. He'll be just landed. I need to call off the search.'

'Shower,' Mary said. Her bathroom was in an extension off the kitchen, in what had been a walk-in larder. She gave me a towel, a round ball of soap and a dark-brown wool robe, like a monk's. 'I'll phone the police and let them know you're safe.'

'Magnie,' I said, through chattering teeth. 'Brae 524. He has Gavin's number.'

I was in the shower when I realised she hadn't said anything about Ertie's bombshell. *It was me mother that killed Keith.* Patsy, who adored him. I kept thinking about that as I washed, dried myself and slipped the robe over my head.

Mary had lit the Rayburn. My clothes were hanging on the chrome rail in front of it, drying already. The kettle was starting to boil on the hotplate. Ertie had slumped onto the couch, his head in his hands.

'I got hold of your man, and told him you were safe,' Mary said. 'He says he'll see you at the house. Magnie's coming to fetch you.'

'I was never in any danger,' I said. I looked at Ertie. 'Irene was desperate for your mam to get away. She caught hold of me at the marina, brought me to your container on the hill, and shut me in there with everything I'd need till morning.'

He gave a twisted smile. 'Much good that did. You found the door behind all the bales of hay straight away.'

'Not quite straight away,' I said. 'I tested the big doors first, and had a cup of tea and a fancy.'

'I'll tell her that. She wasn't thinking straight. Neither of us was. She thought, from something that you said to her yesterday, that you suspected Mam. And as well as that, she said, if you went missing the heat would be off us for long enough, while they looked for you.' He gave me a sideways, apprehensive look. 'So she half-hoisted your sail in the berth. She kent that'd be noticed.' I gave him an outraged look at the thought of my gleaming new mainsail left to flog, and he ducked his head back. 'It worked,' he said hastily. 'The police were straight here, not twenty minutes after Irene got back from putting you in the container, asking if we'd seen you.'

Anders would have stowed my sail properly, I reassured myself, and focused on the matter in hand.

'After Keith fetched the stallion,' I began slowly, thinking it through, 'the day it got loose, he went back to the house. He was the one who'd set it loose, in the hope it'd get lost on the hill, so you could claim the value of it on the insurance. I found the goose-scarer bangers he'd set off, in the grass by the road, up by the container. But it ran the wrong way, onto the road, so that plan had failed. He didn't fit in here, and the harder he tried, the worse it got. *Whatever he did turned out wrong*, he'd said to Emma. Maybe he wanted to try and be family, but it was like he caused trouble every way he turned, with Irene over the horses, with Trevor and Allison over Emma and the croft, and with you over the croft, and him visiting Danielle.'

Ertie nodded.

'So he told your mam he was going,' I said slowly, imagining it. 'She thought he'd come back to stay. She was giving him the croft over your heads, so that he'd settle down here. She was looking forward to him always being here. Her son with her, as she grew older.'

'I was her son too,' Ertie said. His voice was bitter as Patsy's. 'But she never set any store by me. Nor by Allison, though she was the older lass. Nor by Irene, who's looked after her these last months.'

I remembered what he had described on *Khalida* last night. 'Then when he said he was going, just like that, on tomorrow's boat, she remembered how he'd gone away to college and never phoned. Didn't let her come and stay when he moved to London. But she'd kept believing he loved her. She was his mother. Him coming home to help her proved it.' I swallowed, feeling the pity of it; the love she'd poured out on someone who just wanted to escape. *You never loved me.* 'Then he told her he was assigning the croft she'd given him over to Mattie, and going, and she realised that he didn't care at all. And so, in bitter unhappiness, she killed him.' I'd felt the bitterness, when I'd been there. The quarrel had been the night before. Patsy had known he was lying dead in the old house. She'd been waiting for someone to find him.

Ertie sighed. 'Our house was ... stern. Cold. Like Mam had been trapped there.' He flushed. 'Mam was pregnant with me when they married. I wondered if they'd been pressurised into marrying, and she'd always resented it. Coming from being a nurse in Lerwick to being stuck on a croft in Clousta. She fed the animals but she didn't like them. She fed Dad and us. Keith was the only thing she loved. He got all of Mam's attention, all through our childhood. She'd sort of sigh if we asked for anything, but he got whatever he wanted straight off, with a smile. I thought Dad was a bit contemptuous of Keith, because he was a mammy's boy.' He paused to think more. 'I don't think Mam would have told Dad Keith wasn't his. He could get pretty angry about things. I remember Keith being born, just, but I don't remember quarrelling. Even if Dad suspected, I don't think he'd ever have admitted it. He wouldn't have thrown Mam out, I'm sure of that, because that would tell the whole place she'd had an affair, and everyone would be joking about that behind his back.'

His face saddened. 'But Keith didn't love her. He despised her, because he could twist her round his little finger, and he didn't like us because we saw through him. He just wanted to get away and leave us all behind. Make a life of his own, where there'd be excitement and colour and money, and he'd be important to everyone. Only it didn't work out, and coming back here didn't work out either.'

'There was good in him, that he came,' I said.

'I suppose so.' He struck the arm of the chair with his fist. 'I wish I could go back and start all over again. Been a better big brother to him right from the start. Have welcomed him home instead of sulking with my bottle, like a baby.'

'When did you find out that it was Patsy who killed him?'

His face was bleak. He shook his head. 'Only just now. I came into the house a bit after the police left, and she was all dressed as if she was going into town, and then I saw the suitcase open on the table, and stared at it for a moment, then looked at her. "I killed Keith," she said, all matter-of-fact, as if she was saying she'd done the dishes. Just the way she'd told us he wasn't our brother. "I've booked a flight to Aberdeen. I won't tell you where I'm going, and you won't hear from me again, unless the police find me." I stared at her wi' me mouth open. Mam, to kill Keith! Then Irene explained, while she was packing a last few things. She'd worked it out already, that Mam had . . .' He stopped and swallowed before resuming. 'She kent Mam better as I did. She blamed herself for it. She'd heard raised voices even over the book she was listening to, that night, but she didn't want to get involved. She was so, so tired. That was my fault as well as Mam's. I didn't help her, just sat and drank and felt sorry for myself. Irene was worn out with supporting Mam, and Keith, and me, each of us separately, and trying to give Danielle a hand too, and it was all getting too much for her. She thought it was Mam getting on at me again, and she'd had enough. She said she turned the volume up on her book and left us to sort it ourselves for once.' His olive-green eyes met mine bleakly. 'She said that if she'd got up, maybe it wouldn't have happened.'

I wasn't sure what to say to that, and went for the truth. 'It still might have,' I said at last. 'It would have been very quick. She might have found herself in the situation of either helping your mother cover up the murder or phoning the police.'

Ertie thought about that for a moment, then nodded. 'Right enough, she might. Then, she said, it all went quiet, and she went to sleep. When she got up, she noticed, but kinda without noticing, if you know what I mean, that the trolley had been turned around, but she took it that I'd been shifting something. Mam was even more difficult than usual, but she was used to that, and then you came over, and she was busy helping you. It was only later, when I found Keith, and she came out and saw him—' He ducked his head away from me, and was silent for a moment. 'Then, once the shock was over, she talked to Mam. Mam decided she was going, before the police found out too. She'd always wanted to travel, but there was never the money. That trip south, when Dad died, that was the first holiday they'd had, that I could remember.' He was silent for a moment.

'She'll be found,' I said. 'Whatever she does, the police will find her. She'll need money. She'll have a bus pass. Her picture will be everywhere. Someone will spot her.'

Ertie sighed. 'I don't know what she'd planned. But we had to give her a chance. Irene was going to let you out tomorrow. She just wanted to give Mam a head-start.'

'Anders was biding onboard the *Swan*, at Aith pier,' I said. 'He'd start looking for me the minute he saw my boat abandoned like that.'

'He did,' Mary said. 'He phoned Magnie, and Magnie just managed to catch Gavin before the flight took off, and Gavin phoned the police in Lerwick. They'll send a squad car to Sumburgh, to get Patsy and Irene.'

Ertie made an inarticulate grieving sound, and Mary turned to him and spoke firmly. 'As for you, your mother's an adult and fit to take the consequences of her own behaviour. I ken you're no' thinking straight right now, and nor is Irene, after the tiring year she's had, but you've made yourselves accessories after the fact in your brother's murder, as well as nearly killing Cass on the water here, and the only thing you can do is make a clean breast of it to the police, and hope they'll be sympathetic towards you.'

'And you didn't kill him,' I said.

His face lightened suddenly. 'And nor did Irene. That was what I was most faered o'.' He gave me an apologetic look, almost shy. 'I didn't tell you, but they had a massive row about the stallion, after the Viking Show. Annie had found out that mares in Unst were in foal to him, and she told Irene about the dwarfism results. The minute she got him alone, Irene tackled Keith about it. I'd never seen her so angry. She was white in the face, and her hands were shaking. I was mad myself, when she explained what he'd done. It was bad enough that he brought him here in the first place, over her head. The first thing she knew about it was when the horsebox arrived with him, and Robbie, our own stallion, still in his park. We had to find somewhere else for him that very day. He'd have killed Ebony if he'd got at him. Then to find out Ebony was tainted like that, and another stud involved . . . It was a dreadful shock. That was Keith all over. Determined to show off in something he kent nothing about, and being too big to even do the basic checks.'

'What will you do with Ebony now?'

'Keep him for the moment. Annie came out and gelded him on Friday. Irene's going to see if she can turn him into a riding horse, show him south and sell him.' He paused for a moment, shaking his head. 'It's a right mess. Irene tried talking to our insurance, but it was no good. Keith should have had a vet inspection before he bought him, and he didn't, so the liability was his, and now it's ours. We talked it through, then she phoned the stud in Unst that Keith put him to.' I could see by his face that it hadn't been an easy conversation. 'Come next summer, when they're born, we'll pay for all the foals to be tested. The colt foals will be too young to geld in October, when the sales are, but any that carry the dwarfism gene will be sold with a warning, and labelled 'for gelding'. The filly foals will have a warning if they're carriers. The studies are pretty new, but it seems that if the stallion has no trace of it, then the foals will be clear, so buyers might still take a chance on them. We've said we'll repay what they should have made, less the stud fee.' He sighed. 'Let's hope overall prices are low next year. Our own ones, she'll sell the colts for gelding and the clear fillies, and keep the affected fillies. Waterloo Robbie doesn't have the gene. We'll see how they look as they grow, and breed them to him if there's no sign of dwarfism.'

I wasn't sure what I should say next, or if I should say anything at all. He and Irene had to work out their own salvation. Ertie looked dreadful, as if demons were riding on his back, but he didn't smell of drink, and he was looking at Mary as if she was the rock he'd found to cling to. If she could be that for him, he had a chance.

Mary looked at me, and nodded. 'If I could do it,' she said to Ertie, 'so can you. Keep remembering me, and believe that recovery is possible. I'm not saying it'll be easy, but it's possible, if you want it enough.'

'I want it,' Ertie said. He looked across at the square house, with its windows tinted gold in the dusk, and smiled. 'And Irene can have her happy ending now.' He glanced at me. 'She and Annie have been a pair since they were old enough to notice a pair didn't always have to be a boy and a lass. She'd maybe be healthier if she was happier.'

There was the distant roar of an engine. The RIB that we used with the bairns' sailing came planing around the corner and stopped short of the shore. I realised that with so much else going on I'd totally forgotten it was Monday, and junior sailing night. Magnie leant over the engine to lift it, then paddled the boat in.

'That's Magnie now,' I said. I rose and gathered up my clothes and took them back into the shower. My underwear and T-shirt were dry and warm, if slightly sticky from salt, and the sweatshirt and jeans were mostly dry. My shoes were still wet, but then wet feet was a sailor's natural condition. I dressed and hung the robe back up.

I heard Magnie's voice at the door, and Mary replying. He came into the cottage and gave a swift look round. 'Aye, aye, Ertie. I'm vexed to hear of all this trouble that's come upon you, boy, but I hope it'll all work out.' He gave me a flicker of a wink, and said gravely, 'I see you're none the worse for wear. Just a bit damp, and that's normal to you.' I had no doubt he'd noticed the smashed blue skiff on the shore. 'Thanks to you, Mary, but we won't stop. Cass's animals will need fed, and I need to get up to Brae, to supervise the bairns' sailing, once I've put Cass back to the Ladie.'

'Thanks to you, Mary,' I echoed Magnie. 'I hope we'll come to Mass here soon.'

'The third Monday of the month, at ten,' she said. 'God go with you.'

I hesitated, looking at Ertie. 'Good luck,' I said.

Magnie and I walked down the flowered path in silence. 'It's bonny here,' I said at last. 'Peaceful.'

Magnie didn't reply till we got to the beach, then he nodded at the splintered planks of the blue skiff. 'No' like you to be smashing up boats.'

I told him the story as we came between the mussel floats and through Cribba Sound, then fell silent as he opened up the throttle to race through the Røna and round Papa Little to the Ladie pontoon. 'Never you bother about the sailing tonight,' he said, as I stepped onto the pontoon. 'We can manage fine without you. Say hello to your man from me, and see if you can manage to give him a couple of days of peace.'

'Do my best. Thanks for coming to get me.'

'Ah, the RIB needed a decent run anyway.' He backed off, raised a hand and roared away.

I stood for a moment breathing in the soft evening air. It was high water, and completely still. The sun was behind the hills now, but there were slanting gold shafts of light through the gaps in the clouds, and over the soft green hills, and the sound was filled with whisky-amber water. Cat was on his gatepost, a grey oval against the green leaves. He jumped down and came trotting towards the jetty. Kitten followed him, and then Ketling Julie, dark against the grass. She must have found her way out. I headed upwards, swaying slightly. The cats charged ahead of me, Julie leaping exuberantly over Kitten as they went, then turning back to pounce at Cat.

Gavin would be here soon. I'd sort all the animals, so that we could relax together. Sheep. I paused to count them and check the burn. Water running, sixteen sheep, twenty-seven lambs. Horses. Hens. Cats. I wondered how often Gavin felt like this, coming home after a hard day's work dealing with people and forms, to more work with animals. I'd been selfish, leaving it all to him. Yes, he and Kayleigh between them were responsible for us having the horses, sheep and hens, but the cats were mine. From now on, I'd try to do my fair share. At least I'd learned what to do.

I started with the hens. Today it was the cockerel that was agitated and not wanting to be put to bed. I hoped he wasn't seeing a polecat around. I got the hens in and coaxed him after them and shut the door on him with relief. Caedoc and Caitlin accepted being separated for their food; Fergus stamped and snorted in disgust. I picked up the box of eggs I'd collected and headed for the door. There was time to boil some tatties. The little carrots I hadn't used for the show would make a starter with vinaigrette, then a cheese omelette, and the Sandwick cheesecake for a dessert. There'd be wine in the under-stairs cupboard; Maman made sure we were kept well supplied. I found a heavy red and opened it to breathe.

I was just laying the table when I heard the car on the gravel track. I hurried out to meet Gavin, and flung myself into his arms. They closed around me, warm and comforting, and I suddenly realised how frightened I'd been, seeing Ertie's steel boat coming at me to ram the lightweight skiff. Gavin's cheek against mine smelt of Imperial Leather soap. We stood like that for a moment, then he set me from him and smiled at me. 'No damage?'

'Only another swim.'

'So I heard. Well, come and tell me all about it.'

We sat hand-fast on the couch in the sitootery. Gavin sighed, and turned his head to smile at me. 'It's good to be home. So, where did you go to, and how did you end up swimming?'

'I was kidnapped by Irene,' I said. I described it all: the horse blanket, the container, shifting a ton of hay, getting down to the shore and seeing Patsy and Irene leaving, stealing the boat.

'Next time,' Gavin said, 'it might be better to walk firmly in the other direction.' He glanced down at my lap. 'Cat would be seriously upset if you'd been drowned. So would I.'

'Did you know it was Patsy who killed Keith?'

He pulled a face, between yes and a shrug. 'Not sure, no, but Morag and I thought it was moving between her and Irene. It was the sort of case where there was no evidence except the characters and history of the people concerned: all the fingerprints and footprints belonged to the people who lived there.' He smiled. 'No conveniently monogrammed handkerchiefs dropped after the rain stopped at eleven twenty-four precisely. Not even a cigarette end.'

'You'd get one now,' I said. 'Ertie was smoking like a chimney to keep his mind off drinking.'

'The field was wide at first, with Irene and Ertie having grudges against Keith, and Trevor and Allison too, except there was no sign they'd been near Klaufister that night. Morag followed that up after you'd mentioned their reaction to Keith getting the croft. They live in one of the council house estates, and their neighbours were sure nobody took their car out. Then there was Mattie, living just over the headland, with nobody to see his comings and goings. His motive would be either jealousy over Keith, or an attempt to frame Ertie to get him taken out of Danielle's life. As framing, it was circumstantial evidence, but Ertie was on the spot, with a major grudge against Keith, and in the kind of drunken state where he could well have blown a fuse. It wasn't hard for the police to suspect him. When we found out that Keith hadn't been strangled the way we'd thought, and that his body had been moved, that pointed more to someone weaker. It didn't quite rule Ertie or Mattie out, but either of them could have lifted the body, fireman-style, and shifted it more quickly and quietly than messing about with a trolley. It was an indication. Patsy, Irene, or Danielle.'

'But Danielle came forward with an alibi for Ertie.'

'Did it make you more convinced of his innocence, or less?'

'Mmmm.' I thought about that. 'Initially, less convinced.'

'That's what the police thought too; and that flourishing an alibi for him of course gave her one. But Irene was my front-runner. Ertie minded about the croft too, but he was too far gone in drink to really think through his life without it. Irene, though, she was passionate about her horses. If Keith took Klaufister, she'd lose the horses that were her children, and she'd never get another stud. She wasn't strong enough to work for that kind of money, and she wouldn't marry for it. She knew it was the end of all she cared about.'

'But Patsy loved Keith,' I said.

'Yes, but some of the nastiest murders are love gone wrong, like an ex-husband killing his wife. *You never left me* didn't make sense with any of the suspects, but *You never loved me* said to Keith fitted only Patsy or Danielle. Danielle had only known him for five months, and most of that time she'd still been living with her husband. And Patsy could have done it. I think he turned his back on her and wouldn't answer when she tried to talk to him about why he was going, and she saw red and grabbed a dishtowel and strangled him with it. It would have been quick. Then suddenly there she was with her dead son. She had to do something to protect herself. Ertie or Irene could take the rap. She heard voices outside while she was trying to think, Ertie and Danielle, and waited till they'd gone. Maybe hearing them going towards Ertie's gave her the idea of the old house. The trolley was right by the door, and it had a handle like a supermarket one, and four wheels, so it would have supported her as she wheeled it. And there's nothing like weak legs to make you stronger in the arms.'

His phone buzzed. He lifted it, and nodded at me. 'Gavin here.'

I left him to it, and went to get dinner started. I'd done the salad and the potatoes were boiling and the eggs whisked when he joined me. 'They arrested Patsy at Sumburgh, about to get on the plane. They're bringing her back to Lerwick. Irene's going back to Klaufister, for now. Someone'll go out and talk to her and Ertie.'

'Do you need to go in?'

He shook his head. 'I haven't been here, so it's absolutely not my case, however good it was of Morag to keep me in the loop. I'll go in tomorrow and help with the paperwork. We can get this evening together.' He came to put his arms around me. 'I missed you.'

'I missed you too.' I was getting better at making with the words. 'And Gavin, I didn't realise how much work all the animals are. The hens, particularly. There was always one who didn't want to go into the pen at night. I'll try to be more help with that.'

'That would be grand,' Gavin said. He smiled, teasing. 'And you're the mathematician of the family. Once you've learned the dairy work, you can keep being in charge of counting the sheep.'

'No,' I said, as firmly as I could. I leant against him, and suddenly found myself shaking. 'I can't do it, Gavin. I was too close to all this: Ertie, and Irene, and Patsy warped by loving one child better than the others, and Danielle struggling. I don't ever want a life like that.'

His arms were warm around me. I could feel his chest moving as he breathed. 'Cass, dear Cass. My selkie wife. You ken fine I'd never hide your skin in a kist to keep you away from the sea.' He kissed my cheek, then gave me a gentle shake, and set me back from him. 'Don't you?'

I looked up at him, and saw his sea-grey eyes smiling down at me. I nodded. 'I ken.'

'In fact I was meaning to speak to you about that.' He motioned me to the table, and poured two glasses of wine. 'I ken it's no' the same as *Khalida*, but your mast'll be coming down next month, and *Swan*'ll be in dry dock all winter too, so you'll be left with only the *Deuk*. I thought you might like an early birthday present. I was speaking to a man that has a Shetland model for sale. It's a bonny, wooden boat built in the traditional style, with a lug sail. Only five years old. He built her for himself, but he's had a hip replacement, and isn't agile enough. Fourteen foot, with a pair of oars, and I think she'd sail beautifully. We could trail her to the cottage too, if we're having a break there.' He smiled. 'She's called the *Winter's Wark*.'

Acknowledgements

Some books flow out easily, others feel more like hard work. This was one of the hard work ones, not because I was short of ideas, but because I was short of time. I'd had a busy autumn with talks at several crime festivals, and by the end of November I was waking up in my own bed wondering where I was now. I didn't manage to put fingers to keyboard until Boxing Day, and my deadline was the end of June. To add to the chaos, I'd always wanted a Siamese cat, and had discovered that yes, there were breeders who specialised in the old style, like our childhood Chula, who was an imperiously beautiful Seal Point. I met the Wicca Stud cats on a visit to Kent, and was entranced. In March, Philip and I travelled down to Kent and brought two kittens back. Our two tortoiseshells tolerated them while they were small, and bopped out-of-line aristocratic noses as they got bigger. Now at last all four sleep in the same room and patrol the garden together. One plan to keep them away from the road (and visiting tom cats) was taking them for walks, so now the village is entertained by the sight of me heading for the shore with two Siamese cats charging around me.

That I still met that June deadline (nearly) was thanks to many people.

Firstly, my dear husband, Philip, who kept the household running, and even allowed cats in his room to let me work in peace.

Teresa Chris, my wonderful agent, was a huge help in knocking a sometimes incoherent story into shape. Celine Kelly of Headline continued the work with structural edits, and Teresa re-read it after

I'd done those, and made more suggestions. Toby Jones, my editor at Headline, approved the final version, gave it a snappier title than my rather leaden *Death on a Shetland Pony Stud*, and organised another gorgeous cover. Thank you also to the design team. Once the edits were done, editorial assistant Ayana Playle supervised my final corrections, and Jill Cole gave a final proof-check – thank you.

Thank you to John Fraser, who talked frankly to me about life as an alcoholic, and the AA recovery plan which saved him. Thank you to Carol Fullerton, of the Ramanberg Stud, for horsey ideas and advice, and for keeping Milla with her herd; thank you to Lynn Johnson, creator of The Original Cake Fridge and owner of Klingrahoull Stud, for suggesting dwarfism, and of course for her wonderful baking. Thank you to Mona and the Deyell family for allowing me, once again, to use their late father Bertie's wonderful collection of *Shetland Proverbs and Sayings*.

I'd like to say something about Headline's reading initiative (see final page). My mother always read a bedtime story to my sister, Joan, three years older, and me. I'm sure it was that which instilled a love of reading in me. Family tradition has it that I taught myself to read because I wanted to know what happened next in *The Lion, the Witch and the Wardrobe*, instead of having it doled out in chapters. As a former teacher, I know how vital literacy is to children for getting on in secondary: it may be an exam for PE, or Science, but they still need to be able to read the questions quickly and accurately.

All the studies show that being read to as a child makes a difference to a child's love of reading, and the earlier, the better. Please, find time to read to your children right from the start. It doesn't need to be an improving book, or educational, or a worthy classic – those can come later. Find something you both enjoy, and make it your special time. You're giving your child a lifelong gift: the treasure of books.

A note on Shetlan

Shetland has its own very distinctive language, *Shetlan* or *Shetlandic*, which derives from old Norse and old Scots. In *Death on a Longship*, Magnie's first words to Cass are:

'Cass, well, for the love of mercy. Norroway, at this season? Yea, yea, we'll find you a berth. Where are you?'

Written in west-side Shetlan (each district is slightly different), it would have looked like this:

'Cass, weel, fir da love o' mercy. Norroway, at dis saeson? Yea, yea, we'll fin dee a bert. Quaur is du?'

Th becomes a *d* sound in *dis* (this), *da* (the), *dee* and *du* (originally thee and thou, now you), *wh* becomes *qu* (*quaur*, where), the vowel sounds are altered (well to *weel*, season to *saeson*, find to *fin*), the verbs are slightly different (quaur <u>is</u> du?) and the whole looks unintelligible to most folk from outwith Shetland, and *twartree* (a few) within it too.

So, rather than writing in the way my characters would speak, I've tried to catch the rhythm and some of the distinctive usages of Shetlan while keeping it intelligible to *soothmoothers*, or people who've come in by boat through the South Mouth of Bressay Sound into Lerwick, and by extension, anyone living south of Fair Isle.

There are also many Shetlan words that my characters would naturally use, and here, to help you, are *some o' dem*. No Shetland person would ever use the Scots *wee*; to them, something small would be *peerie*, or, if it was very small, *peerie mootie*. They'd *caa* sheep in a *park*, that is, herd them up in a field – *moorit* sheep, coloured black, brown, fawn. They'd take a *skiff* (a small rowing boat) out along the *banks* (cliffs) or on the *voe* (sea inlet), with the *tirricks* (Arctic terns) crying above them, and the *selkies* (seals) watching. Hungry folk are *black fanted* (because they've forgotten their *faerdie maet*, the snack that would have kept them going) and upset folk *greet* (cry). An older housewife would have her *makkin* (knitting) *belt* buckled around her waist, and her *reestit* (smoke-dried) *mutton* hanging above the Rayburn. And finally... my favourite Shetland verb: *to kettle*. As in: *Wir cat's joost kettled. Four ketlings, twa strippet and twa black and quite.* I'll leave you to work that one out on your own... or, of course, you could consult Joanie Graham's *Shetland Dictionary*, if your local bookshop hasn't *just selt* their last copy *dastreen*.

The diminutives Magnie (Magnus) and Ertie (Arthur) may also seem strange to non-Shetland ears. In a traditional country family (I can't speak for *toonie* Lerwick habits) the oldest son would often be called after his father or grandfather, and be distinguished from that father and grandfather and perhaps a cousin or two as well, by his own version of their shared name. Or, of course, by a *Peerie* in front of it, which would stick for life, like the late but *eart kyent* (well-known) guitarist Peerie Willie Johnson. There was also a patronymic system, which meant that a Peter's four sons, Peter, Andrew, John and Matthew, would all have the surname Peterson, and so would his son Peter's children. Andrew's children, however, would have the surname Anderson, John's would be Johnson, and Matthew's would be Matthewson. The Scots ministers stamped this out in the nineteenth century, but in one district you can have a lot of *folk* with the same surname, and so they're distinguished by their house name: *Magnie o' Strom, Peter o' da Knowe*.

Glossary

For those who like to look up unfamiliar words as they go, here's a glossary of Scots and Shetlan words.

aa: all
aabody: everybody
aandowing: keeping a boat still by rowing gently against the tide
aawye: everywhere
ahint: behind
ain: own
amang: among
an aa: as well
anyroad: anyway
ashet: large serving dish
auld: old
aye: always
baa / baw: a rock at sea
bairn: child
ball oot: throw out
banks: sea cliffs, or peatbanks, the slice of moor where peats are cast
bannock: flat triangular scone
(a baaa) bee: (a rock) visible among breaking waves
birl, birling: paired spinning round in a dance
blinkie: torch
blootered: very drunk
blyde: pleased

boanie: pretty, good-looking
borrow: a wheelbarrow
bow: a buoy
breeks: trousers
brigstanes: flagged stones at the door of a crofthouse
bruck: rubbish
burn: a stream
caa: round up
canna: can't
clarted: thickly covered
cloo up: to lock up, put away
cludgie: toilet
cowp: capsize
cratur: creature
crofthouse: the long, low traditional house set in its own land
daander: to travel uncertainly or in a leisurely fashion
darrow: a hand fishing line
dastreen: yesterday evening
de-crofted: land that has been taken out of agricultural use, e.g. for a house site
dee: you; *du* is also you, depending on the grammar of the sentence – they're equivalent to thee and thou. Like French, you would only use *dee* or *du* to one friend; several people, or an adult if you're a younger person, would be you.
denner: midday meal
didna: didn't
dinna: don't
dip dee doon: sit yourself down
dis: this
doesna: doesn't
doon: down
drewie lines: a type of seaweed made of long strands
duke: duck
dukey-hole: pond for ducks
du kens: you know

dyck, dyke: a wall, generally drystane, i.e. built without cement
eart: direction, *the eart o' wind*
ee now: right now
eela: fishing, generally these days a competition
everywye: everywhere
faerdie-maet: picnic food for a long day out
faersome: frightening
faither, usually **faider:** father
fanted: hungry, often *black fanted*, absolutely starving
folk: people
frae: from
gansey: a knitted jumper
gant: to yawn
geen: gone
gluff: fright
greff: the area in front of a peat bank
gret: cried
guid: good
Guid kens: God knows
hadna: hadn't
hae: have
harled: exterior plaster using small stones
heid: head
hoosie: little house, usually for bairns
howk: to search among: I *howked ida box o' auld claes.*
idee: idea
isna: isn't
just: just
keek: peep at
ken, kent: know, knew
kirk: church
kirkyard: graveyard
kishie: wicker basket carried on the back, supported by a *kishie baand* around the forehead
knowe: hillock

lem: china
Lerook: Lerwick
likit: liked
lintie: skylark
lipper: a cheeky or harum-scarum child, generally affectionate
mad: annoyed
mair: more
makkin belt: a knitting belt with a padded oval, perforated for holding the 'wires' or knitting needles.
mam: mum
mareel: sea phosphorescence, caused by plankton, which makes every wave break in a curl of gold sparks
meids: shore features to line up against each other to pinpoint a spot on the water
midder: mother
midgie: the Shetland name for a midge
mind: remember
misanter: an accident, a mishap
moder dy: the underlying sea swell which rolled shorewards (the ninth wave)
moorit: coloured brown or black, usually used of sheep
mooritoog: earwig
muckle: big – as in Muckle Roe, the big red island. Vikings were very literal in their names, and almost all Shetland names come from the Norse.
muckle biscuit: large water biscuit, for putting cheese on
myrd: a good number and variety – a *myrd* o' peerie things
na: no, or more emphatically, *nall*
needna: needn't
Norroway: the old Shetland pronunciation of Norway
o': of
oot: out
ower: over
park: fenced field
peat: brick-like lump of dried peat earth, used as fuel

peerie: small
peerie biscuit: small sweet biscuit
Peeriebreeks: affectionate name for a small thing, person or animal
piltick: a sea fish common in Shetland waters
pinnie: apron
postie: postman
press: cupboard or chest
quen: when
redding up: tidying
redd up kin: get in touch with family – for example, a five-generations New Zealander might come to meet Shetland cousins still staying in the house his or her forebears had left
reestit mutton: wind-dried shanks of mutton
riggit: dressed, sometimes with the sense dressed-up
roadymen: men working on the roads
roog: a pile of peats
rows: rolls
rummle: untidy scattering
rumple: backbone (in 'Row da Boats o Maalie')
Santy: Santa Claus
scaddy man's heids: sea urchins
scattald: common grazing land
scrime: to make out something, e.g. at a distance, or in mist
scuppered: put paid to, done for
selkie: seal, or seal person who came ashore at night, cast his/her skin and became human
Setturday: Saturday
shalder: oystercatcher
sho: she
shoulda: should have
shouldna: shouldn't have
SIBC: Shetland Islands Broadcasting Company, the independent radio station
skafe: squint

skerry: a rock in the sea
smoorikins: kisses
snicked: move a switch that makes a clicking noise
snyirked: made a squeaking or rattling noise
solan: gannet
somewye: somewhere
sooking up: sucking up
soothified: behaving like someone from outwith Shetland
spew: be sick
spewings: piles of sick
splatched: walked in a splashy way with wet feet, or in water
spree: a party
steekit mist: thick mist
sun-gaits: with the sun – it's bad luck to go against the sun, particularly walking around a church
swack: smart, fine
swee: to sting (of injury)
tak: take
tatties: potatoes
tay: tea, or meal eaten in the evening
tink: think
tirricks: Arctic terns
trows: trolls
tushker: L-shaped spade for cutting peat
twa: two
twartree: a small number, several
tulley: pocket knife
unken: unknown
vee-lined: lined with wood planking
vexed: sorry or sympathetic – 'I was that vexed to hear that.'
voe: sea inlet
voehead: the landwards end of a sea inlet
waander: wander
waar: seaweed
wasna: wasn't

wha's: who is
whatna: what
wheech: suggests fast movement
whit: what
whitteret: weasel
wi: with
wife: woman, not necessarily married
wir: we've – in Shetlan grammar, we are is sometimes we have
wir: our
wouldna: would not
yaird: enclosed area around or near the crofthouse
yoal: a traditional clinker-built six-oared rowing boat

Discover more from Marsali Taylor . . .

When an internet lifestyle influencer arrives on Shetland to document her 'perfect' holiday, the locals are somewhat sceptical.

Joining a boat trip to the remote islands of St Kilda with sailing sleuth Cass Lynch and her partner DI Gavin Macrae, the young woman seems more concerned with her phone than the scenery.

But when it's time to leave, there's no sign of her. Despite mounting a desperate search, she's seemingly vanished without trace – from a small island in the middle of the sea.

As a puzzling investigation gathers pace, there are more questions than answers – and uncovering the truth will reveal dark and long-hidden secrets . . .

Available now!

ACCENT

Discover more from Matsuki Taylor

When I managed to get a sullen response from Niall, my
roommate, he turned, before the toilet was unseen to greet.

Sonia, relenting to sign, was asked to sell, I saw the phone
though Cass's sister and her puppet. I'd keep being the voice
woman who your own, and I with her phone than the L spoke.

But soon, if I try to have them in town in
Deep's Christmas. A niche faith. As secretary, waited
with anther company with a haul in the bottle of the sea.

As a reading to me public place, they have this
more matters than you can describe from this
time still never the end tone. Do the even...

...available now!

Crowds are gathered for a concert at Shetland's renowned folk music festival when there's a shocking discovery – international folk legend Fintan Foley has been stabbed backstage.

Sailing sleuth Cass Lynch and her partner DI Gavin Macrae are in the audience and must untangle a complicated case where nothing is quite what it seems. Cass soon discovers that Foley's smiling stage persona concealed links with Shetland. He'd worked here in the 80s, the days when oil brought wealth to the islands.

Has a long-buried secret risen to the surface – and will it make Cass a target for a cold-blooded killer?

Available now!

RAISING READERS
Books Build Bright Futures

Dear Reader,

We'd love your attention for one more page to tell you about the crisis in children's reading, and what we can all do.

Studies have shown that reading for fun is the **single biggest predictor of a child's future life chances** – more than family circumstance, parents' educational background or income. It improves academic results, mental health, wealth, communication skills, ambition and happiness.[1]

The number of children reading for fun is in rapid decline. Young people have a lot of competition for their time. In 2024, 1 in 10 children and young people in the UK aged 5 to 18 did not own a single book at home.[2]

Hachette works extensively with schools, libraries and literacy charities, but here are some ways we can all raise more readers:

- Reading to children for just 10 minutes a day makes a difference
- Don't give up if children aren't regular readers – there will be books for them!
- Visit bookshops and libraries to get recommendations
- Encourage them to listen to audiobooks
- Support school libraries
- Give books as gifts

There's a lot more information about how to encourage children to read on our website: **www.RaisingReaders.co.uk**

Thank you for reading.

hachette UK

---

[1] OECD, '21st-Century Readers: Developing Literacy Skills in a Digital World', 2021, https://www.oecd.org/en/publications/21st-century-readers_a83d84cb-en.html

[2] National Literacy Trust, 'Book Ownership in 2024', November 2024, https://literacytrust.org.uk/research-services/research-reports/book-ownership-in-2024